"Why do you have Autumn?" He didn't take his eyes off hers or release her hand.

"Because she's mine." She wasn't about to let him think for a second Autumn wasn't the daughter of her heart.

"I can see she's yours. That's not what I mean, and you know it."

Infuriatingly cocky, and definitely the Brody she remembered. "I have Autumn because she's yours." Nothing harder than laying her pride at his feet and telling him the truth.

He took a step closer, forcing her to take one back, unable to have him this close when she let her heart rule her mind.

"What are you telling me?" he asked, his voice husky and soft.

"You left. So I kept the pieces of yourself you left behind. They were all I had left of you and a dream I dreamt of us." She tried to turn away. He caught her by the arm and spun her around so fast, she slammed into his chest. His mouth clamped down on hers, she didn't have a chance to catch her breath, only to hold on.

Also by Jennifer Ryan

The Montana Men Series
STONE COLD COWBOY
HER LUCKY COWBOY
WHEN IT'S RIGHT
AT WOLF RANCH

The McBride Series
DYLAN'S REDEMPTION
FALLING FOR OWEN
THE RETURN OF BRODY MCBRIDE

The Hunted Series
EVERYTHING SHE WANTED
CHASING MORGAN
THE RIGHT BRIDE
LUCKY LIKE US
SAVED BY THE RANCHER

Short Stories
"CAN'T WAIT"
(appears in ALL I WANT FOR CHRISTMAS
IS A COWBOY)
"WAITING FOR YOU"
(appears in CONFESSIONS OF A SECRET ADMIRER)

THE
RETURN
OF
BRODY
McBRIDE
BOOK ONE: THE McBRIDES

JENNIFER
RYAN

AVONBOOKS

An Imprint of HarperCollinsPublishers

Excerpt from *Her Renegade Rancher* copyright © 2016 by Jennifer Ryan.

THE RETURN OF BRODY MCBRIDE. Copyright © 2014 by Jennifer Ryan. All rights reserved. Printed in the United States of America. No part of this book may be used or reproduced in any manner whatsoever without written permission except in the case of brief quotations embodied in critical articles and reviews. For information, address HarperCollins Publishers, 195 Broadway, New York, NY 10007.

First Avon Books mass market printing: July 2016

ISBN 978-0-06230602-9

Avon Trademark Reg. U.S. Pat. Off. and in Other Countries, Marca Registrada, Hecho en U.S.A.
Avon, Avon Books, and the Avon logo are trademarks of HarperCollins Publishers.
HarperCollins® is a registered trademark of HarperCollins Publishers.

16 17 18 19 20 OPM 10 9 8

For my family, who put up with late dinners, a messy house, and my never-ending work schedule. You support me despite all that, and a lot more, and encourage me every day to achieve my dreams. I hope you see it as inspiration to reach for yours. I love you.

Chapter One

BRODY WOKE WITH a start, gasped for breath, his hands pressed to his heaving chest where the bullet had slammed into his bulletproof vest months ago, severely bruising his ribs. Used to sleeping in some of the most hostile places in the world, he took in his surroundings with a quick sweep of his gaze. All safe. Adrenaline racing through his veins, he checked his first instinct and stilled his hand, reaching beneath the pillow for his gun. He wished he could shake off the nightmare and memories as quickly as he had sleep.

Alert, he now remembered arriving at the old cabin late last night. Clear Water Ranch. He and Owen should rename the place Mud. Nothing pristine about the blood running through his veins. His father sullied it, along with the McBride name.

Just the thought of being on the ranch again set off a barrage of memories, most of him and Owen running wild. He couldn't pick out one, or grasp the prevailing feeling that went with them. A mixture of happy and sad times, frightening things better left forgotten but relived in Technicolor nightmares, and anger stored up over years, like a river cutting its path until a deep gorge separated them. Instead of spending the last eight years rebuilding bridges, he'd let the gap grow wider.

His stellar military career came with its own kind of horrors, right up until a roadside bomb took out three of his friends and left him wounded, ending his third tour in Afghanistan and his stint with the Army Rangers. He'd stowed them away with the other bad memories.

Two months of rehab under his belt, he returned home to pull the tattered pieces of his life together and mend them into something of a happy future. Hell, he'd settle for dull and normal.

He'd have exceptional if he won Rain back.

He'd blown it with her and let love slip through his fingers. Back then, he had nothing to offer her. Now, he was a different man, the man she always saw inside of him.

Her trail might be cold, but he'd track her, and before she knew it he'd be hot on her tail. That's exactly where he planned to stay until he convinced her his days as a selfish prick were over. He wanted to put the past behind him, prove to himself and everyone else he could be a different kind of man than his father was, and find that all-American dream he'd spent years protecting for others. So long as Rain was part of it, he'd find that elusive happiness.

Judging by the sunlight streaming in the windows, early morning greeted him. A soft breeze filtered up to the loft from what could only be the open door downstairs. Papers rustled, then everything went quiet. Company. His brother had come calling. Time to face his past.

COFFEE IN HAND, Owen had the radio cranked up along with the heat as he drove to his law office on autopilot, his mind on the day ahead. He passed the split in the road that led to the old cabin and spotted the new green truck parked out front. Instinctively, he stomped on the brakes and came to a jarring stop, almost losing his coffee along with his good mood. Eyes narrowed, he glared at that truck and the cabin and knew. Brody was home. Unannounced and unwelcome.

Quickly thinking of what he should do, what he could do, he backed up and took the long driveway to the cabin. Not much changed since he'd come out and put the new padlock on the front door to keep teens from partying and the occasional drifter out. The grass was several feet high. His truck bounced and thudded over the deep ruts and potholes. Garbage, beer cans, and bottles littered the yard. The cabin looked neglected and sad against the backdrop of the Colorado mountains.

Rain had turned sad after Brody walked out on her, just as he'd walked out on this place and left it to the wind and time. With nothing and no one to help, neither was living up to their potential.

With that in mind, Owen walked right in the busted front door and stood in the ruin. This wrecked place suited Brody and the life he'd left behind for others to clean up. Namely him.

Setting his coffee on the rickety kitchen table, he sorted through the contents of his brother's open briefcase.

Shocking. The thought raced through his mind. He had a few friends in the right places, which made it easier to track Brody over the last couple years. Brody found his calling in the military's elite Ranger unit. He'd been on some dangerous missions and served his country in two consecutive tours in Iraq and three more in Afghanistan. He didn't know what several of the medals were for, but the Purple Heart made the reports he'd received all too real.

A grunt and moan carried down the stairs. Concerned, he glanced up to where his brother slept restlessly, caught in a nightmare. He didn't go up, wanting to put the confrontation off as long as possible. Rifling through the other stuff in his brother's briefcase, he listened to the disturbing noises coming from upstairs, ending with a sudden gasp before all went quiet.

Brody padded down the stairs. Owen set down one of the bottles of pills on the table and caught sight of his brother for the first time in more than eight years. Immediately, he was taken back to summer days when they'd run down the dock, feet bare, shirts off, the sun hot on their backs as they took a flying leap into the lake. Brody's hair was that same golden blond, his skin tan—and riddled with scars old and new. Taller, broader, and something else.

The way he carried himself. A mix of confidence, watchfulness, and ease. His eyes had changed. Gone was the sparkle of mischief always just below the surface. Replaced by a steady alert gaze that took in everything around him in one long sweep. A few more lines bracketed his eyes, but he still had that same strong jaw, the muscle working even now as Brody's gaze narrowed down at him.

"Sleeping pills, anti-anxiety meds, painkillers."

"I thought you were a lawyer, not a pharmacist," Brody snapped, a defensive note to his words.

"I've defended enough users to know what these drugs do to people when abused."

"The sleeping pills are nearly full. The others are necessary, and I take them according to the directions so clearly written on the bottle."

Brody moved forward looking larger than life. He'd gained a good twenty-five pounds—all muscle. This Brody was lean and mean. The bad blood between them not forgotten, or even pushed to the back burner for their first encounter. Well, Owen could be just as stubborn and ornery. Hell, he'd taught Brody a thing or two about being obstinate over the years. They'd gotten into a shitload of trouble, usually with Owen in the lead. Brody followed willingly. They both had that same wild McBride streak in them.

"How's the leg?" Owen tossed out, hiding a smile when Brody's eyes narrowed, the muscle in his jaw flexing again.

"Checking up on me, big brother? Is that coffee for me?"

"You refused to return my calls. The coffee is mine."

"I didn't have anything to say. You went your way. I went mine."

Owen had to admit, at first he'd needed the distance from their father, Brody, this town, from a past he couldn't forget or change. The things he'd done and couldn't change. But after everything was said and done, this place always called to him. Good or bad, sometimes miserable, a few times happy, usually somewhere tenuously in-between, it was always home. He wondered if that's how Brody felt. Was it the reason he'd finally stopped trying to get himself killed and come home?

"And the leg?"

"Fine," Brody said through clenched teeth.

"According to these military papers, they honorably discharged you due to medical reasons."

"I'm no longer fit to send off to be killed. You've got to be a hundred percent for that kind of work."

"Is that all it was? Work?" Owen hoped it was something more. That Brody had finally found a direction in his life. Maybe Brody had stopped listening to the recording in his head of their father telling him he was worthless, stupid, and good for nothing and no one. It took a lot of hard work for Owen to shut that voice up. He hoped Brody had managed the same.

"I needed something to do," Brody evaded. "Seemed like a good idea at the time."

"When are you leaving again?"

"Who says I am?"

"You haven't been back in more than eight years."

"I'm here now."

"Which begs the question, why now?"

Until that moment, Brody wanted to tell Owen to go to hell. But that was the old him, the one who didn't answer to anyone, carried around a chip on his shoulder the size of the big Colorado sky and was belligerent just to be a dick and get a rise out of anyone standing in front of him.

With a heavy sigh, he said, "Hi, Owen. Long time no see. How are you?"

Owen crossed his arms over his chest and warily went along. "Hi, Brody. Long time no see. I'm fine. How are you?"

"Doing better. I just got out of a veteran's rehab center. The reason for the pills." He grabbed a bottle and removed a pill from that one and another from a second bottle, popping them into his mouth, downing them without water. "I got caught by a roadside bomb in Afghanistan a few months back. Lost three of my men, another got hit pretty bad by shrapnel. He suffered some burns."

"You took shrapnel and got burned."

"Yeah, well, shit happens. I lost three men. Friends. They had wives, kids. People who loved them waiting for them," he said tightly.

He'd been living his life on the edge, no one to care whether he lived or died. That roadside bomb had been the last straw in a line of near misses for Brody.

"I've been waiting for you," Owen conceded.

Brody figured his changing attitude and Owen's confession were as close to an apology as they'd get. At least, right now.

"I know it. And now, I'm here. Home to stay."

"To stay," Owen repeated, amazed and something else. Brody couldn't put his finger on it.

"Look, Owen, I know you're pissed. I was when I left, too. It's been years. The old man is dead and gone. Can't we let bygones be bygones?"

"You're my brother. If I had the time, we could take this out into the yard and settle a few old scores."

"I'm ready whenever you are," Brody returned with a cocky grin. Owen wasn't really pissed about the past between them. Not if a quick tussle would put the past to rest. Maybe that gaping ravine was just a pissy creek and Brody had been too stubborn to see it for what it was.

No, something else was going on here. Something making Owen angry and edgy.

"I did what you asked. I had the old man cremated," Owen backtracked. "I still have the ashes."

"I told you to dump his ass in a hot fire and let him burn."

"Yeah, well, I thought you might like to be here for that. We could crack a few beers, cuss the man out for being a shitty father . . ." Owen stopped talking and appeared to go somewhere else.

"Man, what is with you?"

"You never answered me. Why are you here now?"

Brody ran both hands through his close-cropped hair, scratched the back of his head, and wished desperately for a cup of coffee and some hot food. He should have stopped before reaching the cabin and picked up a few provisions.

"Listen, Owen, my military career is over. I've got this business thing, but someone else runs the show."

"Silent partner?" Owen guessed.

"Something like that. Anyway, I've got my disability from the military and some savings. The business is doing well, and I can live a comfortable life doing what I want."

"What is it you want? You thinking of turning this place back into a working ranch?"

"I might get a few horses, but other than that, I haven't really thought about it. I have something else I need to do first."

"And what is that?" Owen asked, his voice hard and deliberate.

"I need your help with something."

"Spit it out. Why are you here?" Taking a step closer, Owen fisted his hands at his side.

"I need to find Rain."

Owen cussed, paced back and forth, and rubbed his hand across his jaw.

"I thought about asking Eli where I can find her, but I thought better of it."

"You bet your ass you should think better of it. He'll likely kill you as look at you."

Brody laughed. Small-town people had long memories. After leaving Rain the way he did, and the things he'd done in those last few days, he wasn't expecting a warm welcome from most people, but especially Rain's father, Eli.

Still pacing, Owen went off like a machine gun again.

"Why do you want to find her? What? You want to tell her you're sorry for what happened?"

"Man, get a grip. Yes, I want to make things right."

"What does that mean? Do you know?"

Brody narrowed his eyes. "Know what? Did something happen to Rain? Is she all right?"

Owen took a deep breath and paced again. "You don't know," he said absently.

"I haven't spoken to her since the day I left, but you have." Brody's suspicions rose along with the hairs on the back of his neck. "What happened to her?"

"Is she the only one-night stand you'll look up while you're in town? Or is Roxy on your list of women to find?"

Brody grabbed Owen by the lapels of his suit jacket and hauled him up to his loafer-covered toes. Their faces inches apart, he said very calmly, "Rain was not a one-night stand."

"You tossed her away like she was just another piece of ass." Owen didn't fight the hold Brody had on him.

Brody shoved Owen away and crossed his arms over his chest. He took a moment to remind himself that half the battle to win back Rain stood in front of him. Owen knew how to find Rain, and he'd tell him, or Brody would beat it out of him. The thought held a lot of appeal, but he'd come home to make amends, start a new life, not pound Owen into the mud.

"It wasn't like that."

"No. It wasn't like that. It was worse. You went to Roxy behind Rain's back. Snuck into her bed after leaving Rain."

"It wasn't like I went from Rain's bed to Roxy's. Rain and I weren't sleeping together."

"Only because you broke things off with her and pushed her away for no good reason. You two had been friends for years—more than that, for months. She was eighteen, in love with you, and you decided you'd sleep with that bitch, Roxy, instead of a great girl like Rain."

"Is that what you really think?" Brody asked.

"It's what the whole town thinks. It's what Rain thought."

"Don't you think I know that? The thing is, my explanation wasn't enough to make her change her mind."

This time, Brody paced, then stopped to face Owen and his past.

"Dad ran up a substantial bar tab. He was drunk ... Well, more drunk than usual and about ready to drive home. Roxy called and told me to come and get him."

"She'd done that a hundred times," Owen pointed out.

"Yep, but this time I went into the bar and sat beside him, miserable I'd broken up with Rain. I tried to obliterate her memory from my mind and drink away my anger over the old man dragging me down again. Five shots of whiskey later, Roxy comes by the table and asks to speak to me alone. Bad idea all the way around. I thought she'd give me shit about the amount of money the old man owed her. I prepared to tell her what an idiot she was for letting him run up such a big tab and refuse to pay for his stupidity and hers. Instead, she pulled me into her apartment and everything went to shit."

"She had a thing for you for a long time," Owen conceded. "She was a notorious flirt, but she chased after you with a compulsion."

"Yeah, well, I always blew her off. Don't get me wrong, she was every man's wet dream. She might have been especially hot for me, but she was hot for any guy who walked through the door. I like my women willing, but not like that. Roxy was trouble with a capital T. I got myself into enough trouble all on my own. The two of us together were TNT."

"Yeah, and you took out Rain with the blast."

Brody didn't deny it. He knew exactly what he'd done, why he'd done it. No excuse for his behavior.

Brody sighed. "Rain was different, everything I never thought I could have. I held on to her for as long as I could, praying one day she wouldn't wake up and see what everyone else saw. I was a badass McBride, not good enough for her, not smart enough, or kind enough. Rain didn't think any of those things, but I sure as hell proved her wrong."

Owen remained quiet and watchful, waiting for him to finish his confession.

"So, there I am in Roxy's place and feeling miserable for pushing Rain away. Roxy asks me why I'm drinking alone instead of out with Rain. Stupid drunk as I am, I tell her we broke up. Next thing I know, she's a second skin on me and she whispers in my ear, 'I'll make you forget pretty little Rain.'"

Brody could still hear Roxy's voice notch down a few octaves, feel her tongue slide over his earlobe. Even now, his gut twisted and he felt . . . dirty.

"The thing is, nothing and no one could ever make me forget Rain."

"But you still slept with Roxy."

"I closed my eyes, gave in to Roxy's attempt to prove she could make me forget, and pretended that for a moment I had Rain. Worst mistake of my life."

"That's the fucking truth."

Brody recognized his mistake the second he opened his eyes and saw the wrong woman under him. He zipped his fly and buttoned his jeans and stormed out of her place, hating himself for what he'd done.

Rain showed up at his door two days later, said she refused to give up on them, and jumped into his arms and proceeded to show him why they were so good together. Like he needed to be shown. Nothing ever felt as good as when he was with Rain—no matter what they were doing together.

He tried to cleanse his body and soul with the only woman who'd ever really cared about him. She'd always had a way of making him feel clean and good and worth something.

Too bad making love to her couldn't erase the worst mistake of his life.

"So, you gave up Rain for a cheap fuck."

"Wasn't cheap." Brody planted his hands on his hips, lowered his head and shook it, the sadness welling up his throat. With no more than a whisper, he said, "Cost me Rain."

Brody looked around the ravaged room, a reflection of the mess his life had been in all these years. He wanted a clean slate, but he needed to clean up the past in order to get it.

"That woman cost me a hell of a lot. The old man still ended up wrecking his truck after leaving her bar years later. Killed a perfectly good deer in the process. Who knows, given time away from that place, maybe the old man would have sobered up one day, found religion and some good humor. Maybe I'd have just gotten older and wiser and decided his life wasn't mine. I'll never know because I fucked her and my life. Tossed it all away because I was pissed at the old man and myself for believing I wasn't good enough for Rain. Hell, I was pissed at the fucking world. Why? Because I had a fucked-up childhood. Couldn't pull my head out of my ass long enough to see if I wanted something I had to work for it, earn it, be willing to accept whatever came my way. Doesn't matter now."

"Roxy's a hell of a lot worse than you know."

"Wouldn't surprise me at all." Not much surprised him these days. "Roxy thought she was better than everyone because she knew everyone's dirty little secrets. Most of it was drunken lies told to her chest. Lord knows, her tits were the most interesting thing about her. She is what she is. I made my choices. Paid for them and a hell of a lot more. I've done a lot worse than get drunk and have sex with Roxy to scratch an itch."

"Then why did you come back, knowing that's what you left behind?"

"I told you, I want to find Rain."

"To what end? How do you know she'll even talk to you?"

"Won't know, unless I try. I've seen a lot of bad shit, done even worse. The only time I can remember being happy, truly happy, was when I was with Rain. I want that back."

"You can't go back," Owen snapped. "It's been a long time since you saw her. Things change. People change. Hell, you changed her when you did what you did, and left," he shouted the words.

Brody smiled. "You know where she is." Owen's eyes didn't meet his. "You've seen her. Has she come back to town a few times to see Eli? Where does she live now? San Francisco? Did she stay there after college?"

"You still haven't answered the question. Why do you want to find her?"

"You don't make it easy on a guy." He tossed up his hands and let them fall with a slap against his legs. "She's the one that got away. The one I pushed away. But it's always been her. Wherever I am, whatever I'm doing, Rain is there with me. She got me through Iraq and Afghanistan. She got me through grueling, agonizing rehab."

"And now you want to just find her and say, let's let bygones be bygones."

"I don't think it will be that easy." Half a smile quirked up his face. In for one hell of a fight with Rain, he actually looked forward to it. Rain in a temper was only matched by her passion in bed. Which only proved what a colossal fool he'd been to let her go without a fight.

Hell, he'd made it easy by leaving her before she left him.

That gem of an epiphany hit him while he lay burned and bleeding on a stretcher right after the roadside bomb nearly took his life. Rain had been ready to leave town, take her scholarship and make a real life for herself. He didn't have a single thing to offer her besides more of the same life she was desperate to escape. She had plans, an opportunity to make something of herself, and he didn't fit into those plans. At least, that's what he thought at the time. When the opportunity came to screw everything up royally, knowing it would cost him Rain and any chance to have a life with her, he took hold with both hands. The same thing he'd always done. If you were going to screw him, he'd screw you first. If his old man wanted to get on his case, Brody made damn sure he had a reason. If he was going to lose Rain anyway, he'd sure as hell make sure she knew he didn't need her.

What an enormous lie. He did need Rain.

"I think it'll take a lot of groveling."

"What if she doesn't want to see you?"

"I'll change her mind."

"If you can't?"

"Can't isn't an option," Brody bit out.

"You've got it bad for her. Is that what you want me to believe?"

"Believe what you like. With or without your help, I will find her. And when I do, I will convince her to make a life with me."

"What if she's already married?"

"If she was, you'd have told me that ten minutes ago when I asked about her. You'd have thrown it in my face the minute you realized I came back for her. Because even I know I deserve it."

Brody walked to the open door and stared out at his sorry yard. With his hands braced on each side of the doorframe, he pleaded, "Please, tell me where she is."

Owen shoved Brody out the door and followed him out. "I'll be in court most of the day. Whatever you do, don't come into town. I don't have time to defend Eli against murder charges. Give me today to talk to him before everyone finds out you're back."

"Just tell me where she is, Counselor."

Owen stopped and held on to the door of his truck before getting in. "Make me a promise."

"What?"

"Stay out of town today. In the morning, I'll tell you where she is."

"You're going to call and warn her I'm looking for her." Brody had a pretty good idea she wasn't as far away as he'd originally thought. That would only make things easier. Not that he wouldn't go to the ends of the earth to find her.

"Absolutely." Owen gave him a cocky grin.

"Still playing dirty," Brody said, feeling nostalgic.

"Giving her a fair chance to decide on her own what she wants without you showing up unexpectedly and catching her off guard. A lot has happened since you left. She's not the girl you remember. She has a whole new life."

"Is she happy?"

The play of emotions on his brother's face left him confused. Owen stared out across the yard to the lake beyond. It took him a minute to answer. "There are times she is. Yeah, I guess for the most part she's made the most out of . . . Well, she's fine."

"What the hell kind of answer is that? I thought you'd been in contact with her."

"I have. She's living her life the best she can. What more do you want?"

"For you to stop fucking around and tell me where she is."

"Tomorrow. If you need supplies . . . And garbage bags," he said, scanning the yard disgustedly, "go to Solomon. Twenty-four hours. That's all I'm asking."

"You ask for a hell of a lot. I know she's either in town or close by. Why not just say so?"

"Eli, number one. And she deserves a heads-up. If she doesn't want to see you, you will leave her alone."

"Never going to happen."

"Don't make me give into my urge to pound you bloody." Owen's knuckles went white where he held the truck door.

Owen's odd behavior made Brody agree. "I'll give you today. Tomorrow, you either tell me where she is, or I'll take my chances with Eli." He let that hang for a minute, then added, "I've got my own contacts. One Internet search, and I'll find her."

"Shit! Then why did you ask for my help?"

"Rain isn't the only one I wanted to see." The truth of the matter, Brody thought using Owen to find Rain would be a good way to bridge the gap between them.

"Who are you, and what have you done with my hard-ass brother?"

"Well, Counselor, you aren't the only one who decided to change which side of the law he landed on. Like everyone else, I've changed."

Owen eyed him for a moment before shaking his head. "I'll see you tomorrow. Stay out of town."

"You aren't taking the day off to help me clean up this mess?"

Owen stepped away from the truck and planted his hands on his hips. "Whether you realize it or not, I've been cleaning up your mess for years." He looked at the yard and house a bunch of teenagers had trashed during what had to amount to several rowdy parties at the deserted cabin. "This one you get to fix."

"What the hell does that mean?"

"You'll see. You left a hell of a lot more behind than just Rain and me." Owen gunned the engine and took off.

Owen's final words rang in his ears. His past was coming back to bite him on the ass.

Chapter Two

Trapped in the familiar dream, Rain shifted in the sheets, her subconscious taking her to the one place she didn't want to go. Straight into Brody's arms, his big hand and long fingers clamped around her thigh as he joined their bodies. The dusting of blond hair on his chest tickled her taut nipples just before his chest pressed against her heavy, tingling breasts. Their mouths joined, tongues imitating the thrust of their hips, and their hearts melded together as the heat between them grew hotter than the whitest star, exploding into an ecstasy she'd only ever found in Brody's strong arms.

Rain awoke, gasping for breath as her body betrayed her conscious mind. Ripples of spent passion echoed through her.

Great, Rain. Eight years and you're still dreaming about a man who betrayed you.

But, God, even in her dreams he could make her body

hum. "I need a new dream man," she said to the ceiling and combed her fingers through her long hair. Even in her dreams, she couldn't come up with a new man to stoke the fire in her that was cold as last winter's ashes in the waking hours.

What did she expect? Her only point of reference— Brody. No one but him made her heart stutter. Not that she had the time or inclination to let another man into her life when she devoted all her time to raising her girls. One round with Brody knocked her out of the ring of love. It took years to get up off the mats, dust herself off, and find a way to let go of her dreams and put the past behind her.

Yeah, right. You just woke up in bed with a ghost.

She shivered with an odd sense. Trouble's on the way.

OWEN SAT OUTSIDE Rain's house for a good five minutes before he worked up the nerve to get out of his truck and walk up the driveway to the back door. Without knocking, he walked in and found Rain at the stove flipping pancakes. The smell of coffee hung in the air over the scent of the fresh chopped strawberries on the cutting board.

"Hey, beautiful." Owen eased toward Rain.

Rain turned and smiled. "Hey, yourself."

He kissed her on the forehead, reached around her, and stole a pancake from the platter, rolled it, and took a bite, savoring the buttery taste. "Mmmm, good."

"Want some coffee?"

"Definitely. Where are the girls?"

"Brushing their teeth and hair. They'll be down in a minute."

"Okay." He paced the kitchen, stopping to take his mug of coffee from Rain and the plate of pancakes she'd made for him before pouring more batter onto the skillet.

With her back to him, she asked, "What's wrong?"

"Why do you think something is wrong?"

"It's seven thirty in the morning, and you're pacing my kitchen like a caged animal."

"I have something to tell you, and I'm not sure how you'll take it. It's big. It's about the girls."

Rain turned abruptly, spatula held up like a club. "Is Roxy back in town?"

"Not that I know. It's something else."

She turned back to the pancakes. "Then, just say it. Whatever it is, it can't be that bad."

"Brody's back," he spit out, sipped his coffee, and scalded his tongue on the hot brew. She stood rigid with her head down, watching the pancake batter bubble on the pan. "Flip them over, honey."

She did, but her shoulders remained stiff, her head down. "Does he know?"

"No."

"Why is he here?"

"He's been honorably discharged from the Army." When that didn't faze her, he continued. "He came home to find you."

She turned and faced him, eyes narrowed. "Does he know I'm here?"

"He seemed to think you were probably living in San Francisco, or at least California after you attended college."

"Which I never did." Sadness flashed in her eyes. He hated seeing it.

"He doesn't know that. After we talked this morning, he realized I know where you are, have for a long time, and figured out you're either in town or close by."

"Do you think he means to stay?"

"Hard to say. He's out at the cabin."

"That place is a wreck." She wrinkled her pretty, pert nose.

"Yep. I think he means to clean it up and live there."

"So, there's no getting around it. He'll find out."

"Looks that way. I've bought you a day to tell the girls. He's promised not to come into town. I told him I'd tell him where you are tomorrow."

Rain bit her lip, working her teeth over the rosy flesh. "Do you think he'll try to take them from me?"

Her voice went soft, like a child. Tough and strong, she had to be after everything she'd endured. Brody was the cause of this disturbing change.

"No one can take them from you, honey. You're a great mother."

Footsteps across the floor upstairs, the girls would be down for breakfast soon, so Rain hurried to voice the rest of her concerns. "If he tries to sue me for custody, even partial, will you represent him, or me?"

Owen frowned, not knowing the right thing to do, or if there was a right or wrong. It seemed the longer he practiced law, the more shades of gray he uncovered. "I don't think it will come to that." He held up a hand to stop her from arguing. "If he wants to sue you for partial custody, as is his right, I'll do everything I can to work with both of you to come to some sort of agreement. But I will make it clear to Brody that you're the only parent those children know. He's changed, Rain. We had some words this morning, and things could have gone the usual way."

"With him in your face, both of you ready to trade punches."

"Aw, you know us so well." He teased to bring her out of her dark mood. She didn't crack a smile. "But he didn't. In fact, I won't say he backed down, that will never be Brody's way, but he let the anger pass and opened up about why he's here."

"I don't really care why he's here. The problem is he doesn't know about the girls. He doesn't know about Roxy. How do I explain them to him? They're seven. What if he doesn't want anything to do with them? Do you have any idea how crushed they'll be?"

"You don't owe him a damn explanation. He left you, pregnant with his baby. He didn't call, never wrote, never told anyone where he was for the last eight years. He left you to clean up the mess with Roxy. He should thank you for what you did."

"Somehow, I don't think he'll thank me for keeping his girls from him."

"You didn't keep them from him," Owen said under his breath. Little footsteps pounded on the stairs. "You spent three years trying to find him. It was luck I found out he was in the military. Even then, they were already three and the old man was dead. Brody wouldn't return my phone calls, just sent that damn note. It's his own damn fault," Owen bit out. The two little nymphs came flying into the room with bright smiles on their faces.

"Uncle Owen," they shouted in unison and hugged and kissed him on the cheek. His heart always felt lighter when he saw them.

"Morning, girls. You guys hungry? Your mom made pancakes."

Dawn, ever the inquisitive one, looked at Rain for a long moment. "What's going on? Uncle Owen doesn't usually have breakfast with us during the week."

Rain brushed a hand over her daughter's golden hair. "Uncle Owen came to tell us some news."

Rain turned her sad eyes on him. He wasn't sure how all of this would turn out; he could only imagine how Rain felt.

"What is it?" Autumn asked, pouring syrup on her pancakes.

It always struck Owen how much the two girls looked alike, even though they had different mothers. It was sometimes creepy to see two sets of identical sky blue eyes turn to him, the same as his only brother, Brody's.

"Well, on my way to town today, I stopped by the old cabin." He stalled, knowing there was no way to prepare the girls. "My brother came home last night."

Autumn looked up at her sister, and by silent agreement Dawn spoke for the two of them. "Does he want to meet us?"

"I'm not sure, honey."

Dawn turned to her mother. "You didn't tell him about us, yet."

"I haven't spoken to him, sweetheart. Uncle Owen just told me he's back."

"But you'll tell him. You'll go and talk to him," Dawn said with a hint of demand in her voice.

Rain bit her lip, pushed away from the counter, and came to her daughters. She put a hand on each of them. "I will talk to him. Everything will be fine."

"Does this mean Roxy is coming back, too?" Autumn asked, looking down at her lap, pancakes forgotten.

Rain bent beside her and cupped her face and made Autumn meet her gaze. "I promise you, Roxy will never take you away from me again." When Autumn didn't look convinced, Rain asked, "Don't you want to meet your dad?"

Autumn shrugged and tears filled her eyes. "I guess."

"What's really bothering you?" Rain coaxed.

"Will he take me away because I'm not really yours?"

Rain glanced at Owen and he understood the depth of what it meant to have Brody come home out of the blue.

"Autumn, sweetheart, you are mine. You are my daughter. You have been since the day you were born. God just made a mistake when he put you in Roxy's belly and not mine. But you are the daughter of my heart, and I love you every bit as much as I love your sister. I would never let anyone take you from me. I'm your mommy, now, and forever."

"Promise?" Autumn's lips trembled. One tear slipped past her lashes and trailed over her softly rounded cheek.

"I promise." Rain took Autumn into her arms and stared over her shoulder at Owen.

Owen got the message. He and Brody had better not make a liar out of her. Autumn had been through enough. They all had. Rain spent every day working her ass off to provide the girls with everything they needed, but moreover, she gave them both the love they needed. If Owen— or anyone, for that matter—didn't know Autumn wasn't her biological daughter, you'd never guess by the way she was treated, if not for the fact she and Dawn looked nearly identical. Owen had no trouble thinking of them as fraternal twins. That Rain would love Brody's daughter by Roxy as her own was more than anyone could ask. Rain went to drastic measures to get Autumn—and keep her.

Rain was right, God made a mistake in not putting both babies in Rain's belly. But he'd sure as hell made up for it, giving Autumn a champion in Rain. Autumn had really lucked out when Rain stepped in, and stood firm, to save her.

"Autumn, Dawn, Brody just got back. What you might not know is that he was injured in the military, fighting overseas." Owen cautiously broached the subject.

Unsure how much the girls knew, Rain was very careful about telling the girls too much about their father. She didn't want to get their hopes up for something that might never happen.

"Mom told us," Dawn said.

"Well, he looks fine, but that doesn't mean he doesn't

have bad memories about the war." Owen thought of the anti-anxiety meds and the disturbing way Brody woke up this morning. "He told me he came home to see your mom. I think that's a good sign, girls."

"When will you tell him about us?" Dawn asked, waiting for either him or Rain to answer.

"I'll tell him tomorrow how to find your mom. He thought she moved away years ago. He'll probably come to see your mom . . . and you," he added.

"So, you'll tell him about Mom, but not us?" Dawn asked.

"Your mom should tell your dad about the both of you. No matter what happens, your mom will take care of you. Besides, once your dad gets over the shock, I think he'll be really happy to see both of you."

Owen wanted to laugh at the disbelieving looks on the girls' faces. They weren't too sure about Brody. Both hooked their arms around their mother. "Brody's got his work cut out for him winning over you girls," Owen said with a smile. "He's never met a challenge he couldn't beat." He stood and went to Rain and planted a kiss on her forehead. "It'll be fine. You've got until tomorrow. Tell the girls again about the Brody you loved."

"That's not the man they'll meet," she said defensively.

"Are you sure about that? He was always his best when he was with you. Just look at them. There's something truly good and decent in him, and it shows in them. It showed any time anyone saw the two of you together. That's what she wanted, a little piece of what he was with you." Rain understood he was talking about Roxy. The girls were pretty smart, even at seven. He didn't doubt they knew exactly who he referred to. "The only good she got from him went straight into Autumn." He squeezed her shoulder. "Give him a chance to be their father. Who knows, maybe you can put back together a few of those shattered dreams."

"I've done just fine on my own."

"The operative words are *on your own*. Brody owes you. He's their father. Responsible for them financially, if nothing else."

"I don't want his money."

"Maybe not. But it wouldn't hurt. The girls are getting older, the things they want and need are more expensive. College will be here before you know it." She frowned and the lines on her forehead deepened. "Take today to think of all the possibilities Brody's return presents for you."

"The only possibility concerning me right now is the possibility he'll hightail it out of town faster than he did the last time," she said under her breath. Both girls ate their breakfast, not listening to them.

"I don't think you have to worry about that, darlin'. I do believe my brother has made it plain, he aims to have you back."

With that, he kissed his nieces on the tops of their heads. Rain's astonished gaze followed him as he walked out the door smiling.

Chapter Three

RAIN WALKED INTO the garage bay alone after dropping the girls at school. They'd asked her a hundred questions about Brody and what she thought about him coming home. They worried Brody would try to take them away from her, and would he want to see them and be their dad. She didn't have the answers to those hard questions and tried to explain to the girls as best she could what might happen. She needed to prepare them, but she didn't want them to spend the next twenty-four hours worrying themselves sick over it.

Maybe she should go straight out to the cabin and confront Brody. Nerves raw, her mind scattered. Her heart betrayed her memories, calling out, "Yeah, Brody is back."

She'd loved him once upon a time, and that love bloomed back to life at just the thought of seeing Brody again. She fought hard to tamp down her feelings and concentrate on important matters. Her girls. Her heart could just take a flying leap, because she couldn't afford to be a foolish girl, pining for lost dreams, wishing for happily-ever-after, when she had two seven year old hearts to consider. If Brody didn't want to be a part of their lives, she'd deal with a hurt unlike anything she'd ever felt herself over Brody leaving her. Autumn and Dawn would be devastated. This could change things for them forever. It was one thing to know your father was out there somewhere, oblivious to your existence, but to have him come home, find out about you, and deny you his love and affection was another matter entirely.

If Brody McBride did that to her girls, she'd kill him. No way she'd let him get away with hurting her babies.

But first, she needed to tell her father. Pop had been there for her from the day gossip circulated that Roxy hooked up with Brody and when Brody left. He'd supported her decision when she told him college was out of the question—she was pregnant.

She hated letting her father down, tossing all his dreams for her to the wind. He'd never said he was disappointed, but how could he not be when he'd worked his whole life to ensure she'd have the means to go to college and be whatever she wanted to be. Instead, she'd used her college money to right a wrong. As much as it must have hurt him to see her miss out on college and a different kind of life, he had told her one night over her daughters' crib, them sleeping soundly, he was proud of her and the woman and mother she'd become.

It might not be the life he'd dreamed for her, or she'd dreamed for herself, but she'd made the most out of it. She was happy being a mother. If being a mechanic and helping her father run his garage wasn't as fulfilling as she'd like, it was a good, steady job that allowed her flexible hours to be with the girls when they needed her.

She found Pop in the office going over invoices. Flutters tickled her stomach, spreading out across her taught nerves. He looked just like he had her whole life. That same red ball cap on his dark-haired head, black T-shirt stretched over a broad chest and belly that had only slightly expanded over the years. She knew just how those strong arms felt when they wrapped around her. He'd always made her feel safe and protected.

She leaned her shoulder against the doorframe and crossed her arms over her chest. She took a minute to just look at him before she royally pissed him off. "Hey, Pop."

An easy smile spread across his face. "Hey, yourself. Get the girls off to school?"

"Yep."

"What's with the look?"

"What look?"

"The one you give me every time you have something to say and don't want to say it. So, what is it this time? You need time off to spend with the girls?"

"No. Nothing like that. Um, I had a visitor for breakfast this morning."

Pop sat back in his chair and gave her a knowing grin. "Got a new man in your life?" he teased, knowing there hadn't been a man in her life since Brody. Though he'd hinted, cajoled, and outright told her to go out and find a man, or at least get laid. This, from her own father. He had her best interests at heart, wanted to see her happy and have a full life.

"No, not a new man. An old one," she admitted reluctantly. His eyes narrowed with confusion, and she plunged ahead. "Brody's back in town."

"You saw him? He came to your house this morning?" Angry, his fists clenched on the desk.

"No. Owen came by to tell me he saw Brody this morning at the cabin."

"Does he know about the girls?"

"No. He's been discharged from the military, and he's come home."

"I see." Pop clamped down his jaw so tightly the muscles flexed like a pulse.

"He told Owen he came back to find me," she blurted out.

Pop leaned forward and rested his arms on the desk, staring at her intently. "Is that right? Are you going to take him back?"

Not wavering under her father's steady gaze, she answered, "Whatever Brody and I had is over."

"It's not over. You share a child together, and you're raising his other daughter as your own."

"Then whatever relationship we can manage to have will be as parents to the girls. If he wants them," she added.

"I can't figure out if you're lying to me, or just yourself."

"What?"

"You love him. You've always loved him."

"That was a long time ago. You never approved my seeing him, but knew it was what I wanted. Then. Not now."

"Don't kid yourself, Rain. You still love him. You know how I know that. Because I loved your mother the same way. When I was with her, even after she was gone, I loved her. Every other woman paled in comparison, and I could never see myself with anyone else."

She gave her father a knowing smile, but he ignored it. He still loved her mother, but she knew he'd found a way to move on, even if he kept it a secret. To this point, she hadn't managed to do the same.

"It's been eight years, and I don't think you've ever looked at a man, let alone thought about having a life with one if he wasn't Brody."

"That's not true. I've been raising the girls and working here. There's no time for anything else."

"You've never made time for anything else. Guys come in here all the time, eyeing you and flirting with you."

"They do not," she said, her eyes wide with shock.

"You never notice. It's like other men don't exist."

"I don't get you. You've hated Brody all these years for leaving me, sleeping with Roxy, hiding away, never knowing about the girls. Now, you sit there, tell me I'm in love with him, and act like if he and I picked up where we left off, you'd be fine with it."

"Don't get me wrong, he's got a lot to answer for, but more than anything, I want you to be happy."

"He doesn't make me happy. He makes me angry, furious, ready to kill," she shouted.

"Sounds like a whole lot of passion." He laughed outright when she glared and threw up her hands, pushed away from the door, and moved toward him.

"I remember how happy you used to be with him. When you were with him, you shined.

"You've got every reason in the world to be angry. I hope you give him hell and make his life miserable for a while. But then, I want you to answer something for yourself once and for all. Is what you had in the past still burning bright, or has it faded to a memory? If you still love him, can you forgive him? Or is it over?

"Don't answer now. When you see him, take whatever time you need to discover who he is now, who you are now, and figure out if the two people you've become can make a life together work. Not for the girls, but for you.

"You deserve some happiness and love. If he can give you both, I'll stand behind you like I always do. If he's not the one, you can move on with a clear mind and a heart that's finally free to love again."

Tears filled her eyes and she sniffled them back. "Oh, Pop, I don't deserve you. After everything that's happened . . ."

"None of which was your fault alone. You've done me proud, working beside me, raising those girls, being the best you can be for me and for them. I couldn't have asked for more."

"You've been watching too many old sappy movies again."

"I love you, honey. Doesn't mean I'm not pissed about what he did." The look in the man's eyes told her just how much anger he'd harbored over the years.

"Kill him, or maim him?" he asked, no question he was serious.

"Well, don't kill him. Autumn and Dawn want to meet him."

"How are the girls taking this?"

"They're scared he'll take them."

"Autumn, especially, I guess." Pop understood the girls had been through a lot.

"She asked if Roxy was coming back, too."

"Roxy's got eyes and ears in this town. Once she finds out Brody's back, she'll make trouble."

"It's the one thing she does well. I've already thought of that. I just don't know what I can do to prepare Autumn. As it is, she thinks Brody will take her away from me because I'm not her real mother, and he's her father."

"Brody won't do that."

It helped that Pop believed those confident words.

"I wish I thought the same. The fact of the matter is, he could very well sue me for custody of both of them."

"He won't. He'll know they belong to you."

"They belong to him, too. They're a part of him. I can't help but think he'll want them in his life."

"Of course he will. They're his daughters. What you need to do is come together against Roxy. Don't let her get to him and make a deal, or worse turn him against you."

She spoke one of her deepest fears. "You don't think he'll be pissed I kept both his daughters from him all this time?"

"All he had to do was call. You. Owen. Anyone in this damn town, and he'd have known about those girls. You tried your best to find him. It's not your fault he rambled around for the better part of two years before he joined the military. What was the point in looking for him when he didn't want to be found?"

"I know you're right. I can't help thinking if it were me, I'd have wanted to know about them."

"If that were the case, and it crossed his mind, even for a second he might have gotten you or Roxy pregnant, he should have called to find out."

"What guy would think of that?"

"A guy who loved you and wanted to know if he had a way back to you," Pop said bluntly.

"Well thanks. That just proves the point, he didn't want to come back to me."

"He was just too stupid to think a baby would be a damn good way to stay in your life. When he finds out about Dawn, he'll kick himself halfway to hell for not thinking she was a possibility. Then, he'll realize if he had, he could have had you both in his life all this time. When he knows what happened with Autumn, he'll be angry. After you lay all your cards on the table, Rain, this will hurt him deeply."

"You don't know that. He could just as easily leave town again, never looking back. Worse, he could take Autumn with him, demand partial custody of Dawn, and take her away from me for weeks or months at a time."

"You're borrowing trouble."

"Maybe so, but I have to be prepared for the possibilities."

"You could go to him, find out what he really wants. Tell him about the girls and give him time to settle into the idea of being a father."

"Owen will tell him where to find me tomorrow. Today, I need to be with my girls."

"You've had seven years. You'll have the rest of their lives."

"But today, they're all mine. I'm not sure I'm ready to share. I'm not sure they're ready for Brody." She fell into the chair in front of her father's desk. "Everything will change tomorrow, and there's nothing I can do about it."

"Running from trouble was never your way. I know you're scared and uncertain, but you know Brody better than anyone. You know your girls. You'll know what's best when the time comes. And no matter how hard it is, I know you'll do right by those girls."

Pop watched her while she sat contemplating just what might be the right thing for her girls. And wouldn't you know, Pop knew just what she wasn't thinking about.

"While you're brooding over Brody and those girls, you might find some time to think about what it is you want for yourself. You gave up a lot to raise them. If Brody helped out on the parenting duties, you could get back some of what you lost."

"Think Brody will babysit while I go on a date?" She teased, just to show her father some of her spunk was still alive and well. It would serve Brody right to leave him with two little girls while she went out on a hot date. Too bad she didn't know any hot guys. Life sucked.

"If he's still the Brody we know, he'll kill any man who comes within ten feet of you."

"He's not like that."

"You just never wanted to see it. You only had eyes for him. Face it, you gave him your heart nearly ten years ago. As I see it, this is your chance to either get it back and move on, or see if you still hold his as well and make something out of it."

"Well, aren't you just full of love and wisdom this morning? What'd you stir your coffee with, Cupid's arrow?"

Pop laughed, stood, and came around the desk, pulling her out of her seat and into his arms. Ah, safety and warmth wrapped up with the smell of engine grease, oil, and coffee.

"I love you, Rain. But as your father, I am going to belt Brody one for leaving you the way he did. Then, I'll stand behind whatever decision you make. It's your life." He kissed her on top of her head like he always did, and she felt better for it, despite thinking she didn't need to be coddled like a child. Okay, maybe she did. Just once, she'd like someone else to make the hard decisions. Never a follower, she wasn't about to start now.

When Brody showed up tomorrow, she'd be ready for him. He'd do right by their girls. No two ways about it.

She did think of them as their girls. And that said it all, now didn't it.

Well, shoot.

She walked into the garage bay and set up to rebuild a carburetor. Damn if she didn't hate it when her father was right. She was still in love with Brody McBride, Dawn and Autumn were their babies, and damn if her mind was sprouting all kinds of happily-ever-afters.

Cranking the wrench over a bolt, not concentrating worth a damn, it slipped, nicked her knuckle, and blood welled out of the wound. She sucked on it for a second, then cussed Brody for being the devil, always doing as he pleased, when it pleased him.

Well, not this time. This time, she was ready for him. And she had the mother of all surprises.

BRODY KNEW BETTER than to skip taking his pills. He got through most of the morning without any trouble. But halfway through Walmart his leg acted up. He ignored the pain, had done so often enough when he was in combat, hurt and needing rest and time to heal. The pain he could control. Lock it away in his mind somewhere and focus on something else. Like what color sheets should he buy for the bed. White or blue? What would Rain like? Both, and the white ones with the leaves. She'd like those.

His hands shook, sweat broke out on his brow and down his back. He reached the checkout counter, every noise amplified in his ears. He needed to get out of there. Get home and take his anti-anxiety meds. Quiet his mind, so he could think straight. He didn't want anyone to see him like this. They wouldn't understand what it was like to have a war raging in his head, guns going off, explosions, blood, men dying before his eyes, and none of it real. At least, not here.

Deep, even breaths he told himself and followed through, just like the shrinks at the hospital told him to do. In time, he'd be better able to cope. Time and distance, a normal life would dull the memories and make them seem less real. He prayed for that day.

Mindy, the checkout girl, bagged his items and refilled his cart to overflowing. He'd managed to restock the house with kitchen supplies, including a coffee pot and big can of coffee and cream for Rain. He'd bought new towels, blankets, pillows, anything and everything he needed to settle into the cabin and make it comfortable for both of them.

He refused to let his mind go to that place where Rain told him to go to hell and never spoke to him again. If he had everything ready when he found her, she'd eventually come around and be with him again, right?

Nothing's ever that simple.

Flexing his hands, rolling his shoulders, breathing deeply, he tried to relax and focus on the total lit up on the panel of the little box he needed to slide his card through, punch in his code, and tell the little machine to pay the bill.

"You all right, Mister?"

"Fine." He managed to slide his card, but it took him a second to remember his PIN. He got it on the second try, only adding to his anxiety.

Outside, he scanned the rows and rows of parked cars, trying to remember where he parked. He took a second to find his truck near the end, two rows over on the left from the front doors. Before he stepped into the street, he stopped and tilted his head enough to scan the roofline for snipers. They weren't there, of course, but he felt compelled to check all the same.

The best thing to do was head straight home. He had deliveries lined up all afternoon. A new refrigerator, new furniture for the living room, a new washer and dryer for the mudroom off the back of the cabin, and the all-important brand new mattress set for the old iron bed upstairs.

The landscapers were coming to tame the wild landscape around the cabin. He hired a road crew to grate and gravel the driveway. A contractor was coming to discuss and draw up plans for an addition to the cabin and get started on the necessary repairs that couldn't wait.

But he needed groceries to go in that new fridge. He'd already promised not to go into Fallbrook today, and he needed something to eat at the house. He tried desperately to concentrate on the here and now, the normal, and drove cautiously to the supermarket.

An hour later, his truck filled with new amenities for the house and enough groceries to feed him and Rain for a week at least, he headed home a lot worse for wear, and not because his bank account was several hundred dollars lower.

His leg throbbed, his head pounded, sweat lined his back, making his shirt stick to his skin. His stomach ached and he wished he'd remembered to grab one of the bottles of water out of the case before shoving it in the back of the truck under the tarp. Breathing hard and steady, he rounded the curve before he reached his driveway and everything closed in on him. Just when he was almost home, almost safe, the war came back with a vengeance.

Hunkered down beside his men on a rooftop, M4 held firm to his shoulder and aimed at the enemy several buildings to the north. The *rat-a-tat-tat* of gunfire signaled the start of the fight, smoke hung heavy in the air with the smell of burnt gunpowder. The whiz of a rocket-propelled grenade rang out right before it exploded to his left.

"Move! Move! Move!" he yelled, directing his men to pull back and take cover. Bullets exploded on the walls nearby. They'd go around the other side and take on the enemy from the other direction, while another team moved in behind them. Gunfire erupted from the right as one of his men shoved him from behind, sending him to the floor. His helmet got pushed back, and he cracked the side of his head on some loose debris, blood trickled into his eye.

He wiped it away, opening his eyes, he saw the driveway to the cabin through billowing smoke. Disoriented, everything went black.

Chapter Four

OWEN LEFT WORK early, picked up a six-pack of beer, and headed over to Brody's place to see if he could get a read on what Brody really planned for the rest of his life. He hoped to work children into the conversation, and see if he could gage Brody's desire to have a family. Wanting a relationship with Rain again was a good sign his wild-at-heart brother was ready for a quieter life, but kids might not be in his plans. If that was the case, Owen wanted to give Rain a heads-up before she introduced Brody to the girls and they received a bad reaction from Brody.

He rounded the bend and spotted Brody's truck half in a ditch. The tires screeched to a halt behind the truck. He jumped out on the run, hoping Brody wasn't hurt. The blood on the window frightened him. He pulled open the door and found Brody passed out, leaning heavily to the right. The seatbelt held him upright just enough to make him look really uncomfortable. Blood trickled from a small gash next to his eye and ran over his face, dripping onto his shirt.

"Man, are you all right?" Owen gave him a shake and pulled him upright. "Brody." To his relief, Brody started coming around. He pressed both hands to his eyes and forehead before looking around confused.

"Brody, you had an accident. Are you okay?"

"Owen?"

"What happened?"

"I got caught under fire. Hit my head."

Owen grabbed Brody's face and made him look at him. "Brody, man, you're in Colorado. You've been in an accident. It's me, Owen."

"I know who the fuck you are, asshole," Brody yelled. "My head is pounding." He closed his eyes against the pain. "I need my meds," he whispered.

Owen got the picture. Brody hadn't taken his medicine, and he was suffering some kind of anxiety attack. "Okay, man. Let's get into my truck, and I'll take you up to the cabin."

Brody slithered out of the driver's seat. The truck sat at an odd angle, pitched in the ditch, and Brody had to jump down further than usual. Unsteady, Owen grabbed his arm to keep him upright. "You got it."

"I'm fine," Brody snapped and pressed the heel of his hand to his head. He squinted his eyes and opened them again.

"Yeah, you look it." Owen nudged him toward his truck, sticking close to make sure Brody didn't take a nosedive into the ditch himself. "Come on, let's get your meds."

"Grab the groceries. They'll spoil if you leave them in the truck."

Owen wanted to make a smartass remark, but Brody wasn't in the mood to joke. Pale, sweat beading across his forehead and trickling down the side of his face, the shaking hands got to Owen the most. His strong, kick-ass-and-take-names brother needed help. Owen had no problem putting whatever animosity they'd held on to over the years in the past.

Stowing the groceries and whatever other bags he could fit into his truck, he jumped in and took off for the cabin. Brody sat quietly with his hand braced on his forehead, elbow propped on the door.

Neither spoke until they reached the cabin. A large delivery truck sat parked out front. Two men wheeled the old washer and dryer out of the cabin and up into the back.

"Damn, Brody. You smashed your truck and now they're repo-ing your shit." He made sure to look properly appalled.

Brody turned slowly, looking pissed off and mean. "Seriously?"

Owen busted up laughing. After a moment, the corner of Brody's mouth tilted up in half a smile. Satisfied Brody was starting to relax, Owen got out of the truck and hauled in the groceries, leaving Brody to follow at his own slow pace. He limped heavily on his left leg.

Owen dumped several bags of groceries in the kitchen

next to the brand new stainless steel refrigerator. The cupboard held two intact glasses. Rinsing one out, Owen filled and left it on the table by the bottles of pills, and headed out to bring the rest of the bags in. Brody eased up the steps, his skin a sickly shade of green.

Owen stood among the weeds, pulled out his cell, and called Eli.

"Hey, it's Owen. Can you come out to the cabin? Brody had an accident. His truck is in the ditch on the road just before the driveway."

"Anyone hurt?" Eli asked, concern laced in his deep voice.

"Brody's a little worse for wear, but that has more to do with being a soldier than the accident."

"How bad is the truck?"

"The front right tire is blown, not sure about the rim. I think the radiator is busted. Other than that, I didn't really have time to check it out."

"Okay. I'm on my way. We'll get it fixed up tomorrow."

"Thanks, Eli. I know he's not your favorite person . . ."

"If he'll be driving my granddaughters around, he'll need a safe, reliable truck," Eli answered without giving his opinion on Brody.

"I'll see you soon."

Eli hung up without a goodbye. Owen wasn't sure how Eli felt about the accident, his only expressed concern for Dawn and Autumn. Owen had to admit, he was worried about Brody's condition and whether or not he'd be able to take care of the girls on his own. He'd get that answer before he left tonight. Brody might not want to talk about his messed up head, but he would, even if Owen had to tell him about the girls.

Owen entered the cabin loaded down with bags. He put away the groceries. The refrigerator wasn't quite cold enough, so he left the perishables in the ice filled cooler Brody had packed them in. Brody sat at the table, his head down, a wet cloth pressed to the cut on the side of his head.

"Listen, Owen, I . . ."

"Go up and take a shower. I'll take care of things down here," he interrupted. The delivery guys hooked up the new washer and dryer in the mudroom off the kitchen. He noted the other delivery truck pulling up outside and cocked his head in their direction. "I'll take care of that, you get cleaned up."

Brody hesitated, so Owen pushed. "Give the meds some time to work."

"They're supposed to haul away the old couch, the kitchen table and chairs, and mattresses upstairs."

"No problem. Go," Owen ordered, knowing full well the stairs alone would be tough for Brody to manage. Brody didn't need an audience as he hobbled up one step at a time, the pain etching lines around his eyes.

BRODY SUCKED IT up and went upstairs without a word. Owen directed the guys downstairs on what to do. He took a minute to strip the bed, sending the old sheets over the banister to join the pile of debris below. He'd meant to spend today getting the cabin livable. He'd have to settle for getting the shopping done. Over the last few months, he'd learned some days you had to accept the little victories. He wasn't dead. He didn't crash his truck into another vehicle, or hit someone walking on the road.

Owen was a lawyer, but he didn't ask a hundred questions. In fact, he'd remained calm about the whole damn thing. Brody was grateful for that. Pulling his dirty, sweat-soaked shirt off over his head, he stepped into the bathroom wondering if Owen would call Rain and tell her to stay clear of him. Might be best for her, but it'd be the end of him.

He kicked off his boots, pulled off his socks and jeans, and stepped into the shower's stream. The heat worked its way into his body, numbing his mind to just the sound of the water beating on his head, drumming out the war and the tension.

By the time he stepped out, Owen had left him a cold soda and a new towel sitting on the counter beside the sink. The towel was one of those extra big ones, thick and soft, unlike the thin, threadbare ones that survived the years and party squatters.

It pleased Brody to see the new plastic-covered mattress on the old bed. It wasn't hard to imagine Rain stretched out, her fingers wrapped around the wrought-iron headboard, sunlight pouring through the window, highlighting her beautiful golden skin as he drove himself into her again and again. Now, that was a daydream he could sink into and get lost in.

The place still smelled like stale beer, dust, and some musty smell that just seemed to hang in the air. His brother must have had a hard time dealing with the smell, too. The front door and all the windows on the first floor stood wide open, a soft breeze working its way into the rooms, billowing the cobwebs strewn across the corners and ceiling. He wished it was that easy to clear out his muddled mind.

"You look almost human again."

Brody stepped off the last stair, his leg supporting his weight a lot better after the hot shower and pain-numbing meds. "Getting there. Listen, Owen . . ."

"The washer and dryer are hooked up. I tossed in the rest of the new towels and sheets to get the stiffness out. That washer is so big, you could wash a cow in there." Owen continued to stir the pot of canned chili on the stove with his back to Brody. "Put the groceries up for you. The fridge is cold enough now, so I left the cooler out back to dry out. I have to say, man, the place looks better with the new leather couch and table and chairs. Nice flat screen. The other furniture should clean up well enough. All you need is a cleaning crew to come in here and disinfect the joint, and you'll be good to go."

"Someone will be here first thing tomorrow." Brody took a seat at his new table, watching Owen ignore the elephant in the room. He looked around the kitchen, noted his new coffee pot was set up, coffee can sitting beside it, along with his bottles of pills. Owen had taken the time to wipe down the counters.

Brody scrubbed his hands over his face, noting the scratch of his beard, vowing to shave tomorrow morning before he went in search of Rain. He let out a gust of air in frustration.

"Don't you want to talk about my truck and what happened?"

"Sure. Eli came and took the truck to his garage. You've got a blown tire, cracked radiator hose, busted oil pan, and maybe some other minor damage. He'll fix it up, probably charge you double for the labor, since he thinks you're a prick for dumping his daughter the way you did, and all should be right with the truck day after next."

Owen dumped canned chili into two new bowls. The party people had used the old ones for skeet shooting and target practice in the backyard. Thankfully, their grandmother's silverware was still in the drawer. Owen grabbed a couple of spoons, shoved them into the thick mix, and set the bowls on the table with a thump before grabbing the cornbread out of the oven. "He hopes you'll be a hundred percent when you come to get the truck . . . so he can kill you," Owen finished around a bite of chili.

Brody stared at Owen enjoying his meal like he didn't have a care in the world. Like Brody hadn't lost his mind.

"You should eat something. Taking those pills on an empty stomach isn't a good idea."

"About what happened . . ."

"Brody. Man. Eat. Relax. Take a breath and let it out."

Brody took a bite and his stomach came to life, his hunger grew, so he sat companionably with his brother and ate and breathed. It took a minute for the quiet to sink in before Brody looked around and realized the delivery men were gone, his home was improved if not yet comfortable and clean, and this was the first time he'd sat down to a meal with Owen since they were fresh out of high school. Most nights, it had been he and Owen eating something out of a can, the old man either passed out on the couch or down at Roxy's tying one on. As much as he hated the old man for his drinking and temper, Brody had to admit there had always been something to eat in the house. Maybe not a real, healthy meal, but something. He guessed there were a lot of people out there who couldn't claim the same. Hell, he'd seen enough poverty and hunger in the faces of some of the smaller villages he'd been through during his tours of duty.

Sliding his empty bowl away, Brody caught Owen watching him, his eyes filled with concern. "I have flashbacks. The shrinks say it's post-traumatic stress disorder. I can't control it. They say it will take time to get accustomed to being back. Too much time in a war zone on the front lines, or some such shit."

"So, you're pissed because all the killing and dying left a mark on you?"

"I can live with the scars on my body. I look at them and remember how I got them and let them go. It's no big deal. This is different. I lived through the war once, I don't need to relive it again and again. The pain from the wounds to my body are part of healing what happened and moving on. The flashbacks bring everything back. It's a pain in the ass, and yes, it pisses me off. I just want it to be over. I hoped I could come back, see the old place, see you, be with Rain and it would all go away. Change my focus, change my mindset, and live a normal life again."

"You've spent the last six years at war, and you expect to just turn off those instincts and feelings and what, be a rancher?"

Brody smiled. "I'm not a rancher. Though I do plan on building a new barn and getting a few horses. I own a majority of a company. I can do the work from here," he added, because that's exactly what he wanted to do. Unless it turned out Rain lived somewhere else and didn't want to move back to Fallbrook and live with him on Clear Water Ranch. Actually, the more he thought about those horses he wanted, the more he thought he could make a decent living breeding and selling them.

First things first, he needed to find Rain and get her back.

"As for the flashbacks, can't turn them off. They just happen. The meds help. I left this morning on a mission, and forgot to take the pills with me. I have triggers, things that set me off. Noise, crowds, constantly being on alert, looking for snipers and threats."

Does Owen think I'm as crazy as I sound?

"I know they aren't there, but it's a habit that's hard to break. It becomes a part of who you are, that constant intense alertness to everything around you."

"I get it," Owen said simply. "I've seen news reports about the troops coming home. They need help, and the government, in its slow, inefficient way, is trying to provide the medical and psychological care the soldiers require after what they've been through in Iraq and Afghanistan. So relax, Brody. I don't think you're crazy. I think you're a hero, who deserves whatever time it takes to adjust and settle."

Brody shifted uncomfortably at the term *hero*. Hard to think anything he'd done was heroic. Sure, he saw the big picture and understood many of the people in Iraq were better off. The details of how that was accomplished didn't strike him as heroic, not when a lot of innocent blood had been spilled, and friends and comrades died.

"I'd appreciate it if you didn't tell Rain what happened today." Brody knew full well Owen would tell her.

"Small towns, man," Owen retorted.

"Great. The bastard who left her after sleeping with the town slut comes home off his rocker with a patchwork of scars and a cabin that looks like a garbage dump. Why wouldn't she give me the time of day?"

"I think you've got a shot at a relationship with her. It might not be the way you want it, or for the reasons you think, but Rain is a good woman with a big heart."

"What the hell does any of that mean?"

"You'll see."

Growling with frustration, Brody asked, "Is she in town? Did you see her today?"

"I talked to her," Owen evaded, pissing Brody off even more. "I told her you were back."

"What'd she say?"

"She wanted to know why."

"What'd you tell her?"

"That you're looking for her."

"What did she say to that?" Brody asked through his teeth. Pretty soon, he'd beat the answers out of Owen, until he talked faster than Brody's fists hit him.

"Not much."

Brody made a move to go after Owen, but Owen conceded by holding up a hand and smirking like an idiot. "Okay. She wanted to know why you came home now. She knows you were in the military and got hurt. I kept her up to date on your condition and progress through rehab."

"She knows about the burns and shrapnel." Brody turned his head away. Never far from his mind, he knew one day, if he was lucky enough to win Rain's heart again, she'd see the damage to his leg. He could walk fine, his jeans covered most of the damage to his hip, but in bed, she'd know. She'd see the gnarled, discolored skin and the scars from surgery and shrapnel tearing up his flesh.

"She knows about the gunshot wound, every time you got stitched up for one thing or another, everything."

"How the hell did you find all of this out? I never called you. I never told you I was in the military."

"I was wondering when you'd ask me about that," Owen said, stalling for time. "I left town about six months ahead of you."

"You went off to college and left me here to deal with the old man." Brody didn't hide his anger.

Owen felt that same anger every time he'd had to take care of something the old man fell short doing for himself, for Brody, for him. Owen didn't have a choice but to leave. At the time, it'd been a matter of survival. Brody hadn't hit that mark. No, it took him another six months to reach his rock bottom and see that walking the same path as their father would only lead them down a broken road of misery.

"Your choice," Owen countered. "You could have gone to college yourself."

"I was never interested in school. Got the grades I needed to pass without looking like an idiot."

"Don't pull that shit with me, Brody. You were a good student without using even half of your brain cells. You got straight As on all the college courses you took through correspondence and online while you were in the military."

"How the hell do you know that?" Brody snapped. He couldn't believe the kind of information Owen gathered without so much as a phone call from him. "Did you hire some private detective to ferret out all my secrets?"

"Didn't have to. I went to law school with a guy whose father is a major general. He connected me with your captain. I spoke with him once a month for the last six years."

"Are you shitting me?"

"Do you really think you can be hospitalized in the military and they won't contact your next of kin, no matter how much you protest and tell them not to? That's bullshit, Brody. And a hell of a thing to do to your only brother. I don't care how pissed you are at me for leaving. You had no right to leave without a word, and then not call when you were wounded in action. Not the first time, or the tenth."

Owen took a deep swallow of soda, let his anger simmer, and sat back heavily in his chair. Circling his finger over the wood table, he spoke softly, "I came to the hospital in Georgia. You were unconscious, and I sat with you for a few hours. You didn't want me there, so I made sure I was gone when you woke up. I stayed for a couple of days and made sure you received the care you needed."

Brody felt like shit. One afternoon, he'd woken up with Owen's name sputtering across his lips. He could have sworn he'd heard Owen talking to him. Awake, all he found was a nurse checking his blood pressure. She'd said the oddest thing at the time about calling his brother back. He'd thought she'd meant to call him on the phone. Now, he knew. Owen had been there.

Rain hadn't been far from his mind in those first few days of waking up in constant pain, disoriented and miserable. He'd hallucinated about her many times. It was too much to hope those ghostly images and imagined whispers were truly Rain standing beside him, ordering him to fight.

"I didn't know." He was afraid to ask if those hallucinations of Rain were real. He'd already shown Owen an up-close-and-personal view of how screwed up his head was. He didn't need to give him any more ammo to use against him with Rain.

"You wanted your own life, to stand on your own two feet. I know how that feels, because I left this place determined to be my own man and not the son of John McBride. When I came back to practice law, I did it on my terms. I knew when I'd changed enough, accepted the past for what it was, and moved on to being who I wanted to be. I guess you just needed a little longer."

"You didn't do half bad working for that fancy Washington law firm," Brody tossed out to let Owen know he wasn't the only one who'd done some snooping.

"Yeah, I made some money, but I wanted something more in my life. I like small-town living. I like practicing law here, and I still make a better than decent living."

"All you need is a woman."

"Yeah, well, I've been busy with your woman," Owen said. "If we're revealing all, let's not overlook the fact the little company you own majority share in is worth multimillions and you hold the patent on some very hot commodities."

"Damn, you do know a thing or two."

"I'm a lawyer. Digging up information is my business." Owen gave Brody a discerning look. "How come you know about me, but you didn't look up Rain?"

"You don't miss anything, Counselor."

"Not much. Spill it."

"I did enough damage when I left is the lame answer. I was tied to the military by contract is just another excuse."

"You were afraid she'd turn you down flat," Owen guessed.

"Absolutely. If I wanted even a slim chance of getting her back, I'd have to do it in person."

"It's hard to hang up on a live person all right."

Brody took a deep breath and let out the real reason he'd waited so long. "I didn't want to come home empty handed. She planned to leave for college, would have an education and a great job under her belt. I didn't want to be the dumb hick she loved but had to support, like the old man was to my mother."

"Brody, that was your mother's choice. She knew exactly what the old man was like before she married him. Marrying him didn't make him a different man. He was the same one she'd fallen in love with, for better or worse."

"Seems to me she only got the worse," Brody said sadly.

"She got the better in you. She loved you, Brody. And me," Owen said in all honesty.

"Where's your mom these days?" Brody asked.

"Married to a podiatrist in Florida. Says she can wear heels all day long because the guy's got magic hands." Owen rolled his eyes to the ceiling, his mouth set in a grim line. "I do not even want to know what she means by that," he said miserably.

Brody laughed. "Sounds just like Sharon. So, you see why I didn't want to come back, find Rain, and offer her nothing but my disability check from the military?"

"I get it. But there's something you didn't take into account. Rain." Owen stood and took both bowls to the sink and set them inside with a distinct thud. When he turned around, he leaned back against the counter and crossed his arms over his chest. "She didn't go to college. In fact, she never left town. She's been here the whole time."

"What?" Brody burst out, surprised and confused. "She had her scholarship all lined up. She had the money from her grandparents' and her mother's estates. Eli saved every extra penny he could get his hands on. She was supposed to leave for San Francisco."

"She didn't. Couldn't, really."

"What does that mean? Did something happen to Rain?"

"You did," Owen said in all seriousness. "Things happen, Brody. Life happens. She did the best she could. She tried to find you after you left. Chased you down across three states before she lost you in Arizona. After that, she gave up. You made it perfectly clear by your constant wandering you didn't want to be found."

"Why did she try to find me?"

"You'll have to ask her. The rest of the story is hers to tell. I can only tell you that you don't have to worry about trying to find her, or that she won't want to talk to you. She does. She'll be expecting you when you're ready to go and see her. I suggest you get this place in order, take another day or two to settle in and get some rest."

Ignoring Owen's suggestion to wait a couple of days, Brody asked a simple question and hoped Owen gave him a straight answer for once. "You've seen Rain, talked to her over the last few years you've been back. Do you think there's a chance she could love me again?"

Owen laughed. "She's more likely to lop off your head for what you did to her."

Brody let out a defeated sigh, his shoulders slumped.

"I'm kidding. You've got a shot. She left a window open, even if she did slam the door in your face."

It was too much to hope for, so Brody took in those words and buried them with the rest of his dreams. "What would you do if you were me and you wanted her back?"

"I'd go to her knowing I was the one in the wrong. I'd remember she tried to find me once. As much as you want to explain your side to her, remember she has a side, too. There's a reason she never left town. You have everything to do with that reason." Grabbing his keys from the counter, Owen started toward the door. "I'll leave you to think about that. It might take some time, but I have a feeling everything will work out. If you're not a bonehead," Owen added and shut the door between them.

Brody stood and stared out the window. Owen climbed into his truck and headed for the main house just over the rise. When he turned back to the room, he decided Owen might be right about putting his life and house in order before he went to see Rain.

Rain didn't go to college. She stayed in town because of him. He hated to think he'd hurt her so badly, she refused to take her scholarship and reach for her dream.

But that wasn't right. Rain wasn't the kind of woman, even at eighteen, who'd give up so much for something as stupid as her boyfriend leaving her. It was more likely she'd have gone off to San Francisco with a tilt to her head, her chin out, and a fuck-you attitude toward him with every A she earned.

What would make Rain stay? As he settled into bed that night, the new soft mattress at his back, clean sheets cocooning him, his hands clasped behind his head on his down pillow, he had a very bad feeling he'd done something far worse to Rain than he realized.

Chapter Five

BRODY HATED DELAYING seeing Rain. Knowing she was in town, expecting him even, made it hard to stay at the cabin and get things done. All he wanted to do was find her and put an end to his imaginings about what kept her from attending school eight years ago. Besides, he couldn't have gone to town if he wanted to, unless he walked the fifteen miles. With his leg, he'd likely not make it two miles. His truck was at Eli's garage, and Owen remained conspicuously absent the last two days.

Without wasting any time, he got the road crew working early the morning after Owen left. His driveway was grated and re-graveled within a few hours. Too bad he didn't have a truck to drive over it. He did, however, have a clean cabin. The place was sanitized and scrubbed to the point he could eat off the floors. Then, the contractor and his crew showed up. They'd dug out the new foundation to connect with the cabin and add on another bedroom and bathroom and expand the living room. The landscapers cleared all the garbage from the yard, dug out the dead plants and trees, and cut all the grass down, tilled a few sections under, laid out new sod, planted some shrubs and flowers, and basically transformed the place in two days. It looked like someone actually lived there again.

The lake was the best. The contractor fixed up the dock and the landscaper planted several flowering bushes around the dock and lake border to make it more inviting. He spent most of last night watching the sun go down behind the mountains and eating dinner surrounded by water and the scent of fresh-cut wood.

His peaceful night by the lake turned into a restless night tossing and turning in his empty bed and waking up in a cold sweat, fighting imaginary insurgents. That agonizing dream replaced the one where he'd been sliding his hand up Rain's thigh, his hard cock thrusting deep inside her, as he locked his mouth with hers, waging war with his tongue for total possession of her. And God, he'd been hot and throbbing, her skin pressed to his. He could even taste her. Then everything changed. A bomb exploded, cutting off all sound but that eerie, muffled ringing and the sound of his harsh breaths. Rain was gone, and he was disoriented and surveying his surroundings, gun at the ready, trying to get his bearings and a read on the enemy.

Determined to go into town, he'd stood in the doorway, looking out at his new yard and driveway, drinking strong coffee. As soon as Jim, the contractor, showed up, he asked him to have one of his guys take him to Eli's garage.

On edge, the morning got away from him. After speaking to Jim about the plans for the addition and the work to be done that day, he took several calls for work. By the time Jim's man took him to town, it was past lunch. Before leaving, he took his pills, stuffed the bottles into his pocket just in case, and rode into town with a plan to get his truck, bust down Owen's office door, and demand to know where to find Rain.

His truck wasn't outside in the lot, so he went in through the open bay door. The truck sat in another stall against the far wall. He didn't see Eli anywhere, but a pair of black work boots and legs in coveralls stuck out from under a Buick. Since the boots and legs were too small to be Eli's, Brody figured the guy for one of the mechanics.

"Hey, man, have you seen Eli? I came to pick up my truck."

A tool clinked on the cement before a long silent pause. Brody waited for a response from the owner of the small feet. When a pair of equally small hands grabbed the side of the car and the rest of the person slid out on a rolling cart, his heart stopped. Lying at his feet, Rain, dressed in a pair of dirty coveralls, a black ski cap on her head, and a stunned expression on her heart-shaped face. The garage was cold this time of year, her face was a little pale and her lips weren't quite the rosy pink he remembered, but her eyes were that same shade of sable brown. With her pert little nose and big round eyes, she had always reminded him of a fairy, especially when she smiled. Which she wasn't doing now. One perfectly arched dark eyebrow went up when he just stood staring down at her.

"Pop's in the office. Keys are in the truck," she said in that same husky voice that had whispered to him in the night.

"Rain," he managed on a ragged exhale.

"Ah, you remembered."

She rolled up to her feet in one fluid motion and stood before him a little bit of a thing at five-five to his six-three. Hands on her hips in true Rain fashion, he could only stare at the woman before him. She looked the same. Well, except her hair was all tucked up under that cap. He wanted to snatch it off her head and let her hair fall down her back in waves of deep brown. He remembered exactly how it smelled of sunshine and flowers, how it felt in his hands when he kissed her and held her head to him. The satiny feel of it brushing over his bare chest when he made love to her.

"And here I thought you came home to see me. I must have been misinformed." She tried to hide her nerves under all that sarcasm, but he recognized the tactic.

"I did come home to see you. I just got sidetracked with the truck and the cabin. What are you doing here?"

"Changing the oil on Mrs. Bloomfield's car."

"No, why are you working here?"

"I've worked here since I was a kid. Did my first oil change when I was five. Or have you forgotten?"

She was being obstinate. He deserved that and a lot

more. At least she wasn't screaming at him. Though he wasn't sure about this calm woman standing before him. Something was definitely different about her.

"How's the head, Brody?" She put her hand up to touch the bruise and cut at the side of his face by his hairline. Instinctively, he pulled back, blocked her hand, sweeping his out to push hers away, and regretted it immediately when she let her hand fall to her side. What he wouldn't give to feel her fingers on his skin again.

"Sorry. It's not you, it's just . . ."

"How's the leg? Doesn't look like it's bothering you much. Owen said your rehabilitation went well. He said you have a slight limp . . ." she halted her rambling and just looked up at him. "Sorry. You probably didn't come here to talk about that."

"I have a lot of things I want to talk to you about. The head's just a scratch. The leg's . . . well, it's better. What about you?"

"Oh, I'm fine."

"You look it," he said without thinking. "You're more beautiful than I remember."

Rain let out a nervous laugh, and he caught a glimpse of that elusive smile. She looked down at herself. Didn't matter what she wore, she would always be the most beautiful woman he'd ever seen in his life.

"Thanks."

Someone's shoes scuffed on the ground behind him. Eli. Wasn't hard to imagine what was coming. Rain kept that passive expression on her face when she said, "Turn around, Brody."

The first punch hit him in the jaw, but he expected it and turned his face with the blow, taking much of the sting out of it. He hoped Eli didn't notice. The second one came fast, but Brody grabbed Eli's fist and held it.

"Hi, Eli."

"Sonofabitch." Eli quit pushing against his hand, so Brody let him go. "Looks like you learned a few things over there," Eli said, obviously referring to the war.

He rubbed his jaw, easing the sting. "A few. I deserved the punch and a good pounding, but I'd really rather just say I'm sorry. I hope you'll let me talk to Rain and let us work a few things out."

"Well, damn, boy. You had to go and grow up and ruin my fun."

"Yes, sir."

"Sir, shit. I've known you since you were just a baby. Let's just keep it at Eli." He turned to Rain. "You two have enough time to talk about . . . you know?"

"No," Rain said and looked up at him. "Brody, there's something you need to know. I don't have much time. I want you to hear this from me before anyone else in town gossips to you about it."

"Whatever it is, I'd love to hear all about it. Let's go somewhere and talk." He wanted to get her alone. Somewhere he could just be with her, maybe even kiss her. God, he wanted to kiss her.

"I can't. I'm waiting for a couple of people to meet me here. Brody, when you left, I never got the chance to tell you . . ."

"I took off on you, Rain. I didn't want to leave you, but

after what I'd done, I figured you'd never want to see me again."

"Yes, but there's something you don't know."

"Owen told me you didn't go away to school. Why? It's all you talked about. You had everything planned."

"Yes," she snapped. "I did have it all planned. But life has a way of pulling the rug right out from under you." Hands back on her hips, her cheeks flushed. Pissed off, she let him have it. "After years of friendship, all those months we were seeing each other, growing closer, you went and threw it all away. And for what? A pair of tits half the men in this town have gotten their hands on for nothing more than a 'Come on Roxy, give a guy a little sugar,'" she said scathingly. "Two days after you slept with her, you and I . . ." She stopped herself from going on, knowing full well her father was standing right there discreetly listening to everything. It wasn't lost on Brody that Eli wasn't about to leave them to their privacy. Rain had something on her mind, and Eli would stand beside her while she got it said.

"Rain, this isn't how I wanted things to go."

"Yeah, well, we don't always get what we want," she snapped. She let out a deep breath and added, "Sometimes, we get something better."

"I don't understand what you're talking about."

Stomping her boot against the cement, she said, "Shit. I'm out of time." A car pulled up behind him. The engine cut off. Rain struggled to say whatever it was on her mind.

"Brody, when you left, I was angry. Angrier than I've

ever been. But two weeks later everything changed. I tried to find you. I really did."

"Owen told me you tried to find me," he confirmed, because she looked so lost for a minute. Her eyes went soft and she bit her lower lip. He'd never seen her look this sad and unsure.

Her chest rose and fell with a heavy sigh. "Brody, when you left, I was pregnant."

Brody stilled, rooted to the floor like some great oak. That familiar closing in of his senses took over. The air grew charged. His ears were ringing again. For a minute, he thought his bent mind would take him back to the war and some other kind of nightmare. He wasn't sure he wouldn't welcome it this time, because he couldn't be that bastard who left his woman behind, pregnant, without a word from him for eight years. It just couldn't be.

"No." His voice was quiet, but she heard him. Her eyes were round and sad and pleaded with him to understand.

She'll never take me back, he thought as the world came back with one sentence from a small voice behind him. "That must be him."

Before Brody turned to that voice, Rain grabbed him by the shoulders and shook him to make him look at her. "We have a little girl, Brody. But there's more."

Of course there was more. There was always more, he thought miserably.

"A few months after you left, Roxy started showing, too."

"No," Brody heard himself say. "No."

"She had a little girl, too."

"Rain. How? She. Roxy. Your school. What?" Not a single thought would take hold in his mind and work its way out of his mouth. He couldn't think. Instinct told him to run. Get as far away from this mess as he could. A bigger part of him, a part he had often ignored in the past told him to stay put and hold on to Rain. This could all be worked out. He had a child. Children. Two little girls. His. Looking at Rain, his only thought was, *mine*.

Damnit, this time he wasn't letting her go.

"Brody, you have two daughters. They're standing behind you. They've waited a long time to meet their father."

Taking a step toward her, he said softly, "You gave me a daughter."

Rain took a step back and ran into the car behind her. "Yes. She's right behind you." Her eyes grew wide when Brody advanced on her, grabbed her by the front of her coveralls, hauled her up to her toes, and kissed her.

He felt her shock and the jolt when their bodies touched. She went rigid, her mouth not responding, her eyes wide. But he didn't give up. Not after all this time. He wanted her more than anything in the world. After everything he'd been through, the taste of her eased all the anxieties, crowded into all the dark corners, consumed all the anger and pain and left nothing behind but good.

When she went lax against him, her lips softening against his, he pressed her into the car, his whole body aligned with hers. She returned the kiss with as much heat and demand as he gave to her. This he remembered.

This is how things used to be between them. One touch ignited the fire in both of them.

"Is he mad at her?" a little voice asked behind him.

"No, honey. He's very happy," Owen said with a laugh in his voice.

Brody reluctantly stopped putting on a show for everyone standing behind them watching. With his forehead pressed to Rain's, he tried to rein in his emotions and put words together that would make sense and tell her just what this meant to him. "Thank you. I'm sorry." He kissed her slow and softly. This time, there was no resistance. Her silence made him nervous, but he was just so damn glad to be this close to her. "Thank you, Rain. You don't know what this means to me."

"Is he going to kiss Roxy like that, too?" the little voice asked, and Rain's body turned to stone with a look of pure rage in her eyes a moment before she pressed both hands to his chest and shoved him away. Falling back onto her flat feet, he gave her some space. He needed some, too.

"No." Brody never took his eyes off Rain.

Rain slapped a hand on his shoulder and turned him toward the two girls standing in front of his brother.

Time stopped, everything in him stilled. They looked alike in every way, and so much like him. Blond hair and round faces with little pert noses. They even dressed alike. Both girls wore jeans, pink tops, though one had a darker version, and pink Converse high tops. Rain's influence there, he thought.

One of the girls belonged to Rain. He recognized which upon closer inspection. The one with the light pink shirt had wavier hair and her mother's nose. Looking more closely at the girl in the darker pink shirt, he tried to see Roxy in her. She seemed to be the shyer of the two. Everything about her appearance resembled him. The only thing he could say that spoke to Roxy's contribution was that she was slim and maybe the shape of her eyes was a little like Roxy's. The color was all him and shared by both girls.

He bent on his good knee in front of them, knowing full well Owen, Eli, and Rain watched him closely. The two girls remained reserved, but inquisitive enough to look him up and down.

"Hi," he said and had to clear his clogged throat. "I'm Brody, your dad."

The two girls looked at each other, then Rain's daughter spoke for the two of them. "Do we have to call you Brody?"

"If you want to for a while, that's okay. But it would really make me happy if you called me Dad."

"Because you want us?" Roxy's daughter asked softly.

Brody thought he'd lose it. His throat hurt for keeping the tears from spilling out his eyes. "Yes, honey. I want you very much. If I'd known about the two of you, I'd have come back for you."

"Are you going to take us?"

Confused by the question, he glanced up and found Rain standing close. She went to the girls, stood behind them, and put a hand on each of their shoulders. "Girls, Brody just found out about you. Whatever decisions have to be made, Brody and I will discuss them. But no matter what, I'll always be with you."

"But, Mom . . ."

"Dawn, let it be for now," she said softly.

"Dawn?" Brody asked.

Rain looked down at him and smiled softly. The smile didn't really reach her eyes; too much worry clouded any happiness she might feel. The sadness he read easily. Her heart couldn't stand he'd missed out on knowing the girls. "I think you know Dawn is your daughter with me." She looked down at the other girl. "Autumn is your daughter with Roxy." Rain smiled at her worried little face.

"Dawn and Autumn. Beautiful," he said, meaning their names and the girls themselves. It hit him hard. He was their father. As time ticked by, the meaning of that took root inside of him. A piece of his heart grew two sizes and came to life. His chest ached, he was so full of emotion.

"Well, I guess we'll have to talk with your mom, Autumn."

"No! She's not my mom. God put me in the wrong belly!" Autumn yelled and buried her face in Rain's stomach. Rain wrapped her up in her arms and stared down at Brody, rolling her eyes and letting out a frustrated sigh.

"Brody, Autumn is mine. It's a long story, one we'll get into another time." Cocking her head toward the two girls wrapped around her. "I figured you'd be by today for the truck. I just wanted you to meet them."

Unsteady, he rose to face her. "But, Rain . . ."

"Let it be, Brody. Give yourself and them time to adjust."

Rain moved away, leaving him feeling lost. Dawn and Autumn stood beside Eli. Owen stood near Rain. He was the outsider here. He had a past he'd come home to face with Rain, but the girls made everything more complicated. He owed Rain more than an apology for leaving.

She'd given up everything to be a mother to his children. He wasn't sure why she had Autumn, but it was clear Autumn saw Rain as her one and only mother.

Eli spoke up, trying to defuse a volatile situation. "Let's start with a family dinner. Say, six o'clock at Rain's house?"

Owen smiled wickedly. "I wouldn't miss it for the world."

Rain rolled her eyes and turned her back on all of them. "Let's go home, girls. You've got homework. I've got to cook dinner for six." She left the garage bay with her head up, shoulders stiff. A little girl on each side of her, tiny hands clasped in hers, she'd never looked more beautiful.

Chapter Six

"She's pissed," Brody said, stunned the girls driving away with Rain belonged to him. His girls. All of them. That's how Brody thought of them now. He liked that. A lot. Still, the guilt threatened to swallow him whole. It gnawed at his gut and made it hard to breathe.

"She has every right to be pissed," Eli said, examining the Buick, checking to see where Rain left off.

"What about me? Don't I get to be pissed that I have two daughters no one told me about? Owen?" As overwhelmed as he was right now, his mind grabbed on to the one thing no one had said. "Why the hell didn't you call me? You had my captain's number for the last six years. You knew about my being shot, the roadside bomb."

"Don't blame me. You're the one who slept with two women within days of each other. Normally, I'd high-five you and buy you a beer. But you were reckless and a sonofabitch. You left, never thinking you might have gotten even one of them pregnant.

"People who hide the way you did, usually have a good reason. We all know why you were hiding. Think about how that made Rain feel. You'd rather disappear than face her.

"Imagine how she felt when you took off without a word. Then, imagine how she felt when everyone knew she was pregnant with your baby, and there's Roxy parading around town pregnant as well."

"How did anyone know Roxy's baby was mine to begin with?"

"Seriously? You know what a conniving bitch Roxy can be. She told everyone the baby was yours. Sure, everyone had their suspicions the baby could belong to any number of men in and around town. But she wouldn't shut up about it being yours. It's like she had some sort of grudge against Rain."

"She did," Eli interjected. "Roxy hates Rain."

"Why? Between their three-year age difference and their completely opposite lives, why the hell would Roxy care about Rain at all?" Brody had never understood the grudge Roxy held against Rain.

"Simple. Look at Roxy's life. Look at what Rain's life was supposed to be. Rain had a chance to leave small-town-nowhere behind, go to college, build a dream life with an education behind her and opportunities in front of her. Roxy had been stuck here all her life, raised in that bar by her father before he died the year after she graduated. She wanted more. Never got it. Always looking for the easy way, she never considered working hard to earn it. Then, she set her sights on you. Probably because she wanted to take Rain down a few pegs, or just because she wanted to take one of those good things away from Rain."

"Yeah, I was real good for Rain." Actually, Brody thought, the only person who'd ever thought he was any good was Rain. And he'd had to go and prove her wrong.

"You weren't then," Eli began, "You need to do better now. You've got two daughters to consider."

Brody turned to Owen. "Two daughters you could have told me about any time during the last six years."

Owen frowned. "She asked me not to."

"What? Why?"

"She had her reasons," Owen said, not telling him anything.

"She had no right . . ."

"You weren't around to tell." Eli crossed his arms over his chest. "She spent three years trying to find you, but you made damn sure you couldn't be found. She loved and took care of Autumn like she was her own. The minute she sees you, she tells you about the girls. She didn't hide it from you. In fact, she's terrified you'll try to take them away from her for no other reason than to be ornery about the fact you didn't know about them."

"I'd never do that. I want us to be a family."

"Yeah, I got that from the kiss you laid on her. Not fair, by the way. Since you've been gone, she's been a mother. It's been a long time since she remembered she's also a woman," Eli said, giving him a nod when the shock registered on his face.

His brain was on overload. Brody decided with Eli present, better to stick to his daughters than the fact Rain tasted as good as ice cream on a summer day, and he had plans for that delectable woman. Hot, sweaty plans with lots more kissing.

"Okay, forget everything else. How did Rain end up with Autumn?"

"Because, dumb-shit, you had sex with a viper," Owen said scathingly. "Rain had to—"

"That's for Rain to tell you," Eli interrupted. Owen clamped his jaw shut, daggers shooting out his eyes all aimed at Brody.

Brody bit back a hot retort and the demand someone give him a straight answer. Apparently, the only one who'd do that was Rain. "Okay. What about Rain and the girls? Where are they living? Are the girls healthy? Do they need anything?" He tried to cover all the bases, but he'd just become a father and he wasn't sure where to start. He'd planned on coming here, finding Rain, convincing—*begging*, if he had to—her to marry him, and then they'd have a family. It seemed so easy and brilliant in his mind. Reality sucked. Well, maybe not. He had a child with Rain. Two, by the looks of the bond between her and Autumn. That was his ticket in the door. Now all he had to do was keep her from tossing him out on his ass again.

"The girls are perfect," Owen said, smiling for the first time since Rain left. "They live in Eli's old house. Eli moved to the apartment upstairs after the girls were born."

"I wanted her to have a place of her own, to be on her own. I couldn't give her college and the freedom she'd worked so hard to earn, but I could give her the freedom to run her own household and raise her girls without my interference."

"When I moved back to town, I offered to help her financially." Owen's eyes grew sad. "She wouldn't accept, except a few times when she was short and didn't have a choice but to ask for help."

"So, she's had Autumn since she was a baby?"

"Yes. But that's a long, ugly story. One you'll have to get from Rain. She deserves a chance to tell you herself," Owen said.

"Fine. Owen, are you done for the day?"

"I've got a few things to tie up at the office. Why?"

"Seems I have a family to take care of and provide for. I'll need your help putting some legal matters in order."

"Will you petition the court for joint custody?" Eli asked.

"No. I need to set some things up for the girls. I owe Rain seven years of child support and some kind of monthly support from now on. That is, until I can convince her to marry me," Brody said bluntly to gauge Eli's reaction. Eli didn't give anything away, only stood waiting to hear what came next.

"I own the cabin and half land on Clear Water Ranch. I also own part of a company. If something happens to me, those things will go to the girls."

"Wait," Eli interrupted. "How do you own a company when you've been in Iraq and Afghanistan for the last six years?"

"I had a buddy who was really smart and had a great idea, but he needed the money to get started. The military provided everything I needed, I banked a lot of the money I earned, and decided to invest in my buddy's idea. He started the company and got the patents on a couple of his ideas, but because I financed the patents, I insisted the patents be in my name to protect my investment."

"Sounds like you were the smart one," Eli said, surprising him.

"If Bill Gates can buy an operating system from someone and build a company, why couldn't I do something similar? Anyway, the company took off. I do some of the work, but for the most part, I'm a silent partner. Now that I have the time, I'll get more involved."

"Your degree in business and finance doesn't hurt," Owen put in.

"You know all this about me, but you couldn't make a simple phone call and say, 'Hey, man, come home. There're a couple people you need to meet.'"

"You were overseas most of the time. Besides, not my call to make," Owen said. "Get over it."

"I don't have a choice. I do, however, have to change my plans for the future."

"So, you'll stick around this time?" Eli asked.

"I'm not going anywhere. At least, not without my girls." Seeing both Eli and Owen about to argue, he added, "All my girls, Rain included. If that woman thought I was stubborn before, she hasn't seen anything yet."

Brody let that sink in with both his brother and Eli.

Since Eli didn't seem inclined to kill him or maim him anymore, he asked, "What do I owe you for the truck?"

Eli pulled out a slip from his back pocket and handed it over. Brody looked at the list of parts and their cost. "This can't be the total."

"That's the bill. How do you want to settle up? Check? Credit card?"

"There's nothing on here for the labor."

"According to Rain, we don't charge labor for family."

That hit him right dead center in the heart. "She said that?"

"Yep. Pay for the parts. She did the work. As far as I know, she left your brake lines intact." He winked and Brody almost laughed, but Eli's words held a ring of truth to them.

As much as Rain might want him in the girls' lives, they still had a lot to work out. Rain was a stubborn, proud, strong woman, who could make things difficult if she wanted to torture him. He had no doubt she'd mete out some kind of punishment. He'd just have to take his licks and convince her he may have left a scoundrel, but he'd come back a man ready to settle down into a comfortable life as a husband—and father.

He'd just thought to do those things in that order, not the other way around.

Chapter Seven

BRODY NEVER THOUGHT he'd be afraid of two little girls, but he sat outside Rain's old house afraid to go up the walk and face them. He didn't know them, and they didn't know him. He desperately wanted them to see him as their father, call him Dad, and love him. If he'd been there from the start, he'd have all those things. Coming in halfway through their raising, he'd have to earn it. He had no idea how to go about doing it. The only thing he'd come up with over the last two hours was to win them over, just like he had to win over Rain. If dating Rain turned into love once before, it could again. He could date his daughters too in a sense. It all came down to time. He needed time to prove himself, to his girls and to Rain.

He grabbed everything he'd brought with him, got out of the truck, and made his way up the walkway. Before he knocked, Rain opened the door. She wasn't quite smiling, but she wasn't hissing and spitting either.

"The girls were watching you from their window upstairs. They thought maybe you'd changed your mind about being their dad."

One side of his mouth went down before he answered. "Can't change something that is."

"Don't I know it," Rain shot back.

Unclamping his jaw, he held out the roses to her. "For you. Two for every year I was gone. One for each girl. I owe you a hell of a lot more. Think of this as a peace offering. At least, for tonight."

Although she held the roses in front of her, she hesitated to bury her face in them. She didn't want to like them. Then, she gave in and smelled them before brushing her fingers over the delicate petals. "How on earth did you find purple roses?"

"I'm a resourceful guy," he said with a grin. Memories flooded back. "Whenever you came out to the ranch and we'd walk the fields, you always picked the purple wildflowers. I guessed purple was your favorite."

"They're beautiful."

"Yeah, beautiful," he said, looking at her face. Not quite as long as he remembered, her hair hung in waves down past her shoulders. Her face was scrubbed clean, maybe a touch of makeup on her eyes. She'd never worn much. She didn't need to. Those deep pools of brown remained wary.

It was a moment, her standing there holding the huge bouquet of flowers, their eyes locked, time standing still. He wanted to tell her he loved her. Just say the words, let them fall from his lips and possibly wipe away some of the hurt and pain he'd caused her.

He opened his mouth, only to clamp it shut when his brother appeared behind Rain.

"You guys coming in, or what?"

Rain jumped and pasted that calm, blank expression on her face. She turned and disappeared into the house without another word.

"Was it something I said?" Owen joked with a wide smile.

"You might have given me another minute alone with her," he said under his breath, trying to reel in his temper.

"The girls are tired of waiting."

Magically, the two little ones appeared out from behind Owen's legs. He gave them both a huge smile. He had to admit, he was happy to see them.

"We made spaghetti," Dawn announced.

"You did?"

"Mom said it's your favorite."

"It sure is. Did you help her make it?"

"Yeah. Autumn helped, too."

Brody stared down at his other daughter. Half-hidden behind Owen, looking up at him with her thumb and index finger pinching at her bottom lip. Her eyes were as wary as her mother's. "Hi, Autumn."

"Hi," she said softly. He bent with the pink bakery box held in front of him. "What's in the box?"

Brody smiled, letting her know he wouldn't bite. "Well, now. This here is something special for you and Dawn. Want to peek?"

"I want to see!" Dawn shouted and moved closer,

putting her hand on his shoulder. Nothing had ever felt better than that little hand, so trusting.

Autumn, obviously the more cautious and shy one, he'd have the hardest time winning her over. "Autumn, go ahead, take a look."

She came out from behind Owen's legs and moved toward him. Very slowly, she stretched out her hand and lifted the lid of the box like there were monsters inside. Her eyes grew wide as saucers and she smiled. It was the prettiest smile he'd ever seen, lighting up her whole face. For a moment, he thought she looked like his mother.

Dawn's squeal was ear-piercing. "Cupcakes."

"That's right, sweetheart. For after dinner," he added to Dawn. Fixing his attention back on Autumn, he asked, "Do you like chocolate, Autumn?"

She nodded and bit down on her lower lip.

"Well, how about we go inside and see about dinner. The sooner we eat, the sooner you two can have the cupcakes. Gotta eat all your dinner first," he added.

"You're certainly sounding like a dad," Owen teased. "Come on ladies. Let's eat."

"I want a piggyback ride." Dawn practically crawled up Owen's leg. After Owen hoisted her up, Autumn stared up at her sister riding into the house on Owen's back. The two of them whooped and hollered their way toward the kitchen.

"Want a ride, baby girl?" He wasn't sure if it was the endearment or the fact she really wanted a ride, but she smiled hugely again and melted his heart.

"Can I?"

"Sure." He bent so she could climb up on his back. When she clasped her hands at his throat, he stood with one arm secure under her bottom. "All set?"

"Yep," she said with more enthusiasm than he'd heard from her yet.

The house hadn't changed much over the years. In fact, it was comforting to see most everything was still the same, yet Rain and the girls had made their mark. Along with the pictures of Rain at various ages growing up, several pictures of the girls sat scattered about the mantel and tables. He smiled and felt sad he'd missed so much.

The picture of Rain standing on the porch, a bundled baby in each arm, caught his attention. The smile on her face told him she was happy to bring her girls home, but her eyes held a distinct sadness. He wondered if she was thinking he should have been there. He still hadn't had enough time to really take it in, everything she'd had to do to bring those girls home and raise them on her own. Then he thought of everything he'd missed. The anger bubbled up, but he tamped it down. It wasn't Rain's fault he'd missed it. Still, he wanted to blame someone, and blaming himself only made him angrier.

They made it into the kitchen, Autumn laughing the whole way as he bounced her on his back. Rain turned from stirring a pot on the stove, surprised when she saw him with Autumn. Placing the bakery box on the counter, he went to Rain, not giving her time to move away. "Give Mommy a kiss."

Rain moved close to him to kiss Autumn, her nails

digging into his shoulders. He inhaled her sweet scent and fell into a dozen memories of them as teens. One of her sitting on the tailgate of his truck, her legs kicking back and forth, licking an ice cream cone. He said something that made her laugh, and she leaned into his shoulder and laid her head against him. His gut tightened even now, thinking of the way she made him feel when she laughed, and made him want to join in.

"You look good up there, baby," Rain said, her heart aching. Her daughters had waited a long time to have their father home. Here he was, giving piggyback rides and trying his best to make them feel comfortable. What little girl wouldn't welcome Brody's openness and charming smile? He was just a big kid himself sometimes.

She remembered them as teens in high school. Brody a senior and her a young freshman. She'd run up behind him and jump up on his back, wrapping her legs around his waist. He'd grab hold of her thighs with his big hands and hold her steady, smiling at her over his shoulder and laughing with her. He didn't laugh often, but she brought it out of him. She cherished those fun moments they shared. Moments when he let his guard down. Something he'd only ever done with her.

The purple roses were nice. It touched her that he remembered such a simple thing about her.

She remembered things about him, too. Like he hadn't been quite that well built when he was younger. The military had added a lot of muscle to his tall, lean frame. His hair had always been an unruly mass on his head, golden blond streaked by the sun. It was still the same bright color, but now it was trimmed short around the edges, he'd left the top a little longer. But it wasn't his broad chest or the snug fit of his jeans that took her back. His smile brightened the blue of his eyes until you thought you might actually see that spark of a twinkle in them like some cartoon come to life. Now, that smile had a harder time coming. When it reached his eyes, that spark glowed, but didn't ignite.

Owen spoke to her about Brody's accident and what caused him to veer his truck off the road and into a ditch. Flashbacks from the war. Owen was there when Brody woke from a nightmare. The thought of Brody suffering made her physically hurt. Her chest grew tight and her heart shuddered.

"Rain, are you okay?" Brody asked, bringing her out of her thoughts.

Straightening her shoulders, she answered, "I'm fine. Dinner is just about ready."

She turned her back on him and stirred the sauce. Dinner was done, but she needed a moment. She should have known Brody wouldn't leave her be. He knew her too well.

He leaned into her, put his hands on both sides of her against the counter, his chest against her shoulders. He made her whole body come to life as warm waves of heat radiated out from her lower belly.

"Come on, Rain. What's wrong?"

"I'm fine." She stirred the thick, simmering sauce.

"Mommy gets sad sometimes," Autumn said from over Brody's shoulder.

"She does?" Brody asked.

"Sometimes she gets sad and just stares. Sometimes she's sad after she talks to Uncle Owen." Autumn's fingers slid through her hair, something she did often, and Rain always loved it. When Autumn was a baby, she'd grab fistfuls of her hair and just hold on to her. As if Autumn needed that reassurance Rain would never leave her.

"Autumn, would you and your sister please put the napkins on the table and tell Uncle Owen and Pop it's time to eat."

Brody set the girl on her feet, which gave Rain the perfect opportunity to move away. Distance was necessary to keep herself from giving in to the force that pulled her to him. He'd left her. Alone and pregnant, she'd cursed him for what he'd done, then she'd cried more often than she'd ever admit.

"Rain, honey, why are you sad?"

"I'm fine, Brody. Leave it alone for now. Dinner's ready."

"No. Not this time. Seems to me I've left you alone for far too long." He backed her up against the counter.

Rain wasn't about to put up with it. She planted her hands on his chest and shoved. "You don't get to come in here and ask about me. You walked away, turned your back and left, making it damn clear you didn't want anything to do with me."

"Absolutely. No argument. But . . ."

"No, but—"

"Rain." Owen stepped into the kitchen.

She wanted to say more, but clamped her mouth shut.

"Not now," Owen said low, but urgent. "The girls are at the table. Let's eat."

Rain grabbed the pot of boiling noodles from the stove and dumped them in the colander in the sink. Steam billowed up like the anger roiling in her gut. Owen was right. Now wasn't the time.

Strong hands clamped on to her shoulders. She stood in front of the sink, the window fogged from the steam. Owen leaned in, and she hated that her heart suddenly filled with disappointment that Brody didn't come to comfort her.

"Take a breath. The girls don't need to hear you and Brody hash this out now."

"They'll hear me knock you to the floor if you don't get your hands off her," Brody interrupted in a deadly tone that both Rain and Owen recognized.

Rain held back a groan when Owen kissed her on the head, a gesture she was used to, but was sure to set Brody off like lightning hitting dry grass. Brody grabbed Owen by the shoulder and spun him around to face him. She expected Brody to throw the first punch, starting a brawl right there in her kitchen. Instead, he stood firm, fists at his sides, and glared at Owen before addressing her.

"Are you sleeping with my brother?"

Shocked, Rain took a second to grasp Brody's audacious question. Her anger flashed. Because of him, she'd put her whole life on hold and hadn't had the time or inclination to think about another man.

Oh, who was she kidding? The only man she'd ever thought about was Brody. She'd given him her heart, her love. Everything she was she'd put into loving him and it hadn't been enough to keep him with her—or out of Roxy's bed.

"What business is it of yours who I sleep with?"

"You're my business," Brody growled. "We have two daughters."

"Up until today, I had two daughters I've been raising on my own."

"I should have been here, would have if I'd known."

She ignored the implied accusation she should have told him.

"You want to know why I'm sad," Rain said defiantly. "Because I'm the one who's looked in those girls' blue eyes and tried to be everything to them when all they wanted was their father. Every time I watched them do something for the first time, every birthday they celebrated, every time they hit a new milestone, got a good grade, were happy or sad, skinned a knee, discovered something new and you missed it, it tore another piece of my heart to shreds. Every time they asked about you and wanted you here, I'm the one who comforted them and assured them that if there was anyone you could love it would be them."

"I do love them," Brody snapped, stomping down his hurt and letting his anger reign. "I love you. I've loved you my whole damn life. I never stopped loving you."

"Don't you dare say you love me. If you loved me, you wouldn't have left. You'd have stood on my porch pounding on the door, demanding I come out and face you and everything between us. You would have let me rage and then found a way to get me to forgive you. If you loved me, you'd have known I loved you enough to forgive you anything."

"Then forgive me now." He raked his fingers through his short hair and let his hand fall to his side. His eyes pleaded with her to forgive him, it meant something to him.

"Don't you get it? I forgave you the day I found out I was pregnant, that you hadn't left me all alone in this world. I forgave you again the day I brought both those girls home, even though I was terrified to be left alone with them. I forgive you every day I have them, because they give me everything you didn't. I forgive you for sleeping with *her,* because I have them. After everything we shared, you turned your back on me."

"Rain, I'm sorry." Misery laced his every word.

"Yeah, well, you can take sorry and shove it up your—"

"Mom?" Dawn stood directly behind Brody where no one had seen her.

Rain pulled herself together and shifted her glare from Brody and rested her eyes on her daughter, who looked more and more like her father every day. She took a deep breath and tried desperately to remember she couldn't have an all-out yelling match with Brody with the girls only one room away.

"Yes, honey."

"Why are you yelling at him?"

Rain snuck a peek at Brody. His eyes went soft on his daughter, and he cocked up the corner of his mouth, concerned about Dawn overhearing them fighting. She'd give him credit for understanding they weren't doing the best they could by their children. He cared. She could even imagine how many times he watched his father and mother fight. How often those fights turned into something very ugly—for his mother and him and Owen. She didn't want Brody to fall back on what he'd known as a child. In order to make sure they didn't, she needed to stop goading him into a fight.

"You know what, sweetheart, I don't know why I'm yelling. Your dad and I have a lot to talk about, but yelling won't fix anything, because there's nothing broken here. It is what it is. Can't be changed."

Dawn looked confused, and she couldn't blame her. Rain was confused herself. As much as she wanted to rage against Brody and all the injustices in her life, it wouldn't change a damn thing. "I'm sorry, honey. I shouldn't have yelled at him. Brody, I'm sorry. Let's eat," she said, putting a stop to the whole thing.

Moving to the sink, Rain grabbed the colander and dumped the stringy noodles into a bowl. She handed it to Owen, who'd stood quietly glaring at Brody with a look of disgust. "Owen, take this to the table. I'll bring the sauce."

Owen walked out without a word, making her sigh all the more. Dawn remained next to Brody, watching them both with worried eyes. "Honey, go on in. We're coming."

"Are you going to make him leave?"

"No, honey. We're having a family dinner, and Brody is family." When he frowned and his eyebrows drew together, she thought she might have gone a little too far.

"We aren't done."

"Not by a long shot," she fired back. She turned her back on him, grabbed the ladle and the pot of sauce, and walked out of the kitchen, leaving Dawn looking nervous and Brody trying not to look as angry as he was. Rain tried not to notice the way he rubbed his hand over his left thigh. He was probably in some pain from carrying Autumn on his back. He hadn't complained or told her no. Another thing she gave him credit for. So how come she couldn't put the anger aside and just talk to him? Because she finally had him in her sights and she could take aim with all the things she'd given up to raise their girls.

There it was again. Their girls. It's how she'd always thought of them. Somehow, she'd never really taken it in that every time she looked at the girls she daydreamed of how it should have been, her and Brody raising them together.

She was angry because he hadn't stuck around to make that dream come true.

She'd been eighteen, dreaming of going off to college, marrying Brody, having children, having it all. Part of her wish had come true, but something had always been missing. Him.

She'd given up college reluctantly, but willingly. She could live without it. It was difficult to accept that after everything that happened, she couldn't live without Brody. It hurt too much to watch the girls grow up without him, to have them feel as if something was missing from their life, too.

Dawn took her seat at the table. Rain smiled at the two girls. They'd left a place for their father between them, and Rain's heart melted. Despite her anger toward Brody for leaving her, she made sure the girls knew the Brody she'd loved. They begged her every night for more stories about him. So easy to remember the good times. Meeting at the bleachers for lunch in high school. Afternoons on the weekend, riding horses at his ranch. Watching him play baseball and hitting a line drive down third base, him running the bases with a cocky grin on his face, tipping his hat to her in the stands. Friday night parties with friends, sitting around a bonfire, snuggling together to keep warm—and be close.

She placed the sauce on the table and gave Owen and her father a halfhearted smile to let them know she was okay. She headed back to the kitchen to grab the salad and garlic bread. She caught Brody slipping a pill bottle back into the front pocket of his jeans. The look of shame and guilt on his face hurt her heart. She couldn't imagine how it made him feel to have to need those pills. His father drank himself near to death for most of his life. He'd always hated that his father couldn't get by without the booze. Now, here he was, a man who couldn't get through the day without pills to take away his pain and help him cope with everyday life.

Home, he was fighting another kind of battle. She wasn't exactly showing him she wasn't one of the hostiles in this world. In fact, she wouldn't be surprised if he'd rather go back and fight insurgents, rather than face off with her. This was personal for both of them, and that meant it was messy and complicated. Where he'd been for the last few years, things had been easy—identify the enemy and take them out. Here, they had old wounds, old feelings, past hurts and baggage. The only thing keeping them both from fleeing this field of battle: the stakes were too high. Two little girls counted on them to not be those teenage kids who'd fallen sloppily in love and let it all fall apart—or self-destruct, in Brody's case.

Yeah, that's exactly what he'd done. She'd known him long enough to understand whenever something went well for him, he'd find a way to screw it up. She had just been naïve enough to believe he'd change for her. Stupid. Brody was Brody. And wasn't that one of the reasons she loved him. He never lied or made you think he was anything but what you saw in front of you. He'd never pretended to be her knight in shining armor. He'd always been a badass with a big heart where she was concerned. Too bad that night with Roxy he'd been too much the I-don't-give-a-damn-what-anyone-thinks guy and not the I-only-care-what-Rain-thinks guy. His fault for letting Roxy push his buttons and opening the door for him to be that part of himself he'd tried so hard to leave behind with her.

She approached Brody and put her hand up to place it over his heart, a gesture she had done so often long ago, she didn't even think about it. Until he shied away from her hand . . . again. An unconscious protective gesture not to let anyone close enough to hurt him. She pulled her hand back, but he grabbed it, pressed it to his chest, and kept his own hand over hers. The intensity in his eyes made her catch her breath. His heart pounded against her hand. He wasn't as calm behind the new shield he wore to protect himself. Long ago, he wouldn't have needed that shield with her. It broke her heart he couldn't just be with her anymore.

"It was sweet of you to give Autumn a piggyback ride. It probably hurt your leg to carry her around like that, but you made her happy."

"She makes me feel happy. Well, and a little terrified." He grinned, the one she remembered from so long ago. His chest heaved out and sank, relaxing him a bit beneath her hand and easing the ache in her heart because he was trying. "It's been a long time since I was happy."

Uncomfortable with that familiar look and sound in his voice, she hurried to break the intimate moment. "We should go in. They're waiting for us."

"Why do you have Autumn?" He didn't take his eyes off hers or release her hand.

"Because she's mine." She wasn't about to let him think for a second Autumn wasn't the daughter of her heart.

"I can see she's yours. That's not what I mean, and you know it."

"I do, but now isn't the time to get into it." Before he could make the demand about to leave his lips, she pulled her hand free and held it up to stop him. "We'll talk about Roxy when we're alone and no one's within shouting distance."

"Literally," he said on a laugh.

"Absolutely." She gave him half a smile, because they both knew talking about Roxy only ever ended with one or both of them yelling at the other. "You want to know why I have her?"

"It's why I asked."

Infuriatingly cocky, and definitely the Brody she remembered. Growing serious, she waited a beat to make sure he understood the importance of what she was about to say. "I have Autumn because she's yours." Nothing harder than laying her pride at his feet and telling him the truth.

He took a step closer, forcing her to take one back, unable to have him this close when she let her heart rule her mind.

"What are you telling me?" he asked, his voice husky and soft.

"You left. So I kept the pieces of yourself you left behind. They were all I had left of you and a dream I dreamt of us." She tried to turn away. He caught her by the arm and spun her around so fast, she slammed into his chest. His mouth clamped down on hers, she didn't have a chance to catch her breath, only to hold on.

With his arms banded around her, she slid her hands up his back and pressed them to his shoulders, bringing him close. Her breasts smashed against his chest, the very heat of him seeping into her skin and bones. Cold inside for so long, she didn't even feel it anymore, but she felt him, his heat, and his demand as his tongue slid past her lips to stroke over hers. As demanding as the embrace was, the kiss was the opposite, soft, coaxing, inviting.

He wanted her to know he wanted her in his arms, but more, he wanted her to want to be there, to share in the kiss with as much aching tenderness as he put into it. She responded to that sweet caress of his mouth over hers. She couldn't help herself, had never been able to help herself. When he was close and this open to her, she'd always dived in head first, no matter how deep or shallow the water might be. She didn't care. She just needed. Him.

Her heart wouldn't let him go, or let anyone else inside. And it made her sad.

With a last desperate slide of her tongue over his and her lips pressing to his, she ended the kiss abruptly. Pushing her hands against his shoulders, she shoved herself out of his embrace and took two steps back.

"Don't." Angry, a tear slipped down her cheek. Swiping it away with the back of her hand, she tried to move past him to get the rest of dinner. He caught her by the waist with his arm, his hand planted on her hip, searing her through her jeans straight into her bones.

"I don't think I've ever seen you cry."

"You didn't stick around long enough to see it when I found out what you did."

Swamped with emotions, her mind took her straight back to the morning she woke up alone in his bed, and her heart bled with the pain she felt when she saw the note and realized he left her. *I'm sorry.* All the hope she woke with that morning, the first day of the rest of their lives together, vanished. Her soul turned cold as the sheets beside her. She'd given herself to him, mind and body, she'd poured all her love into making love to him.

She tried. So hard. She put everything she is into loving him. But it wasn't enough to make him stay.

Two weeks later, sad and desolate, she discovered he hadn't left her alone after all. Pregnant, a glimmer of the happiness and love she'd felt the night she shared with Brody woke up again. It bloomed with her pregnancy and a future with her child and helped to heal her heart. Then she discovered not only did he sleep with Roxy, he got her pregnant, too, and the pain tore her apart again. Living without him, dealing with Roxy, struggling to raise her girls and keep them safe, and missing him more and more each day wore on her battered heart.

She couldn't go through that kind of agonizing pain again.

"Why do you cry because I kissed you?"

"Because kissing you only leads to pain."

Chapter Eight

BRODY WALKED INTO the dining room and looked at the table and everyone around it. Rain had set out her best dishes, the ones her grandmother left to her mother and now came to her. Crystal wine glasses gleamed in the fading light from the window. The food steamed in bowls and on platters around the table. Best of all, his girls sat across the table, tentative smiles on their faces, their blue eyes watching him with nervous anticipation as he came around to their side and took his seat between them. He gave each a pat on the head and sat.

"Thanks for saving me a seat."

"Will you come and see our room after dinner?" Dawn asked. "We have pictures."

"I'd love to see your room, honey. What pictures do you want to show me?"

"Of us," Autumn said in her sweetly soft voice as she stared at her hands.

Brody brushed his hand softly down Autumn's golden hair and encouraged her to talk to him. "I'd love to see them, honey. Are they pictures your mom took?"

"She made us books so we could show you us growing up if you wanted us," Autumn said to her hands.

Brody put his fingertip to her chin and tilted her face up to his. Giving the moment and his voice the solemnity it deserved, he said, looking right into her eyes, "I want you very much. You're my daughter. I love you, and nothing will ever change that."

"Roxy didn't want me. Why should you?"

Autumn's bottom lip trembled. A single tear slid down her cheek. Brody glanced across the table, Rain's eyes glassed over, and she slumped in her seat. She'd done everything in her power to be the mother Autumn deserved, but nothing could take away the hurt of knowing your own mother didn't want you. And possibly your father, too.

Brody thought of his own father and the cold way he'd treated him. Brody tried everything to get his father's attention, one elusive kind word, but nothing worked. He'd grown up, thinking he was worthless, but Rain showed him he deserved to be loved.

He scooted his chair back and went with his gut instinct. It had saved his ass a number of times, and he hoped it saved him with his daughter now. Sliding his hands under her arms, he hauled her out of her chair, turned her toward him, and sat her on his lap. Using his finger again, he tilted her wobbly chin up, so she saw the truth in him.

"I owe you an apology."

"Because you didn't know about us?"

"For that, absolutely. I am more sorry than you'll ever know I didn't know about you. If I had, I would have been with you every day. I don't know what happened with Roxy and how you ended up with Rain . . ."

"I hate her. She . . ."

"Autumn," Rain snapped. Brody glared across the table at her. "I will talk to your father about Roxy, honey. It's a difficult story, and better left for me to explain."

Brody noted Autumn's stiff posture and the way she couldn't look at him after being scolded by her mother. He rubbed his hands up and down her arms until she met his eyes again. "Your mom will fill me in about Roxy, baby girl. Right now, I want you to listen. In my life, I've done a lot of bad things."

"Like leaving Mom?" Dawn asked.

Brody turned and gazed down at his daughter and didn't hide his sorrow. "That's the worst thing I ever did. Not only because of you two, but because I didn't want to leave her. As much as I hurt your mom, I hurt myself more."

"Brody . . ."

"What, Rain? Don't tell them we loved each other, and I screwed it all up, left you when all I wanted was to spend my life with you. I missed out on our girls and being with you all this time. Shouldn't they know that sometimes 'I'm sorry' doesn't fix things?" He looked at both girls in turn and told them the cold hard truth. "Sometimes girls, you hurt someone so much you have to do something really hard, never knowing if it'll be enough."

"What?" Dawn asked.

"Earn back their trust."

"How?" Autumn asked him, though he watched Rain.

"That's the hard part, baby girl. I have to show your mom I can be trusted by telling the truth, even when it's not easy. I have to show her she can count on me when she needs me. If I tell her I'll do something, I have to make sure I do it. The really hard one, when I make her a promise, I have to keep it."

"Brody, the only promise I need is the one telling me you'll never lie to these girls, even if you have to tell them you're leaving again."

"I'm not leaving. I came back for you, Rain. Dawn and Autumn may change everything, but it doesn't change the fact I still love you and want you back."

"Brody, don't," Rain warned.

Relenting, they wouldn't settle anything this way. "You see, girls, I haven't earned your mother's trust, so it's hard for her to believe in the words I say. But I will make her believe in them and me again."

"Because you love her," Dawn added.

"Because I love all of you," he told her. Then he focused on Autumn, so lovely and sad under it all. "The reason I owe you an apology, Autumn, I'm sorry I didn't give you to Rain in the first place. I'd never wish you away, baby girl, but I would wish Rain as your mother."

"I guess you got your wish," Autumn said, lifting her face to his. "She is my mom. Please don't take me away from her."

Brody pulled Autumn to his chest and wrapped his arms around her. "I'd never do that, baby girl. I promise," he added, his gaze locked with Rain's.

Rain's throat worked to swallow the knot, the same one in his own. Putting the evening back on track, she said, "Dawn, why don't you tell your dad about softball."

Brody brushed his hands down Autumn's back. She felt so good pressed to his chest. He picked her up and set her back in her seat, smiling when she said, "You're really strong."

"I've been fighting bad guys." He brushed his hand through her golden locks. To ensure no one asked about his military career, he turned to Dawn. "So, baby girl, you play softball?"

"We both do." Dawn warmed to the subject and his attention. "Mom coaches. I play shortstop, like you used to in high school. Autumn plays first base."

Brody turned to his shy little daughter with a surprised smile. "You play first. That's a tough position."

"Mom taught me how to catch and be fast." The warm, genuine smile of pride showed Brody just how much Rain's love had done to help Autumn overcome being born to Roxy. He needed to find out what terrible thing she'd done to his daughter. Whatever it was, it was inexcusable to leave a child feeling the way Autumn felt about herself. As her father, he aimed to make sure she knew he wanted her as much as Rain did.

"When do you guys play?"

"We have practice on Tuesday and Thursday and a game on Saturday," Dawn said around a mouthful of spaghetti. He handed her a napkin to wipe her chin and smiled at her sauce-smeared face.

"Well, I'll be there. I can't wait to see you girls in action."

"Uncle Owen and Pop come to watch us play, too," Autumn added.

"Then it'll be a real family affair." Brody hoped the girls were finally seeing he really wanted to be part of their lives. He hated to admit, Owen had been right. Rain may have shut the door in his face, but she'd left all the windows open for him to come back inside and be a part of this family. He sat back, took a bite of Rain's outstanding spaghetti. Content for the first time in a long time, sitting down to a simple meal, surrounded by his brother, Rain, Pop, and his girls, he finally felt like he was home.

"So, Brody, what are your immediate plans?" Pop asked.

The weight of that question settled over him. As Rain's father, Pop would be the one person watching him closely. Any wrong move, and he'd have to answer. Willing to give him a second chance, Pop wouldn't overlook another transgression. If he stomped on Rain's heart again, Pop would have him paying for it and the past with a vengeance. Nothing Brody wouldn't deserve. This time, he wouldn't self-destruct, he vowed. This time, he'd get it right.

"I'm adding on to the cabin. I've already updated the old appliances, bought a bunch of necessities. Fixed up the yard and driveway over the last couple of days. The place is livable, but not nearly big enough for me and my girls," he said, ignoring Rain's sideways glance.

"Can we come and visit you?" Dawn asked.

"Absolutely. I'll have to work it out with your mom, but we'll spend a lot of time together," Brody promised. Every day, forever, if he had anything to say about it.

"Once the cabin is expanded, I plan on adding a new barn."

"Can we have a dog?" Dawn asked.

When he looked at her and Autumn's bright faces he wanted to laugh.

"Dawn, we talked about this," Rain said through tight lips.

"We can't afford the food and vet bills." Autumn repeated what both girls had obviously been told on numerous occasions. Brody had more money than he knew what to do with, but Rain scrimped by on next to nothing raising his girls alone. Just another reason for her to hate him for leaving her behind.

"How about a horse," Brody said. "It won't be right away, but eventually we'll fill the stables, and you girls can come out, and I'll teach you to ride just like I taught your mother. She loves horses."

"Can we name them?" Dawn asked, her eyes bright, her smile bigger than he'd ever seen.

"Sure."

Rain picked up her empty plate, Owen's, and Pop's, and turned her back on the table and fled into the kitchen. It pissed him off when Owen went after her.

"How's business?" Pop asked, pulling his gaze back from the kitchen door. "Tell me about your company."

Brody spent the next twenty minutes filling in Pop

about the company he owned, helping the girls finish their dinners, and fuming that he didn't know what was going on between his brother and the woman he loved more than his own life.

OWEN WALKED INTO the kitchen behind Rain. With her palms planted against the sink, her head down between her shoulders, she spoke to her feet. "I can't afford to get them a dog, but he can buy them a stable full of horses. Why does that make me feel like such a failure when raising them the best I can has nothing to do with money?"

"You love them and want the best of everything for them."

She stood tall and turned to Owen, her back pressed against the sink. "It hurts, Owen. To know I've done everything I can to give them a good life, and I still come up short. Autumn still feels unwanted."

"You give them the one thing they both need more than anything. You love them. They've never gone without what's really important." She wasn't buying it and he noticed. "I told you three years ago we could file papers and get him to pay child support. You didn't want to."

"You know why I did that."

"Because you needed to protect Autumn. She needed you and the love and stability you give to her. If Brody exercised his rights and took her after what happened with Roxy, that could have been very damaging for Autumn."

"Keep your voice down," Rain admonished and peered

through the door to make sure no one overheard them. "He couldn't take care of her. They were shipping him off to Afghanistan."

"So you sacrificed asking for the money and making life easier. You did that for her. Don't second guess yourself now."

"He has the money to take them away from me. He can hire lawyers, prove I knew where he was and kept them from him."

"Autumn asked him point blank if he intends to take her away from you. He told her no. I, for one, believe him. He wants to build a life with you and those girls."

"Yes, because of them."

"No. Because of you and what you've always given him."

"I gave him a daughter."

"You gave him a hell of a lot more. You see him for who he is and you love him anyway. He knows what a gift that is."

"He didn't want it, threw it back in my face when we were so close to having everything."

"He gave into that voice in his head telling him he's nothing."

"That's your father talking. Not him."

"It's a powerful voice. Look at Autumn. Her mother's betrayal is in her head and in her heart. Words and actions change us. Your love has changed Autumn, allowed her to believe she's wanted and loved. It's what you did for Brody all those years ago. It's what he's looking for now. He's broken inside, Rain. There're new voices in his head. Voices carrying on a war he left behind physically, but can't escape. He loses himself. I think when he looks at you, he remembers who he is. I think he needs that, he needs you."

"You want me to forget what he did and everything that's happened. Forget everything I gave up."

"I want you to remember you gave up those things for Dawn and Autumn, and given the chance to have them back, you'd still choose those girls.

"You can't change the past. You've always known you can't change Brody. If you look close, you'll see he changed himself."

"Yeah, he's come back a war hero and a business tycoon," she said flippantly.

"He's those things and a lot more. He's more the man you saw hiding beneath the surface, he's embraced the good in him. He's ready to atone for the past, where he normally would have told anyone but you to go to hell."

"He did tell me to go to hell the night he slept with Roxy."

"Bullshit. He broke up with you before you broke it off with him and left for school, the old man was doing what he'd always done, and Roxy pushed him over the edge he'd been standing on for months."

"That's no excuse."

"When did Brody have an excuse for anything he did?"

Never. If he stayed out all night with his buddies, drinking and fooling around out at the lake, and showed up late to school or work the next morning, no big deal. "No one died," he'd say. He shoved a boy up against a locker and braced his arm across the guy's throat and growled, "Stop staring at her ass." She pulled him off the poor guy, who'd done nothing but glance at her. Brody looked at her and smiled. "I'm the only one who gets to look." He swept his gaze over her in one long, hot sweep and made her blush. He laughed, unapologetic for his blatant territorial behavior.

When he did something sweet, like bringing her lunch when she worked at her dad's shop on the weekend, he shrugged off her thanks with a simple, "You need to eat." Even though he must have been bored out of his skull, he'd stayed home from school with her when she had the flu and sat beside her bed, holding her hand, trying to make her laugh, even though she felt miserable. "I hate it when you don't smile," he whispered when he thought she'd fallen asleep.

So many memories flooded back. Her eyes glassed over. She tried desperately to blink the tears away.

Owen pulled her to his chest and wrapped her in his arms. She held tight to him because it was easy. So much easier than reaching for Brody.

Brody filled the doorway, his eyes narrowing, and his face turning hard as stone. "This is the second time I've found you with your hands on her. Don't make me ask you again to keep your damn hands to yourself."

Owen kissed her on the head, like always, and stepped away, bracing his hands on her shoulders, boldly keeping his back to Brody. Over his shoulder, he said with a cocky grin. "You have yet to ask."

"Then you should understand the threat. If I have to tell you again, it'll be after your ass is on the ground with my boot on your fucking neck."

"Mom, Dad swore," Dawn said from behind Brody. Since Rain could see the wide grin on Owen's face, the way Brody rolled his eyes after getting caught by his daughter, she figured she had to be the rational one. "Yes, well, he's been stuck in a desert with nothing but rowdy men for company. He can't help himself if he's acting like a wild dog, snapping at nothing."

"Huh?" Dawn asked.

"Nothing, sweetheart. You and your sister finish clearing the table. Brody will help you." She stepped out of Owen's arms and grabbed the near empty bowls Brody held in his hands.

"What's going on between the two of you?"

"I'll tell you . . ."

"Oh, shit. She's going to get me killed." Owen turned to Brody and crossed his arms over his chest, taking a defiant stand.

"Well, let's hear it." Brody took a menacing step closer to Owen, the two facing off with her to their sides.

"I love Owen." Rain shimmied between Brody and Owen, her back to Owen and her hands planted on Brody's chest. "Whenever I needed help or someone to just listen, he always lent a hand or let me bend his ear. Along with Pop, he's been a father figure to those girls. He's been my friend, a damn good uncle to our girls, and a better brother than you deserve. So lay off."

Rain shoved past him. Brody figured, best to let her go. When she was riled up like this, no telling how she'd react. She was spoiling for a fight as much as he was. Holding out his hand to Owen, he waited for Owen's hand to clasp his. He shook, then held on and looked his brother in the eye. "Thank you for taking care of my family while I was gone."

"I'm your brother. Have you ever known me to take something that belonged to you?"

"Never. You always looked out for me," Brody confirmed.

"And you me." Owen let go of Brody's hand now that they understood each other. "It's been one day, Brody. Give her a chance to settle into you being here and what that means for her and the girls. She's been solely responsible for them and answered to no one. Now, you're here and you have a right to be a part of the girls' lives and make decisions with her for them. Whether you believe it or not, you scare the hell out of her."

"Rain isn't afraid of anything."

"Except allowing herself to believe you want to spend the rest of your life with her, only to have you turn your back on her again."

Brody leaned against the counter and pressed the heels of his hands into his aching eyes. Frustrated, he needed to find a way to make things right with Rain in the most expedient way possible. "I meant what I said to the girls. I'll do everything in my power to prove to her she can trust me again. I want forever back." Taking a chance, he added, "We could have something really great, Owen. We have the girls already, but I think we could have the family you and I never had and always secretly wanted."

Owen clasped his hand on Brody's shoulder. "Rain has

let me be a part of this family. Watching her with the girls has shown me what a real mother should be like. She's got a way of disciplining them firmly without making them feel stupid and grinding their self-esteem into the ground like dad used to do. I'll watch her with them when they do their homework, or she's coaching them at softball. She praises them, tells them how good they're doing. Not just for the big things they do, but for the little things."

"Dad certainly never did that."

"You've got an opening here with Rain. Look for the little things she does for you, with you. Build on that, because she won't give you the big gesture you're looking for.

"She's got things to say to you. Terrible things. If she could, she'd spare you the details of the last eight years, because deep down she loves you enough to let you walk in here tonight, forget the past, and let you spend the rest of your life happy with your kids."

Brody ran his hand over the side of his hair and to the back of his neck, squeezing the tight muscles. "How can five minutes of my life screw up everything so badly?"

"Whatever else came into your world, Rain was always the constant you took for granted would always be there. If I was you, I'd make damn sure I didn't lose my second chance, because that's what she's offering, even if those aren't the words coming out of her mouth."

"The only thing she wants to offer me at the moment is my head on a platter."

"Every time you kiss her, there's a moment where she gives in and lets herself feel and believe for just those few seconds that you never left and this is the way life has always been. Then she remembers all that's happened and she pushes you away. Like you pushed her away all those years ago."

"She thinks I'll leave her again, so she's not about to give me a chance to hurt her."

"Sound familiar. Talk all you want, tell her you love her, and you're staying. None of it amounts to shit unless you show her." Owen handed him the bakery box. "So, let's eat cupcakes. Get to know your daughters. Watch Rain. She's watching you."

Chapter Nine

BRODY WALKED INTO the dining room again, Owen at his back. Rain sat beside Pop at the head of the table. They talked about work and a repair job Rain started that day. Brody placed the bakery box on the table and lifted the lid. Dawn and Autumn oohed and aahed over the beautifully designed cupcakes.

Rain stood and tried to pass him. Just because he wanted to touch her, he put his hand on her arm to stop her. "Where you going, sweetheart?" He almost smiled when she glared.

"To get some plates and napkins. You've never seen two little girls make a mess like they do with cake and frosting." A glimmer of a smile touched her rosy lips.

"Yeah?" He gave her a smile, letting his hand slide down her arm until he took her hand. "I bet they've both demolished a cake on their birthdays."

When her gaze came up to meet his, it was plain as day. She regretted every birthday he'd missed.

"When they turned one, I made them each a little round cake and let them go to town. They ended up with more cake on them than in them."

Linking his fingers with hers, he squeezed her hand to let her know he understood everything she wasn't saying. "You loved watching every minute of it."

"Almost," she whispered and pulled free, fleeing into the kitchen. When he looked back at Owen, he caught his brother's nod of approval. He'd connected with her for a second. Now, all he had to do was keep at it, until she no longer wanted to break the connection, but build on it.

Dessert became an orchestrated affair. Rain directed the girls on subjects to talk about, ranging from how they were doing in the second grade, about their teachers and friends, to the things they liked to do in their spare time. It was obvious the girls were not only sisters, but best friends. They did everything together, Dawn usually in the leader's role.

The only times Rain interrupted or stopped them from telling something was when it had to do with Roxy.

Unable to let things go, he had to get Rain alone if he wanted to find out what happened after he left town.

"Dad . . ."

God, how he loved hearing them call him Dad.

"Do you have a computer? Uncle Owen said you have a company, and you'll work from your house."

He was getting used to the way Autumn looked to her sister to be the speaker for them both. He didn't miss the conspiratorial look they shared when they asked about his computer. "I have a laptop and a desk computer. Why? Do you guys know how to use one?"

"Mom got us one for school and to play on some kid's websites. We have some games," Dawn began.

"It was so slow," Autumn added. "Mom got it from the secondhand store and now the screen is fuzzy and half the time it doesn't boot up right and we get weird errors."

"Can we use yours?" Dawn asked, finishing both girls' request.

Brody listened to the girls, but watched Rain. She couldn't afford a new computer. An easy guess. What he didn't get, she made a good living at the garage. Paying for things for the girls took up a good portion of her pay-check, he assumed. She had her inheritance from her family, the money she hadn't used for college. Either she was leaving that money in the bank for the girls to go to school later, or it was already gone. He wanted to talk to her about the money he had, the money he owed her for child support he should have paid. Now wasn't the time, and throwing it in her face he could and would buy the girls a new computer wouldn't score him any points.

"When you come out to the cabin you can use mine." He tried to be diplomatic and not promise the girls something Rain might object to. As far as he knew, at this point he'd get to have the girls at his place sometimes. Shared custody was a long way from the family he wanted, but he'd do what Owen said and take baby steps toward what he really wanted.

"Your dad and I will talk. You have school during the

week, but maybe once he's got the cabin ready for you to visit, you can spend the weekend with him."

"Won't you stay with us?" Autumn asked, her eyes round and worried.

"We'll talk about it, Autumn. No matter what, you'll be safe with your dad."

Brody stared at Rain, the obvious question in his eyes. Why wouldn't Autumn be safe? Did she think he couldn't take care of the girls, his mind was so far gone he'd hurt them or neglect them? Or did this have something to do with Roxy?

Ignoring the elephant in the room, Rain changed the subject. "Girls, why don't you show your dad your room and the photos you want him to see."

Rain grabbed up the frosting-smeared plates and dirty napkins while the girls got up, excitedly chattering at him about coming upstairs. Each girl grabbed one of his hands and pulled.

Rain noted the slow, deliberate way Brody placed his right foot on the stair tread and carefully pulled his weight up.

"He's doing better, Rain," Owen said.

"He knows we're keeping something from him."

Pop grasped her hand. "So, you'll tell him what it is when you're alone with him."

"I don't want to be alone with him." Both men's faces lit up with amused smiles. "Shut up," she snapped. "Do either of you want to tell him what Roxy tried to do with his child?" When both men looked away and frowned, she got the reaction she'd anticipated. "Right. Who wants to hurt him like that after everything he's been through, is still going through. Have either of you noticed how many times he's rubbed his hand over his leg. He's hurting and trying to hide it."

"The doctors said he needs time," Owen said.

"After the accident the other day, I don't want to add to his anxiety by telling him about Autumn and Roxy. It'll only agitate him."

"Roxy will hear he's back in town." Pop reminded her of what she already knew and dreaded happening.

"Do we know for sure where she is now?" she asked Owen.

"Last we knew for sure, living in Las Vegas with an ex-rodeo cowboy."

"That information is over a year old," Pop pointed out.

"It's the best we've got. She stayed in Vegas the longest. I think she finally found a place that suited her," Rain said, scorn laced in every word.

They all fell silent. Every one of them considering the possibilities of Roxy coming back to town now. And the many reasons she'd return. Every dollar she could get her hands on.

"Lay it out for me, Owen. How much could she expect to get from Brody for Autumn?"

"For his daughter." Owen fixed a pointed gaze on her. "You know the answer to that question. You answered it for her the day Autumn was born looking exactly like Brody."

"Every dime he has," she answered her own question.

"Damn. How can I stop her this time? She's stayed away because she knows I don't have anything left. When she finds out Brody is back and he's got some money . . ."

"Not some," Owen interrupted. "A couple million at his fingertips, tens of millions if he sold out his piece of the company."

Rain combed both hands through her hair, pulling the thick mass away from her face and concentrating on her thoughts. Millions. Staggering to think about.

"We can't let her take his money. It's a source of pride for him to come back a success, knowing the people of this town will always look at him first and foremost as the young man he used to be."

"You're fooling yourself, sweetheart, if you think he worked this hard to make something of himself because he cared about what anyone but you thought." Owen pointed out the cold hard truth. It was a truth she didn't want to face. Not again.

"Can we please stick to the subject?"

"You know what you have to do, Rain," Pop told her.

"Why am I the one who has to do all the dirty work and clean up all the mess?"

"You're the mother," her father told her. "And you're a damn good one. You know what's best for those girls and no matter how hard or how many sacrifices you have to make, you'll always do right by them. Tell Brody the whole ugly story. Make him a part of their lives. But this time, honey, take a little something for yourself."

"Sleeping with him is what got me into this mess," she said truthfully, not caring what her father thought of her bluntness. No hiding the way Brody made her feel every time he came near her. She was surprised she hadn't disgraced herself more by drooling over him while he sat across from her at dinner. Every time he pulled her close and kissed her, it was all she could do not to tear his clothes off, kick his feet out from under him, and land naked on top of him.

"If that's all you take from each other, you'll both be shortchanging yourselves. Whether you're willing to admit it or not, Rain, you love that stubborn fool."

"Who's the fool if I go back to him?"

"I'll watch the girls Friday night, so you can talk to Brody alone," Owen called. She walked away without answering to go upstairs and put the girls to bed.

Owen turned to Pop. "Those two are a powder keg sitting in the middle of a thousand firecrackers going off. One spark and they'll ignite."

"Ask me, I think they could both use a knock-down-drag-out fight to get them where they both want to be." Owen waited, knowing the rest of Pop's thought already. "Right back in bed, which will only lead to her giving up her heart to him all over again."

"Why do you think she's the one who's got to give in?"

"All you have to do is look at Brody. He's willing to give her anything, do anything to have her and the girls. This is what he's been working toward, what he came home for. Nothing and no one will stop him from having it. It's too important to him.

"He finally feels like the man Rain always thought him to be. Before, it was a lofty aspiration to achieve the status she put him at. Now, he's got his military background, a business, money, and the pride in knowing he worked his ass off to make himself the man she deserves."

Owen sat quietly and listened to the sounds of the family upstairs. He took a sip of coffee and settled into the realization Pop was right. Brody finally had his act together. All he had to do was convince Rain, get past her defenses, and not screw it up like he'd done in the past.

Chapter Ten

BRODY SAT ON the bed, his daughters on either side of him, the photo album open on his lap. Their comments and delight at showing him the snapshots of their lives was infectious, but with each passing page and years of their lives nothing more than images on paper, he grew sadder and more resigned that he wouldn't be relegated to a weekend father, only seeing glimpses of their lives as weeks passed and all he got were a mere few days with them. He wanted the daily routine, the big and small moments of their lives etched into his memory, not burned into paper for him to look at and not know the feelings and emotions they felt and he experienced when the moment was captured.

"This is the kindergarten play. I was the farmer's wife and Autumn was a carrot in her garden. The play was about vegetables and nutrition."

"Carrots help you have good eyesight," Autumn recited, obviously part of her lines from the play.

"You two were adorable in your costumes."

"Mom made them. She helped us with our lines until we knew them by heart," Dawn said, turning the page.

Halloween pictures, the girls marching in a line at their school in a parade. Their smiles bright. Dawn dressed as Snow White, and Autumn as Tinker Bell. Further along, pictures of Christmas that year. The girls sat on the floor in front of an oddly decorated Christmas tree. Most of the ornaments were clumped near the bottom half of the tree, the part they could reach. The sight of the tree made his heart ache at the same time he wanted to smile.

Each of the girls had a small stack of presents beside them as they tore into one between their legs. Wrapping paper, ribbons, and bows strewn all around them. Owen and Pop sat in chairs nearby, their faces alight with joy and smiles as they watched the girls' exuberance in opening their gifts. Rain wasn't in the picture because she was the one taking them, but he could imagine that behind her smile lay a sadness that he missed it again that year. And would for the next as well. But not this year. This year he'd be there to watch his girls trim the tree, open presents, and delight in the wonder and joy of the holiday like only kids can do.

"I got a doll." Autumn pointed to the picture of her holding up a baby doll with golden curls around her pretty face.

"I got a checkers game," Dawn added.

"Santa didn't bring the bikes we asked for," Autumn said, a little sad.

"Do you guys have bikes now?" he asked.

"They're baby bikes," Dawn said with a frown.

"They're too small for us to ride," Autumn added.

"Mom says they cost a lot of money and we'll have to wait until she can save up enough," Dawn continued.

"Girls, it's time to get ready for bed. You've got school and softball practice tomorrow. You'll want to be rested."

"Can Dad read us books before he goes?" Dawn asked.

Rain gave him a nod, letting him know it was okay with her. "I'd love to," he answered, choked up.

"Why don't you two go downstairs and say goodnight to Pop and Uncle Owen, then come back up and brush your teeth."

Both girls ran for the door. Dawn sailed past her mother, but Autumn stopped and wrapped her hands around Rain's waist and hugged her. Rain ran her hands over Autumn's hair and down her back, then leaned down and kissed her on the forehead when Autumn looked up at her.

After Autumn ran after her sister, Brody said from the bed, "She needs your constant reassurance and show of affection."

"She's not as confident in herself as Dawn. She's sensitive, takes things to heart much more deeply."

"She needs you." Brody picked up Autumn's baby book next to him on the bed. "You've got a good and kind heart. I can't imagine Roxy raising her, crushing her soft heart under her stilettos." He held up the album. "There's not a single photo of Roxy in here."

"I'm her mother."

"The one I would have picked for her," Brody confirmed. "You love her as your own. Because she's mine," he said, knowing she wouldn't answer a loaded statement like that. She surprised him and sat beside him on the small single bed. The mattress and frame creaked under their shared weight.

"I'm begging you, Brody, please don't take her from me. As much as that little girl needs me, I need her. She's my daughter. I loved her the minute I held her in my arms. I've been the only mother she's known."

"You're the only mother she'll ever know. You may not want to hear this right now, but I want us to be a real family."

"Brody, what you're asking . . ."

"Is better left to another time as well. Right now, all I'm asking is that you give me some time to prove to you we can have what we had before. Only this time we'll make it better and last forever. We'll watch our girls grow up, get married, and have babies of their own. We'll have more children."

She shot to her feet and took several steps away toward the window. Opening Dawn's baby book, he stared at the picture of Rain pregnant with his child.

"You were beautiful, all round and glowing pregnant with Dawn." He traced his finger over the outline of her swollen belly. "I'm sorry I wasn't here to help you through the pregnancy. The birth," he said, choked up. "I missed it all. You missed having me there beside you.

"I never got to hold them when they were babies,

never heard their first word, helped them stumble along on unsteady legs as they learned to walk."

"I'm sorry it hurts you to hear about the girls growing up to this point and you missed it. I wish with my whole heart you were here to see and experience it with them."

"I've let you down in so many damn ways. I don't deserve a second chance, Rain, but I'm asking, begging you to forgive me enough to give us all a chance to see if we can make a life together."

"It's not fair to lump the girls into this." She kept her back to him. "All it does is make me look like the bad guy if I don't forget what's happened and let you back into my life and my bed, have the happily-ever-after those girls are hoping for desperately."

"What are you hoping for?" he asked quietly.

"It's been a long time since I hoped for anything for myself. All my time and energy is for those girls, hoping for their happiness and doing my damndest to give it to them. You're a part of that happiness, Brody. Don't think I don't know it."

"So, you'll let me spend time with them, because you know it's what they want as much as I want it. Will you let me spend time with you?"

"Let's start with them, Brody. They're more important than anything else."

"You're important to me. As much as I want to make up with them for missing the first seven years of their lives, I owe you a hell of a lot more."

"You don't owe me anything. I forgave you everything a long time ago. Because of them."

"You're still angry with me for leaving you."

She put her arm up, hand grasping the window casing, and rubbed her cheek against her shoulder. Crying for their past, he thought. He'd wished a thousand times he could cry it all away, but could never bring himself to do it. Rain did it for him.

He wanted desperately to go to her, stand behind her and wrap his arms around her, but the weight of the moment held him back.

Water ran in the bathroom; the girls brushed their teeth and chatted. Time was running out on this intimate moment they shared, and he didn't know how to bottle it and keep it.

The girls ran into the room seconds after Rain quietly left. "Dad, will you read us four books?" Dawn asked. "Please," the girls chorused together.

"Get your pajamas on, girls. You can each pick out two books."

He put away the albums while they changed, unfazed at having him roam about their room, looking at their things, pictures they'd drawn, stuffed animals peeking out of baskets, toys littering the floor and filling a chest. Everything two little girls needed, provided almost exclusively by Rain. A tangible reflection of Rain's affection and love for the girls. His only mark on the room and their surroundings, the three photos of him. One showed him leaning against his old truck, arms crossed over his chest, a cocky, smug look on his face. Another of him prowling after Rain, walking up the dock, a wide grin on his face, his arm outstretched to her. He remembered grabbing her after she snapped the photo. He'd stolen a kiss, tickled her unmercifully before picking her up and running off the end of the dock and into the cool water.

The last photo was of the two of them as teens. He couldn't remember who'd taken the picture. It didn't matter. He'd never seen it before, but he remembered how he felt when he held Rain in his arms like that. Leaning back against a tree, she stood in front of him, his arms banded around her chest, her hands holding his arms. Her face tilted up, and the look in her eyes as she stared up at him was mesmerizing. He could see the love there, captured in that moment as he looked off at something in the distance.

God, had they really been that young once. It seemed a lifetime ago.

If only he'd looked down at her in that moment and seen how much she loved him, maybe he'd never have turned his back on it.

"Dad, are you okay?" Autumn asked tentatively from behind him.

"Just looking at this old picture of your mom and me."

"It's our favorite," Dawn said. "There aren't many of the two of you together. We don't have any new ones of you. Do you have pictures of you in the Army?"

"Some." He turned away from the dresser and the past he was only now seeing clearly.

"Mom said you got hurt several times, but the last time it was really bad. She said you could have died. It made her sad," Autumn confessed from her lavender covered bed. "She cried."

Not wanting to frighten them, he gave the matter a serious answer without all the details. "I was hurt very badly. Some of my friends didn't make it, others were hurt worse than me. But I'm okay now," he added to reassure them.

"Are you going back to the war?" Dawn asked, her lips drawn into a deep frown.

"No, baby girl. I'm staying here with you both."

"And Mom?" Autumn asked.

"Definitely with your mom. When I was in the hospital, I thought about her all the time. I came home to see her, and I found the both of you."

"We were a surprise," Autumn said with a smile.

"Yes, you were, sweetheart. A very good surprise."

"If you'd have come home and I was gone with Roxy, would you have come to get me?" Autumn asked, her gaze on the bed, but her words a desperate plea.

Dawn's eyes blazed. She watched and waited for an answer. Every instinct he had told him Roxy did something terrible to his little girl. He'd make her pay dearly for it.

Easing down onto the edge of the bed beside Autumn, he vowed, "There is no place on this earth she could take you that I wouldn't hunt her down and find you and bring you back to me and your mother."

Her eyes raised to his, her chin trembled slightly. "Promise?" she asked, breaking his heart that such a small child needed a promise like this.

"I swear it." He gave her the words she needed to hear and the vow he swore he'd never break.

Dawn broke the tension by leaping into his lap with her books. "I want this one first."

Autumn's face turned her attention to the book in his hands. The last few minutes tucked away, forgotten for now. "Scoot over, baby girl. Make room for me and your sister."

Brody read the books to the girls, one tucked under each of his arms and pressed so trustingly to his chest. In all his years, he couldn't remember ever feeling this content. Except maybe when he'd had Rain lying down the length of him. Since that one night they'd shared together, all he'd felt was discontent and half-empty without his other half.

After all the books were read and he answered several questions for the girls about following the rodeo circuit when he left town, to joining the military, he tucked them into their beds. He kissed Dawn on the forehead and brushed his nose against hers, making her giggle. Then, he moved on to Autumn. Planting his hands on either side of her head, he leaned down to kiss her. He stopped when her little hands came up and held his face, her right hand softly tracing the cut on his temple.

"Does it hurt?" Her brows drew together. Her worry for him touched a place in his heart he thought long decayed and shriveled up.

"Not so much, baby girl. Not as much as my heart will hurt missing you and Dawn until I see you again." Never one to share his feelings easily, he found it so simple to tell her how he felt.

"You could come to softball practice tomorrow and watch us play," Dawn offered.

He kissed Autumn on the forehead, brushed his nose to hers, and said, "I'll be there."

Standing in the doorway, looking back at them tucked into their beds, both watching him, he took in the scene and sighed. Overwhelmed, he said, "Goodnight, girls. I'll send your mom up to say goodnight. I love you," he added, meaning it wholeheartedly.

"Love you, too," Autumn called back. At the same time Dawn said, "I love you."

He had to sit on the top of the stairs, his face planted in his palms as he tried to get hold of his emotions.

Rain stood at the bottom of the stairs and watched the play of misery all mixed up with love and overwhelming feelings that came along with being a parent cross Body's face. The awesome responsibility swamped her the first time she held Dawn, moments after she'd given birth to her. Looking into her tiny face, she'd realized she was her child's everything. Brody was feeling that right now.

Drawn up the stairs by his slumped form and her traitorous heart, she stood before him and put her hand on his hair, sliding her fingers through the silky strands. Brody's head came up at the same time he took her hand and pressed it to his cheek.

"They're mine," he said on a huge exhale.

"One hundred percent," she confirmed with half a smile.

"How the hell am I going to take care of them and be the father they need?"

"I asked the same thing myself for about the first month I had them home. Two crying babies, both relying on me for everything. Very overwhelming. The only thing I can tell you is it gets easier. Besides, you don't have to change dirty diapers and endure sleepless nights for two and four A.M. feedings."

Holding on to her hand, he looked up to her with earnest eyes. "I would have, Rain. Dirty diapers, late-night feedings, spit up, whatever they'd needed, I'd have done it for them, for you. If you want to have more, I'll prove it to you."

"Be happy with the two you already have." She tried to take her hand back. He wouldn't let her.

"Do you want to have more, Rain?"

"I'll walk you out to your truck," she said, avoiding answering.

"Rain . . ."

"Brody, nothing good will come from me answering that question."

He followed her down the stairs. "Hot sex and a baby will come from answering that question, honey."

"Then my answer is no. I've already had the hot sex and baby that comes with it. Got myself another baby when someone else got the same hot sex." She pushed the front door open and walked out into the cold night air.

Brody grabbed her shoulder and spun her around. His face an inch from hers, he leaned over her, his voice came out rough. "She got fucked and so did I. In more ways than one. Don't ever compare what we had with what happened between Roxy and me. There's no comparison and not a damn thing matches what I had with you."

"Except the end result. Two beautiful girls."

"You got to have both of them, while all I got was a life of living hell without you. My own damn fault, I know. I deserved it."

"If you wanted me so damn much, why didn't you stay and fight with me and then make up the way we always did?"

Taking a few steps away from her, he turned back and gave her the only reason he had and knew wasn't worth anything after how much it cost him. "Because I thought you would walk away from me anyway. You had your scholarship, college, a great future laid out before you and nothing but me and the worst mistake of my life here. I couldn't watch you walk away from me and leave me with nothing."

"You never once thought of going with me?" she ventured.

"You never asked."

"I was working my way up to it, trying to find a way to get you to come with me without you thinking I was trapping you into something you didn't want."

"All I ever wanted was you." Brody took a step to her and reached out to trace his fingers over her cheeks. "I've been to two countries to hunt down and destroy our enemies. The one thing I learned, I'm my own worst enemy. I destroyed myself when I left you and all I want to do is rebuild."

"You're off to a good start with Dawn and Autumn." She let him know she appreciated the effort he was making with the girls.

"How am I doing with you?"

"I don't want to do this with you, Brody. I'm the mother of your children, not some chick you pick up in a bar."

"Did I toss out some line at you?"

"No. You just thought you could come in here, have a few heated words with me, I'd forgive everything, and we'd be right back where we were eight years ago. That's not going to happen. I have those girls to think about. I'm not messing around here."

"I didn't come back to mess with you."

"No, you just want to set up house and play the happy family where I forget everything that's standing between us from the night you slept with Roxy until now."

"Is that so much to ask? You said you forgive me. I get you're still angry."

"You left me."

Brody grabbed her by the back of the neck and around her waist, hauling her body against his, her face inches away. The heat of his breath washed over her lips, his breath coming out heavy with every exhale laced with the anger simmering in his eyes.

"Stupidest thing I ever did. Worst mistake of my life. Saying I'm sorry a hundred times will never make it up to you. But please, after you're done being angry, could you at least try to open your heart to me and see if we could make us work. Make some room for me in their lives and yours. As much as I appreciate all you've done to be a mother to our girls, I want you to be more. I want you to be my wife."

Her body was already melting into his as he held her immobile against him. As much as she wanted to give in to the temptation of his mouth and the hard arousal pressed to her stomach, she couldn't allow herself the momentary pleasure it would bring and the longtime heartache it could cause.

"You ask a whole lot of me. Be your wife. A mother for the girls. Make more babies with you. Fill a house with a family. Nowhere in there did you offer me anything."

"Anything you want, ask and it's yours."

"I shouldn't have to ask. It should be given willingly because you want to give it."

"Damnit, Rain. Everything I have, everything I am is yours already. Can't you see that?"

Before he could crush his mouth to hers, she pressed her fingertips to his lips, pressing to keep him from kissing her. "Don't. Don't kiss me anymore. They're upstairs watching out the window, hoping you and I will fall back in love instantly, get married, and you'll move in and be a full-time father to them."

Brody glanced over her shoulder and up to the black window above her head. "Is this that 'Mom has eyes in the back of her head' deal? The girls are in bed. They aren't in the window."

"Yes, they are. They can be very sneaky when they want to be. Every time they see you kiss me, they plot and plan for happily-ever-after between their parents."

"What's wrong with that?" He let her go before she had to struggle to get free.

"Everything. Especially when there's so much unfinished business between us. Owen offered to watch the girls Friday night. I'll come out to the cabin and you and I will talk."

He frowned and settled for what he could get. "I promised the girls I'd see them tomorrow at softball practice. What time?"

"Four to five at the elementary school field."

"Can I take you all out to dinner tomorrow night?"

"The girls love the pizza parlor."

"I could take you out for something nicer than pizza," he offered, wishing for candlelight, steaks, and soft music, knowing full well he wasn't going to get it.

"Let's keep it simple. Easy."

"For now." He really wanted that intimate evening alone with her. Inspiration struck. "I'll make you dinner Friday night."

"Don't bother, I won't stay longer than it takes to tell you what you need to know. Besides, when you hear what I have to say, you'll lose your appetite."

With his hands fisted on his hips, he studied her. She didn't give anything away. "You won't cut me any breaks, will you?"

"There's nothing I'd like more than to go back to that place where things were easy between us. Where I could take one look at you and see everything you weren't telling or showing me."

"You can still read me, Rain. You knew the minute I saw those girls I wanted to be their father. I mourn every day I missed with them, and I'll do everything in my power to be a good father to them. More than that, when you heard I'd come back to town for you, you weren't sure. Not until the minute I walked into Pop's garage and you saw my face. Then you knew. When I kissed you, you knew I still love you."

"Stop, Brody. Enough."

"It's not enough. Not until you and I are together again. Not until you believe in us again. I'll prove it to you, Rain. We can have the house, the family, the love we once dreamed. It can all come true."

"Goodnight, Brody. Drive safe." She went up the steps to the porch.

"I'll let you walk away from me tonight, because you need time to think. We will lay all the cards on the table and deal with each and every one of them. Starting with the reason our daughter is terrified of Roxy."

"You should be, too, Brody. That woman is evil beyond measure."

Brody opened his mouth to ask her about that last comment, but Rain held up her hand and pointed up, indicating the girls just above them, probably listening to every word.

"I'll see you tomorrow, sweetheart. Dream of me, I'll be dreaming of you," he said, reminding her of just how much her past had come back to haunt her. Those were the same words he'd said to her night after night years ago.

She stood on the porch and he got into his truck and started the powerful engine. She was still standing there minutes after he looked at her and drove away. Wiping the backs of her hands over the tears on her cheeks, she went into the house and up the stairs. The sound of the girls rushing into their beds didn't surprise her.

She kissed both girls, ignoring the fact they pretended to sleep. Dawn's bold voice broke the silence. "Will Dad move in with us?"

Rain answered as honestly as she could. "I don't know. Go to sleep now. You'll see him again tomorrow."

Rain walked into her dark room, light from the street lamp casting the room in a soft glow. The sight of her empty bed, the quiet of the room, the ache in her heart made even the thought of sleep impossible. Curling up with her mother's old quilt in the chair by the window, she gazed up at the stars, her eyes as weary as her mind. Drifting off to sleep almost an hour later, she dreamed of Brody and woke the next morning cussing him for willing her to join him in a place where everything was right and perfect.

Chapter Eleven

BRODY WOKE TO the birds singing outside his window. Their cheerful tune only made the pounding in his head intensify with each squawk outside, echoing in his head. His bad leg tightened into an intensely painful cramp. He could barely move it without shooting pains up into his hip and back or down to his toes. Both of those things were bad enough, but the throbbing erection really had his attention because the damn birds had pulled him out of a dream so intense, he could almost feel Rain on top of him, grinding her hips to his. The weight of her breasts pressed into his palms.

Satisfaction was a hot shower and five fingers away, but the pain in his leg and head made it impossible to get out of bed. Thankful he'd remembered to put his pills on the bedside table, he popped the top, and against his will he took two pain pills instead of his normal one. Even the thought of needing the drugs made him feel weak, like his father. With his arms crossed over his eyes, he waited for the effects of the drugs to take hold and erase the pain.

Over an hour later, he finally made it out of bed and into the shower. Hands planted on the wall, the spray pounding on the back of his neck, he stared down at his damaged leg. The skin grafts looked better. The burns had healed. The doctors told him it could have been a lot worse. He was an excellent healer.

"Like any of that matters when I look like this," he said to the drain. "What the hell will Rain think when she sees this?"

He didn't know, but it was never far from his mind any time he thought about her. His need for her was a living thing inside of him. One day soon, he planned to take her to bed again and find that magical place only they could conjure.

The contractor arrived while he sat at his new kitchen table drawing out new plans for the addition to his cabin. Only this time, instead of adding on a few hundred square feet, he was adding on almost two thousand. A cabin wasn't enough space for him and his family. They needed at least three more bedrooms and two more baths, along with a great room for all of them to enjoy. It would cost him a lot to keep the original cabin structure and build around it, but he felt it important to keep a piece of his past while looking forward to his future. Besides, what was the use of having all that money if he didn't use it for his family?

"Hey, Jim, could you take a look at this?" Brody leaned over the table, staring down at the plans.

"That's a hell of a lot more than we discussed. We've already poured the foundation and put in the subfloor for extending the living room and adding a bed and bath."

"Yeah, I know. But I've got two daughters and I'm hoping a couple more kids in the future." Rain would kill him for talking out of turn, but he needed to make a home for all of them, and that meant working with Jim to get it done.

"Everybody in town's talking about you coming home and finding out about the girls. Can't believe Rain would keep something like that from you?"

Brody ignored the tone, and what Jim was thinking and insinuating. "How long do you think it'll take to make these changes?"

"Six months at the earliest. Probably take a year."

"That's too long." Brody stood to his full height and flexed his ankle and bent his knee to stretch out his sore hip and thigh.

"You're talking about practically building an entire house here, Brody. The cabin will stand as the main entrance and room, but the rest is like tacking on a house to a box."

"If you hired subcontractors for the electrical and plumbing, hired on additional men for the construction, can you cut that six months in half?"

"Brody, you're talking a lot of men and a lot of money to get it done that fast."

"I've got the money. You hire the men and get started right away. I want to see some real progress on this by next week."

"I'll need an architect to look at this and make up some real plans." At Brody's glare for the added time it would take to wait on a set of blueprints, Jim added quickly, "I got a friend who owes me a favor. It'll cost you overtime for him, but he can probably have the plans drawn up in a couple days. A project this big, you want it done right. Besides, that will give me enough time to set up the crews we'll need to get this done in the time you want. Not to mention lining up all the permits."

"I guess that will have to do." Thinking of the aesthetics of the inside and out, he added, "Have the architect call me. This is the basic plan I want, but I'd like his take on making the place look good. You know, change the feel from a cabin to a nice home."

"He's done some real nice work using natural stone and timber from the area. I think he can take this and spruce it up, give it that real custom feel."

"Perfect. Listen, I'll be in and out over the next couple of days, but you need to be gone by five tomorrow. Rain is coming out to talk, and we need privacy."

Jim raised an eyebrow and gave him a knowing smile. Brody dismissed both. He wasn't about to tell Jim Rain planned to ream his ass for what he'd done. And tell him about Roxy. It still nagged at him his daughter was terrified of her own mother. Yet, even he had a hard time thinking of Roxy as Autumn's mother. He didn't see any of Roxy in her, only the kindness instilled in her by Rain.

"We'll be out of your way. So, have you heard from Roxy?"

"No," Brody replied. He hoped he never saw her again.

"Man, she was out for your blood when she found out you left town. Then, she found out she was pregnant and told everyone you'd be back to marry her. When she found out Rain was pregnant too, man, she went nuts. A few of the guys at the bar had to stop her from trashing her place one night. Said she was breaking dishes and tossing furniture, out of control and in a rage."

"That's Roxy," Brody said, frowning, "ever the reasonable one. She was pregnant and in a rage, not thinking a damn bit about the baby she was carrying."

"That's not the best part," Jim said, his delight in telling Brody the sordid story clear to see. "Roxy found out Rain hired a private investigator to track you down. She cornered Rain in the grocery store in front of God and everyone. They were both about five, six months pregnant at the time. Roxy shoved Rain up against the freezer doors and held her there with her arm across her throat."

"What the hell!"

"I know. She was right in Rain's face demanding she tell her where you were. She screamed that Rain found you and you'd pay for leaving her with your brat. Her words, not mine," Jim added. "Roxy said there was no way in hell you were going to knock her up and marry Rain and have the perfect family. When Rain said the detective tracked you to Arizona but lost you, Roxy got really pissed and swore if Rain didn't tell her where to find you, she'd get rid of the baby, she'd make sure of it."

Brody's gut tightened at those damning words. Even though Autumn was alive and well, a chill ran up his spine, thinking of Roxy that far along, making sure she lost the baby.

Jim's silence told him there was a hell of a lot more to the story. "What did Rain say about that bombshell?"

"Nothing. Her whole face turned red. She shoved Roxy back and slapped her. I swear to God, the crack of her hand on Roxy's face was like a gunshot echoing through the store. Everyone gasped. No one moved. Rain pointed her finger in Roxy's face and told her if she did anything to the baby, Rain would kill her.

"Now, about this time the store manager is moving in to put a stop to the whole scene. Can't have two pregnant women fighting in the freezer aisle. Anyway, Roxy tells Rain if you want the baby, you have to pay big time. Rain got real close to her, said something no one could hear, and Roxy smiled in a real nasty way. She walked right out of the store with that smug look on her face she always got when she got over on someone."

"What did Rain do then?"

"Ballsy chick that she is, she finished her shopping. Manager asked her if she needed any help, and she just rolled her eyes. Never seen anything like it, I'm telling you."

"Do you know what Rain said to Roxy to get her to back off?"

"Nope. No one does, though everyone speculated for weeks. Roxy walked around town happy." Jim eyed him, his meaning clear. Roxy was never actually happy. Which could only mean one thing. Something had finally gone right in Roxy's world and it linked back to Rain. So what had Rain said to make Roxy happy? And why the hell would Rain do anything to make Roxy happy after what happened between the two of them?

Jim continued: "What's even more strange, the day Roxy left the hospital after giving birth, the nurse who wheeled her out said she thought someone was coming to pick her up. Instead, when they got to the curb, there was Rain sitting in her car, Dawn in the backseat, and another baby car seat right beside her. Rain got out, took the baby from Roxy, put her in her car, handed Roxy a duffle bag, and drove away. They didn't say a word to each other and Roxy handed the baby over like it was nothing. Roxy got in a cab and left town. At least, that's how the nurse described it to everyone down at the diner."

"So, no one knows why Roxy handed over Autumn to Rain?"

"Rain never said a word. She's just been raising her like her own. Oh, people still talk, but Rain's never said one way or another what actually happened and why. Didn't she tell you?"

"Not yet. But she will." So far, nothing added up, and he had a lot more questions to ask.

"You should ask her what happened a couple years back. The girls were about three. Roxy suddenly came back to town. No one had really heard from her in years. She looked down on her luck, which seemed strange seeing as how she still owns the bar her daddy left her and collects rents on the two apartments upstairs. Anyway, she came back to town and made some sort of commotion at Rain's place when she went to see Autumn. The neighbors called the police because of the ruckus, but Roxy was already gone by the time the cops arrived. The next night, early in the morning really, the cops had to go back. No one knows why. Then Rain went out of town for about five days. No one has seen Roxy since. Some even think Rain might have gone after her and killed her, though that's just crazy talk. The bar manager says he talks to her about the business and rents, though she doesn't call often."

"You sure know a lot about what's been going on between Roxy and Rain."

"Small town, man. Everyone talks. You'll see. Everybody's talking about you coming back and showing up at Rain's last night. Since nobody got shot, people are figuring you two are keeping things civil for the kids. Hell, man, no one would blame you for being pissed she kept the kids from you all this time."

"I'm sorry, what?"

"Well, once Owen came back to town, we were all sure he'd tell you about the kids and you'd come back. Owen mentioned to Bill Radley at the real estate office that Rain told him not to tell you. After the thing with your dad happened, no one wanted to bring up Roxy with your brother."

"What thing with my dad?"

"Well, he was drinking at Roxy's place before he ran himself off the road. Everyone knew how you felt about her allowing him to drink as much as he wanted without the bartender or Roxy cutting him off for his own good. Anyway, I don't think anyone really put it together anyway. Except maybe me, since I was there that night."

"What are you talking about?"

"It was the same night Roxy came back to town and there was that trouble at Rain's place. Roxy was in the bar that night. A real slow night, only a few of us at the bar and tables. She took your old man aside, sat with him in one of the back booths, both of them drinking from a bottle of whiskey."

"Roxy was drinking with my father."

"Looked real intense if you ask me. Your father out-paced her, she seemed to pour two, three for him to her one. He was wasted. Strange thing was, the more your father talked, the angrier she got. Finally, she dragged him out of the booth and shoved him out the door. He laughed at her the whole time, said something that really set her off, and she tossed him out.

"He was still laughing when he drove away. I went out to see if I could stop him, but he took off. Didn't hear until the next afternoon that he'd had an accident. I'm real sorry, Brody. If I'd caught up to him, I'd have driven him home."

"It wasn't your fault. The old man drove home count-less times from the bar. He had more trouble driving sober than he did drunk," Brody added to take away the sting to Jim's guilt.

"That's for sure," Jim said on a laugh.

"Did Owen know Roxy was with Dad that night?"

"I'm not sure. He didn't come back to town at that point, except to take care of your father's arrangements. Seems to me he came back for good not long after."

"Because he found out about the girls," Brody said, mostly to himself.

"Could be."

That was the real truth of his brother giving up his lucrative job at a big law firm. He'd come back to look after Rain and the girls in his absence. Hadn't Rain said Owen had been a better brother than he deserved? Well, here was the hard truth. Owen gave up another life to come back here and watch over Brody's family. But why? He could have kept in touch with Rain by phone, come for visits to see the girls. Something else happened, and every time he came to a dead end, Roxy was right there waiting for him. Everything revolved around her. His father's death, Autumn ending up with Rain, his brother coming back to town.

Brody sent Jim on his way, telling him to have the architect call to go over the details of the new construction. He still had Roxy and Rain on his mind when he drove into the parking lot at the electronics superstore in Solomon. Frustrated, he walked into the store knowing he wouldn't get answers to his questions until he had Rain alone tomorrow night. Well, he might not get his answers, but his girls would get new computers and games to play. He owed them seven years of Christmas and birthday presents, and this was a good start.

Chapter Twelve

BRODY PULLED UP behind Rain's old Jeep Cherokee. It probably ran as well as the day someone else drove it off the lot. An excellent mechanic, Rain would make sure the engine was in top form, even if the paint was worn and scratched from use and time. A good car for her and the girls, but he could do better by her. He would do better by her, but first he had to get her back. Then, he'd spoil her the way he'd always dreamed of doing.

Stepping down from his truck, he noticed two things. Everyone in the bleachers stared at him, and two little blond haired angels ran toward him, screaming "Dad!" Unable to contain the smile on his face, he came around the front of the truck and took a few quick strides before both girls launched themselves into his outstretched arms and he scooped them up.

"How are you, Autumn?" He kissed her on the forehead, then brushed his nose to hers.

"I'm good. You came," she said in a cheerful voice.

"Of course, I came. I said I would." Turning to the other beauty in his arms, he asked, "How are you, Dawn?" Giving her a kiss and a rub of his nose, she giggled and wrapped her arms around his neck, hugging him tight.

"Good. Mom is over there getting set up. She said you're taking us out to dinner after practice."

"I sure am."

"Pizza and ice cream?" Dawn asked, smiling mischievously at Autumn across his shoulders.

"Sure," he said, unsure if he was agreeing to something he shouldn't. Then again, what kid didn't like pizza and ice cream?

Brody walked with the girls in his arms over to Rain. God, she was beautiful. Wearing a pair of tight black leggings, her old softball jersey, and her hair tucked up under her old ball cap, streaming out the back in a long ponytail, she was a sight. Slim and lean as she always was, he had a hard time imagining her pregnant. If he hadn't seen the photos, he'd never guess she'd carried his child. Didn't that thought just do something to his insides every time he imagined her round with his child tucked under her beautiful heart.

"Hi, Rain."

"Aw, are they for me," she said, smiling. "You shouldn't have."

He couldn't help himself; he laughed, and damn if it didn't feel good. This was the wisecracking, fun-loving Rain he remembered and had missed so much.

"I'm glad I did," he teased back with an underlying seriousness. The truth of the matter was that he was happy to have both the girls, despite the circumstances.

Rain's ready smile told him she intended to make this evening easy. As much as he wanted to get to the bottom of the situation with Roxy and Autumn, he much preferred this lighter version of Rain to last night's hostile one. Bringing up Roxy now would only set off Rain's temper.

"You two need to get your gloves and ball caps. We'll stretch before we practice."

Brody set the girls down, straightening out and wincing from the pain shooting up his leg and hip into his back.

"Will you play catcher for us?" Dawn asked, hopping up and down on her toes in front of him.

Brody wanted to say yes immediately, but there was no way he could crouch on his knees with his leg in such bad shape. No amount of pills would help that kind of pain.

"Your dad isn't able to bend down like that, Dawn. Remember, we talked about your dad's injury. His leg isn't healed enough for playing sports. Besides, here's Uncle Owen."

Brody thanked Rain with a halfhearted smile for preparing the girls for his inability to do some things. His leg just wasn't strong enough for much more than getting him around. He worked on his physical therapy, and it was getting better, one irritatingly tiny step at a time.

"Owen plays with you guys?" Brody couldn't hide his annoyance that his brother could do something with his girls he couldn't.

"He's been helping me out the last two years."

"Hey, Brody." Owen walked up. "I'll get them started." He kissed Rain on the head as he passed, smacked Brody on the back with a hard thud, and walked on by.

"Why does he constantly do that?" Brody asked through his teeth.

"Before you came back, he did it because he loves me and wanted me to know he cared." Her eyes went soft as she glanced at Owen gathering up the girls.

"Now that I'm back?" Brody asked, knowing he wouldn't like the answer.

Her eyes met his and the corner of her mouth turned up. "Just to piss you off, because you've made it clear you don't like him being affectionate toward me."

"I don't want any man but me kissing you."

Completely ignoring him, she bent and took out a bottle of water and a granola bar from her bag. "You're limping more today. I saw you take your pills before you got out of the truck. You shouldn't take them on an empty stomach. Drink this and have something to eat."

Touched, he took the water and food. "You taking care of me, Rain?"

"I'm taking care of my children's father."

"I'm him. He's me. You used to take care of me all the time." He tried to pull her back to their past, the place and time when they were happy. God, he missed that, wished he could snap his fingers and have it all back.

"That's me. Always taking care of everyone." He caught the trace of resentment in her voice. That little dig cut all the way to his heart. No one took care of Rain, but she'd taken care of the girls and the mess he'd left behind.

"I have to get the girls started."

She walked away and Brody stared after her. Good coming or going, he thought. Following the sway of her hips, he made his way across the field, gave each of his daughters a kiss on the head, a brush of his nose, and headed to the bleachers to watch.

As he advanced on the seats, he scanned the area, the top of the snack shop building, and the restrooms. No sniper. Why would there be? Just little girls playing ball, but Brody's instincts went on full alert, and he didn't know why. Vulnerable out in the open like this. Perspiration broke out on his face and his anxiety kicked in. While he scanned the outskirts of the park, everyone in the stands watched him. Comical the way they stared from him to Rain and back again, like watching some tennis match. Only they were trying to figure out what was going on between him and Rain. He wished he could figure that out himself.

Stretching out his legs and leaning back against the seat behind him, he put the people around him out of his mind and watched Rain and his girls in action. Focused on them, he could almost ignore the instinct to find cover and safety. When he rubbed his palm over his injured thigh, it wasn't from the pain, but because of his sweaty palms.

Owen grounded balls to some of the girls, Autumn included, helping them practice fielding as the ball bounced off the ground. When the girls missed, Owen encouraged them to hustle and get the ball and throw it back to him. Rain worked with Dawn and another girl on pitching. Dawn had her mother's arm.

The girls took their positions around the field. Owen crouched behind home plate, Rain grabbed a bat, and Dawn and the other girl pitching stood on the pitcher's mound. Autumn took her place at first base.

The crack of the bat drew him to home plate. The ball sailed out past the shortstop to left field. The little girl ran to grab the ball and threw it to Autumn at first. She caught it effortlessly, touched her foot to the base bag, and threw it to Dawn on the pitcher's mound. All the girls showed surprising coordination. Rain had everything to do with that. She'd obviously worked with all the girls to make the game fun, but she put the girls in positions that suited their skills. The longer he watched, the more she and the girls impressed him.

To give the girls a chance to bat, Rain took over field positions as each girl ran to home plate to take their turn. Some of the girls struck out, but got a second chance until they got a hit. All the while, Rain called out directions and encouragement. The other girls followed Rain's example and cheered their fellow teammates on.

A comment by one of the other parents caught his attention, making him frown. "The girl at bat should be dropped from the lineup. She can't hit the ball."

Brody studied her next swing and identified the issue.

Whistling to Owen, he held up his hands and showed Owen the girl needed to spread her hands to give her more leverage and control of the bat. Owen stood behind the little girl and showed her what to do and allowed her a couple practice swings. Dawn sailed in a pitch. The ball cracked off the end of the bat, flew high over second base to the outfielder. The little girl at bat smiled hugely when all the girls cheered. Brody caught Owen's nod of approval before he glanced out to Rain. She touched her finger to the brim of her ball cap, then pointed at him. An old signal she used to give him when he'd come to watch her games. His heart warmed and his chest went tight at the old familiar gesture.

The feeling was ruined as he tuned in to several comments coming from behind him on the bleachers.

"He was shot ... I heard he survived a roadside bomb ... The paper said he was awarded a Purple Heart, another medal for valor, and a bunch of others ... She didn't tell him about the girls ... I read he started his own business ... He's rich now ... No way will he let her keep those kids from him ... He'll probably take those girls from her after what she did ... Wait till Roxy finds out he's back in town ... The paper said he's rebuilding the old cabin and raising horses out on the ranch ... His company is based in Atlanta, but he'll be working from here ... It's awful she's been raising those girls alone without their father ... She's a spiteful bitch, who took another woman's baby and kept them both from their father ..."

The last voice he recognized, but couldn't place the

woman's name. She and Roxy had been friends back in the day. Practice wound down, and he couldn't sit another minute listening to the people around him gossip, thinking they were being discreet and he couldn't hear them.

Rain shot him a concerned look. His confusion and irritation must have shown on his face. Standing, he headed her way. She met him several strides from where the girls did some warm-down exercises with Owen.

He stood over her and said between clenched teeth, "What article about me is everyone talking about?"

"Probably the article in yesterday's paper," Rain supplied, looking as innocent as a bank robber holding a bag of money outside the bank doors.

"Did you talk to a reporter about me?"

"No," she scoffed. "The last thing I want is someone asking me a bunch of questions about you, me, and the girls. I wouldn't give the people of this town anything more to talk about," she added.

"Everyone is talking," he pointed out, "because of some article they read."

Rain rolled her expressive eyes and huffed out a frustrated breath. "Fine. It was me. But not the way you think. Owen knows a reporter at the paper. His friend wrote the article using Owen as an anonymous source. Everyone will talk about us—you and the girls, more specifically. You left town with less than a stellar reputation. I didn't want our girls hearing everyone talk about the old you."

"The old me," he repeated, hoping she really saw the changes in him.

"We aren't those young reckless people we used to be.

I wanted this town to know what you made of your life. No matter what they say about me, what you've accomplished is extraordinary."

"Those people think you're some evil bitch who took another woman's baby and kept the girls' existence from me for spite."

"They're not far off the mark."

"Bullshit." He leaned heavily on his right leg because his left was killing him. Planting his fists on his hips, he added, "There isn't a cruel bone in your body."

"I have Autumn and I didn't tell you about either of them." She pointed out the obvious, but not the whole picture. There was a hell of a lot more to why she'd kept the girls from him. Most of the reason was his own damn fault.

Frustrated, he gazed up at the sky and prayed for patience.

"I wanted the people of this town to talk about your accomplishments. So that when the girls overheard, they'd hear all the good things about you."

"Is this about my company and the money I've made? You want everyone to know I can keep you and the girls in style," he accused.

Too late, he realized his mistake. Her controlled rage was something to see. "You think this is about money. I haven't asked you for a dime. I've put a roof over those girls' heads, fed them, clothed them, paid their doctor bills, made sure they always got the things they need. Maybe I couldn't always afford the best, or they had to go without things they wanted, but I always made sure their needs were met. I don't need to be kept in style and neither do they."

She paced away from him and came back, fire and fury burning in her eyes. "I can't win with you. I've tried to be nice, let you come to the house and see the girls, include you in their lives, bring you into the family. Haven't I?"

He opened his mouth to answer, but she went on without waiting to hear what he had to say. "All this time you thought all I want is your money."

"No." He tossed his hands up and let them fall. He had to rub his palm over his leg to try to ease some of the pain. "I didn't get a lot of sleep last night. That's your fault," he accused, pointing a finger at her. "I'm tired, surly, and in pain, as you very well know. I overheard them talking about the roadside bomb and my injuries and . . ." He couldn't tell her it brought it all back, and all he wanted to do was blank it all out.

"You don't want people talking about what happened to you and your friends." She spoke what was on his mind. "You saved three of your buddies, Brody. You busted out the back window and dragged Tom out of the burning vehicle, even after you were hurt. You gave him CPR until he came back. You never gave up. None of the details were in the article. Only that you risked your life and the military rewarded you with your medals. You're a hero, Brody. Nothing can change that fact, even if you wish away the years you served our country, because of that one terrible day."

"I don't want to talk about it. I don't want people asking me about it." A trace of desperation escaped in his voice.

"You don't have to talk about it. That was one of the purposes of the article. To let people know the facts without them asking you. If they talk to you about it, change the subject, tell them you don't want to talk about it, tell them you left that life behind. Whatever makes you comfortable. Hell, show them a glimpse of the old Brody and tell them to go to hell."

"Wait, how did you know about Tom?" At her guilty look, he said, "Owen couldn't have known those details."

"I guess it doesn't matter if you know now. I was at the hospital, Brody."

"You came to see me." Surprise didn't cover the emotions running through him. He didn't remember her being there when he'd spent every miserable second of agony wishing she were with him.

"Did you think I'd leave you in some hospital to die alone? You scared me half to death." She adjusted her ball cap nervously. "Your burns were pretty bad, but the infection was worse. They kept you sedated those first few days. I met Tom's wife in the hospital. She told me he was holding his own. Alive, thanks to you."

"You saw the burns?"

"The nurses would come in and change the dressing every couple of hours. You must have been in terrible pain." Her eyes went soft, glassing over.

The girls were just about ready to pack up their gear. He didn't have much time before Autumn and Dawn came to them to go to dinner.

"You saw them," he said again. "They've healed a lot, but the skin . . . it's kind of . . ."

Rain put her hand on his arm as he stumbled through trying to explain.

"Brody. Stop. You don't have to say anything. I saw the burns and the other scars on your body. They don't frighten me," she went on to reassure him.

"They're ugly," he admitted, knowing she'd probably feel the same.

Her laugh startled him. "There's never been anything ugly about you, Brody. I'm sure women still fall at your feet. I did," she added when he only stared.

He couldn't speak, didn't know what to say. Reading him the way she always did, she put her hand over his heart in her achingly familiar way. This time, he managed to hold back the instinctive flinch.

"Brody, honey, I see the outside of you with my eyes, but when I really look at you, I do it with my heart. I always have. I didn't fall in love with your handsome face and that outstandingly fit body," she said with a cocky smile. "I fell in love with who you are. The real you, not just the parts I can see.

"Remember my senior year? The championship softball game, and I got beamed in the side by the other pitcher."

"You were the best player. She wanted to take you out of the game."

"She cracked two of my ribs with that pitch."

"You sucked it up and hit a home run on the next pitch and won the game. You were a badass back then. Still are," he added.

"You picked me up for school, carried my backpack for me, did my chores around the house, and helped out at

Pop's shop, until I could do it myself. That's the Brody I fell in love with. The one who can't stand to see me hurt and who drives a half an hour out of town to my favorite Mexican restaurant to buy me tacos just to make me feel better."

"I don't deserve you." Barely able to get the words out for the lump in his throat.

"You don't deserve what I did to you. I'll explain it all to you tomorrow night at your place, but please know, I did it for Autumn. I did it so you could be in that war with your head in the game and not on what you'd left behind."

"You were always with me," he said. "I was fighting my way back to you."

"You made it. The people of this town should know you served them proud. Your daughters know you did."

"I can't believe you came to the hospital." He rubbed his hand over his aching thigh. "Why didn't you stay, so I could see you?"

"You made it clear you didn't want Owen or me anywhere near you. Once I knew you'd make it, I had to fly home to the girls. Owen stayed a few days longer to be sure you were on the mend. We respected your privacy and need to recuperate alone."

"In other words, you knew I'd have a difficult time with the grueling physical therapy and I didn't want you to see me struggle."

"I knew you'd take it on with the same single-minded determination you go after everything you want."

Like I'm coming after you. "You had no doubt I'd get through it."

"Quit. Stop. Lose. These are not words in the Brody McBride dictionary."

"Then why are you fighting me, honey? Be with me again."

"Give me a kiss," she said, and took a step closer.

Just to tease her, he said, "You told me not to kiss you because it confuses the girls."

"I need you to kiss me because Becky Johnstone, previously Long, is on the phone right now with Roxy. She's telling her everything she sees the two of us doing. Now, since a few minutes ago it looked like we were having an argument," she said with a not-so-genuine smile on her face, "I need you to kiss me, so Becky will tell Roxy all is right between the two of us. Hopefully, that will make Roxy believe she can't use you to take Autumn from me."

"How do you know Becky is talking to Roxy?"

"Roxy always knows what's going on with me and Autumn. At first, I wasn't sure how she got the information and details. Through process of elimination of some of the events Roxy knew about, I was able to figure out who was feeding the information to her. Becky is one of those people. Not to mention she's been staring at you since you arrived."

"Not because of my good looks, huh?"

"That's probably a lot of it, and she's telling Roxy right now how good you look in minute detail. So kiss me and give her something to talk about."

Sliding his fingers along her jaw and up to her neck, he leaned in close. "You sure you want me to kiss you?" Her

body trembled, rippling along his fingertips, telling him
how much she anticipated his kiss.

"Why are you making this so hard?" she asked, her
breath catching a bit when he brushed his lips over hers
in a whisper of a kiss.

"Because you're making me hard just standing there
looking good enough to eat." His mouth brushed hers
with every word. He'd like nothing better than to press
her body down the length of his, proving his condition in
blatant reality, but the bleachers were filled with mothers and fathers here to watch their kids play. Though the
only show they wanted to see was him and Rain. So he
kept the kiss intimate but light, a melding of his mouth
to hers as he held her close, but not pressed to him as
he'd like.

"Dad's kissing Mom again," Dawn said behind them,
making him smile against Rain's mouth.

Brody let go of Rain slowly, turning just enough to
see Becky in his peripheral vision. She sat in the stands,
talking furiously on her cell phone and glaring at them.

"Mom, is Uncle Owen coming to pizza with us?"
Autumn asked.

Brody would have laughed at the confused, dazed
look on Rain's face if her lips hadn't remained slightly
parted just waiting for him to kiss her again. Before he
gave into the powerful urge, he turned to Autumn and
Owen. "You coming, man?"

"I'll let you have your girls to yourself. I have some
papers for you to sign before you go."

"You got them done."

"Some of them. I'm not a miracle worker." Owen gave Brody a hearty slap on the shoulder and turned to Rain, who was trying to quiet the girls around her as they asked her for something with a whole lot of high-pitched *pleases*.

"Hey, Rain," Owen called, getting her attention. He pulled her close, kissed her on the head, then spoke quietly. "Becky's in the bleachers talking to Roxy."

"I hope she's telling Roxy Brody and I are getting along just fine. That kiss should tell her he's not about to ally himself with her."

"Why the hell would I do that?" Brody cut in. "I told you I wouldn't take Autumn from you."

"You also told me you'd love me forever. It didn't stop you from sleeping with Roxy and leaving me."

"I didn't want to sleep with her."

"Well, you did," Rain shot back. "And you gave her the means to be a part of your life forever."

"If she wanted that, she'd have kept Autumn. When she didn't, she gave me a second reason to be with you."

"Don't mistake my having Autumn with Roxy giving up on you. She's just biding her time. Now that you're back, she'll do something."

Dismissing him, she turned her back and addressed the girls. Brody clenched his teeth, frustrated she said things like that, then didn't finish by telling him what really happened with Roxy, or what was going on now. He also didn't like people talking about them and reporting to Roxy.

"I won't let her take Autumn. She's ours." He hated

seeing the relief that came over Rain. "Could you just try to trust me? A little bit," he added.

"I don't trust her," Rain said. Not exactly what he wanted to hear, but he'd take what he could get. For now.

"Okay, Owen, let's do a few pitches for the girls before they burst my eardrums with their begging."

Brody didn't know what Rain was talking about, but he definitely wanted the girls to stop jumping up and down and asking her, "Please, Rain, just a couple."

"Stand back." Rain picked up a ball and went to the pitcher's mound. Owen crouched behind home plate, glove at the ready. Rain fired in the first ball, a resounding thud echoed off Owen's glove, and a cheer went up from the girls. Dawn and Autumn stood on either side of him, their little hands tucked in his.

"Mom is awesome," Dawn sang out.

"Too cool," Autumn added.

Brody had to admit, it was an amazing sight to watch Rain pitch, the balls singing over home plate at more than sixty miles an hour. Rain's talent always astounded him. That same familiar guilt came over him thinking about all she'd given up, all that talent going to waste, everything she'd worked so hard to accomplish, so she could go to college, never achieved.

Rain finished the last of several screaming pitches to the girl's cheers. Rain's exuberance and enthusiasm almost convinced him she was happy with her life. Almost. He didn't think someone like Rain—smart, driven, goal-oriented—could be completely satisfied not living up to her enormous potential.

Does she resent working at the garage when she'd had a real chance at something better? Not just a job; she'd had a career mapped out. She'd worked so hard through high school to play her best and earn a scholarship for college, not only for her playing ability, but her grades. Interested in helping people, she'd planned to study psychology, perhaps working with children.

He cursed himself for taking so much away from her.

As they left the ballpark, him in his truck following her to the pizza place, he wondered if there was something he could do to make some of Rain's past dreams come true and still make her his wife.

Chapter Thirteen

———————————————

THE PIZZERIA SMELLED like heaven. Rain didn't take the girls out to eat often, but pizza was always one of their favorites. Brody could probably afford much better. More than likely, he was more used to trendy bistros and steak houses these days. Then again, he'd been eating military fare for the last six years.

The girls climbed into the booth. The place wasn't very busy tonight, but they were already the main attraction.

"What'll it be, girls?" Brody asked.

"I want pepperoni," Dawn said over her sister's, "I want sausage."

Smiling, Brody asked Rain, "Still like the combination?"

"That's fine. You can get the girls a personal pizza and we can share if you like."

"Sounds good. Should I get a pitcher of soda, too?"

"Make it root beer. The sugar is bad enough, they don't need the caffeine, too," Rain said before the girls demanded something else.

"But Mom . . ." Dawn began.

Brody broke in. "Dawn, you heard your mom. Root beer and pizza coming up."

A strange sensation settled over her. It did something odd to her to have Brody on her side and help her with the girls. Normally, they'd have argued with her over the soda, but with Brody cutting Dawn's protest off and siding with Rain, the girls knew not to even try.

Brody stood in line at the counter behind another couple. He scanned all the faces in the restaurant, checked out all the corners and dark places someone could hide, and called himself a fool for not relaxing and enjoying dinner out with his family. Instead, he was looking for a threat that didn't exist. Everyone staring at him didn't help.

Rubbing his palms over his jeans to wipe away the sweat, he took out his wallet and approached the counter.

"Hey, I need two personal pizzas. One pepperoni, one sausage. Then I'll need a large combination and a pitcher of root beer."

"Sure thing, Mr. McBride," the girl behind the counter said, typing his order into the cash register computer. She kept looking at him like she had something on her mind. She surprised him by asking, "Is it true you were in Iraq and Afghanistan?"

"Uh, yeah. I served in both places."

"Wow." The young girl's eyes went wide with astonishment. "I bet it was really scary over there. Lots of soldiers died. They talk about it on the news sometimes."

Brody didn't answer. The sanitized version of the brutality of war didn't tell the true story, or even come close to his memories. He handed over forty bucks to cover dinner, thinking again that he could do a lot better for his family. That's how he thought about them now. They still had a ways to go to being the family unit he wanted, living under the same roof and sharing their daily lives.

"Here's your change. The pizzas will be up in about fifteen minutes."

Brody grabbed the money from the girl. He picked up the pitcher of root beer, uncomfortable he had to use two hands to hold on to it with his sweaty palms. He made his way back to the booth. Rain watched him, her expression worried. Her eyes searched his. How could he tell her this place made him jumpy? His heart raced as the video games in the corner made a loud racket with their sirens, beeps, and explosions. A couple of teenage boys played some shooting game, the *rat-a-tat-tat* unnerving him.

Rain took the pitcher from his hands and set it on the table. He didn't realize he stopped several feet away, lost in his mind and the sounds of gunfire.

"Brody." Rain rested her hand over his thudding heart. "Look at me," she called in his foggy mind. The war tried to pull him back in time, but her voice drew him home.

"Huh," he said, sounding dumb, even to his own ears.

"Hi." She gave him a warm smile.

"Hi. Sorry . . ."

"Don't be." In pure Rain fashion, she made things easy for him again. "Come sit with us."

After Rain slid into the booth, he sat next to her.

"You okay, Dad?" Dawn asked, and carefully poured a glass of root beer.

"I'm fine, honey."

"Mom, can I have a quarter to play one of the games? *Pleeease*," Autumn asked.

Brody dug out his wallet and handed each girl a dollar. "Go nuts." This would give him a few minutes alone with Rain, and he desperately wanted to be alone with her.

Both girls scrambled out of the booth to race across the room to the bank of video games. Brody enjoyed their exuberance and youthful joy. They brought some of that easy lightness back into his life.

"They're great, Rain."

"They're good girls. Things haven't always been easy, but they're resilient."

"It's because of you. You've always been strong. It shows in what a great mother you are. They're happy." He didn't know how to give her the words to describe how it felt to see his children happy when his life as a child was rarely so carefree. Which explained why he's spent so much time with her as a kid rather than going home.

"I hope so. From the day I found out I was pregnant, and when I brought them home, it was my biggest worry. How am I going to make sure they have a happy and healthy life? As you sink into parenthood along with me, I'm sure you'll find it's the one thing you want for them and the hardest to ensure."

"Harder when you're doing it alone without the education you thought you'd have. You were so young when you had them. I should have been here," he said, taking her hand. "Maybe you could have still gone to college," he added.

"Brody, stop wishing for a past we can't get back. The girls are seven. Enjoy them now, because they're growing up so fast."

"What about the dreams you worked so hard for and had to leave behind?"

"Things change, Brody. I learned that really fast when you left. When one dream fades, you dream a new one."

"You can't tell me you're happy being a mother and working as a mechanic when you had almost a full ride to college."

"Why not? I almost had that life. Now, I have this one. You almost had a different life here. Instead, you went away, joined the military, went to college, started your own business, gained some knowledge and wisdom, grew up and became the man you are now. This is your life now. Don't tell me you'd give it all up, them, to have that life back. Think of all you wouldn't have, your military career, the education and life experiences you've had, your business and the secure future it provides you."

"Much of which you gave up yourself."

"Look what I gained. You said it yourself, they're amazing. I love being a mother. I always knew I wanted to have children. Not as early as it happened, but sometimes when something is taken away, you get something so much better. I haven't exactly given up on school. I've taken courses here and there. Over the last seven years, I've completed two years of college."

"That's a long time to cover such little ground, Rain," he said to illustrate how hard he'd made her life.

"Well, college is expensive and I don't have a lot of time. I can't take more than one class at a time when I've managed to save up enough to pay for the course and my books. I did it because it's important to me, but not more important than taking care of them and being a good mother."

"It really doesn't bother you to sacrifice everything you worked your ass off to achieve." He read it in her eyes, heard it in her voice, and knew it was there in her heart. She loved her daughters more than anything, including the future she might have had. "You don't resent them for what you lost. You don't even seem to resent me for getting you pregnant and leaving you."

With a nervous laugh, she answered him honestly. "Don't get me wrong. I've got a lot of pent-up anger for you and what happened. I've also had a long time to look at the situation for what it is . . . in my more rational moments," she added with a smile. "Plenty of times I wanted to rage at you, call you every dirty name in the book, and I resented the hell out of you for going off and living your life without a care for me, or what you'd left behind."

"That's not exactly true, Rain. I thought about you all the time."

"Let's not have a fight right now."

"What's that supposed to mean," he said defensively.

"You say you thought about me, would have come back here if you knew about the girls. I tried to find you.

You left as fast as you could and never looked back. Every report I got back from the investigator always told me the same thing. You held some random job to get cash and there was always some woman you left behind. You were living with someone before you shipped out overseas," she accused. "So don't give me the 'It was always you, Rain' crap. For all I know, she's back there waiting for you to come home."

Brody took in everything Rain said, felt her anger and the bitterness she dished out with her words and the accusation behind them. Everything she'd said was true. Well, almost.

"You're right. I ran away from you and what I'd done. I tried to erase your memory and what we'd shared by sleeping with other women and hoping they'd make me feel . . . something. Anything that wasn't the hatred I felt for myself and what I'd done to you. If I could just find that feeling you gave to me when I was with you, I could let you go for good. You were better off without me. Nothing left here for me but a whole lot of bad memories. All the good ones, I'd already tarnished and destroyed.

"As for the woman living at my place . . . Well, I don't really know what to say about her. She wanted things I couldn't give her."

"Not at the time maybe," Rain said. "Now, you've got money coming out your ears and you're out of the military. You two could have the big house . . ."

"Damnit, Rain. She was nothing more than a distraction and a convenience. Callous, I know. I'm a sonofabitch. Always have been. Except with you, up until my monumental fuck-up. It would have never worked out with her . . . or anyone . . . because I couldn't give her my heart. You already have it. I gave it to you when I was thirteen and we kissed for the first time at the lake."

"You kissed me." She remembered the occasion fondly because that had been a simpler time.

"Hell yes, I did. Ever since then, it's always been you."

"Not always," she said sarcastically. "I may have been your first kiss, but I wasn't the last."

"I'm a guy. I sowed some wild oats after that."

"We could plant a whole field with the number of oats you sowed."

"Doesn't matter. When you turned eighteen and I kissed you again, I wasn't experimenting with my best friend, but kissing the woman I wanted."

"Until you didn't."

"It's always been you."

"It hasn't been me for a long time. Face it, Brody, you moved on with your life. It's a good life you've made for yourself. Which makes me wonder why you're back now."

"And you accused me of making things hard."

"I believe you accused me of the same already," she said with a smile. "Come on, Brody, you show up out of the blue, announce to your brother you're moving back home, and you want me back. Is that about right?"

"Sure. That's the watered-down version. Interested in the muddy version?"

"Hit me." Her chin propped on her hand, elbow on the table. Her attention focused on him, his on her and the creepy-crawly nerves dancing up his spine with every loud noise coming from the people and video games. In the last ten minutes, three more families and a bunch of guys getting off work arrived. His mind tracked them and everything else in the place, making him lose focus on Rain while sharping in on the noise and nuance in the room.

"Have you ever felt like you were out of place?" he asked, hoping she would understand. "I don't mean just feeling uncomfortable until you had a minute to settle in, but really out of place and needing to go somewhere familiar again."

"Sure. I guess so. Being in the war, a foreign country, the sounds and sights so completely different, I guess you'd want to be back here around the things you know."

The tightness in his chest eased a bit with her understanding a small part of what he was trying to tell her. "That's part of it, but I'm talking about even before I joined the military and went overseas. I'm talking about feeling that way in my own skin."

"Brody, I have a hard time believing you ever felt out of place. You've always been so confident."

"I made people believe I am, and for the most part it's true. It's those times when it's just me, alone with my thoughts. When I was a kid, well, the things that happened with my old man ... I always felt like I wasn't good enough. We've been friends since we were little kids. When I was with you, something inside me shifted and changed and I could leave all the bad behind, block out all the suffocating thoughts in my head, and I could breathe. I never felt out of place, or like I had to be something I wasn't ... or couldn't live up to. Not with you."

"Brody, are you okay? You're sweating." Rain placed her hand over his. He slapped it away and pulled back from her, a learned response he wished he could forget he ever needed to be that protective of his personal space. Lately, he needed the space and distance, like he needed air to breathe. He didn't want to be this way with Rain. He wanted to pull her close and keep her there.

"Brody, what's wrong?"

The room and noise closed in on him. He wanted to hang on to Rain before he lost her and himself.

Rain gasped when Brody's hand clamped on to her arm just above her wrist. She tried to pull free of his punishing grip, but he only held tighter and his eyes went blank. Her only thought was she'd lost him and she needed to bring him back. She couldn't leave him lost in his own mind. Struggling against the pain, trying to look calm as Dawn and Autumn made their way through the tables toward the booth, Rain thought fast.

Wrapping her arm around Brody's shoulders, she leaned in close to his ear and whispered, "Brody, come back to me. Come on, honey. It's Rain. Come back to me. Let me go," she added, hoping he'd understand he was hurting her. Instead, he must have thought she wanted him to let her go for good, because he only held on tighter. Tears stung the back of her eyes and she had to swallow the yelp she wanted to let loose from the back of her throat.

"Brody, baby, please listen to me. Hear me. It's Rain. You are safe and home and with me and Dawn and Autumn. You're safe, Brody. You're home."

"Mom?" Dawn's voice was tentative, her eyes scared as Rain leaned against the side of Brody. He stared off into space, seeing something she could only imagine. His whole body vibrated against hers. Sweat beaded his brow; his skin went pale beneath the sheen.

"Autumn, go up to the counter and ask the girl to box up our pizzas. Ask her for a few paper cups for our drinks. We'll have a picnic," Rain said, trying desperately to sound normal and not frighten the girls any more than they already appeared.

Dawn moved closer after Autumn left to do as she was told. She approached her father, hesitating more than once before she reached his other side. "Dad, let go of Mom. Please, Daddy. You're hurting her."

Rain's heart broke. "I'm okay, sweetheart."

Dawn grabbed Brody's hand where it clamped over her arm. She tried to pry his fingers away, but Brody held firm. Rain was desperate to get them out of this situation before the others in the restaurant took notice.

"Brody, honey, come back to me. You're home, safe and sound with us." She let her voice sound slow and soothing. Rubbing his back softly in small circles up to his neck where she squeezed the rock-hard muscles. She kissed his cheek and along his jaw to his ear and whispered, "I love you. Come back to me. Please come back."

Just like that, Brody snapped out of whatever trance he'd been in, shaking his head and looking around like he couldn't remember where he was or what he'd been doing. Dawn struggled with his hand, still gripping her arm.

"Let her go, Daddy," Dawn pleaded.

"Rain," Brody spoke for the first time, his eyes shifting to focus on them.

"I'm right here." She hugged him to her and he turned his face and pressed his cheek to hers. "Let go of my arm now, Brody." Just like that, he let go and wrapped his arms around her.

"I'm sorry. The noise . . ."

"It's okay. You don't need to explain. We'll walk out of here as a family. The park is only a block up."

Autumn slid the pizzas onto the table and Rain backed away from Brody. Still pale, he took a deep breath and pressed the heels of his shaking hands into his eyes. She slipped her sweatshirt on, covering her arm, and zipped it up. Dawn, ever the observant one, watched her with eagle eyes. Rain gave her a smile to reassure her everything was okay.

"Slide out, Brody. Let's go, girls."

Brody stood just outside the booth. When she stood up in front of him, she went up on tiptoe, wrapped her arms around his neck, and held him close. With her cheek pressed to his and his arms wrapped around her, she whispered, "I'm here. You feel me with you."

Brody held her tighter, burying his face in her neck and inhaling deeply. "I feel you."

"Stay with me." She hoped he'd hear more than the words and the meaning of the moment, but her heart's desire.

When he didn't say anything, she leaned back. Such raw emotion filled his eyes. Placing her hand on his cheek, she gave him a smile to let him know she understood. He'd been a lost child, living in a tumultuous house with a drunk. His teenage years had been wild and unruly, lacking direction for a young man who had a lot of potential and no outlet. After leaving his home, he'd found a career, excelled in the military, earning him medals and honors, but he was paying a price for his service. Laced through all the times of his life, she'd been the only thing he'd held on to of home.

Rain gave up the fight to keep him at arm's length. She loved him, had always loved him, and was ready to concede the fight.

His hand locked on hers, she walked out of the pizzeria with him beside her, the girls trailing behind. She grabbed a blanket out of the back of her car, and they all walked down the street toward the park. Brody remained quiet, turned into himself. When she leaned into him, he wrapped his arm around her and pulled her closer. She wrapped her arm around his waist and held on. His body relaxed in her arms. Nothing was said. Words weren't necessary or needed when you were where you belonged and everything was right. For now. Tomorrow, she'd tell him about Roxy and Autumn. As much as she wanted to hold on to this bond they'd just forged, it was tenuous and malleable. Their talk would either strengthen their bond, harden it into something lasting, or break it, leaving them both adrift in their separate lives again.

Chapter Fourteen

RAIN STOOD IN the kitchen, staring out the window at the fading light of day. Shadows moved across the yard, masking the vibrant colors of the blooming flowers. Much like the darkness enveloping Brody's mind at times. She'd been concerned about his car accident, knowing he'd had some sort of episode while driving. Unreal, but not so serious or dangerous at the time. Especially since he'd only received minor injuries. But seeing him last night, up close and personal, concerned her even more. What if one of the girls had been in the truck with him? What if he'd grabbed on to one of them? She glanced down at her bruised arm and flexed her fingers, working the sore muscles.

"Hey, sweetheart." Owen walked into the kitchen behind her. As always, he came to her and kissed her on the head. "You look a million miles away."

"Just thinking."

"What's wrong with the girls? I thought they'd be all riled up and rowdy, ready for dinner and a movie. Instead, they look like someone died."

"They're worried about me seeing Brody tonight."

"Is Autumn worried about what he'll say about Roxy and what she did?"

"Yes," she said absently.

"Why won't you look at me?" Owen put his hand on her shoulder. She leaned her cheek on it for a second, gathering her thoughts. "Come on, Rain. Tell me what's going on," he coaxed.

"We went out for dinner last night," she began.

"Yes, I know. What happened?" he asked, his voice tight. "Did you two get into a fight in front of the girls?"

"No. Nothing like that. In fact, we had a really good talk. A little heated, but we were getting someplace."

"I thought once you guys spent some time together, maybe the old spark would flare to life again. So, what happened last night? Did you decide you don't want to be with Brody?"

"Not exactly," she stalled, trying to sort out her thoughts.

"Rain, if you want me to go lawyer on you and ask a lot of probing questions, fine. Otherwise, spit it out."

"I lost him," she blurted out.

"Lost him? He loves you. He came back for you."

"Yes. I believe he did. I just didn't understand how necessary I am to him."

Owen took her by the shoulders, turned her, and made her face him. "What are you talking about, sweetheart?"

"I'm not explaining this very well."

"You haven't explained a damn thing." Owen's frustration with her evasive answers came out with his words.

"We were sitting in the booth talking. He's different. Not confrontational, but controlled. Even when I told him the cold hard truth, things he didn't want to hear, he didn't lash out at me, didn't fight back."

"He took a breath and said something to defuse the situation."

"Much more disturbing," she said, only half teasing. "He opened up to me, told me how he's felt all these years. Since he was a kid really," she added.

"Okay," Owen said, tentative about making any further assumptions. "After that?"

"I lost him. He was talking to me one minute and just gone the next."

"He blacked out." Owen ran his hands down her arms to her hands. Unfortunately, he didn't miss her wince in pain when his fingers brushed over her forearm and wrist. "What the hell?" He took her hand and pulled the sleeve of her sweater up. "What the . . . Did he do this to you?"

"This was done by a man desperate to hold on to me and home and not get lost in a dark and scary world pulling him under against his will."

"You lost him," Owen repeated her sentiment. "He had a flashback."

"Owen, it was the scariest thing I've ever seen. He was sitting beside me, his body trembling, sweat breaking out on his skin, and I couldn't reach him. He couldn't hear me, respond to me. Everything in me knows he was holding on for dear life because he wanted to be with me. Not there, not lost."

Owen pulled her into his arms and held her tight, close. "Okay, sweetheart. I get it."

"I don't think you do. I can't explain what it was like to see someone like Brody in that state. He's strong, determined, smart, sturdy as they come. Kick ass and take names, that's the Brody we know. I look at him and he's still the same, even bigger and stronger than before."

"Yeah, the military bulked him up. Physically, he's well."

She took a step away and ran her fingers through the side of her hair. "It's his mind, Owen. Part of him is locked in that war and the horrible things he's seen and done. It sucked him away from me."

"What happened when it was over? What did he say about your arm?"

"I didn't let him see it," she confessed and frowned. "I made sure he didn't see it. You should have seen how lost he looked. I got him out of there as fast as I could without making a scene. We went to the park. I thought keeping him outside and in the open would help. Instead, he was quiet and kept searching everywhere for something."

"Probably the enemy."

"That was my thought, too. The girls tried to engage him, and he made an effort to respond, but you could see he wanted to leave. He didn't want us to see him like that."

"He's probably worried about what you think, or that you'll never want to be with him because of this."

"This. What is this? Post-traumatic stress. I expected him to be the same but a little distracted, depressed, short-tempered. Those were the things the doctor warned us about. But not this, Owen. Not him falling away blank, sinking into nightmares when he's awake."

"I know you're scared for him, Rain."

"Scared doesn't begin to cover it. You know Brody. He won't deal with this well."

"Are you afraid he'll hurt himself?"

"I'm afraid for the girls to be alone with him. I'm afraid for him to be alone with himself."

"Are you afraid to go see him tonight? To be alone with him? Because if you are, we can all go. I'll distract the girls while you talk to Brody."

"No. It's not that. He wouldn't hurt me." Doubt infused her voice, and she hated that it was there.

Owen took her hand and raised it between them. Blue and purple bruises encircled her arm in a perfect imprint of Brody's hand and fingers. "He did hurt you."

She snatched her hand back. "You know him. I know him. He'd never hurt me on purpose. You didn't see him."

The tears fell down her cheeks, silent at first, but she couldn't hold back the sob as Owen took her into his arms. His big hands rubbed up and down her back and he held her and let her weep all over his shirt. When she finally brought herself somewhat under control, she leaned back and looked up at him.

"Have you ever wished for something so hard and for so long you thought it would never come true? It was too far out of your reach and too much to ask for anyway, because you can't erase the past."

"Brody has always been yours, Rain. You knew it when you were kids, you know it today. Whatever came between is just life. It's in the past. Do you want to live there, or find a way to really live now and have everything you ever wished come true? It's within your reach. Grab it. Hold on to it. Life has given you enough hardship and grief. Find some happiness. You know, the kind you only ever had with Brody."

"Right up until he screwed it all up. And Roxy, too," she added bitterly.

"That's the past, Rain. Move on."

"Move on. Just like that?"

"Why not? For once, take what you want. Do something foolish because it makes you feel good. You've been taking care of everyone and everything for too long. You've forgotten that you deserve something for yourself."

"Between the shop and taking care of the girls, there's nothing left for me," she admitted. "I'm afraid I don't have enough to give to Brody. What if he needs more than I have to make him better?"

"It's not your job to make him better. He knows what he needs to do."

"What is he supposed to do to make this go away? The

physical therapy will rebuild his muscles and strength. What will rebuild his mind?"

"Time, Rain. It's only been a couple of months. He needs time and distance from that other life. Being with you and the girls will give him a new focus. It's got to be stressful to come back here and try to win you back, find out he's got two daughters, and figure out how to go forward with all of you, knowing things might not work out. He's got a hell of a lot more to lose than the woman he loves. There's a lot at stake, and he knows one mistake on his part could ruin it all. He's got to make up for the past, earn back your trust, be a father to two little girls who have grown to the age of seven without him.

"He spent too long living on the edge. That's become his normal and he's trying to get back to a regular kind of life. I think you know that, and maybe it makes you a little scared to think Brody's need for a wife and family to help him feel sane again is more than you can wish for right now. It's what you both want and are scared to make a reality. He's afraid of losing you and you're afraid of being hurt."

"It's not like I don't have reason to be," Rain snapped.

Worn out and resigned, she sighed out her frustration. Owen's words came out softly behind her.

"Listen to your heart. Take a deep breath and be brave. As much as you know he needs you, you need him, too. More than anything, I think that scares you the most. Knowing you need him, and fearing he'll let you down again. Because he let you down when you needed him the most and you were pregnant with Dawn and everything that came after that. You'll never know if he'll let you down or stand beside you for the rest of your life unless you try."

"Dammit, Owen, you're not going to let it go until I make the first move toward him."

"I'm doing this for you and him. After last night, he'll push you away. With the way things have been going for him, he's probably convinced himself you're better off without him. Don't let this happen, Rain. It won't be good for either of you."

"How do you know?" she asked, her mind a whirlwind of thoughts.

"Both of you are miserable without each other. Imagine how empty you'll feel if you spend the rest of your lives apart."

She didn't want to think about it. It had been on her mind since the day he walked away. How she'd spend the rest of her life feeling empty and alone, like a piece of her was missing. Because it was. Brody had her heart, and only when she was with him did she feel that vibrant love and completeness he brought to her life.

"Sonofabitch." She gave in. "Fine. I'll go see him. I'll tell him about Roxy and Autumn. We'll see how things go after that."

"I'll take your bed tonight." Owen's cocky grin mocked her in the dark window above the sink.

She turned and scowled. "You assume I won't be home tonight."

"I assume you'll make it clear to Brody that you want

to work things out and make a life with him and the girls. The only way to have everything is to lay your cards out on the table and take a risk."

"I just might come up bust," she said.

Owen kissed her on the head and shoved her toward the door. "You might win the pot if you play your cards right."

Chapter Fifteen

BRODY STOOD OUT on the dock, looking at the water and waiting for Rain. The sun descended, setting over the mountains, the sky bright with vibrant colors ahead of him as the dark of night grew behind him. He wanted to stay bathed in the last light of day, soaking it up before he got lost in the dark. This evening would tell the tale between him and Rain. They stood at a crossroads, both of them coming from different directions and standing in the center to decide which path to take. They'd been in this position before, only that time, he'd turned his back on her and they went their separate ways. He hoped this time he could convince her to walk the same path, because he couldn't stand to think of spending the rest of his days without her, all of her, on his side, by his side.

Last night weighed heavily on him. They needed to talk about his losing his mind in the middle of the pizza parlor. One minute he'd been talking to her, and the next he was lost in the middle of war, bombs exploding, gun-fire piercing the air. Adrenaline pumping through his veins, he knew his job. It had become second nature, a reflex to the situation. Survival at all costs, the most important thing. He'd used his strength, his skills, a gun. Then. But not now. Now, survival hinged on getting Rain back and making a life with her and his daughters. He wished the how of it was as natural to him as holding a gun in his hand.

She brought him back last night. He hadn't told her he'd heard her say she loved him. It was too much to hope she meant it in a deeper way than just a tribute to their past friendship and because of the children. Without a doubt she had feelings for him, long lasting and deeply felt from years of shared experiences. Beautiful memories he wished could be reality now.

He didn't know how she felt now, or what she thought of his diminished mental state. Humiliating and maddening, it scared him to think Rain might be put off enough to not let him see his kids as freely as he'd like. Ashamed and embarrassed his children witnessed his behavior last night, all he wanted was to be with them, have a normal family life, and love them.

So much at his fingertips, he wanted to grab hold and never let go. Like reality, it seemed to slip through his damn fingers just when he thought he had a handle on it.

Lost in thought, he didn't hear Rain drive up, but the sound of the door slamming shut caught his attention. He tracked her footsteps over the gravel drive, almost silently across the new grass, then padding down the wood dock toward him. She stopped a few feet away and stood in the quiet with him for a moment. He let the night settle around them.

Once they started talking, things would turn heated. They still had a few things to hash out, and he and Rain had always done that, everything, with a lot of passion. Like the time they made Dawn. What he wouldn't give to have Rain beneath him again. Right now, they stood apart in more ways than one. He wanted it all and was willing to go through this mess in order to get there.

"Beautiful night." Her voice broke the silence. Not the opening he expected. Her soft, sweet voice surprised him as much as her words. He expected direct and curt, but he'd take her cue and hold to it as long as he could before the sparks flew and someone got burned.

"When I was gone, I missed this sky. You can't see stars like this anywhere else," he commented, keeping his back to her.

"I wouldn't know about that."

A shaft of guilt ripped through him. This had been the only place she'd ever known.

"I'll bet the desert sky is beautiful at night."

He thought she'd make a dig about missing school because of him. Her voice and the comment about the desert were more inquisitive.

"Hard to appreciate it with bombs going off," he shot back. So much for soft and sweet. He didn't know why he was being antagonistic when all he wanted was to talk to her calmly, rationally.

Well, there's your problem. Your mind's a long way from calm and rational. Fucked up is more like it.

"I imagine so, but that place is far away and here we are, underneath this sky. Together," she added, her voice still tranquil, making him wonder about her strange behavior. He wanted to turn and look at her, see the expression on her face, and know what she was really thinking. Instead, he stood still, waiting for that first spark to flash, so he could get through it, get it done, and have her back in his arms.

"When I was pregnant with Dawn, sometimes I'd drive out here at night to be close to you. I'd stand on this dock and look up at the stars and I'd talk to you."

Surprised, he turned to her then, but her gaze was on the sky above, and she was a million miles away as those stars.

"Rain . . ."

"At first," she said over him, "I let my anger reign. I'd scream at you in the night and tell you how mad I was that you'd slept with Roxy. As time went on, I realized what hurt the most was that loving me wasn't enough to keep you from sleeping with her."

"Rain . . ." he tried again.

"Then, I fought my way through all the anger and dissecting everything that happened and was happening in my life and realized there was only one thing that really hurt. The only thing that mattered. You left me." Her face turned from the sky to him. Her eyes shimmered with unshed tears. "I wanted you back. In the end, that's the only thing I really cared about. You aren't a cheater,

Brody. I can't defend or explain what you did, but as much pain as it caused me, Autumn has brought me infinitely more joy. It's taken me a long time to realize I'd rather have her than to erase what you did."

"Then you know how I feel. As much as I'd like to take that hurt away from you, erase that day from my life, I don't want to because I love that little girl."

"I know you do," she said, a soft smile curving her lips. "So, here we stand."

"I just want to put the past behind us, but I have no idea how to do that, Rain. I have so much to be sorry about, so much to prove to you."

"You don't have to prove anything to me, except that you want to be a part of my and our daughter's futures."

"I do, but saying so isn't enough to convince you."

"Then let's settle the past." An easiness laced her voice and softened her face.

Brody took the piece of paper out of his back pocket and held it out to her.

"What's that?" she asked.

"You said, let's settle up. So, this is for you. I should have given it to you a couple days ago, but I had to settle some matters with my accountant and have Owen draw up some legal papers."

She took the paper from his outstretched hand. Once she opened it, her passive expression turned hard. "What is this?"

"Child support." He waited for the smile to bloom on her face when she saw the check, for her excitement to show. When she did the opposite, he crossed his arms over his chest, defensive at her less than exuberant response.

"Are you trying to piss me off?" she demanded.

"I don't know what you mean." His voice cold as the pit of his stomach.

"This is a hell of a lot more than child support."

"It's a quarter of a million dollars. If you want more, you can have it. Take it all. I don't care. It's just money, but it's money owed to you for caring for our children alone all these years. You have your inheritance from your grandparents and your mother, but even if you and I weren't together, I'd still have to pay you child support. I've made a lot of money over the years. Considering that and what a court would have me pay, I'm giving you that check. If you want more, I'll give it to you."

Crushing the check in her fist, she pressed the back of her hand to her forehead. "I don't have the money anymore."

"Excuse me?"

"My inheritance money," she explained. "This is so strange. You handing me a check for all this money, it's so unbelievable."

"I have a lot of money, Rain. What I don't have is the woman I love and my children living under one roof. I can't buy that, but I can make life a hell of a lot easier for you and the girls until I make that happen."

She sucked in a deep sigh, that far-off look coming over her again as she stared up at the stars. "When you came back, you thought I'd be living in California, a graduate from college, working on my career."

"It bothers me you lost out on your dream." he admitted.

"Your understanding about how important school was to me helps. It really does. I resented you for a long time for going off and living your life the way you wanted when I was stuck here with two babies."

"One that didn't belong to you," he added, watching her closely.

"I really wanted to go to college. More than anything . . . except being with you."

"You were all set to leave in the fall," he said, remembering how he'd been so afraid of losing her. Much like he felt now. Only this time would be worse, because she had his children and losing all of them would destroy him.

"More than anything I wanted you to come with me."

"Why didn't you say anything?"

"Think back to those days, Brody. Things between us were moving so fast. Everything was moving in the right direction, but I had to be sure you really wanted to come with me. As the summer drew on, and we got closer to fall, you pulled away, so I tried to pull you back to me."

"The night I brought you home after we went to the movies. Your dad was out. I told you we needed to talk. We went up to your room. You kissed me. I thought we'd set the house on fire. You stepped back, pulled off your shirt, and said, 'I'm ready. Are you?' God, I wanted to grab you and never let you go."

"But you didn't. You pulled away and said it would never work, that you'd made a mistake thinking we could be anything more than friends. Before that night, you'd always been hungry for me, but patient and understanding about my wanting to take our time. Yet, you didn't go through with it when I finally made the decision to make love to you."

He rubbed his hand over the back of his neck in frustration. "Before I picked you up that night, I talked to my old man and told him I thought I'd go with you to San Francisco. He laughed and asked me why the hell any pretty co-ed with a campus full of men to choose from would want a guy with no job and no future. I barely remember the movie, because I couldn't stop thinking about the truth in what he said. The city is no place for a rancher. What was I going to do? Find some lame job that barely paid anything, scrape by on construction jobs, or worse, find myself unqualified for anything and ask you to support me until I found something?"

"Better to leave me before I left you."

"The second worst thing I ever did."

"Yeah, because breaking up with me sent you straight into Roxy's bed. Two days later, I couldn't stand the distance you put between us. I came to this cabin to show you how much I loved you and wanted you back."

"I opened the door and you threw yourself into my arms. You kissed me with the same desperation I felt for you."

"I felt it in the way you held on to me. That day, neither of us would have settled for anything less than being with each other completely." A pretty blush flushed her cheeks.

"The guilt over what I'd done ate at me. I loved you so damn much and if you found out, you'd never want to be with me again. If I could just make love to you, you'd know how much I love you and nothing else would matter. Stupid reasoning, but I desperately wanted to bind you to me."

"You did. Dawn binds us together forever."

"It's not enough." He wished she would get it, because he couldn't seem to string the words together to convince her.

"Well, let's stick with settling the past before we talk about the future."

"Do we have a future?"

"One thing at a time, Brody."

"Just answer the damn question," Brody demanded, ready to lose it if she didn't answer him.

"Back off," she snapped back. "How can we move forward when we're anchored in the past? Let's finish this, put it to rest once and for all, so we can stand together in the future knowing there was nothing left unsaid, nothing left undone."

"The only thing that needs to be said is that I'm sorry." Brody turned his back on her, overwhelmed by the moment. Knowing he had to, he faced her when he said the rest. "I'm sorry I broke up with you. I'm sorry I ever walked into the bar that night, more sorry than I can say. I followed Roxy upstairs knowing she was playing me. I'm sorry I did something I didn't want to do and can never take back. I'm sorry I hurt you and made you mad. I'm sorry I made you think everything between us meant nothing to me. You have to know that isn't the case. I love you, have always loved you. I can't tell you why I did it . . ."

"You went there upset you broke up with me when you didn't want to, thinking I was leaving you, and frustrated because you had a scared virgin for a girlfriend . . ."

"I never regretted that. You were mine. Only mine. It meant something . . . everything to me. And I threw it away. Don't you see? I don't want to look back. I want to make things right now."

"All I'm asking is that you look at what happened, knowing what you know now."

"I want to leave it buried and never look at it again. Don't you see, Rain, that night cost me everything."

"It gave you so much more." Her voice pleaded. "It gave you Autumn and Dawn."

"I might not have had Autumn otherwise, but I'd still have you and Dawn."

"Maybe," she conceded. "Who's to say? But we need to talk about what happened and how we ended up here."

"We're here because I'm an asshole. End of story. I walked into her room, drunk and missing you so damn much. I was pissed off you were leaving and that you had every right, because I had nothing better to offer you. I wanted you so damn bad, and if I couldn't have you, well, I could pretend she was you. But she wasn't. No one is you. I was a fool to believe that anyone could take your place."

"So you took her to bed and left her afterwards without a second thought?"

"I was drunk and pissed and confused and miserable without you. I never even took her into the bedroom."

"Oh . . . I just thought . . ."

"What? That I took her to bed and made love to her the way I made love to you?"

Why wouldn't she? She'd never made love to anyone before him. He didn't want to think about her making love to someone after him. She couldn't know, and had probably spun quite a tale of him with Roxy . . . like he'd been with her.

"I only thought . . ."

He hated to do it, but she had to know how little Roxy meant to him. "I kissed her to shut her up. I didn't want to hear her voice. I closed my eyes so I didn't see her, but you in my mind. I fell on top of her on the couch. I never even took her clothes off, just pulled up her skirt. She wasn't even wearing any underwear. That's the Roxy you remember, the woman who'd fuck any man she could get her claws into and take whatever she could from him. A woman who doesn't even wear panties and is ready the minute her back hits a firm surface.

"You think I left there without a second thought. God, that's all I had. I might have been drunk and not thinking clearly, but in the back of my mind I knew she played on my overwrought emotions and lead me straight to hell. I still followed, even though I knew how many men she'd been with. I felt as dirty as she is. If I caught something from her, well, I deserved it. Later, I worried about it, you, until I knew I was healthy, which meant so were you.

"See, another dickhead thing I did to you. I hated myself for it. I didn't protect you, and I should have because you mean more to me than my own life.

"Sleeping with her ruined any future I might have had with you. I had you. Fresh, clean, bright, smart, kind, loving, beautiful," he said, taking her face into his hands and looking deep into her eyes. "You were everything I wanted and needed. My best friend, the woman I loved more than anything in my life. Everything in my mind was dark, and I couldn't shake the feeling I'd lost everything good and decent in me doing what I did. Then, two days later, you came to me. One look at you, the only thing good I'd ever had in my life, and I had to have you. I needed desperately to feel your love and kindness, to fill myself up with it."

He gave into his need, brushing a soft kiss against her lips. "I made love to you like I never wanted to let you go because that's exactly how I felt. I knew you'd hate me when you found out what I did. I needed to show you how much I loved you. I poured everything in my heart and soul into showing you how much I cherished you, needed you, couldn't breathe without you."

"Why didn't you stay and tell me that instead of leaving with nothing more than a note that said, 'I'm sorry.' I had no idea for days what you meant. Sorry for sleeping with me?"

"Never. I couldn't face you and tell you what I'd done and see the hurt and misery on your face and in your heart, knowing I did that to you. The best thing for both of us was for me to leave. I figured you'd go off to school, have the life you dreamed and planned, and I'd be a distant memory. You being pregnant never crossed my mind. Roxy pregnant with my child was the last thing I wanted. I couldn't stay here, or I'd kill her."

"You might want to once I tell you what happened after you left."

"It couldn't have been easy for you to see her pregnant, too. The whole town talking. Someone told me the two of you had a pretty heated argument in the grocery store."

"We did. If you think I was angry about you leaving, she was livid. After five months, she realized you weren't coming back for her or me."

"I can't tell you how many times I picked up the phone and started dialing your number. I'd sit in my truck, the engine idling, and I'd desperately want to turn in your direction and come home. But I thought there was nothing and no one waiting for me here. I thought you'd gone off to school, some college jock dating you, sleeping in your bed . . ."

"I didn't go to college, not because I was pregnant, but because I gave all my money to Roxy," she blurted out, leaving him stunned.

"What?"

"The argument we had in the grocery store," she began. "She cornered me and demanded to know if I'd heard from you. She didn't like my answer. She thought if she could find you, you'd come back for the baby. What she hadn't counted on was my being pregnant, too. Somewhere in her demented mind, she knew if you found out about the pregnancies, you'd still choose me and our baby over her."

"Damn right I would."

"After five months, she was tired of the pregnancy and not being able to . . . do the things she liked to do," she finished lamely.

"Threw a wrench into her drinking and whoring, did it?"

"More than that. You know how much she loved attention. Everyone was talking about us, but she got the worst of it. People were betting the baby wasn't yours, talking about the way she got you into bed, and how you'd snubbed her afterward. Your dad wasn't a big help, he made some rather nasty comments to her about tainting the McBride bloodlines."

"Like he can talk," Brody admitted bitterly.

"Why don't we finish this inside the cabin?"

"Can't," he said quickly.

"Why's that?" she asked.

"There's a bed in there," he said with a self-mocking laugh. He liked it that she smiled.

Chapter Sixteen

THE SMILE ON Rain's face disappeared and she turned serious again. "Brody, your father came to me when he found out I was pregnant. I don't think I've ever seen him so . . ."

"What?" Brody wished they could go back to light-hearted teasing instead of hashing out their past.

"Soft."

He almost laughed at the thought of his old man being anything but mean and nasty for no other reason than he wanted to be.

"Soft? He must have been really wasted."

"Not at all. In fact, it was quite early in the day."

"You think that means he was lucid and sober?"

"Would you stop. Listen to me. He came to ask if he could see the baby when it was born."

Surprised his old man even cared, he asked, "He did? He wanted to see the baby?"

"Very much. I don't think I've ever seen someone look so . . . regretful," she said after taking a moment to think of just the right word. Her thoughtfulness made Brody think twice about the old man.

"The conversation was very short, but before he left, he said something I think you need to hear."

"Anything he had to say isn't worth knowing."

"Brody, he was your father. For better or worse, he loved you in his own way."

"Bullshit. That man didn't love anyone."

"Then maybe what he had to say will make a difference for you. He turned back before he left and said, 'Anything good in me went into my boys. It grew in them and made them who they are. If Brody put half the wealth of good he has into your baby, I'll have a fine grandchild.'"

Brody actually took a step back, covered his mouth with his hand, and slid his fingers over his jaw before dropping his hand to his side again. "He said that?"

"Whatever else was between you, he was proud of his sons. In that small moment, I saw it in his eyes, Brody. He regretted not being a good father to you, but he knew you and Owen had taken what little he thought he'd given to you and made something of it.

"After Dawn was born, he came to see me again. He stared at her for the longest time. Barely said more than a few words to me. Then, he picked her up and held her in front of him. He apologized to her for playing a part in your leaving," she said, her eyes never leaving his.

He couldn't move, couldn't believe what she was saying could really be real.

"He turned to me then, to let me know the apology was meant for me, too. He sang her a lullaby, said it was one he used to sing to you and Owen when you were small."

Brody choked back the lump in his throat. "He liked to sing when he was drunk," he said, filling up the awkward moment.

"He had a nice voice. Dawn fell asleep, content in his arms. He left after that. I didn't see him again until the day after I brought Autumn home. He stared at her with this strange look on his face. When he spoke, it was with such reverence. He told me she looked just like your mother."

"She does. When I saw her, I was taken back to my childhood when my mother was around."

"He didn't stay long. Before he left, he held her for a few minutes, then looked at me with so much sadness in his eyes. He said, 'The worst thing a man can do is leave a good woman, or make her leave him. You're a good woman, Rain. Brody left too much of himself behind. He'll be back, or spend the rest of his days in misery as it should be for any man willing to let love go.' I'll never forget his words, or the way he said them."

Brody turned away toward the dark, his back to the truth. He couldn't believe his father had been so different with Rain from the man he knew.

"Brody, did you ever wonder why your father drank so much? Maybe it would help you to reconcile who your father was if you considered how he truly felt about your mother. I don't know much about their relationship, but

I gather he loved her very much and didn't know how to show her, or tell her. It's my impression she was very different from Owen's mother, softer, sweeter of nature. Maybe a counterbalance to your father's more gruff and hard personality. I think he regretted damaging her and driving her away. I think he lived in misery, trying to drink away his memory of her and what he'd done, because he'd let love go."

"What does this have to do with anything between us?"

"I don't want to see you make the same mistake your father made when he pushed your mother away and spent the rest of his life punishing himself for letting her go. I don't want you to punish yourself for what happened, or take it out on the people around you. I don't want to see you turn your back on us because you're having a hard time right now."

"Is that what you think I'm doing, punishing myself?"

"I think you believe you deserve to be punished, and for more than just what happened with us."

She was talking about what happened while he was in Iraq and Afghanistan. "I haven't been a very good man," he said by way of an explanation and an excuse.

"I don't believe that at all. You've made mistakes. Ones you're willing to take responsibility for and try to make right."

"I do want to make things right with you. I want that more than anything. And if you tell me how to do that, I'll do it, anything to make you happy and love me again."

"Again isn't necessary. It's always been, Brody. But Roxy is still standing between us, and I need to know if you'll stand by my side when she comes back for Autumn."

"What makes you think she will after all this time?"

Rain held up the check in her hand. "She'll want you to give her one of these, too. She'll take as much as you'll allow her to take from you. Once she's used it all up, she'll be back for more."

"How will she know about the money?"

"If I cash this check, everyone in town will know about it in a matter of days." He frowned and she went on. "The teller will mention to someone I deposited a huge check drawn on your account back east. She won't even have to say how much, it'll just be out there. One of Roxy's spies will hear about it and call her. They've already told her you're here and about the article in the paper, listing all your accomplishments. She probably already knows about you fixing this place up and hiring a contractor to build an addition. This will only add to her curiosity and plotting to find out how she can get what she can from you and use Autumn to do it."

"Now tell me what you're avoiding saying and used that little story about my dad to delay telling me. Why did you give Roxy money?"

"I'd think that's obvious. I paid her for Autumn."

"She sold you Autumn, my daughter," he said, not believing anyone could be so cruel and callous.

"Yes. The scene in the grocery store, her breaking down under the stress of being pregnant and realizing you weren't coming back. Also the fact I told her I had no idea where you were and didn't care."

"Is that how you really felt?" he asked, afraid she did and might still.

"I think you know it's not, but I needed her and everyone else to see I was okay on my own."

"Eighteen, alone, and pregnant. Yeah, I can see why you'd want to convince them and yourself you could do it."

"I did do it, but it wasn't easy. Anyway, she cornered me and after a few choice words, she told me she wanted to get rid of the baby. She made it plain she'd do anything to be rid of it. I had a life inside of me, could feel our child growing and moving. One look at her round stomach and I knew just how precious that life was, it was my child's sibling."

"You couldn't have known that for sure," he bluntly pointed out, hating the fact he'd slept with Roxy along with a horde of others. None of them meaning more to her than the pleasure of the moment, or a means to an end.

"I couldn't take the chance the baby wasn't yours, so I made her an offer. I told her if she kept the baby, I'd pay her. Since we were in the store, she agreed to meet me later and discuss the details. We met privately and discussed terms."

"Terms. Like it was nothing more than a contract to be negotiated, not an unborn child. Disgusting." The thought so foul, he actually tasted his bitter revulsion. "It cost you everything you had." The hate he held for Roxy spilled out with his every word.

"Twenty-five thousand to get her to carry out the pregnancy," Rain confirmed. "Dawn came two weeks early.

I like to think she wanted to be your first, even though you'd gotten Roxy pregnant before me," she said.

He didn't know how she could look back on this mess with any kind of humor.

"Roxy went into labor fifteen days later. Pop watched Dawn while I went to see Roxy and the baby at the hospital the next morning. I took one look at Autumn in the nursery and I knew she was Dawn's sister."

"They don't look exactly alike," he pointed out.

"Not exactly, but there was no doubt she was yours. So I went into Roxy's room and negotiated." Rain's voice turned hard, which meant Roxy had really stuck it to her, made it impossible for Rain to do anything but give in to her demands. Roxy probably made sure if Rain didn't take the deal, she'd do something to Autumn, like put her up for adoption or sell her to some desperate couple. Worse, Roxy might have kept Autumn for spite. He had no doubt his daughter wouldn't have been safe and loved in Roxy's care. A chill went up his back just thinking about it.

"Roxy wanted out of this town. She owned the bar, every dime she had invested in the business. Whatever else she'd made, she'd squandered away. So I paid her for Autumn and gave her a way out."

"She hated knowing you had plans to leave for college. I'll bet she gloated about you having to stay here."

"And a lot of other things," Rain confirmed.

He just bet Roxy had really gone after Rain, embellishing what happened between the two of them. He wanted to hit something.

"I paid her the money she needed to get the hell out of town. I wanted her gone from my sight for good."

"How much?"

"Twenty-five thousand for the pregnancy. Thirty-five thousand for her to give me Autumn."

"She sold my child for sixty thousand dollars." Disgusted with himself for ever laying a hand on the woman, or letting her get under his skin and using him.

"Yes," Rain began, only he cut her off.

"How the hell have you been making ends meet?"

"It's not easy. I do okay at the shop, but there have been a few times Owen bailed me out of a tight spot. I owe him about three thousand dollars. Pop helped me pay for the private detective I hired to track you down. So thanks for the check, that'll go a long way to paying Owen and my father back for their help."

"I'll pay them whatever you owe."

"I feel strange taking your money as it is. I'll pay them."

"This is my fault, my mess to clean up," he told her, and meant it.

"There's more, Brody. Roxy came back to town when the girls were three. She'd gone through all the money I'd given her. She came back, thinking you owed her, blaming you for all the bad in her life. This time, she went to your father to find you. Your father could be nasty and meaner than a rattlesnake when he wanted to be."

"Truer words," he said, agreeing with her.

"She told me later he laughed at her and told her if you wouldn't come back for me and your children, you certainly wouldn't come back for her. It's all she needed to turn her cruelty on your father."

Yeah, he knew all about it. "She got him drunk," he said. "Well, more drunk than usual and sent him home. He hit a deer and the tree and died."

"After, she worked herself into a rage and came to my house."

"The cops were called." Small towns, word got around quickly.

"A neighbor overheard us fighting. She tried to take Autumn. When I wouldn't let her, she asked for more money."

"Money you didn't have," he guessed.

"Not the kind of money she was asking for, and I didn't have any idea how to contact you. Both those things really pissed her off, but not as much as Autumn coming down the stairs and calling me Mommy."

"Like she cared," he spat out. "She sold you her child."

"I got her out of the house with a promise to scrape together whatever I could."

"Why would you pay her more?"

"I had no choice. All she had to do was take Autumn. Legally, she's her mother and has every right to her child."

"Any judge would have given you custody after they found out you'd paid Roxy for Autumn."

"How could I prove it? I paid her cash. She never signed anything giving me legal custody, or allowing me to adopt her. All she'd have to do is tell the judge she asked me to care for Autumn, but wanted her back now."

"What a mess."

"It gets even worse. The next day, she snuck into the house and took Autumn. I'm telling you, Brody, there is nothing scarier than having your child go missing. I was frantic. Dawn saw Roxy take her, so I called the police. They sent an officer to the house, but once I explained who Roxy was to Autumn, they shut me down. I didn't have any legal right to keep Roxy from taking Autumn. I was able to get them to agree to find her and make sure Autumn was safe. Not any great comfort, because it would be a low priority since there was no reason to believe Roxy would harm her own child."

His heart slammed into his chest and thrashed against his ribs. The thought of Autumn at Roxy's mercy made him sick. He could only imagine the pain and anxiety and fear Rain must have felt not knowing where her daughter was or if she'd ever get her back.

"How did you get Autumn back?"

"Roxy waited three days to call me. It was agony not knowing anything about Autumn, or if I'd ever see her again. Dawn was a mess without her sister. She stopped talking the second day, and on day three she stopped eating. Brody, I'm telling you, I've never felt fear like I did watching my child living in misery, knowing my other child was out there with that selfish, conniving bitch."

"There's no end to the amount of pain I've caused you."

"Brody, stop doing that. Stop taking everything that's happened onto your shoulders when Roxy has a lot of the weight to carry all on her own."

He dismissed her words all together. "How did you get Autumn back?"

"Roxy asked me to meet her at a fleabag motel outside Solomon. If you think the cabin looked like a dump, it had nothing on this place."

"This is where she had our daughter?"

Rain put her hand on his chest over his heart. "Thank you for that, for believing she's mine and yours."

He took her hand and kissed her palm. "There's no getting around the truth. Is there, Rain?"

"No. I guess not."

Rain sucked in a shuddering breath and spilled the rest. "Roxy was there with some seedy-looking guy. The room ... Oh, Brody, just the thought of Autumn being stuck there for three days in all that smoke and filth and seeing and listening to Roxy and that guy smoke and drink themselves into oblivion. Roxy was a complete stranger to her. She was so scared."

He lost Rain to her memories and the emotions she couldn't hide from her expressive eyes. Offering what little comfort he could now, he kissed her palm again and held her hand to his heart, waiting for her to go on.

"Long story short, I paid Roxy another eight thousand dollars. It wasn't as much as she wanted, but it was all I could come up with, everything I'd saved for the girls to go to school someday."

Still holding her hand, he gave it a squeeze to let her know he understood how important that money was for their future. Pennies scraped together by Rain to make sure the girls had every opportunity.

"The whole time, I was frantic. I didn't see Autumn anywhere in the room. I thought maybe they'd made her wait in the bathroom. Then Roxy went to the closet door and opened it. Autumn was curled up in the corner in the dark."

Tears streamed down Rain's face, every one of them tore his heart to shreds. "She's just a little girl, afraid of the dark and monsters. I can't imagine how terrifying it was for her to be locked in there for three days."

"What? How do you know they didn't just put her in there before you arrived?"

"Autumn told me later at the hospital."

"Hospital?"

"I've never seen anyone so listless. They'd barely fed her, just some French fries and pancakes. They hadn't given her anything to drink. She was severely dehydrated. Roxy had slapped her. Autumn's cheek was bruised. I'd never even given her a little swat on the butt." Rain swiped at the tears on her face and went on. "I grabbed her and headed for the door. She held me so tight, like she was terrified I'd leave her there.

"The guy blocked my way out and said the eight grand had only bought me time enough to make sure Autumn was in one piece. They wanted more, and I didn't have it."

"How'd you get out of there?"

"Sheer determination and force. When I tried to shove past the guy, he grabbed me and Autumn. I struggled and managed to knee him in the balls, but Roxy grabbed me just as I got the door open. I don't know what came over me, but I punched her in the mouth, split her lip and made her scream. It was all I needed to get past them and haul ass out of there."

"What the hell. That bitch. Unbelievable."

"I'd have done anything to get her back."

"Of course you would, but that bitch didn't think twice about hurting you or Autumn." He vibrated with the need to find Roxy and that guy and make them pay. "If something happened to you, to her, I don't know what I would have done."

"I took Autumn to the hospital. I could barely get her to open her eyes. After answering a lot of questions and getting my hand looked at . . ."

"What happened to your hand?"

"I broke it when I popped Roxy." She went on like it was nothing. "The cops asked a lot of questions about Autumn's condition and why she lives with me. I called Pop to check on Dawn and tell him what happened. He told me Owen was in town dealing with your father's death. Pop spoke to him and sent him to me at the hospital. Being Autumn's uncle and a lawyer went a long way to the cops leaving me alone and letting me keep Autumn."

"Why didn't you have Owen call me then?"

"He wanted to, but I talked him out of it."

He shoved his hands into his jeans pockets and stared over her shoulder at the lights of the cabin behind her. Dark as it was outside, he could still see everything, including the regret and need for him to understand written all over her face.

"Please listen to me, Brody. I wasn't trying to punish you by keeping them from you. You were about to be shipped overseas to Afghanistan. Your response to Owen about your father's death told us just how much you wanted to leave this place behind. I don't know what it's like to be a soldier, but I know enough to realize you didn't need to worry about two kids and what Roxy was doing back here."

"I could have helped you, sent you money."

"Helped me from a country halfway around the world where you were facing life and death each and every day. How would you have been a father to those girls? By sending them letters? They were three years old. They didn't know who you were, except for a picture in a frame. How could I explain to them anything you'd written when they didn't know who you are, or if you were coming back?"

"Better for me to die over there never knowing I had them," he shot back.

"What do you want me to say? I made the best choices I could for those girls. Autumn was in no condition for you to come rushing back, a stranger in her life, who might take her away from me, too."

"I'd have never taken her from you," he said, furious she'd even think it.

"I couldn't take that chance," she shouted back. "I couldn't risk her mental state at that time. Brody, please understand, after I got her to the hospital, she was a mess. She wouldn't speak. She clung to me, and I had to stay in the bed with her, or she'd scream. Her voice was so hoarse, and she'd have nightmares.

"After a week with a psychiatrist, I decided to take her home. She wasn't responding to him. I had a long talk with the doctor, he gave me some advice on how to handle her. When I brought her home, I got a few books and I worked with her. She didn't speak for almost a month. When she finally started coming around, it was at night when we'd lay in bed together. She had to sleep with the light on and always with me.

"You have to understand, before this happened she was a happy little girl, always ready with a smile. She wasn't shy, but exuberant, like her sister."

"There's a definite difference in their personalities."

"There always was, but Autumn never used to be so reserved, afraid of shadows. Roxy changed her, made her something she'd have never been, except for those three days with Roxy that stole the little girl I'd raised until then. It took a lot of patience and time to discover what happened those three days."

"I have a feeling I don't want to know," Brody confessed.

"If you don't, I'll keep it to myself. The point is that Roxy can never take her from me again. Autumn won't survive. She's sensitive, has always been that way. Roxy has no idea what she did to that little girl because she only ever thinks of herself."

"What did she do to Autumn?"

"Besides locking her in a dark closet and slapping her more than once for crying. Autumn was terrified. She didn't know Roxy and that man. They scared her, yelled at her, mistreated her. Locked in that closet. Autumn heard what she thought was Roxy being hurt, maybe killed. She thought she was next."

"What?"

"It took me a little while to sort it out from the snippets of information I gathered from Autumn over several days. I think she heard Roxy and that man having sex. Rough, loud, sex. Imagine a little girl hearing those kinds of sounds. Not loving gasps and sighs, but flesh slapping, dirty talk, and a lot of moans and gasps and you're three and locked in the dark with people you don't know and all you want is your mommy."

"Holy Christ," Brody swore.

"No matter what, we have to protect Autumn from her. Under no circumstances can Roxy ever be left alone with her."

"You'd actually let Roxy see her?"

"I might not have a choice. She's Autumn's mother."

"You're her mother. Roxy was just an incubator. I swear to you, Rain, I'll never let her take Autumn from us again. I'll do whatever I have to, to make sure that never happens."

"Sign over guardianship to me. It's the only way I'll have any say in what happens to her."

"Marry me," he countered. "Then you'll be her stepmother legally. You can adopt her."

"Seriously, Brody. Just like that, standing in the dark, no flowers, candles, dinner, you on bended knee with a ring. Nothing. Just forgive and forget and be my wife for Autumn's sake."

"I'll give you all of that and more if you say yes." He would, too. He'd give her anything. Still, he knew she wouldn't. Not now. Not yet. "And it's not for Autumn's sake alone. It's for mine."

"Wow. Lucky me," she quipped.

"Tell me what you want, Rain."

"I want the girls to be happy and healthy the rest of their lives. I want a normal life. I don't want to have to worry about money," she said, then held up the check he'd given her earlier. "Check," she said, signing it in the air. "One item down."

Brody wrapped one arm around her waist and pulled her close. With his other hand, he brushed the wisps of hair from her cheek. "Tell me what you want from me."

"I want what anybody wants, what you want. To feel safe and loved. To know nothing can ever come between us again. I want to trust you and know that when I have my back turned you won't jab a knife between my shoulders and into my heart."

"Brutal, honey."

"Then you have some idea of how I felt when you left me."

"You know how I felt being away from you," he countered. Taking her hand, he not so gracefully kneeled down in front of her on one knee.

"Brody . . ."

"I got it," he said, wincing in pain. "Will you do me the honor of coming inside and having dinner with me?"

"There's a bed in there," she teased.

"I know," he said with a small groan. "I'll behave myself and work on rebuilding the trust I shattered."

"All right, dinner." She smiled down at him.

"Mind helping me up?" he asked, only half kidding.

"Oh, Brody." She made a grab for him as he stood. His forehead hit her chin, cracking her teeth together, making her let go and fall back. He grabbed her as they both stood and pulled her to his chest, their eyes locked.

"Man, that hurt." Her hands gripped his biceps as she worked her jaw to ease the sting. Unable to help himself, he leaned down and kissed the side of her face, planting soft kisses along her jaw to her chin, then moving up and taking her already open mouth in a deep, sensuous kiss. Her grip on his arms grew tight and she drew him in with a tentative slide of her tongue over his. She opened to him and pressed her body down the length of his.

He wanted to devour, to take everything she offered and more. That's why he gently brushed his lips over her parted ones, taking in the breath that escaped her lips in a soft sigh before he let her go and put her away from him. His whole body screamed in agony from the separation, but he owed her a lot more than one long talk and taking her to bed without any of the trappings that went into a relationship. He'd cheated her out of so much. He couldn't bring himself to give into what he wanted without thinking first of the things she'd asked from him. Trust. Feeling safe and loved. Knowing he'd never pull her close, only to turn away from her again.

"Come up to the house. Talk to me about our girls."

"Will you tell me about . . . everything?"

"Everything?"

"What your life has been like these last years. Where you went, the things you've seen and done."

"I don't think you want to know the things I've done," he said, thinking of everything he could tell her but would only hurt her more. She knew about the other women. He wished she didn't. Then, there were the things he'd done in the military in the name of freedom and democracy. There were a lot of good things he'd done, he guessed.

"Can't you tell me a story without starting with '. . . There was this blonde . . .'" she said with half a smile.

He couldn't help himself, he laughed. It was an old joke between him and Owen going back to the early days in high school when they'd tried to one up each other with the girls. Rain had been just his friend back then, and whatever trouble he and Owen stirred up, the story always started with ". . . There was this girl . . ."

Teasing, he said, "Actually, she's a brunette." The softness in her eyes told him she knew he was talking about her. It seemed everything meaningful in his life started with her.

Chapter Seventeen

BRODY WALKED RAIN up to the cabin, her hand safely tucked in his. By silent agreement, they didn't speak, but let the words they'd already exchanged settle. Lord knew Brody needed time to let the anger simmering in his gut fade. He'd thank God every second of every day Rain had gone to such lengths to keep his daughter safe, unharmed by the woman who'd carried her for nine months and given birth to her.

He didn't know how any woman could carry a life inside of them, give birth to that child, and toss it away without a single thought, except to how much money she could get for her. Every dime left to Rain by her family members. The money she needed to raise his children.

"Nice floor."

Rain's voice pulled him out of his dark thoughts. He squeezed her hand and glanced at the foundation and subfloor the contractor finished and now had to rework with his new floor plan.

"You like it? It'll be a little cold in the winter, but hey, you can't beat the view." His gaze rose to the brilliant stars and surrounding trees and mountains.

"Planning on sleeping alfresco?"

"I want to sleep wherever you're sleeping." She glanced up at him through her lashes. Just to rile her, he added, "Well, not really sleeping. A whole lot of loving."

"You think so."

"God, I hope so." He helped her up onto the subfloor, pulled her to the center and into his arms. He held her close and started with a step to the left, a step toward her, and then a step to the side with his left. She followed, matching him easily as they danced under the stars to the sound of crickets chirping and the occasional fish jumping in the lake. For several long minutes, they danced around the wide open floor, until he steered her back to the center and just swayed softly.

She felt so good pressed against him. The citrus scent of her hair surrounded him, drew him in. He raised his hands to her face, cupped and tilted her chin so she was looking up at him. He brushed a soft kiss on her forehead, the tip of her nose, her cheek, along her jaw. His lips pressed to her soft skin. When he reached the corner of her mouth, she sighed. The whisper of breath fanned his cheek and warmed his heart. She still loved him, responded to his touch. She gave him everything she had.

Her lips parted, and God, how he wanted to press his lips to hers and slide his tongue deep into her mouth. Taste all her secrets, erase every bad memory with something good and sweet and sultry. If he took her mouth now, he'd drag her to the floor and bury himself deep inside her. Hard and throbbing, in painful agony, the ache still nothing compared to the hurt in his heart, knowing she didn't trust him and wasn't ready to be his wife.

Leaving her sweet mouth, he kissed his way to her ear. "You are so beautiful." His hands left her face, mapped her neck and skimmed down over her chest to the swell of her breasts. She sucked in a quick breath when he slid his hands over the two rounded, soft mounds to her ribs. His thumbs traced the underside of her breasts back and forth while she settled into his touch, got used to the feel of his hands on her body again.

Her head fell back, eyes closed; he kissed the column of her throat, the sweet spot near her shoulder. "You smell the same. Something sweet and flowery, like a meadow in spring." He cupped her breasts, his thumbs brushed over her taut nipples. She squeaked and her breath hitched. When he tugged gently with her nipples caught between his index and middle finger, she sighed his name. That was just the beginning of what he wanted. Her soft moans and his name on her lips as he touched her, ignited a spark of what they'd shared before. "I carried your scent with me everywhere I went. In the desert when it was hot," he said against her throat, "I'd think of you, suck in a ragged breath and smell you. I'd be so hard, I'd ache to be inside you again, my hands on your skin, your breath on my face, our hearts pressed together and me driving into you until you called my name."

"Brody," she called breathlessly.

He wrapped his arms around her and picked her up off her feet. The entire length of her body pressed against his, her toes scraping against his shins. He buried his face in her neck and held her tight with her arms locked around his neck and her face pressed against the side of his head.

"I've missed you so damn much," he confessed. "There were days I thought I'd never breathe again without you. In my happiest, normal, saddest, darkest moments, I held on to your memory. You were with me every second of every day. God, how I begged for you at times. Just to hear your voice, see you smile, smell your skin, feel your body pressed to mine. Anything. Everything. I needed you so damn much. You were the keeper of my heart and without you, I wasn't whole. This. Right now. I feel whole."

Her arms wrapped around him tighter and he held her close, his face buried in her mass of brown hair. "I'm here, Brody. Right where I belong. I swear, I'll never let you go again."

Just those simple words and all the air went out of his lungs. He crushed her to him. Her body tensed at the powerful embrace, but she held tight, knowing he needed her.

"I'll never leave you again, Rain. I can't live without you. I can't breathe, think, be. Not in any kind of way that exceeds existing. I want to live and be happy the only way I can when I'm with you."

"Okay, Brody. It's okay."

"I'm sorry about the past. I'm furious with Roxy about what she did, what she put you and Autumn and Dawn through. I promise, I'll never let her hurt you or the girls again. I swear, I'll never hurt you again."

"Enough," she said, her words choked out on a soft sob.

"It's not enough until you love me again. Until you're mine again."

"Not again, Brody. Always. I've loved you my whole life, since the day I met you in the school nurse's office. You were sick and I'd skinned my knees because that awful boy pushed me down."

"Scott. You asked if my mother was coming to take me home."

"You were green. You confessed you didn't have a mother or a father who cared. We swapped stories about how your mother left you and my mother died. The nurse let me sit with you until after school and I asked my dad to drive you home. The next day, you stayed close while I played on the bars. When Scott tried to pick on me again, you shoved him to the ground and told him to leave me alone."

"He was terrified," Brody remembered.

"You were older and six inches taller than him. He never bothered me again. No one did, because they didn't want to go up against you. I worshipped you from that moment on.

"I'm yours, Brody. I always have been and I always will be. There never was and will never be anyone else but you."

She was his. He was the only man who'd ever touched

her, loved her completely. The only man she'd ever loved. He'd make damn sure he was the last.

He took a step toward the house and his leg gave out with their combined weight. He fell forward, but she caught him when her feet thudded to the floor. She took his weight, braced her hands on his shoulders, and helped him stand on his own again.

Looking at the floor and the toes of his boots, he said, "Sorry. I guess I'm not up to carry you off to bed."

She took his face in her hands and made him look at her. "How about dinner then?"

"Are you going to keep making things like this easy on me?"

"Your body still needs time to heal. Of course, I'll give you a break and be there for you when you need me. More important is the fact that in addition to your leg, you're hurt here," she said and took his head between her hands. She placed her right hand on his chest over his heart. "And here."

"Rain. You have no idea how it feels to stumble on my leg or lose myself in a war that isn't there. My world falls away and I'm in a living nightmare and I can't escape."

"The only thing I ask is that if you can't take care of the girls on your own, you let me know. No recriminations, I'll just be sure to be there with all of you."

"Why are you being so cool about all this? You have every right to use my past against me, use my muddled mind and my injuries to keep them from me."

"Punishing you only punishes me. Isn't that what you've finally realized you've done to yourself the last eight years? Isn't that why you really came home? Because living apart is a torment for the both of us."

"I wish I knew what I did to deserve you. I'd do it every day for the rest of my life just to keep you."

"The only thing you need to do to keep me is love me. And our girls."

"I do love you. With everything I am. I won't screw this up again. I promise."

"Don't make that promise, Brody. We both know you're going to do something supremely stupid that I'll have to forgive."

"But you will forgive me because you love me." This time, the cocky grin came easy. He squeezed her hips where he held her close.

"I can forgive you most anything, Brody. I have before. But don't ask me to forgive you sleeping with another woman. I just don't have it in me to live through that again."

"Never. I don't want anyone but you. I swear it, Rain."

"Will you do something for me?"

"Anything." He leaned down to kiss her upturned mouth. Before his lips met hers, she said, "Feed me." To prove her point, her stomach rumbled, making them both laugh.

"Come on. I've got most of dinner ready. You can set the table while I toss the steaks on the grill."

"Perfect."

"Yeah, you are," he said under his breath and followed her to the door.

Chapter Eighteen

BRODY WALKED INTO the kitchen through the mudroom, a platter of steaks and baked potatoes in his hand. He stopped and stared at Rain as she leaned over the table and set a glass of iced tea in front of a place setting. The table looked great. Rain simply took his breath away. Two candles burned in the center. Their soft glow highlighted her long hair, sparking off the reds and golds throughout the thick mass. Her red sweater fit snug over her breasts and hugged her body to her slightly curved hips. Her breasts were still high and round. Her hips tapered to lean thighs. She'd held her athletic physique all these years. Probably from running after two active little girls.

She caught him staring at her. Without a word, she came to him and took the platter. He hadn't seen the slice of carrot in her hand, but she popped it into his mouth and patted his cheek.

"Let's eat, big guy. I'm starving."

"Me, too." It had nothing to do with the food on the table and everything to do with her. She made his mouth water.

He took his seat and looked at the dishes she'd set out.

"I like the new dishes and glasses you bought. They're lovely."

"I thought you'd like them. The place is kind of a disaster right now . . ."

"Not really. The new furniture is great. I see you've set up your computers in the living room."

"Yeah, I've got some work I need to do. In case you haven't noticed, the back wall is nothing but plastic sheeting."

She gave him a lopsided smile and looked thoughtful at the same time. "I thought there was something different."

A bite of steak disappeared into her mouth, her lips skimming over her fork. He swallowed hard. "I'm meeting with an architect. When I arrived, I thought I'd just expand the living room and out the back, adding another bedroom, bathroom, and expanding this room. But when I found out about the girls, I knew we'd need a bigger place."

Her fork stopped halfway to her mouth. Potato and sour cream suspended in midair. Her face stilled, her eyes narrowed on him. "We need a bigger place?"

"I know you like your house, but it's kind of small for you and the girls. I don't know how Eli feels about living over the garage. I thought he might like to have the house back and you and the girls would live with me. I have plans for this place and building the new stables. I thought we could do it together. I have a condo in Atlanta. I'll have to go there a couple times a year for business. I thought you might like to go with me. Sometimes it's necessary for me to travel here and overseas. Maybe you could come along when it's convenient. You could see some of the world. We could see it together."

"What about the girls?"

"They can come with us when they aren't in school. Or, we could take them out for a few days, a week, and give them a real adventure. Life experience."

He took a big bite of steak and smiled broadly. He'd taken her off guard. He'd made it plain he wanted her back. She just hadn't realized that he'd also made plans for their future.

"You're serious."

"As a heart attack, sweetheart. It's easy to talk about having a life with you. I want you to understand I didn't come back on a whim. I'll admit, I've had to adjust my plans to include the girls, but I have to say, they're a wonderful bonus."

"I can't just travel with you."

"Why not? Eli and Owen will babysit the girls. We could hire a full-time nanny if you want. Hell, we could bring the girls and a nanny. That way you and I can do the town at night while the girls sleep. I'll get my business done, and we'll all get a chance to see some interesting places around the world."

"Like where?"

He had her attention now. Her tentative question didn't mask her interest and curiosity.

"I have to go to China in a couple of months. We've got a new prototype and we'll work with a manufacturer to mass produce the product."

"China," she said, astonished.

"Of course, I'd like you to take a look at the blueprints for the expansion of the house. I don't expect you to just agree with my plans, but tell me what you want and need, so we can work together to make it happen. I want this to be our home."

"You mean that?"

"Yes. What good is building this place if you're not happy here, or you hate it."

"What are your plans?"

"The entire back of the house will be blown out. We'll expand the kitchen and living room into a huge great room. I'll have an office downstairs. There'll be a bathroom and a couple of closets. Upstairs, we'll have a master suite and three or four other bedrooms. Two or three more bathrooms depending on the number of bedrooms. I figure we'll need the bathrooms when the girls get bigger. I'd really like to have another baby with you. More if you'd like.

"What do you think?"

"The kitchen will need to have a breakfast room and an island. The stove should have burners and a griddle. The girls like pancakes for breakfast several times a week. Keep the mudroom, but enlarge it so there is space to fold laundry and keep the baskets. The master suite and four bedrooms upstairs. The girls will want to share for now, but eventually they'll want their own room. Maybe," she said thoughtfully. "They're really close. And, yes."

"I'm sorry, yes?"

"Yes, I'd like to have another baby. Maybe two. We'll see. Oh, and I'd like to paint the house white with dark blue trim. Hardwood floors and a stone fireplace that you'll make love to me in front of when the girls stay at Uncle Owen's house for a sleepover."

She forked up another bite of steak and chewed, a thoughtful smile on her face.

"I'm having a hard time believing you're just going along with this."

"Between now and the house being done we still have a lot to work out. Owen goaded me into coming tonight, laying my cards on the table, and taking a risk. Because of what we once shared, and the future I think we can create together with our girls, I'm betting on us.

"Besides, the only thing I had planned was a softball game on Saturday and grocery shopping on Sunday. Your plans are much more detailed."

She barely contained the smile creeping up her face. Her eyes sparkled with suppressed laughter. His heart felt lighter knowing she wasn't fighting him anymore. Whatever her reasons for putting aside her anger and thinking about a future with him, he didn't care. He hoped this was the start of many conversations about joining their lives permanently.

She leaned forward and her eyes turned serious again.

"Just because I agree doesn't mean it'll be easy or happen overnight. We have to consider the girls. They want us to be together, for you and me to be their mom and dad and be a happy family. You and I have a lot of catching up to do before we make any promises to Dawn and Autumn."

"Every time they see the two of us together, their little faces look so hopeful."

"Didn't you ever wish for your parents to be back together when you were a kid?"

Brody thought about it. "I wished my mother would come back and take me with her. Then again, I didn't want to leave Owen. My life growing up wasn't anything like normal. I'd like the girls to have normal at the minimum. If you and I can find our way back to happy, they'll have extraordinary."

Tears gathered in her eyes and he reached out and took her hand. He brought it to his mouth and kissed her palm. He held her hand against his cheek and met her glistening eyes. "I know you missed your mother. Probably wished a million times to have her back, but never so much as when you found out you were pregnant. I bet you wished she was there with you."

"Pop was great. My rock as usual. But I really wish I'd had my mother there to give me advice about being a mother. How did . . ."

"I know you. We both grew up with only our fathers. I was always jealous of you and Eli. Of course, you shared him with me. He always welcomed me into your home. Even when he realized I wanted to sleep with his daughter."

She smiled, remembering those months Eli seemed on edge, always watching them like a hawk. "You did make him nervous. You should have seen him trying his best to give me *the talk*." She giggled. Her whole face lit up with a smile bright enough to banish the darkest night. "I've never seen him sweat so much, or stumble over his words like that. By the time he was finished, I didn't know what to expect, but I knew he had enough faith in me to let me make my own choice."

"What did he say?"

"He told me the basic technique using a very strange baseball analogy."

"Whatever he told you, you blew my mind that night."

"You didn't give me much time to think."

"You knocked on the door and the next thing I know, you jumped into my arms and kissed me like your life depended on it."

"It did. You pushed me away and I needed you back. I had to prove to you we belonged together."

"I could have gone slower, been more careful. I knew you were a virgin. I was so far gone, I couldn't stop myself, even if the house was falling down around us."

"You were slower, more careful later that night."

"I knew you were probably sore. I wanted to give you as much pleasure as you gave to me. You were so . . ."

"Wanton," she supplied.

"Free. Open. Trusting."

"I knew you'd never hurt me, felt how much you needed me that night. I didn't know the why of it. At the time, I didn't care. In my limited experience, I'd say no other woman has been loved that well her first time."

"You thought I was that way with . . ."

"Don't say her name. This is our first date. Dinner was lovely. The company, handsome and charming."

"Not charming enough. We're still at the table and not in bed."

She laughed, but didn't take the bait. "Tell me about your company. What do you do?"

They sat for an hour swapping stories about work, the girls, his life in the military, movies, the everyday things that filled their lives over the last eight years. They kept things simple and settled back into that comfortable friendship they shared so long ago. She laughed about the story of him and his buddies holding a karaoke contest for the worst singer in the squad. Brody came in second. Brody went through a range of emotions listening to the stories she told about the girls as babies and growing up. She brought the missing years to life for him, and he vowed he'd never miss another moment. Interested in his company, she asked several questions and listened to him explain his plans for the future. She warmed to the idea of traveling. They daydreamed of taking a family vacation. Something fun for the girls, like Disneyland or Hawaii.

"I didn't think tonight would turn out this well. I'm glad I came," she admitted, making him smile.

She picked up her glass of iced tea and held it up to clink with his. For the first time, he noticed she'd put his medicine on the table behind his glass. He tapped his glass to hers and stared at the bottle of pills.

"Take the ones you need, Brody. You've had a good meal. Don't be reluctant to take them in front of me. I want you to be well." She placed her hand over his fist on the table. He turned his hand over, her palm pressed against his, her fingers lightly stroked his wrist. So easy for them to be together like this, now that they'd shared some of their lives together with quiet conversation, the animosity and anger dissipated now that everything was out in the open.

She stood and grabbed both their plates. "You cooked, I'll do the dishes."

She stared at him for a moment. He took the bottle of pills, read the label to make sure he had the right one, and took one of the pills. He grabbed the bottle of pain meds and took one of those. After he downed his iced tea, she walked into the kitchen.

He grabbed up the rest of the bowls and glasses and carried them to the sink. He dumped the rest of the salad into a plastic-covered bowl and stuck it into the fridge while she rinsed plates and put them in the dishwasher. Moving in behind her, he kissed and nuzzled her neck, making her giggle and wiggle.

"Brody, I'm trying to clean up here."

"I just wanted a little something sweet for dessert." He kissed her neck again to rile her. "Sweetheart, you're getting your sweater all wet." He grabbed her hand and pulled up her sleeve.

"No! Don't!"

Too late, he saw her arm and the nasty bruises. "My

God, Rain. What happened to your arm? That's gotta hurt like hell."

She tugged down her sleeve, shut off the water, and moved away from him, never meeting his eyes. "It's fine. It's nothing. Really." Her words came out quick and nervous.

Stepping around her, he stopped her in her tracks before she left the kitchen. She wouldn't look at him. "Rain." When she refused to raise her head, he put his finger under her chin and made her. "Did that happen last night at the pizza parlor?"

He read it in her eyes. The sad way she looked at him, imploring him to drop it.

He raked a hand through his hair and tried to remember everything that happened before Rain dragged him out of the restaurant and down the street to the park. Completely out of it, he followed her lead and prayed he didn't frightened his daughters when they saw him disoriented.

Wait. His daughters. He remembered. "Dawn begged me to let you go." He took two steps away from her, but she came after him and grabbed him by the front of his shirt.

"Don't you back away from me. Don't you shut me out."

"I hurt you." His voice barely made it past his lips.

"You slipped away from me," she began. "We were talking and this look came over you. Right before I lost you, you grabbed on to me."

"I hurt you."

"I tried to bring you back."

"I hurt you! I put those marks on you. Is your arm broken?"

"No, and you didn't mean to."

He threw up his hands and let them fall along with his sarcastic retort. "Well, if I didn't mean it, then it's fine to hurt you like that." He took a deep breath and took a step back. This time she let him. "Oh God, I feel sick." He put his hand to his stomach. He couldn't believe he'd hurt her. "You have to go. Go home, Rain. You have to go. Please. Get away from me. I shouldn't have come back. It was too soon. My mind . . ."

"Brody. Stop it. You aren't sending me away."

"I don't ever want to hurt you again. You have to leave. Go. Please." His lungs grew tight. Hyperventilating, he grabbed the back of a chair.

"Brody, honey, please. Take a breath. Calm down. You're scaring me."

"You should be scared. Look what I did to your arm."

She threw herself into his chest, wrapped her arms around his neck, and pulled his mouth down to her. Her lips were insistent, and without a conscious thought his whole body responded to her. He slid his hands up the back of her sweater, over her soft skin, and pulled her close. Her tongue swept across his lips. He opened his mouth and devoured her. He'd been unable to breathe a minute ago; now, he breathed her in and held on to her warmth.

With intense tenderness, they held the kiss. She broke free and touched her forehead to his. Eyes closed, her voice no more than a whisper. "Do you love me, Brody?"

The muscles in his arms contracted and he held her closer. "More than anything."

"Would you ever consciously hurt me?"

"I'd rather cut off my arm with a dull blade."

"Please let this go. I have. You knew you were being taken somewhere you didn't want to go. All you did was hold on to me."

"That's all I want to do. But I never meant . . ."

"I know."

"You said you love me. I held on to that and pulled myself out of hell, hoping I'd hear you say it again."

"I love you." She kissed him softly.

He set her away and looked her in the eye. "Did the girls see your arm?"

"They saw you last night. I've talked to them about what you're going through and that you need time to get better."

"Dawn tried to pull my hand away from you."

"She knew you weren't really there. You saw her at the park. She was her usual self."

"She takes after her mother, overlooks my bad behavior."

"She has complete faith in the fact that her father would never hurt her mother on purpose."

"What about Autumn? She's so sensitive and takes everything to heart."

Rain smiled softly. "She crawled in bed with me late last night, took my arm and kissed the bruises. She said, 'He didn't mean it, Mommy.' She tucked my arm close to her chest and held on to me while we slept."

He took her hand and held it up between them. Gently, he slid her sweater up her arm and really looked at the damage he'd done. He traced his fingertips over the darkest bruises. "Does it hurt bad?"

"I'm a tough girl."

"That doesn't answer my question."

"It's sore. Seeing your reaction to it, I understand how you must feel. It must be very hard for you to reconcile being the badass boy you used to be. Nothing ever touched you. The world could go to hell. You lived your life on your terms. After everything you've been through, to be a man now and find yourself unable to control the images and nightmares that come to you. I know you're frustrated, Brody. But it's just your mind's way of trying to deal with something that is terrible and inconceivable. The things you must have seen and done. At the time, you didn't have the luxury of processing it. That's all your mind is trying to do."

"My mind is stuck in a loop of nothing but endless battles. I left that world behind. I wish my mind would do the same."

"Give it time."

"It's been months." His voice was rough and angry. He hated seeing her face take on that strange look. "Sorry. I get agitated sometimes."

"It's to be expected."

"Now you sound like one of the shrinks at the VA hospital."

"Maybe you should take their words to heart and understand that you can't just flip a switch and make this go away."

"So what, because I can't do that I should be allowed to use it as an excuse for snapping at you"—he pointed to her arm—"hurting you."

"Not an excuse. A reasonable explanation for your condition and the things that happen that are beyond your control."

"Yes. Beyond my control. Which is why you shouldn't be around me."

"That's not what you really want." Ever patient with him when he was being unreasonable.

"I want you to be safe. I never want to hurt you . . . in any way," he added softly.

"Then stop telling me to go away and stay away, because nothing hurts me more than being without you."

Silence. They stood not two feet apart. He wanted to close the distance and take her in his arms, take her upstairs to bed and show her how much her admission meant to him.

The ringing of his phone broke the silence and the intensity of the moment.

"Why don't you go sit in the living room and answer that. Get off your leg and rest while I finish cleaning up the kitchen."

For the first time, he noticed he was absently rubbing his bad leg and the throbbing wasn't easing. He'd done a lot of work that day, helping out the crew clearing space for the addition and walking the property to determine the best spot for the new stables and fence lines for the horses.

Without another word, Rain turned and went back

into the kitchen. He limped over to the couch and picked up his cell phone from the side table.

Not wanting to talk to anyone but Rain, he halfheartedly said, "Hello."

"Hey, man, it's Jim. You'll never guess what I just overheard."

Chapter Nineteen

A RIPPLE OF dread went up Brody's spine. Whether the words or the tone alerted him, he knew Jim wasn't calling about the work on the house.

"What's up, Jim?"

"Some of the crew and I came down to Roxy's for a few beers after work at your place. I was waiting at the bar for the bartender to refill my beer when I overheard the manager talking to him. He said they needed to be ready in a few days because Roxy's on her way back to town."

"Did he say exactly when she'd be rolling in?"

Rain's back went rigid and she braced her hands on the counter. Brody wanted to go to her, comfort her, promise her Roxy wouldn't get anywhere near her or the girls. Especially Autumn. Too bad that was a promise he couldn't keep, and she would know it was an impossibility. Roxy was a force unto herself. No way to stop her when she set her mind to something, and it seemed every time she set her mind to something it ended in devastation. Look what she'd done to his life, Rain's, Autumn's. He couldn't allow her to wreck the tenuous bond he'd built with Rain. He absolutely couldn't allow her anywhere near his daughters.

"I only heard them say in the next couple of days. Nothing definite. Sorry, man. I wanted to give you a heads-up. If I hear anything more, I'll let you know."

"Thanks. I owe you."

"You want me to call and warn Rain?"

"No. She already knows."

"Huh."

"I'll see you tomorrow. Thanks for the heads-up."

"Yeah, sure, man."

Brody never took his eyes off Rain. She'd finished with the kitchen and stood leaning against the chair across from him, one leg crossed over the other. Tight jeans hugged her trim hips and thighs. Her arms crossed, pushing up her pretty round breasts, making them mound and tease him at the V in her sweater. Her hair was slightly tousled from their earlier kisses and his fingers sliding into the thick mass. Her eyes were like liquid chocolate. Beneath the steely determination he caught a glimmer of fear he hated seeing in their depths.

He opened his mouth to speak, but she beat him to the punch.

"Call Owen. Tell him Roxy's coming back to town."

"Jim, my contractor, said she wasn't due for a couple of days."

"Might be true. Maybe that's what she wants people to think. If we aren't expecting her for a few days, we won't guard Autumn as closely."

Brody punched the speed dial for Owen's cell phone.

"How's everything going there?" Owen asked.

"Listen, Owen, I got a call from Jim. He's the guy I hired to work on my place. He was down at Roxy's place tonight and overheard the manager saying Roxy is due back in town in a couple of days."

"Shit!"

"Rain thinks it's possible Roxy just wants people to believe she won't be back for a few days, that she could actually be in town now. Maybe pull some stupid stunt, like coming to the house and trying to see Autumn."

"Or worse." Owen spoke Brody's own thoughts. He just didn't want to say it out loud in front of Rain. The evening had been going so well.

"Make sure the house is locked up tight."

"I already checked, but I'll make the rounds again, make sure all the windows are locked up, too. I'll take a look out the upstairs windows, make sure all's quiet on the street."

"Anything happens, you call me."

"You know I will. Hey, put Rain on."

He held the phone up to her. "Hello."

"Goodnight, Mommy," her two little girls voices cheerily came over the line.

"What are you two still doing up? It's late."

"Uncle Owen let us watch a movie and eat popcorn and have hot chocolate," Dawn announced. In the background, Owen told the girls not to tattle on him. Smiling, the phone jostled and Autumn's voice came on the line. "Mom, did you talk to Dad?"

Brody pulled Rain down onto his good leg. His hand slid under her sweater and glided over her stomach as he nuzzled her neck. Every nerve sparked to life at his touch.

"Yes, honey. I had a long talk with your dad."

"Is everything okay?"

"Everything is fine, honey. He understands what happened and how important it is for you to stay with us. We'll do everything we can to make sure what happened before never happens again. Uncle Owen is there with you tonight. I'll be there when you wake up in the morning."

"Promise."

Rain pinched the bridge of her nose and tried to hold back the tears. Autumn had been doing so well this last year. She went for long stretches without thinking or fearing Roxy. Brody's return stirred it all up. The first year after Roxy took Autumn, the little girl could barely cope any time Rain was out of her sight for more than a few minutes. Preschool had been difficult. Autumn had a hard time making friends and interacting with the other kids. She'd clung to Dawn and used her as a shield. Dawn had become Autumn's protector.

"I promise when you wake up, you'll smell breakfast, and I'll be there waiting for my morning hug."

Brody took the phone. "Hey, baby girl."

"Hi, Dad."

"Are you having a good time with Uncle Owen?"

"He's a lot of fun."

"We had a lot of fun when we were kids. Listen, baby girl, would you like me to come and have breakfast with you and Dawn in the morning?"

"Yeah. Can I have another piggyback ride?"

"Sure, baby girl. Pretty soon, I'll get some horses here at the ranch and I'll take you girls riding."

"That sounds awesome."

"Great. Now you make sure Uncle Owen reads you three books before bed and you sleep good. I'll see you in the morning."

"Okay. And Mommy will be here."

"Yes, baby girl. Mommy will be there. I promise."

They said goodnight again to both girls and Brody set the phone on the table. Rain leaned against him, the silence in the room lengthening.

"I came back because I wanted to make a life with you," he said quietly. "I thought it would be so easy."

She cast him a sideways glance and he smiled sheepishly.

"Don't get me wrong. I thought we'd have a few knock-down-drag-out fights. You'd yell, cuss, call me every dirty name in the book. Stomp your pretty little foot and hiss and spit at me."

"I sound like a terrible shrew."

He laughed, the rumble in his chest absorbed by her back. He wrapped his arms around her and squeezed her tight. "Not a shrew. A woman scorned with a rightful wrath I deserved, but didn't exactly want to face."

"I think I've been quite understanding and forgiving so far."

"You're a saint. I really thought you'd make my life a living hell. I figured I'd at the very least have to buy you some expensive baubles and kiss your pretty feet."

"You really have a thing for my feet."

"In the summer, you'd paint your toes. You had a sexy little ankle chain. Gold with a star charm."

"I lost it in the lake the summer before you left. The clasp must have broken."

Brody's hand slid up the inside of her sweater. He made lazy circles up her spine and massaged her sore muscles. His hands were magic. Her nerves danced to life. Heat pooled in her lower belly as he both relaxed and woke up her body, tuned it to his sensual touch.

"You said my coming home would bring Roxy back. Until tonight, I didn't understand what that meant for Autumn. I'd do anything to keep her safe and happy. Erase the fear in her voice tonight because you aren't with her. If I thought leaving would keep Roxy away, I would. It would kill me, but I'd do it for you and the girls."

"That isn't the answer, Brody. I've dealt with Roxy the only way I could over the years and paid her off. You hold the real power. You're Autumn's father. You can keep her from Roxy."

"That's exactly what I plan to do. I have a few ideas of how to accomplish that, but I'm not sure how far Roxy will go to manipulate the situation."

"You mean try to get as much money as she can out of you."

"It's not the money I'm worried about. It's her dragging me to court and tying this thing up for the next few years. It's the thought of her being given visitation rights that kills me. We can't let that happen. Autumn's so fragile now. Her only sense of security is you."

"If you're concerned she won't feel safe with you, Brody, it's only a matter of time. She's just met you. Give her a chance to know you."

"She saw me hurt her mother."

"I don't want to go backward. Let's move on to the fact that you're Autumn's father. She needs you. Dawn needs you."

Brody's arm circled around her back. His hand slid up her ribs until he cupped her breast. Leaning up to her, his breath feathered over her skin and he whispered in her ear, "Do you need me?"

Her mouth fell open on a sigh when his thumb brushed over her straining nipple.

"Lace." His warm breath caressed her ear. His tongue traced her earlobe before he nibbled the sensitive skin behind her ear. "What other surprises do you have for me?"

Rain stood and took a step away. He looked so good slouched on the couch. His strong legs spread wide, his jeans molded to every contour of muscle. His navy blue T-shirt stretched across a wide expanse of chest, the sleeves tight over his biceps. She liked his shoulders. Strong, rounded, tapering up to his neck.

"Like what you see, honey?"

Ah, that same cocky, confident attitude when it came to women, her, looking at him with such appreciation. She loved that about him, because once, now, he was hers. She was the woman he wanted, needed. She'd always known something special existed between the two of them. It had taken her until now to realize he spoke the truth. She was the keeper of his heart. Just as he held hers.

"You've always been the sexiest, most handsome man I've ever seen. You know what I like best about you?"

"What?" He leaned forward, planted his forearms on his knees, let his hands dangle between his legs. His eyes on her. She thought of a predator hunting his prey.

Gazes locked, she pulled her sweater over her head and let it fall to her side and land at her feet. "The way you love me," she said breathlessly.

Heat surged through her body from her face down her throat to her breasts, the same journey his hungry eyes made over her skin. Her breasts tingled, her nipples tightened to small buds. She ached to have him touch her.

"I haven't loved you well."

She knew what he meant, but she'd decided she was only moving forward. To something good. Something wonderful.

"You gave me a night of extraordinary love. I want more."

"I don't think I can be that gentle with you right now. I'm too hungry for you. It's been a long time, and I need you desperately."

"I've waited a long time for you. I have no doubt you'll find a way to make it up to me later."

"I thought you needed to get home. Make breakfast for the girls in the morning. Autumn needs you."

"While I find your concern for her truly heartwarming, tonight is about you and me. We need this, Brody. Besides, if you send me home, I'll be sleeping with Owen. He took my bed tonight."

She almost laughed at the feral look in his eyes.

"Forget it, you're staying with me." He stood and stalked her as she stepped back for every step he took toward her.

She smiled seductively and undid the button on her jeans.

"Don't. I want to undress you, discover what other secrets you've got hiding under your clothes. More pink lace?"

"Take me to bed. Find out."

"Quit backing away from me."

She started this, but making love to Brody again made her nervous and giddy all at the same time. "If I don't, we'll never make it to the bed."

"Would that be so bad?"

Ah, that smile. The lighthearted spark in his eyes. God, how she'd missed both.

"I want to be lying on something soft when that hard body comes crashing down on me."

"Oh, baby, I've got something hard for you," he teased, his eyes closing to slits as he stared at her breasts. His tongue swept across his bottom lip. She stumbled over her own feet and hit the last tread on the stairs. She hit her bottom and fell back as he came down on her and took her mouth in a deep kiss. She opened to him, his tongue taking possession and he held himself above her on his hands. Since he'd left some room between them, not wanting to crush her back into the wood stairs, she slid her hands up under his shirt and splayed her fingers wide. Tentative at first, she grew daring and mapped her hands over the contours of his flat belly, up over sculpted muscles and back down. Desire bolstered her boldness. One hand went over his lean hip, the other slid over his rigid erection pressed along the length of his fly. Her fingers traced the length of him, big and thick; her palm smoothed down and back up. He groaned and hissed in a breath when she did it again.

This is the Brody she remembered. All power and strength mixed with infinite patience, giving her time to settle in and reach for him.

Free from the kiss, she scrambled up from underneath him and made it up two steps before he grabbed her from behind. One of his hands splayed across her belly, pulling her back against him, his erection pressed to her bottom. Her head fell back against his shoulder, her breasts rising into his hands. She reached back. With her hands on his hips, she held his body to hers, rubbed against him, and his hands cupped, molded, teased her breasts. He took her taut nipples between his fingers and plucked and played until she moaned.

With his lips on her neck and a nudge from behind, she took each step plastered to the front of him. When they reached the loft, he turned her in his arms, hauled her up to her toes, cupped her bottom and brought her slamming into his chest, their hips pressed together, his cock nestled in between her thighs. He rocked against her, and the heat in her lower belly flared. His mouth found hers. Locked in a passionate kiss, he walked her backward to the bed. His lips trailed down her throat to her breasts. His tongue traced the lace trim of her bra and her hands fisted his short hair. She held him to her, probably hurting him, but he didn't seem to care as his tongue made the same journey over the mound of her other breast. He kissed his way down the valley between her breasts to her stomach. With each warm and soft and wet kiss his tongue flicked out to taste and tease.

He landed hard on his knee when he kissed her navel. Bending down wasn't good for his injured leg. When his hand pressed against her chest, she dropped willingly onto her back on the bed. He stood to look down on her. She scooted back to the pillows and thought he'd come down on the bed and lay beside her. Instead, he took a minute and just stared. Never uncomfortable around him—in fact, his gaze lazily traveling over her body heightened her anticipation.

He stalked toward her along the side of the bed. The outline of his rigid cock drew her gaze as his hands went to his jeans and undid the button. He slid the zipper down and freed his swollen flesh still hidden behind his black boxer briefs. She bit her lower lip and met his eyes.

He sat, reached out and brushed her hair from her face, his hand smoothing down her neck to her breast. He took it in his palm, his eyes hungry, watching as his hand molded and played.

His hand dipped low on her belly and traced the edge of her jeans, his finger sliding just under the material before—fingers splayed—he smoothed his hand up her body to her breast again.

"You're so beautiful. I want to see you when I make love to you, but I don't want you to see me."

He turned his back to her and reached up to turn out the single light beside the bed. Kneeling behind him, she stayed his arm and pulled his hand back.

"You bought candles." The table beside the bed held three pillar candles, one taller than the next. A wooden box gleamed in the light from the lamp.

"I wanted to give you a little romance. I thought I'd have to seduce you to get you here."

Tension infused his big body. "Brody, I swear to you, the scars don't matter."

To prove it, she bit the meaty part of his shoulder at the base of his neck and smoothed her tongue over the small hurt. Her hands glided up and down his arms and shoulders.

"You're so strong. I love the way you feel. All hard and tight and smooth." She kissed her way up the side of his neck, her breasts brushing against his back until she got to his ear. "Light the candles, Brody. Watch me burn and come alive while you make love to me."

"Ah, God, Rain. You don't know what you do to me."

"The same thing you do to me every time you look at me, touch me, want me the way you do."

She waited while he opened the wood box and took out a pack of matches and laid a condom on the table. "Aren't you prepared," she quipped.

"Yeah, I'm a boy scout. Actually," he said over his

shoulder, "this time I didn't want to leave anything to chance. Before you and after, I was always careful."

Except that one other time. The words hung in the air between them. God, how she wished . . . wishing wouldn't change anything.

She turned off the light herself. The candlelight danced on the walls and his face.

"From this moment forward, there's just you and me."

His whole body deflated with a deep exhale. He reached down and quickly untied his work boots and kicked them off, pulling his socks off afterward. He reached back to pull his shirt over his head, but she grabbed the bottom and pulled it off for him, tossing it to the floor. It only took a second to unclasp her bra and dangle it over his shoulder before she dropped it, and her breasts pressed against his back. His body tensed at the intimate contact. Skin to skin, the peaked tips of her breasts grazed his skin, so sensitive now, she gasped.

She wrapped her arms around his chest and leaned into him, her chin resting on his shoulder. "If I wrap my legs around you while we make love, will I hurt you?"

"No." More hesitantly, he added, "I don't think so."

To keep him from getting too anxious about it, she teased, "If it does, we'll find another way. I'm sure there are lots of ways you can teach me to love you." She made her voice husky and he responded, turning his face to hers and kissing her hard and deep.

"I don't deserve you."

"I'm yours all the same." She fell away from him with a smile on her kiss swollen lips and landed on her back on the bed.

His eyes locked on her bouncing breasts. Arms settled next to her, completely relaxed, she smiled invitingly and waited for him to come to her. Her fingers went to the button on her jeans and she pulled it loose.

"I told you I wanted to do that."

"Well come here and do it."

That taunting tone and smile would probably be the death of him. As it was, he'd stalled all he could to cool his ardor and hopefully have some control and finesse when he loved her. He stood with his back to her about to pull off his jeans. Instead, he turned and faced her, knowing the candlelight would highlight his damaged leg. He stalled for just a second before tearing his jeans and underwear off. That's how long it took him to realize this was Rain. She loved him despite all the bad things he'd done in his past, all the wrongs he'd committed against others, the most damaging against her.

There she was, pretty as a picture, half-naked, lying on his bed waiting for him to love her. She didn't care what he looked like. Appreciated it, yes. That's not why she loved him. She loved him despite knowing everything about him, the good and the bad. Standing before her naked, fully aroused, his leg bare for her to see, he wasn't self-conscious in the least. Instead, his usual confidence and cockiness returned.

This was Rain, and she only knew how to love one way. Unconditionally.

Lying on the bed beside her, his hard shaft pressed to her hip, he looked deep into her eyes. "I love you."

Cupping his face between her hands, she drew him to her. Against his lips, she said, "I know."

She knew. She believed him, in him. That's all he needed. He dove in, taking her mouth, his tongue sliding in to taste her. Nothing else tasted so good. He dipped his head, cupped her breast in his hand, and brought her nipple to his lips. He flicked his tongue over the taut bud, she arched her back, and he took her into his mouth. Yeah, this was better. He laved and suckled, loving her every moan and sigh as he moved from one breast to the other. He slid his hand down her slim belly, over her jeans, and cupped her mound in his palm. Her hips rocked into his hand, demanding his attention, but he didn't want to leave her sweet breasts.

Throbbing, aching, he wanted to bury himself in her heat and lose himself and find the man she loved so completely.

He unzipped her jeans and skimmed his fingers inside over her panties. He smiled against her breast.

"Lace," he said, though he could only feel it.

"Pink," she confirmed, her hips rising to his touch.

He caught sight of her pretty breasts, rosy nipples wet from his tongue. His cock jerked with a surge of passion.

He ripped her jeans and that nothing of a swatch of lace off her legs and tossed them away without a second thought. Kneeling between her legs, he slid both hands up over her firm thighs, to her hips. Her belly was warm and resilient against his lips as he planted kisses over her silky skin. The smell of her intoxicated him. He dipped his hand lower, and he swept his thumb down over the soft flesh, dipping between the folds, her desire slicked over his skin. Her breath caught when he brought his thumb back up and found that sweet spot that had her arching her back off the bed, her thighs spreading with no more encouragement then a soft touch of his hand on the inside of one of her thighs, the other following suit, until she was bared to him. So wet, so ready for him. His whole body throbbed, desperate to cover her and sink into her deep and hard.

He reached for the condom on the table. Since he was over her, she took him into her hands and stroked down and up the length of him. She cupped his balls in her palm, clutching her fingers around him and massaged gently. He hissed in a breath and groaned when her hand slid up, her fingers wrapped around him, all the way to the top where her thumb found the bead of liquid and circled and smoothed it over and around the round head, slowly killing him.

Ready to explode, he leaned back on his heels, ripped open the condom package with his teeth, and sheathed himself.

"I'm sorry, baby. I really wanted to make this good for you. I'm afraid, I just can't wait any longer."

Rain never took her eyes off him and when he came down on top of her, his body pressed to hers, his erection pressing at her entrance, her eyes went wide and she tensed at the intrusion.

Taking nipping kisses at her lips, he eased his body into hers in aching slow motion.

"Relax. It's just me." He held her gaze as she let out her breath; her whole body relaxed and allowed him to slide into her to the hilt in one long, fluid motion. "Am I hurting you?"

She didn't answer. She didn't have to with words. She rocked her hips into his and then away. Satisfaction lit her eyes, ripples of passion trembled through her body, and his mind shut off and his body rode that wave of pleasure. He pulled out almost all the way. She made a disappointed grunt, dug her fingers into his back to pull him in again. He thrust back into her hard and deep. He did it again and her head fell back and she arched her back, her breasts grazing his chest. He watched her expressive face, thrust into her again and again, trying to go deeper, his release riding him hard, but he tried to hold back. Nearly over the edge, she pulled her knees up and wide and he sank back into her so deep, she sent him over the edge. Two more deep hard thrusts, her fingers digging into his hips, she pulled him to her, his whole body rigid, he spilled himself inside her. Wave upon wave of contractions from her body fisted around his and wrung him dry.

Eyes closed, breathing heavily suspended above her on his fisted hands, he collapsed on top of her, his face buried in her fragrant hair. Completely spent. Happy. Home.

Her arms and those gorgeous legs wrapped around him, she hugged him with her whole body. It had been a long time since he'd felt this good, this safe. She'd always been the one place he could be and know he could let all the walls crumble, shed all his protective instincts, never fear she'd hurt him with her words or deeds.

Rain, his island of peace. Without her, life wasn't worth living.

Chapter Twenty

SOMETHING WOKE RAIN. Sleepy and disoriented, she searched the surrounding darkness. The candles had long ago been extinguished. The room was dark but for the moonlight seeping through the gauzy curtains. Brody's bed, his hard body down the length of her. Her leg thrown over his, her head pillowed on his shoulder, his arm wrapped around her back and side.

Brody's whole body twitched and shook her. He must have done it before and woken her up.

Caught in a nightmare, Brody mumbled in his sleep, his arm tightened around her and his legs kicked and thrashed in the bed. Hating to leave him at the mercy of some awful memory, she scooted up and brushed her fingertips over his forehead and raked them through his hair, crooning, "Brody, honey, wake up for me," over and over again.

He didn't respond, but grew more agitated, kicking and flailing his arms. She slid over on top of him, her legs straddling his hips. His hands came up to fight off his imaginary attacker, but she expected something like this, so she dodged his arms and lay down on top of him her mouth finding the pulse in his throat. She licked, her lips sucking gently. She nibbled her way up his throat to his ear and whispered, "Brody, love me."

She'd swap one kind of dream for another.

Easing back down his chest, her bottom came down and she pressed against him. She rocked her hips and within moments, he was hard beneath her. His breathing slowed and his hands found her thighs, slid up to her hips, and encouraged her to move against his swollen flesh.

"That's it, baby. Come back to me. Love me."

She nipped at his chin and brushed her breasts over his chest. Warm, hard, so handsome, she couldn't help but rub against him, feel his heat seep into her, pool in her lower belly, and spread out like a wildfire across her nerves.

The wood box sat open on the bedside table. She reached in and found another condom. Mapping his body with kisses from the bullet-wound scar high up on his shoulder, over his chest, down his rippled belly, she detoured and found the long scar that ran across his stomach and around his side. She traced it with her tongue, her hands roaming over his chest. Her hair fell in a curtain over him and she sank lower and found his thick erection. Not really knowing what she was doing, she circled the head with her tongue. Brody's whole body went tense and his fingers dove into her hair, his fingers curling in the strands. Encouraged, she slowly took him into her mouth.

"Ah, God, Rain."

His voice was sleep husky and ragged. He groaned, and she worked her mouth over his flesh, learning the contours and taste of him with this intimate loving. His big hands combed through her hair, down her neck, and over her shoulders, encouraging her to touch and taste as she pleased.

Desperation in his voice, he called to her in the night, "Rain, baby, I'm so damn close. I want to be inside you."

Swiftly unwrapping the condom, she slid it over him and crawled back up his body, kissing, nipping, and a love bite on the meaty part of his chest before his hands cupped her face and he drew her to his open mouth. His tongue dove deep. In a frenzy, he pulled her higher so he could take possession of her breast, his tongue sliding over her tight nipple a second before he took the rigid peak into his mouth and suckled deep. One hand on her other breast, teasing and tugging on her nipple, the other slid over her belly, down until his finger thrust into her, nearly sending her over the edge. On her hands and knees above him, he played her body like an instrument, bringing her to soaring heights with his mouth and fingers.

Both desperate for the other, Brody grabbed her hips and brought her down hard. Seated on top of him, she paused just for a second and his hips came off the bed, his cock buried deep inside her. She rocked forward then back and he fell back to the bed, holding her to him as she moved.

His hand moved to where they were joined. She moved over him and his fingers dipped and found that sweet spot. Her head fell back, her hair brushing her skin as she bounced and moved and Brody sent waves of pleasure through her system until she exploded with an intense orgasm, her body contracting around Brody's. He lifted her and thrust deep, his cock pumping as he groaned long and deep. He settled back into the bed; she fell on top of him completely limp. Her chin rested in the crook of his neck and shoulder, her lips just below his ear. She kissed him softly and fell into a deep sleep with his arms banded around her and their bodies still joined.

The sun's first light began to take over the night, but that's not what woke her. Brody spread her thighs wide and entered her achingly slow. Filling her, he pressed his hips hard to hers and stopped moving. Just paused, their bodies locked together.

She opened her eyes just enough to see him staring down at her with such love. His fingertips brushed over her cheek, traced it up to the corner of her eye, where he slipped a strand of hair away from her face.

"You're so beautiful when you sleep." He pulled back. She gasped when he almost left her completely. "Soft." He entered her again in that long, slow invasion that made her sigh. "Warm." His body moved away and came back into her again and again in that slow, sweet loving. "Mine." His mouth was warm and wet on her neck, his hand brushing up and down her thigh.

This was the perfect way to wake up in the morning. The man she loved had finally come home. Not only that, he'd come back for her. Her heart felt so full. She put all her heart into making love to him. Her hands roamed up and down his back, her fingers digging in to firm muscles. Their mouths melded, their loving went from leisurely to something more serious and basic, all need and demand.

What had been building between them over the last few minutes exploded through her system. She held tight to Brody's hips as he thrust into her hard and deep, his jaw locked, head thrown back, and he spilled himself inside of her. His pulsing body deep within hers set off a second wave of ecstasy. Her body contracted around his in sweet aftershocks. He fell on her with a deep groan, his lips pressed against the pounding pulse in her neck.

"You're lethal," he said against her skin. His warm breath sending a shiver through her.

She laughed. Eyes closed, she enjoyed having his weight on her, pressing her into the bed. He felt so good, she drew her hands over his tight butt, up his lower back and down again. Satisfied, lazy, and feeling quite content, she lay beneath him in a haze of spent passion.

"You don't have to touch it just to convince me it doesn't bother you," he grumbled, his voice deep and filled with irritation.

Her hands stilled on his hips and lay against his skin. At first, she wasn't sure what he was talking about. Then, she realized her right hand lay over his damaged hip and thigh. The skin felt rough, rippled in places where the burns had healed into knots and lines of scar tissue.

"Until this moment, I hadn't realized what I was touching was anything different than touching you.

I cannot believe after everything we shared last night and two minutes ago, you could think so little of me. I wouldn't care if your entire body had been burned. What it looked like, or felt like." She turned to look at him, eyes ablaze. "What I care about is the terrible pain you must have been in, the pain you're still experiencing. I wish I could take it away. I wish you believed what you look like doesn't matter to me. I love you. If you think the scars change that or diminish it in some way, then you don't understand my love for you, because it has no boundaries. I don't want there to be anything that keeps us from being completely open and honest with each other."

Her eyes held his. She hadn't moved her hands, and she knew he could see the anger in her eyes, feel it in her body beneath his.

"You mean that."

"You're damn right I do."

His forehead touched hers and he kissed her softly. "I'm being stupid."

"For a smart man, you say some stupid things," she agreed, and was happy to see a slight smile cross his face.

"I thought when I came back, the scars, my mental state . . . other things would be another black mark against me."

"I'm not keeping score. I don't have a blackboard in my mind where I'm ticking off things for and against you."

"It's me. It's just that getting you back is the most important thing I've ever tried to do."

"Mission accomplished. Scars, past deeds, everything between our past and present doesn't seem to matter more than the fact that I love you. I don't want to be sad and angry and lonely anymore."

Brody rolled to his side and kept her pulled close to him. They lay face-to-face. "You'll never be lonely again, sweetheart. I'm sorry I left you alone to raise our girls. The sacrifices you made, all the hard work and care you've put into raising them. They're beautiful, smart, happy little girls because of you. Autumn is safe and knows she's loved because of you. I'm sorry and thank you doesn't seem to be enough to show you how much I appreciate what you've done. From now on, you won't have to do it alone."

"Good. Because the scariest thing is knowing if Roxy pushed for her parental rights, I'd lose. We can't lose, Brody. For Autumn's sake, we have to end this and make sure Roxy never takes Autumn again."

"We will, sweetheart." He kissed her forehead and held her close, the morning blooming brightly through the window above them. "We need to get up and go have breakfast with the girls. We'll talk to Owen this morning and start planning our strategy."

"Spoken like a true military man going into battle."

"If we're dealing with Roxy, you're damn right it'll be a battle. She never makes anything easy, and usually makes matters worse."

"Enough about her. You take a shower, I'll make the coffee."

"Deal." He smacked her on the bottom, threw off the covers, and stood next to the bed stretching his arms high over his head and leaning side to side to stretch his back.

When his arms came down, he automatically rubbed his hand over his thigh.

"I don't know how you could possibly think something so small could take away from how sexy and beautiful you are." She lay in bed, her eyes devouring every inch of skin stretched over taut, well-defined muscles. The scars and burns were there, but she didn't really see them as she took in the whole of him.

He turned back to her. This time, no apprehension in the way he moved or in his eyes. "Remind me never to buy you the pair of glasses you so obviously need." He planted his hands on either side of her shoulders, leaned down and kissed her with such reverence tears came into her eyes. Her hands came up and smoothed over his shoulders. As he stood, her hands slid down his arms until their hands met. He held hers, gave them a squeeze, then walked to the bathroom, completely unfazed by her intent gaze.

She'd helped him get past his uneasiness over his physical injuries. Now, if she could only help him with his anxiety and those terrible nightmares he had when he was both awake and asleep. She'd find a way to bring him peace. She'd surround him with love and family. They'd make a home and a life together.

First, they had to find a way to keep Roxy out of their lives.

Chapter Twenty-One

AUTUMN AND DAWN screeched with excitement when they came down to the kitchen that morning and found Brody sitting at the table, watching Rain make breakfast. Both girls ran to him and threw their arms around his neck. Rain's heart melted seeing them with their father. They'd waited so long to have him in their lives and Brody didn't hesitate to pull them close, engage them in conversation, and, of course, provide the promised piggyback ride for Autumn. Not to be outdone, Dawn got hers, too.

Owen came down just as Rain put breakfast on the table. "What's going on down here?"

Rain stood in the doorway, her shoulder propped against the frame. The girls attacked Brody, wrapping their arms around his hips and legs. They stood in the living room surrounded by shredded wrapping paper and ribbons. Their shriek of delight filled the room and her heart.

"Brody bought the girls new computers."

Owen came to stand beside her. He kissed her on the forehead. "Good morning, beautiful."

Brody kept his eye on them, despite the girls begging him to set up the laptops immediately. A ripple of pleasure coursed through her seeing that small show of jealousy.

"Morning. Did you sleep well?" she asked.

"I slept alone." He pointedly looked at her clothes, the same ones she had on last night. "Did you?"

"She slept with me and will from now on." Brody planted his fists on his hips and glared at Owen.

Rain's cheeks flushed immediately. Owen smiled broadly. The girls looked at each other, then Dawn asked, "You slept at Dad's last night?"

Before she left last night, she hadn't told the girls she'd stay at Brody's. She wasn't sure she would, or if it would be a good idea to give in to her need for him when there was still so much unsettled between them. Besides, she didn't want to get the girls' hopes up too much.

"Your dad and I had a lot to talk about last night. Let's have breakfast. We need to talk to you about a few things. Your softball game is later today. When we get home, your dad can set up your computers."

"Ah, Mom. Can't we set them up now? Just one game?"

"You heard your mom. After the softball game. Let's eat. I'm starving." Brody smiled to let her know he was on her side. They were a team.

"I'll bet you worked up quite an appetite," Owen said with a knowing grin.

"Jealous." Brody took his seat next to Rain at the table and brought her hand to his lips, kissing her palm. She brushed her fingertips over his cheek and smiled.

"Actually, yeah. She's been mine for more than four years."

The truth of Owen's words settled into her heart. They'd been a family these last years, Owen helping her out with the girls, picking them up from school, coaching softball, breakfasts, dinners, Saturdays at the mall, or out for a movie. He didn't have romantic feelings for her, but still, they'd been close. If the girls couldn't have their father, he was the next best thing because he was there, and he told the most wonderful Brody stories.

Rain wanted to say something to add weight to Owen's casually spoken words. Brody spoke first, showing her just how much he'd changed. Gone was the wisecracking, take-next-to-nothing-serious man he'd been. This Brody understood where his brother was coming from, because Brody understood everything he'd missed with the girls and everything his brother hadn't.

Brody leaned forward and braced his forearms on the edge of the table and looked Owen in the eye. "I know it seems like I'm taking your place in the girls' lives."

"You're their father. Your place is with them."

"It's where I'll stay, but that doesn't mean there isn't a place here for you. I'd really like it if you and I could stick together to take care of them. We may have had our differences, but we've always had each other's back. What you did for Rain and my daughters while I was gone, well, there are no words to thank you enough. We always wanted to have a real family when we were young." Brody looked at all of them sitting around the table, pancakes, eggs, and bacon piled on platters. "This is it, Owen. We finally have it."

"This is your family, Brody. I don't want to get in the way of that."

"It wouldn't be a complete family without you," Brody admitted.

Rain hadn't ever heard the two brothers talk like this. They'd never been so open and honest. At least, not in front of witnesses.

"Brody's right. We need you, Owen. Who else will play catcher, or take the girls out on dates. They love spending time with you."

"She's right," Brody added. "I can barely make it upstairs. There's no way I can play ball with them."

"I look forward to the time we share, having breakfast together, sharing our days over coffee. You've got the juiciest gossip in town," Rain added.

Owen laughed. "Is that a roundabout way of saying I'm your best girlfriend?"

Not rising to the joke, she gave him the serious answer. "You're my best friend. You have been all these years. Just because Brody's back and we're trying to work things out, that doesn't mean I don't need my best friend. Besides, if he gets out of line, I expect you to come to my defense."

"Seems only right," Brody said around a bite of syrup-dripping pancakes.

"Uncle Owen is really good at playing checkers. He lets me win," Autumn said, and gave her uncle a huge smile.

"He said we could sue David Murphy for defamation of character if he called me ugly on the playground again," Dawn added, and everyone laughed.

Smiling, Owen conceded. "Well you, my little hothead, will need me to defend you if you stomp on his foot and pull his hair again." Owen grabbed Dawn and hugged her to his side and gave her a kiss on the head. "You're your father's daughter."

"Mom taught me the foot-stomping thing. It works real good." Dawn gave Brody a huge smile, her eyes pleading for his approval. When he gave her back a huge smile, she sat even taller in her chair. Rain laid her hand over Brody's and squeezed it to let him know she appreciated his show of pride in their daughter's less than reputable, but very much like their father's, behavior.

"Yeah, David couldn't play kickball for two days." Autumn nodded her approval to Dawn and both girls shared one of those looks that says so much without saying a word.

"Eat your breakfast, girls." Rain had trouble eating her own. She kept looking at Brody and everyone else at her table, wondering how they'd gotten to this point so quickly. She'd been so angry with him for what he'd done. Yet, she'd found it easy to forgive him, fall back into bed with him, and start planning a life with him. Well, not really plan. They'd only had a few words about the future, but still, it seemed so set in her mind. Here they were sitting around the breakfast table. So normal. She had no trouble imagining this is how things would be from now on.

Thinking forward, she pictured them in the house Brody was building. The girls in their own rooms. Brody would have his office and work from home. He'd be there when the girls came home from school. They'd have dinner together and talk about their day. She'd sleep in his arms every night.

Memories of last night surfaced. The way he'd been so apprehensive about her seeing his scars. How they'd come together with such intense heat and need. The feel of his hands, his mouth on her breasts, the weight of him covering her, his heat sinking into her bones, the way he filled her body and at the same time her heart to the point it went beyond pleasure and into some kind of melding between their souls. Maybe that's what happened years ago, but in her youth she hadn't recognized it for what it was.

She's spent the last several years waiting for him, because for her, he was her everything.

Brody's fingers slid along her cheek and into her hair. He pulled her head to his and whispered into her ear. "If you keep looking at me like that, I'm going to eat you up rather than my breakfast." His hand dropped between them and he squeezed her hip and sent heat into her belly.

"Mom, are you okay?" Dawn asked.

Brody let her go, his hands not leaving her without touching every inch of her skin at his fingertips.

Turning to Dawn, she smiled softly, her mind still spinning with thoughts of Brody and the future. A future they had to plan carefully because their daughters' happiness needed to be considered.

"I'm fine, honey. I just got lost in thought. It's been a crazy few days."

"Because Dad's back."

"Yes. Your dad and I had a long talk last night, but we still have a lot to discuss and work out. Nothing has really been settled."

"Although I'm home, it'll still take time to earn your mom's complete trust. We need time to get to know each other again," he said to the girls. "I'm adding on to the cabin, turning it into a real house. Eventually, I'd like your mom and you to come live with me on the ranch."

"With the horses?" Dawn asked.

"Eventually. The house and stables will take time to build. During that time, we'll get to know each other. Your mom and I will plan our future, learn to live with each other."

"Are you going to get married? She'll be my real mommy then." Autumn's eyes held so much hope.

Dawn leaned forward, waiting for Brody's answer.

Rain loved Brody as much today as she did years ago. More. Not just because of their daughters. Since the moment she'd seen him lying in that hospital bed, burned and so near death she could feel it in the room, she'd known her life, her happiness, her reason for being was him. When she'd seen him at the shop the day he'd come to pick up his truck, she'd seen the pure joy and wonder and gratitude when she'd told him she'd had his child. She'd also seen the relief that Dawn bound them together. He needed her, and she needed him, too.

"Autumn, baby girl . . ." Brody began, and paused searching for the right words.

It was a loaded question, and Brody didn't want to make promises when things were so fresh and new between them. They had a foundation of love, but they still needed time to build on it.

Roxy was coming back. Brody knew as well as she did that meant trouble.

Frustrated, Brody ran his hand over his hair. He opened his mouth, but closed it again. Rain didn't say a word. She'd spent the last four years trying to console Autumn and make her feel safe. Nothing worked for long. Something always made Autumn feel like any minute Roxy would pop out of a dark corner and take her back to hell. This time, Autumn had a very good reason to fear, and they hadn't even told her Roxy was coming back to town. No doubt to see Brody. Maybe to try to get him back into her bed. Certainly to get as much money from him as she could.

"Rain, you want to help me out here?"

He'd never outright asked her to marry him, even though he'd made himself clear on what he wanted. Her. So she smiled and said, "I believe Autumn just asked what your intentions are."

"Maybe we should get Eli over here, too. I'm sure he'd like an answer to that question."

"Oh, I think he's got your number." Owen gave Brody a wolfish grin. One brother always loved seeing the other backed into a corner.

"Okay, baby girl, you want to know if your mom and I are getting married. The answer right now is I hope so." Autumn and Dawn both wanted to interrupt, but Brody held up his hand to stop them. "I love your mother. I love her more than anything. I came back to find her and a way to take the best of our past and see if we can turn it into a future together. Your mom and I talked last night and even managed to take a step toward that future, but a couple of dinners and one good long talk isn't enough to build the future I want with her."

"Why not? You said you love her." Autumn's eyes remained intent on Brody. It had been a long time since Rain had seen her this worked up and forward.

"I love both of you, and I love her. I know your mom. I believe she forgives me for what I did to her. I also know she needs time to think about what my coming home and being a part of her life means to her."

"You'd be our dad all the time. We'd live together and Roxy couldn't take me. It would be two against one. We'd win then."

"Autumn is right," Brody. I need your help this time. I have possession of Autumn. I've raised her as my own. She's my daughter as if I gave birth to her myself.

"Roxy is still her biological mother. She has rights." Rain kept things vague so as not to frighten Autumn, but the message was clear. A judge could grant Roxy visitation, or the unthinkable, full custody.

"You have to marry him," Autumn burst out. "You have to. You can't let her take me." Sobbing, Autumn flung herself into Rain's lap and wrapped her arms around her neck, holding tight. Dawn's eyes were glassy, the tears ready to fall for her sister's pain and anguish. Rain had no doubt she wanted what Autumn wanted: she and Brody married to save them from Roxy. Too bad life was never that simple.

Brody looked wrecked. He shifted uncomfortably in his seat. Like most men, he had no idea what to do with a crying female, especially one so small and traumatized.

"Sssh, baby. It's all right," Rain crooned to Autumn, rocking her in her arms.

"Baby girl, listen to me. Marrying your mom will not make Roxy stay away. As much as I want her to be my wife, I want her to marry me because it's what we both want more than anything and not because it will make things easier in dealing with Roxy."

"She'll marry you. She wants to. Tell him, Mom."

Rain held Autumn away from her and smiled softly. "I've told you and your sister how much I will always love your dad."

"See," Autumn said over her shoulder to Brody.

"Listen to your mother," Brody replied, reading Rain as well as he used to.

"Your dad and I aren't saying we aren't getting married. We're saying we need time. I haven't seen your father in eight years. I'd like some time to get to know him again. Discover all the wonderful things about him I fell in love with years ago, all the new things I don't know yet. I'm sure your father would like to discover those things in me."

"You're easy. We live in the same town he grew up in. Only now you're our mom."

Rain tried not to laugh, but some of it escaped. Leave it to a child to put things so simply. What more was there to her than the fact she was their mother. They didn't see her as anything more. Maybe that was the safety and security every child needed.

"He knows what being your mom has meant to me over the years. Besides being your mom, I'm a woman. That's very different to a man than being a mother."

"You mean the kissing stuff," Dawn said, her cheeks turning pink and her lips turning into a sour pucker. Brody, Owen, and Rain laughed.

"The kissing stuff along with a lot of other things. When your father and I get married, we'll live together for the rest of our lives. Before we do that, we both should make sure that's what we really want. What if he leaves his socks on the floor and puts mushrooms in the spaghetti sauce?"

"Ew," both girls chimed.

"Well, the military has drilled into me how to be neat and organized, so I don't leave my socks on the floor. Who would put mushrooms in spaghetti sauce? Yuck," he agreed with them, earning a giggle from both girls. "So, those two questions are answered, but your mom and I have a lot of other things we need to learn about each other. This won't happen tomorrow, but we aren't saying it won't happen soon."

Brody gave her a look that told her he agreed with them taking some time, but he wouldn't be patient for very long. Rain had a feeling he already had a timeline in his head. Look at the way he was dealing with the cabin. He intended them to live in the house within months. A house with several extra, unfilled bedrooms. Brody had come home intending to win her back, make her his wife, and have babies with her. She had to admit the more she thought about that house, those empty bedrooms, carrying his child again, the more it grew on her. The girls were getting so big. They'd gone from babies to second graders in the blink of an eye. She'd been an only child and dreamed of having a family with several children. Time to stop the spinning, settle all her thoughts, and figure out exactly what she wanted. Soon, Brody would ask her to answer that question, and she needed a good answer, or he'd tell her what she was going to do, because he already knew what he wanted. His wife and children under the same roof.

"Be patient girls. We aren't saying it won't happen." Rain laid her hand over Brody's where it rested on her knee.

Hugging Autumn close, Rain kissed her temple. "Autumn, your dad and I have something to tell you. I know you'll be upset, but I want you to know we'll keep you safe."

"Roxy is coming back." She guessed the news easily. "Because Dad came home."

"That's part of the reason. Your dad has worked very hard to open and run a very successful company."

"So he could come back and be with us?" Dawn asked.

"I started out helping a friend of mine," Brody answered. "But in the back of my mind, I knew if the company did well, I could come back and prove to your mom I had grown up and was responsible. I can take care of her . . . and you."

"Because you have a job?" Dawn asked.

"Yes. And with that job I earn a very big paycheck."

"Roxy wants more money." Autumn spoke the cold hard truth. Even a child understood the bottom line when it came to Roxy.

Rain cupped her face and met her wary gaze. "Yes, baby. She wants money."

"She never wanted me." Autumn's lips trembled and her eyes filled with tears.

Rain's heart ripped open and bled. Her own eyes glassed over, but she fought the tears. "I'm sorry, baby. I know it hurts you a lot to know Roxy didn't want you. Always remember I want you very much."

Brody kneeled beside her chair and rubbed his hand up and down Autumn's back. "I want you, baby girl. More than anything. I love you so much. If you ask me, you got the best mom in the world. You're a very special girl, and you deserve to have a great mom. I want you to know something else. If I had known Roxy was pregnant with you, I would never have left you with her. I would have taken you and made sure she never hurt you in any way."

"Really."

"Yes."

"But you were gone."

"That's why I'm so grateful Rain raised you and loved you until I came back to love you, too." Brody wrapped his arms around both of them and kissed Autumn on the side of the head. He slid his hand up Rain's back and cupped the back of her head and drew her to him. His lips brushed hers. "Thank you," he said against her lips.

He kissed her then, slow, soft, a wealth of love seeping into her skin, spreading warmly through her system. She melted.

Brody ended the kiss. Before he stood to take his seat again, she ran her hand over the side of his head, his short hair brushing her palm and fingers.

"So, Autumn and Dawn, I want you both to be extra careful when we're out. If you see Roxy, you let me know. The two of you stick together. Stay close to us. When Roxy arrives, your dad and I will talk to her. We'll settle this once and for all. Okay?"

"Okay," both girls answered.

"Why don't you both go and watch TV. Your dad and I need to talk with Uncle Owen."

Rain waited for the girls to leave the kitchen. Cartoon music and high-pitched character voices played on the TV in the family room. She took her plate and coffee mug to the sink. Her gaze fell on her garden blooming outside the window in the bright sun. The sight usually made her cheerful. Not today. A black cloud had descended, overshadowing everything in her world.

"I'm going up to take a shower. I'd appreciate it if you guys cleaned up the kitchen. When I come back, we'll talk about Roxy's invasion."

She turned from the window, detoured from walking upstairs, and went to Brody instead. He wrapped his arm around her waist and looked up at her waiting. She didn't know what she wanted to say, what there was to say. "I'll be back soon."

"I'll be waiting for you."

She leaned down and met his lips. Aware Owen was watching them, she kept the kiss brief. She needed to taste him, feel his breath on her face. The special connection they shared vibrated around them. She rested her cheek against his, her fingers digging into his shoulders, and whispered into his ear, "Take your medicine."

She stood when he said, "You taking care of me again?"

"I can't seem to help myself."

"Want to do it every day for the rest of your life?"

"Probably."

She stepped out of his light embrace and left the room. The girls were on the couch, sitting close together, watching a show. When Autumn saw her, she got up and came into her arms.

"It'll be okay, baby. I promise."

Rain swore to herself Roxy would not make a liar out of her. If she touched one hair on her daughter's head, she'd kill her.

Chapter Twenty-Two

BRODY AND OWEN cleaned the breakfast dishes in silence. Brody needed the space and time to collect his thoughts, think about what happened that morning and last night. What to expect when Roxy arrived, and the impact it would have on Autumn—and his tenuous relationship with Rain.

"Things seem good between you two." Owen broached the subject with tact, even if his voice held a lot of concern, but Brody had no doubt he wanted the real scoop.

"Last night started off kind of rough."

"She told you what Roxy did to Autumn."

"The whole sordid story. She sold my child." Anger laced every word and vibrated through him. Without an outlet for his rage, he took a deep breath and sat heavily in his seat at the table.

"Best thing that ever happened to Autumn . . . and you."

"Rain is the best thing that ever happened to Autumn and me. She's . . ."

"Exceptional," Owen supplied.

"Absolutely. After what I did, I thought the most I owed her is a huge apology, show her I've grown up, taken responsibility for my life, changed my ways."

"You've done all those things. She accepted the apology. After all, time has a way of putting things into perspective."

"The fact we share two children doesn't hurt," Brody admitted.

"Definitely makes it easier."

"I'm afraid the obstacle between Rain and me is her."

"Huh?"

"She gave up college, every cent she had, her freedom"—Brody hated to admit the next part—"dating, finding a man to love and marry, have a family with on her terms."

"The last she did with you. Any other guy would have been a substitute."

"Thanks for the vote of confidence."

"Can't get around the truth, man. It is what it is."

"She's smart. She shouldn't be working in her father's garage. There's no challenge in it for her."

"She loves working with her dad. Maybe it's not what she wanted to do with her life, but she's good at it. The hours are flexible. She can be with the girls when they have school events and other activities." Owen leaned in. "Did you ask her what she wants to do now that you're back?"

"Not specifically. We talked about the house, her living with me. We skimmed the topic of having more kids."

"Stop sweating it then. If she agreed to all that, you're golden."

"We didn't make any definite plans. Given time, and the money I gave her, she may decide she wants something else."

"Are we talking about the same woman who not half an hour ago kissed you, told the girls you two were getting married sometime in the near future, and who did everything she could to keep this family intact?"

"She gave up all her dreams," Brody said, frustrated Owen didn't get it.

"So, I'll dream a new dream," Rain said from the door. "Owen, could we have a moment alone."

"I'll get the paperwork Brody asked me to complete."

Brody bowed his head for a moment. When he faced her, she stood in the doorway, her shoulder propped against the frame. God, she was beautiful. Her hair softly waving down past her shoulders. Dressed for the softball game, she wore black leggings, a billowy white top that skimmed the tops of her thighs, and white socks. Her black high-top Converse shoes dangled from her hand. The bruises on her arm stood out against her satin, cream skin. A touch of makeup on her eyes highlighted the understanding in the brown depths.

"I don't want to force you to do anything you don't want to do," he said.

"You never forced me to do anything I didn't want to do in the first place."

"You wanted to go to school."

"I wanted to be a mother more."

"You didn't have a choice."

Rain's eyebrow shot up. She pushed away from the doorframe and walked toward him, standing just out of reach. "Every decision we make has a multitude of choices. We make the best ones we can and live with the consequences. The choices I made are the ones I could live with without regrets. Given the choices again, I'd do the same thing."

"I'll take you anywhere you want to go."

She smiled softly, more to placate him than anything else.

"You seem to think I gave up everything and gained nothing. That simply isn't true. The things I wanted when I was sixteen aren't the same things I want now. Life, time, experiences change the things we want and our perspective on the things we decide are worth giving up for something else."

"You wanted me then. Has that changed?"

"How can you ask me such a stupid question after what we shared last night?"

"Because I feel guilty about the mess I left for you to clean up. Because if it was me, I'd resent the hell out of you for having the life I'd wanted and never got to have."

She came to him then. The weight of his guilt settled like a lead brick in his gut.

"Maybe things happened for a reason. Maybe you needed time to realize the dreams I had for myself were dreams you could have for yourself. You always thought you weren't smart enough, or good enough. Your father had a lot to do with that, and maybe if he'd given you the words he gave to me when the girls were born, things could have been different for you. Whatever the reasons for the way things happened, there was a reason. I've had a lot of time to imagine how things could have been if you'd stayed. Can you imagine how tumultuous our lives could have been if you'd stayed?"

Too easily Brody conjured images and scenarios of how Roxy would have made their lives a living hell. How he and Rain would have fought and grown apart because of what he'd done and because Roxy would never leave them alone to raise the girls. She'd have been a constant thorn in his side, gangrene eating away everything good in his life until everything was poisoned and dying. Not to mention the life Autumn would have endured.

"Exactly," Rain said, reading his mind. Not difficult. They both knew what Roxy was capable of doing. Rain maybe more so.

"I've been thinking a lot over the last few days."

"Why doesn't that sound like good news to me?" he asked, only half kidding.

"Probably because, like you, I've had to deal with a lot of changes in a short time. It's not easy to make decisions when you're bombarded and your thoughts are scattered."

"Great sex will do that to you."

He loved it when she laughed like that.

"I'll have to take your word for it. You're my only reference."

"Another thing I boxed you into."

"When you've had the best, you don't go looking for mediocre."

He'd been with other women and shared an apartment with one of them. He'd had a lot of less than mediocre because none of them had even come close to her. He couldn't say that to her.

"Brody, stop worrying and analyzing the life you had away from me with the life I had here with the girls. They aren't the same because you and I aren't the same."

"I'm the asshole who left the best behind, left a trail of not-worth-mentioning behind me, and lived out several of your dreams."

"You're also the man who went off to war, defended our country and the rights of others to have a life free from tyranny and hate. You came back to face me, knowing I might slam the door in your face again. When you found out about the girls, you didn't hesitate to claim them as yours, love them with your whole heart, and take on being a father without blinking."

"That was easy. You're scary as hell."

"Why, Brody?"

"Because I don't know what you want."

"I'm a simple girl. I want the same thing I wanted when I was ten and you kissed me for the first time. I want you, Brody. I've always wanted you."

"You said *when* we get married."

"You caught that, huh?"

"A drowning man needs a lifeline."

"I'd never let you sink."

"No, you wouldn't. So, tell me what you want, and I'll make it happen."

"You want a list," she asked on a laugh.

He stood and closed the distance between them without actually touching her. Somehow, that smart remark made him feel better.

"That would be very convenient. I could mark them off one by one until I had you."

"Oh, Brody. You have me." She stepped to him and put her arms around his neck, her body pressed down the length of him. She smelled like flowers and citrus. Warm and pliant in his arms, he drew her even closer with his hands at her lower back. His whole body woke up to her. His hard cock was painful against the fly of his jeans.

"I never thanked you for what you did last night," he said, kissing her temple, inhaling her sweet scent.

"I think I should thank you." She nibbled at his lips with each of her words. "Once, twice, and again, four times, five."

His laugh burst free when he tried to keep a straight face. "You're a couple up on me, but I guess I owe you."

"Big time," she agreed, pulling him close and kissing his neck.

He tightened his hold on her hips and rocked his erection into the V of her thighs. Not good. That made the throbbing worse. He wanted to strip her bare and bury himself in her right here on the kitchen floor.

Serious again, he stopped playing and waited for her eyes to meet his. "I meant the way you brought me out of the nightmare last night."

"Oh well, that was my pleasure," she purred.

He grabbed her shoulders and held her. Completely serious, he refused to let her joke away the significance of what she'd done for him.

"I mean it, Rain. Every night I lay down knowing what's waiting for me in the dark. Most nights, I'm lucky to get a couple hours of sleep, which makes the anxiety that much harder to control. Having you with me last night . . . you not only chased away the dream, you made me forget it entirely. Though we didn't get a lot of sleep last night, it was the best sleep I've gotten in months. Even when I was overseas, it was hard to get more than a few hours of sleep sometimes, but I never could rest. This morning when I woke up . . . I felt better."

Her hand lay over his heart and he took in the comfort of it. Sometimes when he came back in from a dangerous mission, hopped up on adrenaline and a good healthy dose of waning fear, he'd sit among his men and pretend he could feel her hand over his heart, her love magically seeping into him. Two minutes of that and he could breathe easy again, put the mission out of his mind and fill it with images and memories of Rain.

"Brody, you're having a difficult time adjusting. We haven't really had time to talk about what happened to you, the things you saw and did. We'll need to soon, because I need to know how I can help you."

"You help me just by being with me." That didn't seem to take the troubled look out of her eyes. "You're worried about me."

"Of course I am."

"You're concerned about me being around the girls, that I might . . . that something might happen."

"I told them if something happened, where you weren't responding to them, or acted strangely, they should get me or Owen immediately."

"What if you're not around?"

"I told them to stay away from you, but watch you to make sure you didn't hurt yourself."

"Great. What mom has to tell her kids to stay away from their father because he's lost his mind?"

She grabbed the front of his T-shirt with both hands and shook him.

"You listen to me, I don't want to hear you talk like that. Not to me and not to the girls. You haven't lost your mind. You've been through a series of traumatic events. You've been shot and cut up and nearly died in an explosion." The last was said at the top of her lungs.

Tears ran down her cheeks, stunning him. Her hands shook against his chest. For the first time, he realized she'd been here, probably hoping and praying she didn't have to tell their girls their father was dead, and they'd never get to meet him.

He pulled her close, wrapped her in his arms, and laid his cheek on her head. "Sssh, sweetheart. It's okay. I'm fine. Nothing's wrong that won't get better," he assured her.

Oddly, he believed it himself, because he had Rain. He wanted to be well for her, Autumn, and Dawn. He'd do anything to never see the look in Rain's eyes he saw when they'd been walking out of the pizza parlor. He'd scared her then, too.

"I thought you were going to die," she sobbed.

"Ah, Rain. No way I'd leave you thinking I'm a complete bastard. You're the reason I put myself through that grueling rehab day in and day out. My military career is over. I'm staying here with you."

Rain had a lot of pent-up emotions. He'd been wrong about what she'd been holding inside. He should have known the things that bothered her the most about the past had nothing to do with her. As always, her concerns were for him. Always, everyone else in Rain's life came first. He needed to do something to show her how much he appreciated her.

Chapter Twenty-Three

OWEN ENTERED THE kitchen and cleared his throat to get their attention. Brody kissed Rain, long and deep, telling her with his mouth how precious she was to him. Owen clicked open his briefcase behind them. He hated to let her go, but he had to . . . for now. He ended the kiss with a brush of his lips over hers. Her eyes still closed, he swept his thumbs over her cheeks, taking away the drying tears.

"I love you," he whispered.

"You've said that more to me in the last few days than you ever did in the past."

"I took you for granted. Let's face it, you carried the bulk of the relationship while I sat back and figured we were together, what more did you want. It took me leaving to realize the reason I believed you wouldn't forgive what I did was because I hadn't done enough, loved you well enough, to give you a reason to want to forgive me."

"You know that's not true. I always knew you loved

me. That's why it was so hard to believe you'd throw it all away for her."

"Not for her. The reasons are too stupid to go over again. This time, I'm not taking anything for granted. If I do, I want you to tell me. I want to make you happy, Rain."

"To that end"—Owen drew their attention—"how about we discuss how to eliminate a very big threat."

They made their way to the table. Brody smiled when Rain took a second to peek into the living room to check on the girls. Engrossed in their show, neither paid attention to the adults about to discuss something that could change all their lives.

Rain sat next to him. Because she was close, he smoothed his hand down her thigh and rested it on her knee.

"Okay, guys, tell me what you've been plotting behind my back." Rain's eyes fell on him and moved over to rest on Owen. "You guys look so guilty. Come on, tell me what you're thinking."

"We all agree she wants to get paid," Brody said.

"How much will you give that bitch?"

"As little as possible and still get her to give me what we want," he answered.

Owen placed a document on the table in front of them. "I've drawn up these papers. If you can get Roxy to sign them, they state she relinquishes her parental rights to Autumn. This document will open the door for Rain to adopt Autumn officially." Owen took out another document. "If Brody can get her to sign, these are the adoption papers for you to sign, Rain. We'll have a court date, and a judge will make the adoption official. I don't think we'll have any trouble convincing a judge you're the best mother for Autumn. We have all the proof and documentation you've raised her since she was a baby."

"Wait. I can adopt her even though we aren't married?"

Brody's chest went tight. Nothing in that question indicated she had any intention she planned to marry him. If she'd just said, married *yet*.

"You adopting Autumn isn't contingent on our getting married. You're her mother. Adopting her will give you parental rights. No one can take her from you. It will also give Autumn a sense of permanence and safety knowing she's yours forever."

"Without my marrying you," Rain said again.

"Yes," he said irritably.

"You said you wanted to get married."

Brody slammed his hand on the table, frustrated and short-tempered when it came to this.

"Damnit, Rain. You don't have to marry me just for the sake of the kids. I want you to be my wife because it's what you want, not so you can have a piece of paper and a judge say what's already true. You're Autumn's mother. We'll make it legal, whether you marry me or not."

He ground the heels of his hands into his eye sockets and tried to relax and believe his plans would all work out in the end.

"Brody, I was just surprised. I figured you'd make Roxy give you permanent custody and you and I would raise the girls together."

"As husband and wife, or co-parents?"

"You keep talking about us getting married, but you never actually asked me to marry you."

He opened his mouth to ask her. If that's all it would take, fine. Easy. She slapped her hand over his mouth before he got a single word out. Inches away from his face, her eyes burned a hole into him.

"Don't you think after everything that's happened between us I deserve to be asked properly? Shouldn't we have something special, something we do right? We shared one night, made a baby together, and then you were gone. I went through labor and delivery with my father by my side, but not the father of my baby. Can't we do something the normal way for a change?"

He pulled her hand away, so he could answer with more than a nod of his head. "Okay, okay. I get it. You're right. I'm a jerk."

"Sometimes," she agreed, but with little sting behind it. "Slow down, Brody. Take a breath. I've been in this house my whole life. I'm not going anywhere."

"I'm sorry."

"Nothing to be sorry about. It's kind of nice to know you want to marry me that bad."

"In the worst way," he confirmed, and cocked up one side of his mouth in a lopsided grin.

Owen drew them back to the main topic. "So, once we have her signature on these papers, Roxy has no legal right to Autumn. If she takes her again, it will be kidnapping."

"How will you boys get her to sign those papers?"

"Money," Brody answered, but never really looked at her. He didn't want to involve her in the dirty details right now. He had a couple of ideas. The last one depended on Rain and was absolutely a last resort. No matter what, he'd keep his family safe.

"The money alone won't do it. A one-time payment won't be enough, not once she discovers how much you're worth."

"I'm hoping she won't find that out until it's too late."

"You're underestimating her. She's a manipulative, self-serving bitch. She's looking for the big score. She'll lie, cheat, and steal to get what she wants. She may even try to seduce you again."

"Nothing she says or does will ever make me leave you. I promise."

Brody kissed her on the mouth, slipped his tongue past her sweet lips and tasted her. His tongue glided over hers and she gave herself over to the kiss and the slow, intimate pace he set. He wanted her to feel they had all the time in the world. No reason to hurry, they could just exist in this moment. He ended the kiss nibbling at her lips a few times. His face inches from hers, he smiled at the dreamy look in her eyes.

"Owen, why don't you show Rain how serious I am about staying and making her a part of my life."

Owen slid the papers to him and he set them in front of Rain. Sorting through several documents, he found the one he wanted to begin with. "This is my new will. As it stands now, I've left the girls everything, except for a large sum of money for you. Enough for you to live more than comfortably on for the rest of your life. You'll be the trustee for the girls, until they're of age. At which time, they'll receive portions of my estate in increments at age eighteen, twenty-five, thirty, and when they turn sixty."

"You didn't want them to be spoiled trust-fund babies," Rain said with a huge smile.

"I didn't want them to blow it all before they turned thirty." He laughed with her. It felt good to talk to her like this. The tension of moments ago gone after that sexy-as-hell kiss they'd shared.

"Okay, these papers we'll sign if we get married . . ."

"When," she said, and it took him a second to get her meaning.

The air squeezed out of his lungs in a gust.

"You have no idea what that means to me."

Her hand came up to rest on his shoulder, her fingers lightly tracing back and forth over his neck.

"These papers change the will if we get married. You'll then get the bulk of the estate and the girls will have trust funds that will pay out lump sums on the birthdays I said before, but the trust should grow and last their lifetimes. These last papers are the most important to you. If for any reason you and I don't stay married before the girls turn eighteen, you'll not only get a large settlement and my estate will go to the girls, but you will retain custody of the girls, and I'll be granted visitation rights. Mostly weekends, a couple weeks in the summer, and we'll swap holidays from year to year."

"It makes me very sad you had those papers drawn up."

"They're to protect you and Brody both," Owen tried

to explain. "If you divorce, you won't be entitled to the bulk of his estate."

"But I take his girls away from him."

"No. They stay with the mother who's raised them their whole life. I promised you I'd never take them from you. This is your guarantee."

"I only needed your word."

"I wish that were true."

She meant it, but deep down she was relieved to have the papers spelling it out.

"You've lived in fear, believing at any moment Roxy or I could show up and take the girls away. Once I get Roxy to relinquish her rights to Autumn, you'll never have to worry again. She'll be yours legally, and after we get married, if you divorce me, she'll stay with you."

"If *I* divorce you?" Rain's eyebrow went up and she frowned.

"If you marry me, as far as I'm concerned, it's forever." He shrugged his shoulders. "Hell, even if you don't marry me, it's you and me forever. No one else wants a guy who's crazy about another woman."

"You're crazy about me?"

"Crazy, stupid. Head over heels. Desperately, hopelessly, one hundred percent in love with you."

Owen stuck his index finger in his mouth and made a gagging sound. "You two are making me sick. Go back to yelling at him, Rain. I like that better." Owen tried, but couldn't hold back the laugh. "Okay, the paperwork is done. I'll hold on to it until you get married. Brody, you hold on to the papers for Roxy to sign."

"What if she doesn't sign them and wants to go to court?" Rain asked.

Owen took a thick file out of his briefcase. Brody hadn't seen it before, but he was interested in the stack of papers inside.

"We have enough evidence to show you've been caring for Autumn since she was born. You've taken on the expenses to clothe, feed, and shelter her. You've paid for all her medical and dental expenses. We have the ER and psychiatrist's reports for the one and only time Roxy saw Autumn four years ago. She's never called to check on Autumn, gone to a parent-teacher conference, seen her play ball, sent her a birthday or Christmas gift."

"Well, I feel like shit. Thanks for that overview," Brody said irritably.

Owen laughed and slapped Brody on the shoulder. "You didn't know you had a daughter. Roxy did, and still she didn't do a thing for her."

"Except terrorize her for three days."

"My point is that we have a lot of evidence that shows Rain has been her one and only parent for the last seven years. Brody will back you up."

"What if she says I stole Autumn from her?"

Owen smiled and cocked his head to the side. "Rain," he said at length, "everyone knows you've had Autumn since she was a newborn. Roxy never filed a police report that you'd stolen Autumn. There's nothing she can say that will reflect badly on you. Autumn is proof you've been an exceptional parent."

"The judge might not like the fact I bought her."

"Roxy will have to prove you did. Besides, the judge would toss her in jail for admitting she sold her child to you, so that's in our favor, too. When we hear Roxy's in town, Brody will go and speak to her."

"Actually, I thought I'd head her off at the pass and go down to the bar and leave her my card with my cell number. Let her come to me."

"Then what will you do?"

"Find out exactly what she wants. Once we know that, I'll know how to proceed. The goal is to get her to sign the papers for as little money as possible."

"What if she wants more than you're willing to pay?" Rain asked nervously.

"I imagine there'll be a whole lot of arguing back and forth. If she refuses to make a deal, I have another plan, but it's a last resort. If it comes to that, you and I will have a serious talk about how far we're willing to go to keep Autumn away from Roxy."

"All the way," Rain responded. "Whatever it takes."

"That's my girl." Brody squeezed her hand on the table.

Owen put all the papers away and snapped his brief-case closed. "I'll meet you two down at the ball field in half an hour."

"We'll see you there." Owen gave her a kiss on the head before he left the kitchen, saying goodbye to the girls on his way out.

"You never said what plan B is."

"We'll talk about it if it comes to that. It's a wild idea,

but it may be the only option, depending on how far Roxy is willing to take things."

"She doesn't give up easily."

"I don't back down and I never give up," Brody said. "Look how I'm wearing you down." He pulled her out of her seat and into his lap. His lips were a breath away when Dawn's voice intruded and he smiled at Rain instead of kissing her.

"Mom. We need to get ready to go."

"You and Autumn go upstairs and put on your uniforms."

"Dad, are you coming to the game?"

"Absolutely," he said over his shoulder.

"Mom, why are you sitting on Dad? You might hurt his leg."

Brody's heart warmed at his daughter's concern. "I wanted to hug her," he explained. "She's not hurting me at all."

Dawn's arms wrapped around his neck from behind, her chin rested on his shoulder. Tears filled Rain's eyes in front of him. "I'm glad you're home, Dad."

Brody turned to her and kissed her on the head. "Thank you, baby girl. There's no place I'd rather be."

Rain brushed her hand over Dawn's head, leaned down, and kissed her. "Go get ready," she said softly.

The girls pounded up the stairs to their room. He pulled Rain against him and hugged her fiercely. "I missed so much. Every time I'm with them, I realize more and more how different things could have been if I'd been here with all of you."

"You're here now. That's all that matters."

"I'll make things up to you. We'll take care of Roxy and have the life we want. I promise."

Brody hoped he wasn't making promises he couldn't keep. He could make a good life with Rain and the girls, but Roxy was an unknown at the moment. If she didn't sign the papers, that changed the game considerably. He'd have to resort to drastic measures, and that meant the life he wanted with Rain and the girls . . . well, it didn't bear thinking about.

Chapter Twenty-Four

RAIN DROVE DOWN the long driveway toward the cabin amazed at how much progress the contractors had made in only a week. They'd have to stop calling the place a cabin. She'd seen the plans, but seeing the size of the foundation up close was something else entirely. The place was huge. With all the trucks, equipment, and noise, no wonder Brody had decided to move in with her and the girls. Not that he'd had any intention of not staying with her. He'd told Owen they'd slept together and would from now on. He wasn't kidding.

After the softball game last Saturday, he came back to the house with them, the girls excited about their win. Brody barbecued and Pop and Owen joined them for dinner. Autumn remained on guard and quiet, afraid Roxy would show up any minute. When the girls found out Brody was staying, they were both excited, but Autumn seemed mostly relieved. Brody's presence in the house made her feel even safer. As she'd said, it was two against one, them against Roxy.

Rain exited her car and headed for the portion of the cabin still standing as part of the new construction. Jim stood off to the side, talking to some of the men near a cement truck. He waved to her. She entered the main room and found the girls at the kitchen table playing a game on each of their laptops. The noise of construction wasn't much muffled as the side and back walls had been torn down and sheeted with plastic to keep the weather and dust out during construction. Heavy canvas tarps draped over Brody's furniture.

"Mom!" both girls shouted.

"Hey, guys. Where's your dad?"

Silence. Neither of them met her eyes. Not a good sign. They'd all seen how Brody could sometimes lapse into silence for long periods, become short-tempered for no reason, and check the locks on the house several times before coming to bed. The girls heard him in the night when a nightmare overtook him and he thrashed and yelled in bed. Sometimes she woke him easily, distracted him by making love. Other times, he'd come out of it in a cold sweat and not want her to touch him or be near him. He'd leave the room and sit on the back porch in the cold, until he was calm and under control again. She felt inadequate to help him. It took a couple of days for her to realize that as the days went by without a word or sighting from Roxy, the worse he got.

"Dawn, where is your father?"

"He left."

"Where did he go? His truck is outside."

Dawn looked to Autumn and both girls remained silent. Rain went to them and kneeled by their chairs. "Dawn, you have to tell me what happened. Is he okay?"

"He was acting strange. His hands were shaking. His face got all red and sweaty. He kept covering his ears."

"Do you know why?"

"Well"—she bit her lip—"they were doing a lot of sawing and hammering. He helped for a while, but then he came in for lunch and the noise bothered him."

Rain kissed Dawn on the forehead and did the same to Autumn. "Where did he go?"

"He walked off toward the trees, past the lake."

"Okay. You two stay here. I'll be back soon."

"Mom?" Autumn's small voice stopped her. Her big, pleading eyes nearly made her stay. She hated to leave the girls when they were scared for their father.

"He'll be fine, honey. We need to give him time to heal. The bad things in his mind aren't like a cut through the skin. The mind doesn't heal as quickly. Autumn, you know how it feels to have something terrible in your head and you can't make it go away. At first, it was real hard for you to forget, but over time, you could forget for long periods of time, and not think about it all the time. Your dad is still thinking about the war and what happened. The few hours he's able to put it aside and not think about it will change to days and weeks and months, until one day he'll think about it again and it won't hurt him so much."

"Hugging you makes him feel better. His face changes

when he kisses and hugs you. He's not so sad and upset. He smiles," Autumn said.

"He needs me and you and Dawn to remind him of good things."

"He only checked the locks and out the windows three times last night," Dawn said, hopeful that was a good sign.

"He had to live his life for a long time watching for the enemy, making sure no one snuck up on him and his team of soldiers. It's very hard for your dad to stop a habit like that. It's become a part of who he is."

"That will get better, too," Autumn said, because she too had spent many nights checking to make sure the door was locked, the nightlight was on, and no one was hiding in the closet or under her bed. Rain remembered those nights and Autumn's irrational fears. In those moments, Rain knew those fears were very real for Autumn. Just like Brody's fears were real for him. Sometimes too real.

"Yes, honey. There have been a lot of changes in Brody's life lately. All the changes have made it hard for him to settle. But he will, with our help."

Both of them looked reassured. Autumn's eyes didn't look quite so fearful. "I'll be back shortly. If you need anything, Jim is right outside. Do not leave the cabin until I get back unless it's an emergency. A lot of men and trucks are outside. You could get hurt if you, or they, aren't paying attention."

Rain got the nods of agreement she expected and both girls turned back to their games.

She waited on the porch while her eyes adjusted to

the bright sunlight overhead. Jim ended his conversation with another man and headed her way. She met him halfway.

"Brody took off about fifteen, twenty minutes ago. He looked a little worse for wear. Told me to keep my eye on the girls, make sure Roxy didn't show up and try to take Autumn. Said you'd be by soon. Everything all right?"

"The war," she said by way of explanation. "All the noise gets to him sometimes."

Jim nodded, placed his hands on his hips and stared at his boots. "I have a cousin who served a tour a few years back. I swear when he came home, he was an entirely different person."

"Thanks for understanding. I'd appreciate it if you'd keep this between us. If people started talking, well, it would only make things harder for Brody."

"You got it. Brody's a good man. This project is a real good opportunity for me and my guys. I know he wants it done fast, but we'll do it right. He's a real hero and deserves the best, and that's what we'll give him. And you. He sure does talk about you an awful lot. The two of you look real good together. Especially when you're with the girls. It can't have been easy for you to do it on your own."

"No, not easy, but my pleasure all the same. We're happy he's home."

Not wanting to waste another minute away from Brody, afraid of what condition she might find him in, she asked, "Which way did he go?"

Jim pointed to the trees off to the left of the lake. "He

headed that way, straight into the trees. I'll keep a real close eye on the girls until you get back."

"Thanks, Jim. We'll be back soon."

"No problem. Hey, in a couple of days, we'll have some walls up. Then, you'll really be able to see the layout of the place."

"Can't wait," she called, and headed toward the trees and Brody.

Chapter Twenty-Five

RAIN ENTERED THE tree line and tried to maintain a straight course. Unable to spot Brody's tracks in the dead leaves and brush, she went forward on instinct, sidestepping trees and saplings, something inside her zeroing in on Brody's location. The trees weren't dense, but she was suddenly surprised to reach a small clearing. Shade dappled green grass and wildflowers carpeted the oval. Butterflies flitted from one flower to the next. A soft breeze ruffled the leaves overhead. Beautiful, this little piece of heaven was quiet and serene. And across the short distance sat Brody, his back to a tree, knees up, hands and arms covering his head. Desolate.

She didn't want to startle him, so she walked to him without trying to conceal her presence. When she was only a few feet away, he put his hand up to make her stop, but he never looked up at her. She didn't stop, but hunched down in front of him and put both hands on his head, his hair sliding between her fingers.

Her touch was all it took for Brody to come to life. Rolling forward, he wrapped one arm around her back and took her mouth in a fierce kiss. She landed, him on top of her, in the soft, sweet-smelling grass. The branches overhead softened the sunlight streaming down on them. Brody was hard and heavy covering her. In a frantic need, he peeled away clothes and tossed them aside. His mouth never left hers, except when he ripped her lavender shirt over her head. He pushed a frustrated growl through his teeth when he sat back on his heels and not so gently ripped her jeans, underwear and all, down her legs.

Giving in to his speed and demand, she reared up, grabbed the back of his black T-shirt and hauled it over his head. She went for the button on his jeans. Too much in a hurry to have her, he took over and pushed his jeans down his thighs. His flat palm latched on to her breast as he shoved her back to the ground. His other hand clamped on to her thigh and pushed it wide. Two of his fingers plunged inside of her, deep. He pulled them out and slicked the wetness over the soft folds of her entrance. Not foreplay, but a concession to not hurting her in his desire to be inside her this second. Now.

The thick head of his penis nudged her entrance, and he thrust hard and deep, his breath coming out harsh against her neck. Pulling back, his mouth clamped on to her hard nipple. He suckled and nipped and licked. Her back arched and her fingers dug into his shoulders as he left one breast for another in an all-out assault on her body. The more she responded, the hungrier and more demanding he became. She panted and moaned, her body heated to Brody's touch. They'd never been like this together. Brody had never been this out of control, driving into her again and again. She loved the way they made love together, but this was altogether different. Primal. She let herself go. Gave herself over to Brody without reservation. Relished his possession of her body.

Brody clamped his hands over her hips, pulled himself back on his heels, his knees widespread. Her shoulders were still on the ground, her breasts bouncing with every thrust of Brody's hard cock into her as he pulled her hips to his, her legs lying over his thighs and wrapped around his back.

His intense gaze skimmed over her face to her bouncing breasts. One big hand took possession, squeezing the round orb. He clamped her nipple between two fingers and squeezed, plucking at the swollen flesh. She arched into his touch and moaned. His hand slid down her belly, fingers splayed wide to touch as much of her as possible. His thumb found her sweet spot where they were joined and ruthlessly rubbed over the nub, his hips grinded against hers. Heat flared and her body tightened around him. The building explosion gathered energy. Ready to detonate, his harsh voice demanded, "Give it to me, Rain."

Fingers digging into his calves, she had no choice. Her body exploded in an intense orgasm. Brody stilled, his teeth clamped shut, the muscles in his jaw working. He released a feral sound deep in his throat, holding back his own release.

Her body relaxed, but he didn't let her settle. With another hard, deep thrust, he brought her body back to the brink. Eyes locked with hers, something powerful in their depths. His jaw hard, he demanded, "Again."

"Brody." She reached up to his chest to soothe him, but he didn't let her touch him. Instead he repeated the order. "Again." His hands digging into her thighs, he pulled her hips to his and grinded against her. Heat, lust, pure passion raced through her again. She grabbed both his forearms and used them as leverage to maneuver her body against his. He groaned as she shifted her hips to take him deeper, create a delicious friction as her body slid against his.

Breathing hard, panting out moans, she gave herself over to Brody's dominance and jumped over the edge, her body locking around his in wave upon wave of contractions.

"Brody." She called him to join her, but he stilled, waited for her back to lie flat against the ground as he watched her. A self-satisfied look came over him, but he didn't smile. His face still hard and impassive, he adjusted their position enough to lean down and lick the underside of her breast in one long sweep of his tongue. His teeth toyed with her tight nipple before his hot mouth clamped down and suckled hard. She moaned and rubbed her hands over his shoulders, up his neck and over his head, holding him to her as he feasted.

His hands slid around from her bottom, over her skin, to the underside of her thighs as his body moved over hers. He spread her thighs wide, his hips seated between them, his cock pressed deep inside her, full and thick and heavy. He mapped a trail of wet kisses up her chest and neck until his teeth bit into her earlobe. His breath was hot against her ear.

"Again."

With her legs spread wide, he pulled out and thrust hard. This time, she gripped his hips and pulled him to her again and again. Without mercy, they went at each other in a ferocious battle of lovemaking. He growled something fierce at her ear. His teeth bit into her flesh where her shoulder met her neck. He soothed the small hurt with his tongue, sliding over and over the spot, his lips nipping the sensitive skin. Her head turned away as he licked the column of her throat and kissed his way back down.

A subtle change came over him. Unable to hold back now, he drilled into her. His hand clamped over her knee, drew her leg up, tilting her hips to him even more. She matched the angle with her other leg and met his every thrust, pressing up to him. Her body vibrated, heat pooled low in her belly again. The orgasm came over her in a blazing fire radiating out to her toes and head. Brody thrust again and again as her body contracted around his. With a guttural shout, he emptied himself, his cock pulsing, spilling his seed deep inside her.

Brody's harsh grunt scattered several birds from the trees. He collapsed on top of her. Both of them breathed hard and heavy. Time passed in silence, their breathing evened out, and Brody moved down to rest his head on her breast, his mouth and chin nestled against the other.

Her hands lay on his strong shoulders. She savored the feel of his hard, lean body lying down the length of hers. For the first time, she realized Brody's jeans were bunched at his ankles. Her feet were hooked over his calves, her toes brushing the material.

The grass smelled sweet, crushed beneath them, soft beneath her back and bottom. She could lay here all day with Brody in her arms, the sun on her face, her body sated, and her heart full of love.

Brody's silence didn't bother her. He needed time. Right now, they had all the time in the world.

"Fuck."

Brody planted his hands on either side of her and levered himself up.

"Again," she teased, her lips turning up into a soft smile.

He stared down at the raw, red marks on her breasts where his beard stubble had grazed her soft skin. A red mark at the base of her neck would turn into a bruise. He drew away from her. Her hands slid down his arms and landed limply on her ribs, her thumbs just under her pretty pink-tipped breasts. So lush and full, so sweet to taste. He held back a groan and made himself sit back, away from all that tempting skin. No use, he couldn't stop looking at her. Eyes closed, face soft, her cheeks rosy, lips kiss-swollen. A long expanse of creamy skin, marred by stubble rash, red against the white of her skin. He skimmed over her flat belly to the wet, glistening thatch of curls at the top of her widespread thighs. His eyes feasted on her sex, the way her legs lay soft and supple spread around him. He wanted to have her again, but as enticing a picture as she made, he couldn't get over the red marks on her hips and thighs from his fingers digging into her skin.

He opened his mouth to apologize profusely, beg her forgiveness for treating her so poorly. Her words stopped him.

"Promise me, Brody, we'll do that again someday soon."

She stretched lazily in the grass and tiny flowers, her arms up over her head. She went lax in the sun again. God, she was beautiful. Relaxed, completely at ease with him staring down at her.

He opened his mouth to say something, but closed it because he wasn't sure what to say. He went with what he'd felt for the last hour when his mind turned on him and he'd left his daughters in the cabin, unable to trust himself around them.

"I knew you'd come," he began.

Her bright smile took him off guard. "Several times," she teased him again.

She had to know he'd been out of his mind when he'd come out here. Why wasn't she angry with him for treating her the way he had, pushing her to her back, stripping her bare in the middle of the woods, grabbing and bruising her . . . Oh God, driving himself into her again and again until she moaned his name over and over. The best sex ever. Hands down. She'd brought him out of hell again and shown him heaven. What had he done, betrayed her trust. He couldn't control his baser needs when he was near her and feeling so foul and dark all he wanted to do was touch some of her goodness, take it into him and shine with a bit of the light inside of her.

He bent forward and rested his forehead on her belly at her navel. "I'm sorry. I'm sorry, I'm sorry, I'm sorry."

Her hands slid into his hair and she combed her fingers over his scalp. "Brody, honey, it's okay. Everything is okay."

"No. It's not." He shook his head back and forth on her belly and sat back and looked her in the eyes. She deserved that much from him.

"I came out here to escape the noise, but I couldn't escape myself. I left the girls behind."

"You left them at the cabin with Jim and a dozen other men watching out for them."

"I shouldn't have left them at all. Roxy could be anywhere."

"True, but there's no way she'd get within a hundred feet of the house without being seen by one of the guys."

"I yelled at Autumn when she spilled juice on the table next to her computer."

"She should be more careful."

"Damnit, I can buy her another one if she dumps the whole glass on it and shorts it out. That isn't the point."

"What is the point, Brody? You got upset because she spilled juice. Believe me, I've yelled at both of them for a lot less. Some days, I have endless patience for them, others, I'm on a short fuse."

"I used to be mellow."

"You were wild," she countered, not deterring him one bit. "You'd pick a fight because you wanted one."

"Damn right. I was in control. I chose. Now . . ."

"You're under a great deal of stress. You've come home to find yourself the father of two children by two different women, you're building a house the size of Texas, you're working long distance and helping with the house, trying to be there for me and the girls. You're recovering from a severe injury, you're in constant pain, and your mind sometimes thinks there are snipers on the roofs. You have nightmares, which make it impossible for you to sleep. Being tired makes your anxiety worse and you become grumpy and short-tempered. A good bout of sex among the trees and forest creatures should have relaxed you and made you feel like me, completely satisfied and smug. Instead, you're trying to make me mad at you for something that isn't your fault."

"I didn't use anything," he said bluntly.

He placed his hand over her stomach, imagined her belly swelling with his child. Shouldn't he feel more penitent for taking her again without a thought to the consequences? She'd asked him for time. Settle things with Roxy, build the house, be together and get to know each other again. But no. He had to move into her house not even a week after seeing her again. He had to take her in the damn grass, in the wide open, demanding she give him everything. Again, and again, and again.

"While your timing in these things is incredibly accurate, we'll see what happens."

"We'll see what happens." His voice might have gone up an octave there at the end. He was too completely taken off guard by her casual words. She knew he hadn't used anything. When? Before he slammed into her? After?

"Spilled milk." She rose up to lean on her elbows, her arms lying down her sides in the grass.

"What?"

"Spilled milk. Spilled juice. Either way, there's no reason to get upset."

"This isn't something we can wipe up with a paper towel and toss in the trash like it never happened." He stood, pulled up his jeans to his hips and zipped before he tripped himself, and paced away from her and then back. "How can you be so calm about this? You told me you wanted to wait. Take things slow. Since the first time we made love when I came back, you counted on me to supply the condoms and use them."

She sat up and wrapped her arms around her up-drawn knees. "Who said it was your sole responsibility? I could have said, hey, Brody, don't forget the condom."

"I didn't exactly give you a chance to say anything."

"That's it." Rain bent her head and combed her fingers through both sides of her hair to the back of her head and gripped her fingers into a fist. It had to hurt to pull her hair like that, which told him he'd pissed her off good this time. She finally understood what this romp in the grass could mean. He'd pushed her too far this time.

She rolled up to her feet, naked and gloriously furious. Nothing compared to Rain in a rage.

"You can't control the way the images in your head take over your mind, but you can sure as hell control the crap that comes out of your mouth."

She jabbed him in the gut with her fist to get his attention. He sucked in a breath, the muscles in his belly going taut just as her fist connected.

"Since you got here, all you've done is tell me how you want things to be between us. You tell me you love me, make love to me like I'm everything you ever wanted or needed."

"You are," he ground out, just as harshly as her words came at him. She had to believe he loved her, needed her.

"Yet today, after you make love to me like you can't live another second without being close to me, a part of me, you say you're sorry over and over. For what? Loving me. Needing me. Wanting me beyond all thought. Why couldn't you just lay in the grass, savor the moment with me, tell me how much you love me? Why couldn't you say, 'I got so caught up in my need for you, I forgot the condom. We didn't plan this, but if you're pregnant, I'll be the happiest man in the world.'

"Can't you find it in you to see the good? We shared something wonderful. We might be gifted something amazing. Couldn't you find the words to match what your body shows me every time we come together?

"Instead, you want to apologize for something I'm not even mad about. You want me to be angry and punish you. For what? A past that's over and done and can't be changed. I've told you numerous times, I forgive you, Brody. I wish you could forgive yourself."

They stood for a moment staring at each other. He didn't know what to say. Everything she said was true. He hadn't forgiven himself. He always seemed to be waiting for her to turn on him, tell him to get the hell out of her life, and he could never see his kids again. If he kept this up, that's exactly what she might do.

He reached out and cupped the back of her head, drawing her to him slowly, his mouth descending to cover hers in a soft, slow kiss. One turned into two, turned into many as she melted against him. One hand buried in her hair, the other splayed over her lower back, pulling her close.

He kissed her lips one last time, her cheek, her forehead, her nose. He cupped her face and turned it up to his. "I am the luckiest man alive, because you love me. I love you so much, and if we made a baby, I swear to you, I'll be by your side through everything. Nothing in this world would make me happier than for us to have another baby."

"Better," she said. The smile on her lips didn't quite meet her eyes. He'd ruined the moment and making up for it at her demand wasn't quite what she had in mind.

"I can't seem to talk to you the way I used to."

"Yes, you used to be such a charmer. Sweet-talking me was one of your favorite pastimes."

"I can't get past what I did to you. I want to make things right so bad, but all I do is make a mess of it."

"Not true. You love me and want to have everything perfect. Right now. You seem to think that if I marry you and we live together that will somehow erase all the years between. It's not like that, Brody. As far as I'm concerned, we're starting from here. I love you. I want to be with you. I will marry you. Settle into that. Take it in and live with it for a while. Enjoy the newness of being together again, discovering the changes in both of us, and the luck and wonder that the love between us is deeper, stronger. That's what I'm doing."

"You're amazing. I guess I've been trying so hard to hold on to you, I'm crushing you."

"A little bit. Being out here with you was like being teenagers again with no worries. Sneaking off into the woods, making love in the grass under the trees. For a little while there, you weren't thinking about anything but me and you. Try to do that more."

"I will. Your way of looking at things is a hell of a lot better than mine these days."

Rain stepped away and gathered her scattered clothes. He couldn't help himself: he stared at her ass as she bent over to pick up her jeans. His eyes fell on her breasts, slid lower to her flat belly. Yeah, he'd be the happiest man in the world if he'd gotten her pregnant.

His eyes remained glued on her as she shimmied her panties up her thighs to hug her hips. She pulled her jeans up her legs and fastened them. Bra in place, cupping her breasts, rounding them over the lace edge, she walked to him and stopped when they were mere inches apart. Her hand went to his bare chest over his heart.

"What is it?" she asked, understanding he still had more on his mind.

"I don't want to screw up what we have because of what's wrong with me. I want to be a good father. I don't want the girls to be afraid of me."

"They aren't."

"Sometimes they are." He had counseling while he was in the hospital, but he'd been so focused on his physical injuries, his mind was the least of his worries. Now, it was interfering with his life and his family.

"They understand."

"That doesn't change the fact I left them at the cabin because I couldn't cope, was afraid I'd do or say something that would harm them."

"You'd never hurt them, Brody."

"I hurt you." He touched her healed arm, the bruise he'd left on her neck today, traced his finger over the stubble rash he'd left across her breasts, and she flinched. "I love you so much. The thought of hurting you makes me sick."

He put his hand over hers on his chest. "I did some research and found a doctor who specializes in post-traumatic stress disorder. He's ex-military. His office is three hours away, but he's willing to do sessions via webcam. I'll drive to his office twice a month. He comes highly recommended. His credentials are impeccable."

"Brody, that's great. You need someone to talk to about what happened to you overseas. I've tried to help you in my own way, but it isn't enough. I see you suffering and it kills me. I hoped that when you settled in with us at the house you'd relax, feel safe and protected with us surrounding you. But you don't, Brody. You're getting worse."

"I hope this guy can help me, but if he can't, I'll find someone else."

"Whatever you need, Brody, whatever it takes. I support you. I'm here for you."

"I feel like I'm enduring life, instead of really living it with you and the girls. I want to experience everything with you without all this anxiety and stress underlying everything I do."

"I just want you to be well and whole."

"I know you do, sweetheart. I want that, too, so I can be the best man I can be for you and the girls. To that end, I've also set up a schedule with a physical therapist at the hospital. I've been doing all my exercises, but I need help with some of the movements. As I get better, he can help me build the strength back in my leg."

The pain and lack of strength frustrated him. He'd do a lot better with a therapist. He'd be able to do more with the girls if he could walk and move better. His mind would take longer than his leg.

He had plans to help make Rain's life easier, more comfortable, but he hadn't followed through. He had a surprise planned for the girls and Rain, something to make up for the years he was gone, but he hadn't done it yet. Why not? Because he couldn't think straight and get from point A to point B without taking several detours. Not anymore. He would follow through with the doctor and therapist, and this week he'd complete his plans for his family.

"This is good, Brody. I'm so glad you're doing what you need to do for yourself. We should get back. Do you know what happened to my shirt?"

He smiled and searched the area. Her shirt landed several feet away behind a clump of purple wildflowers. He picked it up and plucked a flower from the plant. After she pulled her shirt on, he tucked the flower in her hair at her ear. He kissed her softly. "You're so beautiful. I love you." He held her in his arms and hugged her.

"I love you, too."

With a deep breath and her in his arms, he settled into the moment like she'd asked him to do. The wind rustled the leaves overhead, birds chirped, and the peace and quiet of this place worked its way inside of him.

He took her hand and they walked back to the house. "I like it here. We'll have to come back and make love under the sun again."

"Okay," she replied. That was his Rain. Easygoing, ever ready to be with him again. "Brody?"

"Yeah?"

"I really enjoyed today," she admitted shyly. It went a long way to easing his conscience about the marks he'd left on her.

"Me too. I needed you, and I knew you'd come." He took a deep breath and let it out. "This thing with Roxy is really getting to me. I want it to be over, so we can live our lives without her hanging over our heads."

"I know how you feel. It's the last piece of the past to settle, so we can move on. Clean slate and all."

"Exactly. I wish she'd call, so I can finish it."

He should have known better than to wish Roxy back into his life.

Chapter Twenty-Six

MONDAYS SUCK. AND this Monday particularly sucked. Brody spent half the morning on the phone with his office in Atlanta. His partner insisted they needed him in China in three days. He told them in no uncertain terms, hell no. He had too much going on. More than he could handle, and leaving right now wasn't an option. He made it clear he wouldn't take any trips for the next three months. He needed this time with Rain and the kids. So he spent hours working long distance without having a proper office and supplies, like a fax machine and a secretary to keep track of everything he was supposed to do. Someone who could type faster than his henpecking fingers.

He kept the laptop at the house with him, but he needed his desktop computer at the cabin to retrieve files and put them on the laptop, which prompted his early afternoon jaunt to the cabin where he'd been working for two hours, the sound of progress on the house keeping him from concentrating on his work. He made several mistakes and had to go back and fix them, which made something simple turn into something maddening.

His focus lately wasn't great, but with all the noise, he couldn't seem to keep a single thought in his head for longer than a few minutes. He should have emailed himself the files and gone back to Rain's place to do his work. He pressed the heel of his hand to his eye socket and rubbed. The headache that started this morning pounded away.

Rain left this morning looking tired. His fault. He'd kept her up again last night. He woke her up at some point every night. She needed a break, but every time she sat down for more than five minutes he or one of the girls needed her for something. They'd tried to have a quiet evening last night, but the girls were restless and kept giggling and talking in bed instead of sleeping. Rain must have gotten up four or five times to quiet them down. She missed half the movie they had been trying to watch.

Eli called late that night. Sick, he'd asked Rain to go to the drugstore for some cold medicine. She came back over an hour later, Eli fully medicated, his belly full of canned soup she'd made for him while she was there.

She climbed the stairs with Brody when she returned to the house. In her sluggish daze, it took her nearly as long as it took him on his bad leg. Two hours after getting into bed together, his arms around her while they slept, he woke her up during one of his nightmares. He'd tried to tell her he was sorry, but she didn't want to hear it. She clamped her hand over his mouth, laid her head on his chest, and lay there with him in the night. She didn't go back to sleep until his heart stopped slamming into his ribs and he finally drifted off. She never did.

The girls began the morning fighting over who got the last bowl of fruit O's cereal, only to discover they were out of milk. Dawn settled on cinnamon toast, but Rain used the last of the bread to make the girls' lunches. Tired, frustrated, and on her last nerve, she shoved granola bars into both girls' hands and told them to get in the car. Five minutes after leaving for school, she came back through the door, slammed it, and found Autumn's forgotten backpack. While checking to be sure Autumn's homework was inside, she found a note from the teacher. Autumn had a bad week at school, prompting the teacher to ask for a parent-teacher conference. Rain and he both knew why. Autumn couldn't concentrate, became quiet and withdrawn, not participating in the lessons. Roxy coming home terrified her. She worried something bad was going to happen.

Rain left again, saying, "Your first parent-teacher conference. Welcome to fatherhood."

Great. How could he explain his monumental screw-up was coming back to haunt him? Easy, everyone in town knew Roxy's reputation. The teacher would understand. He should probably tell her to make sure Autumn didn't leave school with anyone but him, Rain, Owen, or Eli.

Trying to concentrate on the email he needed to send to the manufacturing manager in China, he blocked out the hammering and sawing and attached the file with the specifications for the changes they were making to their product. For once able to focus on the task at hand, he hit the SEND button and checked off one item from his list of things to do. He hated this new habit of having to write everything down, but it was necessary.

Reading over his ten new messages in his inbox, he jumped when his cell phone rang for the hundredth time that day. He snagged if off the desk, continued reading an email, and answered absently, "Brody."

"Now, that's the deep, seductive voice I've been missing."

Brody leaned back heavily in his chair, pressed his forearm to his aching forehead, and looked up at the ceiling. "What the fuck do you want?"

"Is that any way to talk to the mother of your child?"

"I speak to Rain with the utmost respect and admiration for being an outstanding mother to my children." After everything she'd done, just the sound of Roxy's voice sent a volcanic burst of rage through his gut.

"I'm Autumn's mother. Not that bitch you're shacking up with."

"Bullshit. Even you don't believe that lie."

"Whatever she told you is a lie."

"You've lost your touch. You used to be better at this kind of thing."

"We need to meet."

"Tell me what you want and let's get this over with, the sooner the better."

"I want to see you. We have things to discuss."

"I don't give a shit what you want, but you're right, we need to talk. Where should we start? With the way you got my father drunk and let him drive home, or how you kidnapped my daughter, starved her, and locked her in a damn closet for three days?"

"I have every right to see my daughter any time I damn well please. Whatever Rain got her to lie about isn't on me. You'd do well not to piss me off. I might not be so agreeable when we meet."

"You've never been agreeable a day in your life."

"I'm at the bar," she hissed, and hung up.

Finally, the moment they'd all been waiting for. Time to set his plan in motion. He stood, but sat again and hit the speed dial on his phone. He wanted to keep Rain out of this, but because of her, Autumn hadn't grown up with that viper.

"Hey, honey, how are you?"

Reassured, he smiled, because just the sound of her voice made him happy. "I'm having one hell of a day, but right now, this minute, I'm good. What are you doing?"

"Rebuilding an engine," she said matter-of-factly. He liked that about her: she took for granted the skills her father taught her from birth. Most women couldn't even change a tire. Her voice kicked into low gear when she asked, "What are you wearing?"

"If you were here with me, it'd be nothing at all."

"Then, I can't wait to see you," she purred, making him smile even more.

"Rain." He put all his emotions into her name. He wanted nothing more than to drive to town, bypass Roxy's bar and go straight to Rain, take her in his arms, strip her bare, and make love to her for the rest of the night.

"What is it, Brody? Is it the visions? Do you need me?"

"I always need you."

"I need you, too. Tell me what's going on. Talk to me."

He took a deep breath and spit it out. "Roxy called. I'm headed down to the bar to talk to her."

"Do you want me to meet you there?"

"No. I think I'll get farther if I go alone. Besides, I'll only have to bail you out of jail after you kill her."

"True. Brody, I'm worried."

"You've taken care of our girls alone for more than seven years. Let me take care of all my girls this time. I promise, I won't let her hurt you or the girls."

"Okay. Will you come straight home when you're done?"

"There's no place I'd rather be." He meant every word.

"Do you have the papers for her to sign?"

"In my truck. Not that I'm confident I'll get her to sign them at this first meeting."

"Why would you have to see her again? Make her the offer and get her to sign."

"Right now, she thinks she's got me by the balls, calling and telling me to come to her. I want to see what she wants. Once I know what her demands are, I can start negotiating."

"Autumn is not on the table."

"No way," he confirmed. "Let me do this, Rain. I'll play it her way at first, get a read on her and what's going on in her life. If she's desperate enough, we might get this done quick."

"What do you want for dinner tonight?"

"You."

"I'm dessert."

She yawned and it reminded him again how little sleep she'd been getting, the stress she was under taking care of all of them, and this thing with Roxy.

"How are you, Rain?"

"I'm fine. Don't forget we're meeting Autumn's teacher before school tomorrow."

"I know. You'd tell me if something was wrong, right?"

"You know why Autumn is upset. Once this mess is cleaned up, she'll get back to normal. We'll help her to feel safe again."

"It'll be over soon, but I was talking about you."

"I'm fine, Brody." His name came out on another yawn. She took care of all of them, but he hadn't done a good job of taking care of her.

"How about I bring home dinner tonight? You can rest until I get home."

"Sounds great."

"I love you."

"I know you do. And, Brody . . ."

"Yeah?"

"Don't let Roxy piss you off again."

"Never again. Are you pregnant?"

She laughed. "How am I supposed to know that already?" she teased, because of his anxious need to know. "Maybe," she conceded. "We won't know for a couple weeks."

The last two nights, they'd made love without using protection. He'd grabbed a condom, but she'd tossed it back on the bedside table.

"Let's make a baby," she said.

"You'll have to marry me, then. I'm not having any more babies with you unless you become my wife."

"You still haven't asked me."

"I will," he said against her throat. He'd joined their bodies in one powerful thrust, all talk of marriage stopped, and the baby-making was his pleasure and hers.

He came back to the conversation, hoping they'd made a baby. "You'll tell me when you know."

"You'll be the first. If I do get pregnant, I'd like to wait to tell the girls."

"We'll tell them the day we get married."

She didn't say anything. After all, he hadn't asked her. Yet.

"I'll see you tonight. Oh, and Brody . . ."

"Yeah?"

"If you get arrested, I'll bail you out."

"You always do, whenever I need you."

Brody checked his watch. They'd been on the phone for twenty minutes. It would take him another twenty to get into town. Roxy should be good and mad, thinking he'd hop to it and drive down to meet her immediately. Calling Rain had been a great idea. He felt better, less anxious, his anger under control.

"Make her sign the papers, even if you have to stand on her neck to do it."

"You're brutal, honey."

"I'm always sweet to you."

"Yeah, you are. I'll see you soon."

After their goodbyes, he tucked his phone in his pocket, transferred the rest of his files, and closed out his email. He'd finish work at Rain's place after dinner.

Before leaving the cabin, he spoke to Jim one last time, noted the perimeter walls were up on the new foundation. The guys had done a fair amount of work that day, and he'd survived their constant pounding and sawing. The construction company putting up the barn and stables would begin next week. Everything was moving along.

The house would be finished in a few months. Long before the baby arrived. He and Rain needed to set a date for their wedding. Soon. First, he'd have to ask her. He knew just what he wanted to do, but before he'd have his wife and family under one roof, he had to take care of his fucked-up past.

She was waiting for him at the bar.

Chapter Twenty-Seven

BRODY PULLED INTO the parking lot of Roxy's bar nearly an hour after she'd called him. The parking lot wasn't full, but several cars lined the front of the two-story building. The neon sign glowed blue; at night it would cast an eerie light over the solid double wood doors with the horseshoe handles. The windows were high and filled with neon beer signs.

Brody checked out the cars in the lot. Some he recognized as the usual crowd. A late-nineties Camero caught his eye. Red. Roxy's favorite car color. The windows were tinted near black. Taking a few steps toward the front end, he noted the Nevada plates. Looks like Roxy was still residing in Las Vegas. Her kind of town. It matched the information Owen dug up on her over the last week.

Just past five on a Monday, the bar wouldn't be very busy until later. Good. Not as many witnesses. Of course, in a small town, his being at the bar with Roxy would spread faster than a phone call crossing the wires all the way to Atlanta.

He thought of Rain and the last time he'd been here. He'd let her find out from someone else how badly he'd screwed up and betrayed her. Not this time. The consequences then had been devastating. Losing Rain and his girls again . . . he'd rather die.

By the time Brody walked the short distance to the door, he was near to being in a rage. Everything Rain told him came back in a rush. He'd have to keep his emotions in check, deal with Roxy without strangling her.

Roxy leaned over a table, giving some guy a full view of her abundant cleavage spilling over a purple tank top. Tightly hugging her tits and body, it outlined every roll in her belly to her hips. The skimpy jean skirt barely covered her wide ass. If she leaned over any further, he and everyone else in the bar would know whether or not she was wearing underwear. He'd lay odds against it. The thought of confirming that suspicion made him cringe. Some things never changed. From her wild mane of reddish-brown hair to her cowboy boots, nothing much had, except she'd put on some weight. He wondered if it was left over from the pregnancy or hard living. When she turned and locked eyes on him, the lines at the corners of her eyes and around her mouth told him she'd been living hard and fast for a while now.

A smile came to her face, despite the predatory look in her eye. He remained passive, not giving anything away. A skill he'd perfected in the military. He waited for her to make the first move. She stood straight, her shoulders back, breasts out, showing off her best feature. Too bad they'd looked a lot better in her younger days.

Rain's image came to mind. Her body still toned and supple. Her breasts high and round. Not overly big, but a nice full handful. Her legs were slim and strong, probably from playing softball with the girls and running around after them all the time. Not a single line marred her pretty face, and when she smiled, she lit up a room.

How could he have ever betrayed her with a woman like Roxy? Because he'd been a monumental jackass. Not anymore. Older, wiser, desperate to keep Rain and his girls, he'd never make a stupid mistake like that again.

Roxy bobbed her head toward the back stairs that led up to her apartment. Without waiting for his acknowledgement, she sauntered to the stairs and started up. He let her go, stood his ground below with his arms crossed over his chest and waited. When she reached the landing, she turned back and her head whipped to him. He gave her a feral smile and tilted his head toward her office door just past the bar. Everyone in the room watched the play-by-play. Brody didn't give in, even when Roxy cocked her hip and waved him to come up. Furious, she stomped down the stairs, crossed in front of the bar, and walked straight to the office. He followed, but took his time about it, not wanting anyone to get the idea he was anxious to see her.

She stood at the entrance and waited for him to draw close before she said for everyone to hear, "Afraid to be alone with me upstairs?"

"No. I came to talk about my daughter, not fuck the local whore."

Smiling inside at her outrage, he walked past her and stood by the desk.

"She's our daughter."

"Autumn belongs to Rain. What are you doing here?"

"Want a beer?"

Brody wasn't deterred, but he'd let her take the lead if it took him where he wanted to go. "No thanks. I don't drink." Not with all the meds he took.

"Rain's got you on a short leash. Too afraid you'll turn out like your old man."

"I'm not like him." So easy to say and believe now that he had some life experience under his belt.

"I heard something about you getting hurt."

"I have a few new scars."

"I heard you're not quite right in the mind."

Brody didn't take the bait. "You called me. What do you want?"

"I want to see my daughter."

"She's not your daughter. Rain bought and paid for her."

"I gave birth to her."

"You sold her," he shouted.

"What was I supposed to do? You left me."

He actually laughed, despite his anger. "Left you. You. Get something straight, Roxy, any guy who'd fuck you while drunk out of his mind isn't thinking about having anything with you past the three minutes he takes to get himself off."

"You're a real cold-hearted bastard."

"You're a cold-hearted bitch, who sold her own child."

"Well, then, we're suited for each other." She reached up to touch his face, but he grabbed her wrist and held tight.

"Don't touch me."

"Oh, come on, sugar. I just wanted to soothe your ruffled feathers. You're looking real fine, Brody."

She fisted her hand and tried to pull away. He didn't let go.

"So much strength. You know you want to throw me up against the door and pound into me until I scream your name."

He flung her hand away. "The only thing I want to do is wrap my hands around your throat and squeeze."

"So much violence and rage. What you need to do is release all that passion, sugar. Rain must be some sorry piece of ass to have you all wound up like this."

"Have you seen her lately?"

She glared and crossed her arms over her middle. Not in a defiant way, but to hide her plumper figure. Yeah, she'd seen Rain, hated her for the way she looked and the life she made for herself despite Roxy's efforts to wreck it.

"God, she's more beautiful now than she was back then."

He leered at her from top to bottom, the look on his face making it clear he found her lacking.

"The two of you looked real cozy after the softball game Saturday. Hard to believe your precious Rain would forgive you for leaving her behind pregnant."

So, she'd been in town long enough to spy on them. He wondered what else she'd been doing, or watching them do.

"She's got a big heart."

"I'll just bet she jumped at the chance to forgive you," Roxy said, baiting him.

Eyes narrowed, he replied, "She loves me more than I deserve."

"Yeah, sure. Your company has nothing to do with it."

"You know about that, too."

"Even I read the paper."

Brody bet she'd heard the news from someone in town. She wasn't one to watch the news, let alone read the paper.

He sat on the corner of the desk, crossed his arms over his chest, and faced off with her. "How's Vegas?"

"Expensive."

"Especially when you've got a boyfriend with a gambling habit, and you both have an aversion to steady work."

"You've done your homework." She took the chair in front of him, her thigh brushing against his leg.

He stood and moved away, looking at some of the open files and papers on the desk. A couple of her suppliers' bills were past due. Her liquor license was up for renewal in a couple months. Interesting.

"Know your enemy," he said vaguely.

"I'm not your enemy," she said, her voice husky. "Well, I don't have to be."

"Let's cut the crap, Roxy. I don't want you as an

enemy. I don't want you in my life, or Autumn's. What do you want?" He enunciated each word to let her know he meant business.

"I want to take Autumn back to Vegas with me. You'll pay me child support, and you can visit her any time you like."

"Not going to happen."

"Why not? I'm her mother."

"You were an incubator. You don't want to be a mother to her."

"That's not true. I never got to be a mother to her."

"Because you sold her. You threatened to end the pregnancy and kill her. You kidnapped her and threw her in a closet. You scared and tortured a three-year-old little girl. The child you gave birth to," he growled.

He stood over her, his face inches from hers. Her eyes were wide, her mouth slightly open. He stood up tall again and took a breath.

"Autumn isn't going anywhere with you. She stays with her mother."

"I'm her mother," Roxy spat out.

"Rain is the only mother she knows. She's the only mother Autumn will ever know."

"You can't keep me from her."

"Yes, I can. I will. Nothing is more important to me than the happiness, safety, and protection of my family."

"I gave birth to your child. You owe me."

"Rain paid you sixty-eight thousand dollars. She's paid to raise Autumn all by herself. You never gave her a dime for food, clothes, her medical and dental expenses, the roof over her head, softball uniforms, birthday and Christmas gifts . . ."

"You didn't either."

"I didn't know I had any children."

"I'll bet you gave Rain a fat paycheck."

"I owed her child support for seven years. Any court would have made me pay."

"I guess I'll have to take you to court then."

"For what? I don't owe you child support. You didn't raise my daughter."

"A judge will give me custody. I'm her mother."

"How will that play out? Will you walk into court and ask a judge for custody after what you did? How will you explain selling Autumn to Rain?"

"I don't have to. She paid me in cash. No records."

"Do you think a judge will take your word over Rain's when she raised Autumn for the last seven years? You never made a single phone call to check on Autumn. Not for a birthday or holiday. You never took her to her first day of school, or picked her up when she was sick. You never sent her a gift, or even a letter. You never sent any child support. Rain can prove she's been with Autumn for everything. She's got albums of pictures. She has receipts for everything she's bought for her. She has an entire town who knows what you did and what it's taken for Rain to raise those girls on her own."

"A judge will side with me because I'm her biological mother. The courts favor the biological parent."

"No way in hell will I ever let that happen. If you take her to court for custody, I have no doubt Autumn will tell the judge she wants to stay with her mother. If that isn't enough, you can bet I'll walk into court with as much evidence as I can dig up on you to prove what an unfit mother you are. I'll parade in half the male population of this town as character witnesses, maybe even some of their ex-wives. How many homes have you broken up over the years?"

"You can't do that."

"I can, and I will. I'll do whatever it takes to keep you from being within a hundred miles of Autumn. She didn't speak for over a month the last time you took her. She's been terrified the last few weeks thinking you're coming back to steal her from her family. You think I'd risk her health and safety again? Never.

"Quit bullshitting me. You don't want anything to do with Autumn. She's just a means to an end. Always has been to you. How much do you want?"

"Just like that," she said, not believing he'd make things so easy.

Tired of playing games and dealing with her, he wanted to finish this. Quick.

"Name your price."

"A million dollars."

He laughed outright. "Not going to happen."

"Why not? You own a company."

She didn't know how much he was worth. She only knew what she'd learned from the Internet probably. The company was privately held, so she couldn't get all the financial information. He downplayed his role.

"I own a small part of the company. You're asking for what I don't have. I'll give you twenty thousand cash."

"That's a drop in the bucket. I'd get more in child support."

"Keep up. You'd never get custody, and you know it."

"I know you've got money. Look at the place you're building out at the ranch. New stables and buying horses, those things take serious money."

"Exactly. I've tied up what I have in the house and ranch."

"For her. So, she'll finally have everything. You, the kids, the big house, and all your money. It's the only reason she'd take you back after sleeping with me."

He didn't believe that for a second. Rain loved him. Enough to forgive him and want to make a life with him.

Not giving anything away and allowing Roxy to believe Rain was using him, he only shrugged. "Face it, you'll never have what Rain has. You don't even want the same things."

"Half a million." She threw out the figure, hoping he'd bite.

"Fifty. Cash."

"Brody." She pouted, frustrated he wouldn't just give her what she wanted.

"You don't have a leg to stand on. I'm offering you enough money to pay off your bills," he said, indicating the stack of papers perfectly visible on the desk. "You'll have enough left over to live a few months."

"It isn't enough, you bastard. I have things to take care of in Vegas. Plans."

A flash of desperation crossed her eyes. Problems were waiting for her in Vegas. Probably an unhealthy dose of trouble, too.

"One hundred grand. Cash."

Her eyes lit up a bit at that figure.

"For that kind of money, you'll sign off on your parental rights, and you'll stay away from Autumn."

She opened her mouth to ask for more, but he cut her off. "That's my final offer."

With a feral smile, her sharp mind latched on to the one thing she could use to get what she wanted.

"You want me to sign something giving Autumn up for good?"

"You gave her up more than seven years ago. This will make it official, you'll have no rights to Autumn."

"Maybe going to court would better serve me."

"Try it. You don't have the money it will take to go up against me. Take Rain out of the picture entirely. I'm a war hero and a businessman. Autumn is living with me. Who do you think the judge will choose? You or me?"

Her eyes narrowed as she thought about it.

"When I marry Rain, we'll be a family. Do you think the judge will choose to send Autumn with you, a single mother with no job or means of supporting her, or keep her with the only family she knows? She'd have a mother and a father, plus a sister."

"Why do you have to be such an asshole?"

"It serves me," he said, using her words. Roxy was all about serving herself and leaving others to starve. "Take the offer. Take us to court, piss me off, you'll get nothing."

"Fine. How soon can you have my money?"

"Since it's after five and the bank is closed, tomorrow morning. First thing."

"I'm busy tomorrow. The day after," she suggested.

"Tomorrow. I want this done."

"I have something I need to do. The day after."

He didn't know why she'd stall on getting her money, but he'd go with what she wanted if it got him what he wanted.

"Fine. You'll sign the papers, or you won't see a dime. Clear?"

"Crystal."

He walked out of the office, Roxy on his heels. "That's it," she said.

He turned back and glared. "Day after tomorrow we'll meet. You'll get what you want and I'll get what I want. After that, I don't ever want to see you again."

"Is being around me too much of a temptation?"

"Don't push me," he said, knowing full well everyone was listening to them. "You won't like the outcome. You'll lose what little you've gained from me."

She crossed her arms and glared at him. Apparently, she didn't believe him. He had one last card to play. He walked to her and stood toe-to-toe. In a low voice, he threatened, "If you play any more games with me, I'll put Rain and the children on a plane and we'll leave the country. My company does business all over the world. We can be gone in a matter of hours and there's nothing you can do to stop me."

Her eyes showed him she understood. Leaving was the last resort. Rain would agree to keep Autumn safe. She'd always wanted to travel. They could settle in another country as well as they could on Clear Water Ranch.

He turned on his heel and walked out. Every eye in the place on his back. Just before exiting the door, he caught a glimpse of a man sitting in a booth. Pure hate and rage shown in his eyes. His hands fisted on the table. Roxy's boyfriend. Another player in this strange game.

Another threat.

Chapter Twenty-Eight

BRODY WORRIED ON the way home. Roxy was unpredict-able at best. Toss in a boyfriend feeding her impulsive, volatile ways and it could spell more trouble. The last thing he wanted.

He made a couple of pit stops on the way home and walked in the door carrying two bags and a bouquet of flowers. The girls were on the couch watching a movie.

"Dad!" they yelled when he came in the door. They both ran to him, throwing their arms around his legs and hugging him.

"Hey, you two. Did you have a good day at school?"

"Yeah," Dawn answered.

Autumn didn't respond. He set the bags down and picked her up, handing her the flowers. "Want to give those to Mom for me?"

"Okay."

"Don't worry, baby girl. Your mom and I will talk to

your teacher tomorrow. She'll understand why you've been upset."

"Did you see her?"

"Yes."

"Is she coming here?"

"No. She'll leave real soon."

"Promise."

"Yes, honey. I won't let anything happen to you."

Rain appeared in the entry from the kitchen. She leaned her shoulder against the doorframe and stared at him. Her eyes spoke volumes. Fear, reservations, resignation, relief at seeing him. He didn't know which to address first, so he walked to her with Autumn in his arms. She immediately handed Rain the flowers. He kissed Autumn's cheek and set her down. His hands reached out for Rain, and she moved toward him. He kissed her, buried his hands in her hair and tilted her head back so he could take the kiss deeper, the scent of roses surrounding them.

"They're kissing again," Dawn said from behind him.

Smiling against her mouth, he opened his eyes to the laughter in hers. "I missed you today."

"You saw me this morning."

"I miss you whenever you're not with me."

"Brody." She took a second to look down at the roses. "What are the flowers for?"

"You. I'm so lucky to have you in my life, Rain. You're so beautiful, and you have the biggest, best heart. You've had a hard couple of weeks, you're tired and worried about this situation and how it's affecting Autumn. You do everything for all of us, and I haven't spent nearly enough time making things easier for you."

"Everything went well?"

He hated her suspicions, but deserved them after what he'd done in the past. Meeting Roxy without her stirred up old wounds and hurt feelings again.

"I think I got what we wanted. We'll see in a couple of days. I'll tell you all about it after dinner and when the girls are occupied."

"You're angry," she said, the flowers held in front her.

He shook his head that he wasn't, but she added, "You took two full steps away from me and stuffed your hands in your back pockets. If that doesn't say you're pissed, I don't know what does."

He stalked her as she backed away from him. He came through the kitchen entry. Owen sat at the table reading over some papers. "Get out," he said between clenched teeth. Owen read his mood and tone, stood and left without a word.

Rain's back hit the counter. He grabbed the flowers out of her hands and tossed them aside. Planting his hands on the counter at her sides, he leaned over and looked her in the eyes.

"Brody, I—"

"My turn." He cut her off. "I'm not mad at you. I've had one hell of a day. I have a pounding headache."

"I'll get you some ibuprofen."

She tried to move past him, but he kept his arms caged around her, leaving her nowhere to go.

"I don't want you to get me anything. If I want something, I can get it myself. I want you to relax, take a break from taking care of everyone but yourself. I feel like I've done pretty well with the girls. I help them with their homework, have even put them to bed a few nights for you. We're getting closer, they treat me like I've been the dad in the house all this time, not like a stranger anymore. You and I share the same house and bed. We've mended fences, but I'm sorely lacking in the taking-care-of-you department. You're always there for me, day and night. I need you so damn much, I forget you need me, too."

"I'm fine . . ."

"No, you're not. You don't sleep because I keep you awake. You work a full day and still make time for me and the girls whenever we need you. You're the first one up and the last one to bed. The house is clean, the meals prepared and cleaned up, and you run all the errands in between everything else you do. Every night you come to me, give yourself to me with so much love and passion. Sometimes during the day, too, when I need you, like Saturday in the woods."

He stood tall, grabbed her hips, and lifted her onto the counter, stepping between her thighs and pulling her hips to his. His erection pressed into the V between her thighs and came into intimate contact. He rocked forward and her eyes dilated, her fingers dug into his shoulders.

"I stepped away from you before because all I want to do is drag you upstairs to bed. If I kept kissing and touching you, I would have taken you right there in the living room. This house is too full of people, and all I want is to be alone with you."

Her hands slid up his neck to his jaw. She held him and leaned down to kiss him, her tongue traced his bottom lip, he groaned, and she dipped her tongue inside his mouth, smoothed it over his. They lost themselves in the kiss, the closeness they shared whenever they touched.

She pulled back, wrapped her arms around his neck, and hugged him with all her strength. He wrapped his arms around her and held her close. She needed this. Just to be close and held and loved.

The girls were getting restless in the other room. Owen told them twice dinner would be in a few minutes. Rain leaned back and traced her fingers over his forehead to his temples where she rubbed softly to help ease his headache. "You can't help yourself, can you?"

"Taking care of you. No. I love you."

He planted his lips over hers, slipped his hands under her hips, and picked her up with her legs wrapped around his waist. Still kissing her, he carried her to the table. Without breaking the kiss, he released her legs and let her body slide down his. When her feet hit the ground, he placed his hands on her shoulders and pushed her down into a chair, ending the kiss. "Sit."

He moved to the cupboard and piled plates and bowls. He carried them to the table and placed them at each spot. Over his shoulder, he called, "Owen, girls, dinner."

Owen brought in the bags of food and pulled out the cartons of Chinese take-out.

"You got me chicken chow mein?" Rain asked.

"Your favorite, if I remember right."

"I love Chinese food."

Body filled a vase with water, unwrapped her flowers, and placed them inside. He carried them to the table and set them in the center. Autumn and Dawn were already digging into the food. A fortune cookie sat in front of each of their plates.

"I know you do. That's why I got it. Eat, honey."

He sat next to her and for a while they all ate in silence. Owen looked preoccupied and kept checking his phone.

"Waiting for a call?"

"A client," he said and frowned.

"Something serious?"

"I helped her with her divorce. Her ex was just released from jail. She's nervous."

"She have reason to be?"

"And then some," Owen answered.

"Let me know if you need some help."

"It's fine. She's fine," he said, though it sounded like he was trying to convince himself as much as Brody.

"Did you get those papers signed?" Owen asked, changing the subject.

The girls had no idea what they were talking about, but Rain's head snapped up and turned to him.

"Not yet. Day after tomorrow."

"Why not sooner?" Rain asked.

"Bank was closed, plus she set the day, not me. Believe me, I wanted to get it done sooner."

"How much did it cost you?" Owen asked.

"One hundred."

"A hundred dollars," Dawn said, a touch of awe in her voice.

"Eat your food," Rain admonished. "We'll talk about this later," she added to him and Owen.

Brody set up a movie for the girls and made them a bowl of popcorn after dinner. He figured all the crunching should keep them from overhearing the conversation in the kitchen. They knew something was going on, but best to keep the details from them.

Rain sat with her hands wrapped around a cup of tea. He came in behind her and clamped his hands down on her shoulders. Tense, he rubbed the knots in her neck and between her shoulder blades.

"I met Roxy at the bar. She tried to get me to follow her upstairs."

Rain's shoulders went rigid beneath his hands, but he kept rubbing and kneading while he spoke.

"I waited in the main part of the bar for her to come back down the stairs and talk to me in her office."

"I bet that ticked her off," Owen said with a smile of approval.

"Bet your ass. I did it on purpose to piss her off. Every person in that bar will blab the story all over town. I refuse to have people talking about how the past repeated itself, even though I'd never be that stupid again."

He brushed his hand over Rain's hair to show her how precious she was to him.

"We went into her office. A bunch of bills were piled on the desk, including the renewal for her liquor license.

I think she's hurting for money. The bar does okay, but it could do a lot better if she put some money into the place. Owen, I'd like you to find out what the bar is worth."

"Why do you want to know?" Rain asked, turning her head up to him.

"I want her out of our lives and out of this town for good. If I buy the bar, she'll have no reason to come back, even after she signs the papers for Autumn."

"Do you think she'll sell to you?"

"I'll set up a dummy company and buy it under that name. Owen can take care of the paperwork, get a realtor to make an offer, and she'll never know it's me. She may guess, but she won't be sure. If my guess is right, she's desperate for money, and since I didn't meet her million-dollar demand, she might jump at the chance to get more money through the bar."

"She asked you for a million dollars?"

"That was her opening offer." He dug his knuckle into a knot between her shoulders and worked the stiff muscle. Rain leaned against the table, her forearms braced as he pressed hard against her back.

"What was yours?" Owen asked.

"Twenty grand. Cash."

"Did she laugh?" Rain asked.

"Not when I threw it in her face she'd already been paid. She countered with a half million, I offered fifty and made it clear if she went through with her threat to take Rain to court to gain custody, she'd lose. She backed down a bit, but in the end, I had to use my trump card to make my point."

"What was your trump card?" Rain asked, nearly lying on the table now as he massaged her neck, her hair falling over one shoulder.

"If she didn't take my offer, I'd put you all on a plane and take you out of the country where she and the courts couldn't touch us."

Rain turned completely in her seat. "What?"

"I won't let her ruin what we have, or have a judge say she can visit Autumn. As it happens, that threat was enough to get her to take one hundred thousand and sign the papers. I'll get the bank to issue the cash tomorrow, meet her the following day, and we're done.

"Owen, can you get the info on the bar tomorrow? Find out about any outstanding loans or liens. Anything that will make it easier to get the bar and her out of town."

"I'll get to work on it first thing in the morning. I'm glad you got her to agree."

"Yeah, well, I'm not celebrating yet. She wasn't happy with the amount and stalled the payoff another day. She seemed nervous and desperate. She made a couple passes, even though I'd made it clear I wasn't interested. I down-right insulted her, played up my relationship with you, Rain, and how you've made quite a life for yourself despite Roxy trying to ruin things for you."

"You said that to her?"

"Damn right. But as I was walking out of the bar, I think I spotted her boyfriend. He looked like he wanted to kill me. Whether that was because Roxy and I were in the office for a while, or because she's fed him a bunch of bullshit, I don't know."

"You think he's a problem?"

"My instincts say Roxy isn't one to make things easy."

"She took the money I offered her and left," Rain pointed out.

"Not the second time. When you went to get Autumn, she didn't just take what you offered. She demanded more and didn't want to give Autumn back."

"It was only eight thousand dollars."

"She knew you didn't have more. Maybe her plan was to take what you had and find me, hoping to get more."

"She didn't know where you were," Owen said.

"No? These days, it doesn't take much to find someone. Rain couldn't find me because I was on the move. Roxy could have hired a PI, used my social security number to find out I was in the military. Maybe she already knew."

"It doesn't matter now. You made the offer, she accepted. We'll wait and see what she does next when she comes for the money." She rolled her shoulders, loosening the muscles he'd already worked.

"Why don't you go sit with the girls and watch TV. I'll clean up the kitchen."

"What have you done with my Brody McBride?" she asked, joking.

He pulled her up and into his arms. "I'm all yours, sweetheart." He kissed her and Owen groaned behind them.

"You two are really starting to make me sick."

"Jealous." Brody gave him a big smile and gazed down at Rain. She surprised him and laid her head on his chest and held him around the waist. He wrapped her up tighter in his arms and looked over at Owen. Owen was at a loss, too, and shrugged. It wasn't like Rain to be so quiet and cling.

It took some doing, but he got Rain to relax on the couch with the girls. Before long the three of them were laughing and having fun while they watched the princess movie. He and Owen cleaned up the kitchen and went over the plan for giving Roxy the money, getting the signature they needed, and how they could covertly buy the bar to keep her away for good. Irritated everything was still in the planning and waiting stages, nothing finished, like the end would never get here. Maybe that's how Rain felt too, only she'd been waiting years to end this. No wonder it was taking such a toll on her.

"I'll catch you later." Owen slapped him on the back and headed out the back door.

Brody walked into the living room and took charge. "All right girls, you got to stay up an extra half hour with your mom. It's time for bed. Upstairs, brush your teeth, and get two books each."

Both girls got up, but he stopped them before they headed up. "Kiss your mom goodnight."

Rain stood, hugged and kissed each of them. Brody hugged them before they pounded up the stairs. He went to Rain and pushed her back down to the couch.

"Wait here for me."

He handed her the remote and climbed the stairs. The girls were changing clothes, giggling and talking in their room. He went to his and Rain's room and into their bathroom. He ran the water in the tub and poured in some of the scented oil from the tub shelf. The room filled with the smell of lavender and white lilies. Soft, sweet. He lit the candles near the tub, grabbed the ones out of the bedroom and brought them into the bathroom, too. Done filling the tub at the same time the girls finished brushing their teeth, he met them in the hallway.

"You guys get your books. I'll be in to read in just a second."

They dashed off and he went to the head of the stairs. "Rain, come on up. I have a surprise for you."

She appeared at the foot of the stairs and made her way up to him, looking tired and moving slow.

"A surprise."

"Yep. Come with me."

He took her hand and pulled her down the hall to their room. Once inside, he closed the door and turned to her. "Strip."

"Excuse me," she shot back, one eyebrow going up.

"You're right. I like to do it myself."

He reached for her and brought the hem of her shirt up and over her head. Lucky for him, she didn't argue or stop him. His fingers dipped inside the top of her jeans and skimmed over her belly. He unbuttoned them and slid the zipper down. He leaned forward and kissed the swell of her breast over the lace bra and tugged her jeans and panties down her hips and legs. She helped by kicking them off, and he undid her bra and brought it down her arms, dropping it on the pile of other clothes at their feet.

Standing back for a moment, he looked his fill as she stood before him, perfectly content to allow his perusal. He took her hand and pulled her toward the bathroom door.

"Brody, what are you doing?"

He opened the door, revealing the candlelit room. The soft sent of flowers wafted out.

"Oh, Brody, you . . ."

"Wanted to do something nice for you," he finished, because he didn't want to hear her say he shouldn't have. He should have done a lot more. "Get in, honey. Relax. I'll take care of the girls and lock up the house."

She snagged a clip off the counter, piled her hair on her head, and with a hand from him, stepped into the tub. She settled into the fragrant, steaming water and closed her eyes on a sigh. Satisfied she was happy and relaxing, he headed out to read to the girls.

She stopped him before he left. "Brody, thank you."

Leaning over the tub, he kissed her on the forehead and whispered, "I love you." He wanted to dip his hands in the water, smooth them over her soft body. Instead, he let her have her peace and quiet.

It didn't take long to read stories and settle the girls in their beds. He walked back into the bathroom and found Rain lounging in the tub, her eyes closed, perfectly relaxed and half-asleep. His heart eased, his shoulders relaxed just seeing her content. So beautiful, his eyes traced the column of her throat, down her chest to her rounded breasts tipped with soft pink nipples. He knew how she tasted, wanted to fill his mouth with her even now. Her belly was flat, her hips slightly flared. He imagined her swollen and round with his child, sorry he'd missed it with Dawn and hoping to see her heavy with pregnancy soon. He skimmed over the thatch of dark curls. Tonight, he wanted to keep his passion in check and allow Rain the rest she needed. Still, her legs were a lovely sight. Trim, strong, well-defined muscles, firm when he grasped them and drove himself inside of her.

Detour. Back to admiring her, not lusting after her, he thought.

With a heavy sigh, he pushed the drain down and took her hands. Her eyes opened and held a dreamy quality. Compliant to his coaxing, she stepped out of the tub and stood while he softly wiped the water from her skin with a thick towel. No words were spoken; they weren't needed as he scooped her up and carried her to the bed and laid her on the cool sheets. He pulled the blankets over her and stripped off his own clothes and rounded the bed. Naked, he slipped beneath the covers and pulled her close. Her back to his chest, her hips snug against his erection, he draped his arm over her and took her breast in his hand. Her heart beat against the heel of his palm and she sighed and snuggled closer. He kissed her shoulder, trailing kisses up her neck to her ear. He whispered, "I love you, sweetheart. Sleep."

Her whole body relaxed against his and within moments her breathing evened out. Listening to the quiet night, Rain's soft breathing, and the feel of her body against his eased all the tension he'd carried with him all day. He didn't think about work, Roxy, the future or the past. He gave himself over to the sweet contentment of being here with her, let it fill his heart and soul, and all the dark corners. He slept soundly, dreamlessly, the whole night.

Chapter Twenty-Nine

RAIN WALKED OUT the double doors and descended the steps to the walkway below. Squinting her eyes, she looked up at the bright sky and let the sun warm her face. Brody's hands clamped over her shoulders, the heat of his body warmed her back.

"That was terrifying," he said, a laugh in his voice.

"I was twenty-three the first time I walked into a classroom and had to remind myself I wasn't the student, but the mother of the students. Their teacher was at least ten years older than me and had a picture of her three-month-old on her desk. Very bizarre."

"I became a father at twenty-eight. It's hard to imagine being twenty and having them. I know I'd have felt too young and irresponsible."

"You were," she teased.

"You too," he said, his voice serious. "Eighteen and the mother of two."

"Old enough," she said, and turned to face him. "Thank you for last night and this morning. You're spoiling me."

"You're just a little soft, not quite spoiled. I'll have to keep working on it."

She laughed. Last night and this morning, Brody had gone out of his way to help her and make her feel treasured and loved. She'd slept in his arms and woken up to him kissing her neck and holding her close. Warm and hard behind her, she'd wanted to make love with him, but he'd gotten up, put on his sweats and gone down the hall to get the girls up and ready for school. By the time she came downstairs, they'd had breakfast. He handed her a cup of coffee, told her to sit at the table and eat her breakfast, eggs and toast with strawberry jelly. Her favorite. While she ate, he helped Dawn and Autumn get their backpacks and lunches ready. He walked them to the school bus.

Every chance he got, he touched her, kissed her, said something complimentary.

"I mean it, Brody. Yesterday, I was really feeling run down and tired. I appreciate you taking care of dinner, the girls, and me. It meant a lot. The bath, lying in your arms . . ."

"Sleep," he added.

"Yes, sleep. All of it. I needed it. You. I can't remember the last time someone treated me so well."

"I don't want to be one more person you have to take care of, Rain. I'd like you to count on me. Lean on me when you need to, and ask for my help. Anything you want or need, it's yours."

"Right now, I need to get to work. What are you doing today?"

"I'm headed for the bank to withdraw one hundred grand in cash," he said with an odd smile on his face. "This is strange," he went on. "I grew up next to poor, always scraping together cash to pay for gas, beer . . ."

"Taking out girls," she added and smiled, because back then she'd loved Brody's wildness and his go-to-hell attitude. She'd always been special to him, even when they were only friends. She'd always adored him. He'd always been drawn to her because he could be himself with her. One day, they'd looked at each other and saw something more. He didn't see a little girl and his best friend, but the woman she grew into and he loved, even though he'd never thought himself capable. She saw the man she couldn't live without.

"Yeah," he admitted easily. "Now, I can buy anything I want."

"Like your daughter's freedom from Roxy."

Frowning, he answered, "Sad, but true. Necessary. What do you want, Rain?"

"Lunch with you," she answered easily. "If you're working at the house, I'll meet you there in a couple hours."

"Actually, I thought I'd come by the garage and bring you lunch. Something's been rattling on the truck. I thought you'd take a look at it."

"I'm sure I can fit you in between the tire rotation I'm doing and replacing a fender on Miss Bertie's Cadillac."

"Did she hit something again?"

"Hopped the curb and hit a light pole."

"She's, what, eighty-three? When are they going to take her license away? She's a menace."

"Two new bumpers and four fenders. Still, she's never hurt anyone."

"Thank God," Brody said, smiling.

"Her son promised me he'll sell the car before her next birthday. Otherwise, I told him I'd disable it."

"You threatened him?"

"No." She laughed, incredulous he'd think she'd do such a thing. "Miss Bertie's a formidable lady. Her son's afraid of her, so I said I'd help him out by making sure the car didn't work."

"Sneaky."

"Necessary." She repeated his earlier thought that some things aren't always pleasant, but needed.

"Do you like working at the garage?"

"You know I do. Pop and I have always had a good time together."

"Is it what you want to do? You don't have to work, you know."

"Why? Because you have money?"

"We. We have money. You could go back to school. We could travel. Stay home and take care of the girls and organize and decorate the new house."

"How about a little of all of that, plus a few other things?"

"What things? Tell me what you want and it's yours."

She put her hand on his chest over his heart and looked up at his earnest face. "Brody, the only thing I truly want is you and our children. You don't have to buy me things to make me happy. I'm happy with you.

"The truth is, I'm looking forward to working on the house, making it a home for us. I can't wait for the stables to go up, so we can buy some horses."

"You love horses."

"You used to take me riding."

"You used to beg me to take you riding," he remembered with a smile.

"I thought we could get the girls a dog. A big tomcat for the barn. I think I'd like to be a rancher's wife."

Brody scooped her up and swung her around right there in front of the school. "You're the best."

Since she was above his head, she leaned down and held his face in her hands and kissed him. "More than anything, I want more of what we had last night and today. You and I in tune with each other and being there for our daughters."

He set her down and combed his fingers through the side of her hair. "Things have been kind of hectic lately."

"Don't I know it. I'll see you later."

They left each other with a kiss. When she got to the garage, she lost herself in work, though her thoughts always circled to Brody. Recently, her thoughts were about the baby they might have made over the last week. She wouldn't know for sure for a couple more weeks, but everything inside her wanted Brody's baby. It would be so nice to have a baby in the house again. More than anything, she loved being a mother. In her heart, she'd always regretted Brody had missed seeing the girls grow and develop from birth to little girls. She wanted to share it with him. A baby would be a beautiful start to their new lives.

So many changes lately. Brody coming home, building a new house, a new business starting at the ranch with the horses, no more worries about money, and finally, the elimination of the threat of Roxy taking Autumn.

Life was good and getting better. Soon, she'd marry Brody. She'd secretly dreamed of it for years, planned the ceremony in her mind, and held that dream close to her heart. She'd put Brody off on that front because she wanted everything in their past settled and done, but she couldn't wait.

Her father came out of the office, took his hat off, and scratched his head before saying, "Brody just pulled up outside."

Rain peeked around the hood of the car she stood bent over. Brody got out of a brand-new Chevy Tahoe. Odd, a tow truck sat idling in front of the SUV. Rain came around the car, wiping her dirty hands on a rag. She stuffed it in the back pocket of her coveralls and cocked her head at Brody as he stepped up close, smiling like an idiot.

"I thought you said you were bringing your truck in for me to look at."

"I lied. I brought you this." He held out his hand to indicate the new vehicle.

"What's wrong with it?"

"Nothing. It's yours."

"You bought me a car." Unable to believe what was right in front of her, she stood stunned.

"Like it?"

"I, ah . . ." She stood there dumbfounded. No one had ever bought her a new car. She'd never owned a new car.

"Rain, honey," Brody coaxed.

"You bought me a car," she said again.

"I'll buy you a whole fleet of cars if you'll smile."

"Don't you think Roxy will hear about this and try to get more money from you?"

"I don't give a shit what Roxy hears or tries to do."

"Yes you do, because you want to keep Autumn safe."

He frowned and reached out to trace his fingers over her forehead and threw her hair. "I did this to make *you* happy. But you're right. Keep the car hidden here at the garage until we finish this nasty business with that bitch." All the fun sucked out of his surprise, he asked, "Do you even like it?"

She leapt into his arms and kissed his face over and over again from his cheeks to his forehead, on his nose, and finally a big smacking kiss on his lips. "Thank you. Thank you. Thank you."

"Now that's more like it."

He set her down and she ran to the open driver's door and leapt inside. She took in the leather seats, all the buttons and gauges, the navigation system, MP3 and CD players, and, of course, that new-car smell.

Brody leaned in the door and put his hand on her thigh. She covered his hand with hers and gazed up at him. "Thank you, Brody. I love it."

He leaned down to her ear and said for only her to hear, "It seats eight. You, me, the girls, plus a car seat will fit perfectly."

"Yes, we will." He'd thought of everything. Her old car would be cramped with a baby seat between the girls in the backseat. This would allow for all of them . . . and then some. A baby now, another down the road. Sounded like heaven to her.

"You did good, Brody. That's a fine car for my girl," Pop said from the open back door.

"Only the best for my girls," Brody answered. He stepped away from the car and pulled her out to stand beside him.

"Eli," he began, and Rain had no idea why he looked so serious. "I want to thank you for taking care of Rain, Dawn, and Autumn. I know they're family, but you went above and beyond to see they had a roof over their heads, Rain had a job and her independence."

"She's my daughter. Like you do with yours, I want to be there for her and make her happy."

"You knew I made her happy, and even if you didn't think I was the right guy for her, you always welcomed me into your home."

"We both saw the good in you, even when you did your best to prove us wrong. You just had some growing up to do."

"I've done that, and part of growing up is taking responsibility and thanking those who've helped you along the way. My father taught me what kind of man I didn't want to be. You showed me the kind of man I could be."

Rain's eyes stung with unshed tears. Her father shifted from one foot to the other, uncomfortable with the emotions evoked by Brody's words.

"I hope I someday live up to your example. To thank you, I bought you this," he indicated the tow truck. The driver pulled the brown paper taped to the door and revealed the painted insignia. ELI'S TOWING was scrawled across the door in bold red letters outlined in black against the yellow background.

"Ah, now, son, that's a beautiful thing."

"It's all yours. The old truck's getting up in years. I thought you might like a new one. Expand your business a bit, hire on some help."

Pop came to Brody and wrapped him in a huge bear hug, slapping him on the back and shaking his hand. "I love it. Thanks. Thanks a lot."

"Go, check it out." Brody smiled wide.

Rain hadn't seen him this relaxed and carefree in a long time.

The men got a kick out of playing with all the gadgets, lifting and lowering the tow bar, checking out all the amenities. She looked too, but spent most of her time watching her father and Brody interact, like two little boys with a new toy. Once the delivery guy went over everything and handed Pop all the paperwork, they came back to her, standing by the large bay door.

"Rain didn't know about the truck, but we talked about it and we have something else for you." Brody took out the envelope from his back pocket. "Two tickets for a ten-day cruise to the Caribbean. She thought you might like to ask Sherry Osborne from the bank to go with you."

Pop turned to her, his mouth agape. "You know about her."

"You've always been very discrete about the ladies you've dated. You've always said Mom was the great love of your life, but that doesn't mean you can't find love again. I don't want you to be alone. Sherry is very nice. I think the two of you make a nice couple together."

"You do?"

"Does that surprise you?"

"Kinda. I do like her a lot. We've been seeing each other for several months. Taking a trip is a big deal."

"Think about it. You and her on a boat at sea, visiting exotic islands. By the time you come back, you can move back into the house again. You'll have the place to yourself. Or . . ." She left the rest hanging. From the odd look on her father's face, he was thinking. His cheeks went ruddy and a soft smile tilted the corners of his mouth.

"Thank you. Thank you very much." He walked back to his office, studying the tickets in his hands.

"Want to bet he's calling to make a date with Sherry?" Brody wrapped his arm around her shoulders and pulled her to his side.

"He'll surprise her over dinner," Rain guessed, watching her father pick up the phone and talk to Sherry. He smiled and used his hands. His whole face lit up when Sherry said something to him, probably agreeing to go to dinner that night.

"Thanks, Brody, we made him happy today."

"Yes, *we* did."

Brody didn't say it, he didn't have to. She finally saw them as a couple. They may not be married—yet—but they'd gotten to that place where it was no longer "me" and "you" separately, but "we and us" together.

She slid back into the Tahoe and turned the key. The engine hummed and she rubbed her hands over the steering wheel and took a moment to savor the new car and the excitement tickling her belly. She drove the short distance and parked it in the garage bay. She grabbed the duffle bag off the seat and got out, handing it off to Brody. He leaned down and kissed her softly on the lips, the smile never leaving his face.

"Is that Roxy's money?"

"That's Autumn's safety and freedom."

Chapter Thirty

TODAY WAS THE day. He'd pay off Roxy and finally be able to tell himself he'd taken care of his family, kept them safe when they needed him. The tension inside him grew more and more difficult to keep at bay.

Brody picked the girls up from school and brought them out to the ranch so they could see the progress on the house. He needed to sign for the steel beams being delivered today at the site of the new stables and barn. The foundation and beams would go in next week. Once the skeleton was erected, the contractor could begin finishing off the shell and interior rooms. As much as they loved seeing the construction on the house, the main reason he brought them with him was he needed to keep them close.

He wished this day would end, the girls tucked in bed, Rain lying in his arms, and everything right in their world. Still three hours until he was due to meet Roxy.

Rain was on her way to the cabin. They'd all drive back to town, have dinner out, and he'd drop them off at the house before heading over to the bar.

Sleep escaped him last night. Rain slept in spurts beside him. Grateful the construction crew had left a half hour ago, he wrapped the quiet around his frayed nerves. If he didn't have the meeting later, he'd go off by himself and settle down. As it was, he needed to keep an eye on the girls and get through this day without letting the past swamp his mind and drag him under, so he fought it hard. Rain would understand if he needed his space tonight and tomorrow.

The girls ran around the corner of the unfinished house and came barreling toward him, screeching and yelling as Dawn chased after Autumn. Autumn grabbed his waist and swung around behind him as Dawn feinted left then right to tag her sister.

"Girls. Enough. What have you two been doing?"

"We were skipping rocks into the lake like you showed us. I got three," Dawn announced.

"I got the most. Four skips." Autumn smiled up at him, triumphant in her victory over Dawn.

"You two are fast learners. We'll have to show your mom when she gets here."

"Can we go inside and get a soda?"

"Sure, but you have to split a can. We're going out to eat and Mom will kill me if I let you two ruin your appetite on sugar."

"Okay, we'll share," Dawn answered, and they took off for the cabin.

He finished checking out the framing and the rough-in for the plumbing. Things were moving along smoothly on the house. Walking through the open room, his footfalls echoing on the subfloor, he wasn't sure what set him off. His whole body went tense. He scanned the area around him for . . . snipers he knew weren't there. Screams pierced the air, sending him to a crowded market in Kandahar, Afghanistan. Insurgents set off a bomb, gunfire erupted in the crowd, and he dove for cover, crawling along a low wall for a better vantage point. A door slammed nearby. A child screamed. Someone gunned an engine and the tires kicked up gravel. His lungs billowed in and out, deep gasps of air. He needed to move. Something was very wrong.

A car crash, metal against metal crunching in the distance.

RAIN DROVE HER old car out to the ranch. Brody called this morning to let her know one of the guys on Jim's crew wanted to buy it. The outside wasn't much to look at, the paint was chipped and faded, but the inside was clean, the seats worn, but not overly so. Of course, the engine ran perfectly and she put new tires on last year. A good deal for the money.

The radio boomed out classic rock, but Rain shut it off, preferring the quiet and her own anxious thoughts to the annoying music. Her stomach clenched, tied in knots since yesterday and getting worse with every passing hour. She hated this waiting game. Why did Roxy hold off on her big payday?

Still, it gave Brody and Owen time to investigate Roxy's financial situation, so they could buy the bar out from under her and send her away for good this time.

Roxy agreed to the amount, but she had to know it would take a hell of a lot more money to set her up for any length of time. She'd jump at an offer for the bar. She had to. Roxy wasn't one to put her business before her own fun and needs.

A plus for Rain, Roxy didn't have the money to hire a lawyer and fight them in court either. Brody swore if she managed to take them to court, he'd hire the best lawyers in the country to ensure Autumn never stayed a minute alone with Roxy. A great relief, but Rain had a creepy feeling dancing up her spine every time she thought about Roxy's desperate situation and putting off getting her payment so long. Why?

The last two times she'd needed money or a way out, she'd come to Rain. The last time she'd been desperate enough to kidnap Autumn. What would she do this time if the money paid her wasn't enough? That question haunted Rain all day yesterday, long into the night, and followed her everywhere she went today. Brody would pay her more. Roxy didn't know that, and wasn't smart enough to just ask.

Rain slammed the flat of her hand on the steering wheel. "Why do we have to pay her at all? She doesn't even want Autumn."

Easy answer. Roxy only understood money and doing as she pleased. She never thought of anyone else. She certainly didn't have Autumn's best interests at heart. Hell, Roxy didn't have a heart.

That was her last thought as she rounded the corner into Brody's driveway. Roxy's red Camero tore down the gravel road toward her. Autumn's terrified wide eyes stared at her from the center of the backseat.

Rain sped forward in a deadly game of chicken. A game Rain intended to win. She angled the car across their path at the last second. Roxy's car slammed into the side of hers with a jarring crunch of metal and shattering glass.

A LITTLE GIRL pulled Brody's arm. Her face changed, shifted, Dawn, someone he didn't recognize, Dawn again. He squeezed his eyes closed tight and opened them again. He looked up at Dawn from the floor of the unfinished room, his back against the two-by-fours of the framed wall. Tears streaked down her bright red cheek.

"Please, Daddy. Get up. You have to get her back. Please, Daddy." She pulled on him again and again, trying to make him stand up.

"Daddy. Come back. Daddy!" she screamed at him.

Shaking his head like a wet dog, the hollowness in his ears vanished. Her voice came through loud and clear.

"Daddy, they took her. Daddy," Dawn wailed.

He grabbed her arms and pulled her close, her face inches from his. "Who took her? Who hit you?"

"Roxy and some man. They took her. Go get her."

He picked her up, ran for the front of the house, jumping off the raised foundation floor and nearly falling when his bad leg couldn't support his weight and Dawn's. Adrenaline kicking in, he gained his balance and ran.

RAIN'S HEAD SLAMMED into the side window, splitting open a gash that poured blood down the side of her head. She moaned and pressed her hand over the wound. Her heart raced, pounding against her ribs. Everything inside her told her to get out, save Autumn. Her movements felt stilted. She shook her head to clear the fog and encroaching darkness, grabbed the handle, pushed open the door, and nearly fell out. Adrenaline and her mother's instincts kicked in. She ran to Roxy's side of the car and pulled open the door. Stupid woman didn't have her seat belt on. Luckily, they hadn't been going fast enough to kill anyone. Or maybe too bad.

She grabbed Roxy by the hair and dragged her out of the car.

"Autumn run. Run back to Daddy." Autumn scurried over the center console into the front seat. Her wide eyes looked up at Rain, tears streaked down her pale face. Roxy's boyfriend made a grab for her, but Autumn batted at his hands and managed to pull away at the last second and get past him and out of the car.

"Run, Autumn. Now."

Autumn stomped on Roxy's foot, like her sister had done to David Murphy when he called her ugly.

"Ouch, you bitch."

Autumn ran and Rain held tight to Roxy when she tried to go after Autumn.

"Let me go," Roxy shrieked. Rain dragged her around to face her.

"You came here to steal my daughter, you're lucky I don't kill you, you stupid cow."

"She's my daughter," Roxy spat out.

Rain had put up with a lot of shit over the years. Having Roxy claim Autumn as her daughter sent her over the edge. She cocked her arm back and slammed it forward, her fist connecting with Roxy's nose. A satisfying crack sounded a second before blood burst out of her nostrils, spraying through the air. Her head whipped to the side.

"You broke my nose," she wailed, but the words were muffled behind her cupped hands. She dropped her bloodstained hands and mumbled, "You'll pay for that."

Roxy staggered, but Rain wasn't finished. She hauled her arm back again and this time smashed her fist right into Roxy's jaw, snapping her head back and sending her to the dirt with a thud. At the point of impact, the bones in Rain's hand popped and gave way with a snap. Rain fell off balance and went down, too, landing on her hands and knees. Pain zipped up her arm from her broken hand, and she screamed in agony.

Roxy's boyfriend's boot-clad feet appeared in front of her. She scrambled back, but he made a grab for her and hooked his hand around her upper arm, hauling her to her feet. His fingers dug into her skin, punishing and bruising, his eyes dark with rage.

"Stupid bitch. That girl was my meal ticket." He shook her and pulled her against his chest. She thumped against him, even as she tried to pull away.

"If he was willing to pay a hundred grand for the brat, imagine what he'll pay for a fine piece of ass like you."

His breath stank of whiskey, coffee, and cigarettes. She wanted to gag from the smell and the nausea created by the wound to her head. Dizzy, she tried to stay on her feet, think straight, and figure a way out of this mess.

She planted her hands on his chest and shoved him away. The only thing she accomplished was hurting herself more. His hold on her arm tightened painfully. Shifting her weight, she sent her knee to his groin. He sensed her movement and moved his leg to block her. She grazed her target, making him groan. All the air whooshed out of him. He shoved her over his leg, taking her off her feet. She flipped around in the air to her back and landed hard on the gravel. Sharp tips and jagged edges gouged at her shoulders and back.

"I'll kill you, bitch."

She believed him. He landed hard on top of her. Her hands shot up and grabbed his wrist as he plunged the hunting knife down toward her chest.

BRODY JUMPED INTO the cab of his truck and tossed Dawn into the seat beside him. He gunned the engine, threw the car into gear, and stomped on the gas, sending rocks flying as the tires bit into the road. Not far from the crash, he needed to get there as quick as possible. He rounded the soft bend. The scene in front of him sent his heart pounding and his stomach into his throat. The blood drained from his face. His heart nearly stopped when Rain, blood running down her face and hair, grabbed Roxy by the head and dragged her out of the car. Autumn scrambled out a moment later, stomped on Roxy's foot, and ran toward the truck.

He felt the pride, seeing his quiet little one stand up for herself against the woman who had terrified her for years.

The pride faded behind his fear for her and Rain.

He jumped out on the run and scooped her up, holding her close, just as Rain punched Roxy in the nose. Momentarily stunned, he got another shock when she cocked her hand back and punched her in the jaw, knocking Roxy out cold.

Autumn cried hysterically in his arms. He ran her back to the truck and sat her in the seat beside Dawn. The girls clung to each other. Two tearstained, pale faces with huge round eyes stared up at him. Brody grabbed his cell phone from his pocket and dialed 911. He handed it to Dawn.

"Tell 911 we need police help at Clear Water Ranch."

"O-k-kay," Dawn sputtered out and nodded. He waited to make sure she put the phone to her ear and spoke to the dispatcher.

Pure rage swamped him when he turned back to help Rain and the guy he'd seen in the bar shook her, making Rain's head snap back and forth like a bobble head. She tried to fight off his hold, but he was bigger and stronger. Rain got in a good shot as Brody ran to her, but she ended up on the ground. A glint of sunlight glared off the knife as it plunged toward Rain. She grabbed the guy's hand just before the tip of the blade sliced into her chest. She fought, but he knew she'd lose. He couldn't let that happen.

The tip of the knife pressed into her chest, pierced her skin, and sank in. Rain used the last of her strength to push against the inevitable. Brody's big body flew over her in that moment, taking Roxy's boyfriend with him, the knife slicing through her as he pulled it out. The two men scrambled over her legs and toppled away in a tumble of arms and legs.

Rain struggled to sit up, legs spread wide, her hands lying limp, shoulders slack. Brody gained the top of the other man and landed a body blow just under his ribs. The man drew the knife down toward Brody's back, but he shifted just in time. The knife sliced through Brody's dark blue T-shirt and the chunky part of his shoulder. Blood oozed out and left a snaking trail down over his bicep to his elbow.

Brody punched him in the side again. The man grunted with the impact. He clamped his left hand around the guy's right wrist and bashed it against the ground. Once, twice, and on the third blow, the guy released the knife. It thumped and landed a foot away.

Rearing up onto his knees, straddling the man, Brody punched him in the face. The man reached up, tried to grab Brody's shirt to hold him off, but Brody wouldn't be stopped. He shoved the guy's arm aside and punched him in the face again. And again. His head snapped to the side, his face swollen and bloody, Brody hit him again.

"Brody!" Rain yelled.

He didn't stop. He landed another blow. "Brody! Stop!" she tried again, but he'd gone to another place and didn't respond to her calls.

Rain tried to get up, but her legs were like rubber. Her head spun, her eyesight went blurry, her chin fell to her chest and she saw the blood running down her white top.

The man grunted again, his feet sliding in the gravel.

"Brody. Help me!" Rain screamed.

Silence. Brody stilled, two hands fisted in the guy's shirt, holding him partially off the ground. He shoved him away. He rushed to her side. Her head fell back, sending her onto the ground, her head thumped into the gravel. A shaft of splitting pain arced through her brain.

"Rain!"

Brody slid to a stop on his knees beside her. He took a second to scan her face and body to see where she was hurt the worst. The blood on her head, face, and chest terrified him. With trembling hands, he cupped her face and leaned over her.

"Rain, baby, open your eyes. Please, honey."

"Brody." His name came out on an exhaled whisper.

"Yes, honey."

"Get the girls," she ordered. "Get them out of here."

"I'm not leaving you." He ripped her bloodstained shirt to reveal the deep gash in her chest, just above her breast. Seeping blood, he pressed the heel of his hand over the wound to stop the bleeding. It gushed through his fingers.

"*Rrrrr. Aaaaah.*" The sound of agony that came from her shattered his heart.

Roxy stirred behind him, whimpering and crying. Every once in a while, she let loose with a string of cuss words and obscenities.

"You hear the sirens, Rain. Help is coming."

Her eyes fluttered open, pain clouded the depths. "Take care of the girls. They're scared. Go to them, Brody."

"You're bleeding."

"I'm fine. It's just a scra-atch," she slurred.

"Bullshit."

"You're bleeding, too," she pointed out.

"I didn't get to you in time."

"I'm still breathing. You got to me in time."

"I should have . . ."

"Go see the girls. I can hear them crying. Please, Brody. They need you."

"You need me, too."

She reached up and traced her fingers over his cheek. Tears he hadn't realized he shed wet her fingertips. "I'm fine. Just a broken hand. My head hurts."

"You broke your hand?"

"Roxy's got a hard head."

He couldn't help himself, he laughed. "Please tell me you're going to be okay."

"I am. Now please go to the girls."

Brody leaned in and kissed her softly on the mouth. When he let up the pressure on her chest, the wound didn't bleed. He gently picked up her broken right hand and laid it on her stomach. Swollen and bruised badly, her knuckles raw and bleeding, she'd need a cast. She gri maced in pain, gritted her teeth, and clamped down her jaw when he touched it.

"I'll be right back."

"I'm not going anywhere."

Brody ran to the truck. Dawn and Autumn stared at him through the window. He had to point at the lock to get them to open the door. They fell into his arms and held him tight. Their little bodies shook as they bawled.

"Is Mommy . . ." Dawn began, but couldn't finish the words as she cried harder.

"Mommy is just fine. She's a little hurt, but she'll be okay."

"You promise."

"Yes, baby girl."

Three sheriff's cruisers and an ambulance came to a jarring halt just past the crashed vehicles. Officers swarmed the area, taking Roxy's boyfriend into custody just as he came awake, sputtering obscenities and demanding they arrest Brody for assault.

An officer shoved Roxy up against the side of the wrecked Camero. A paramedic looked at her broken nose and handed her a wad of gauze to staunch the bleeding.

"Hey," he called to the other paramedic about to help Roxy's boyfriend. "She needs your help. She's been stabbed in the chest and broke her hand." He indicated Rain, lying on her back in the gravel, an officer kneeling beside her who looked very familiar.

"Sweetheart, what happened here?" Brody's cousin, Dylan, asked Rain as Brody approached with Dawn and Autumn in his arms.

"Dylan? What the hell are you doing here?"

"I guess Owen and Rain didn't tell you I came home. I'm the new sheriff." Dylan glanced at the scene around them. "I see nothing much has changed."

"Bullshit. I didn't start this fight."

"Owen filled me in about what happened with Rain and Roxy years ago when I came back to town."

"Good, then you're up to speed and know that Roxy has no rights to Autumn. She kidnapped her from the house and tried to take her. Rain"—he nodded to her on the ground—"stopped them from leaving. I don't know the guy's name, but he got out of the car and tried to kill Rain with that knife." Another officer held up the long bone-handled blade. "I knocked him off her, and we got into a scuffle."

"He slice open your shoulder?" Dylan asked.

"Yeah. Rain needs to get to the hospital. She banged her head during the car crash and broke her hand on Roxy's face."

"Mommy," Autumn's tremulous voice called out.

"I'm okay, baby," Rain called back as the paramedic placed a bandage over the wound on her chest and staunched the blood again, making Rain clench her teeth to stifle the moan of pain.

"I'm sorry, man, Mom and Dad never told me about the way your father died, or the girls," Dylan said.

"They don't exactly keep in touch with me and Owen," Brody said, knowing his aunt and uncle looked at him and Owen as the black sheep of the family. Their father's drinking caused a rift between the two brothers. Brody and Owen barely saw Dylan when they were kids. Still, they were family.

"Well, I'm glad to see you finally came home."

"Me, too."

"Owen should have called me and let me help you," Dylan admonished.

"I wouldn't have wanted to get you involved and jeopardize your job with all this business of buying children and payoffs for signatures on legal documents."

Dylan shrugged that away. "We're family. No matter what, I've got your back."

"In that case, lock those two up and throw away the key."

"I'll contact Owen and we'll sort out this mess."

Brody had no doubt about that as they lifted Rain on a gurney into the back of the ambulance. Roxy sat inside on the bench, glaring at him. An officer ushered her boyfriend to a police car and stuffed him in the backseat.

Dylan took them in his car to the hospital. Brody called Eli from the backseat, while Dylan spoke to Owen on his cell up front.

Let Dylan and Owen sort things out with Roxy. He needed to be with Rain.

Chapter Thirty-One

RAIN WOKE UP disoriented. The bright morning sun shining in her eyes, her tongue thick and dry. Brody sat beside her, his image shifted hazily, doubling, then returning to his normal, handsome form. He looked haggard, his face pale, dark circles marring the underside of his eyes. His cheek rested against his fist, his elbow propped on the arm of a chair as he watched her. When it registered she was looking back, he leaned forward and laid his hand on her shoulder.

"Hey, honey."

"Hey yourself. Where are Dawn and Autumn?"

"Outside in the hall with Pop. I didn't want them to wake you up."

"What happened? Everything's a little fuzzy."

"You have a mild concussion. They set your arm in a cast. You broke three bones in your hand. I need to teach you how to throw a proper punch."

"I did okay." She defended herself. "Did you see Roxy's face?"

That got her a smile. Not a big one, but the corners of his mouth went up.

"Yeah. She was screaming in the ER while they reset her nose and taped her up. She's got two black eyes to go with it and a nasty bruise on her jaw."

"Did you see Autumn stomp on her foot?" Rain didn't hold back the smile.

"She got her good." Brody let his pride show in his voice. "Her mama taught her well."

His fingertips slid from her shoulder over her chest to the bandage taped to her skin.

"They put in eight stitches." His voice grew husky with emotion.

"How many did you get?"

"None. The cut wasn't so bad. It'll heal. They cleaned it and put a bandage over it. It'll leave a scar, but hey, you love my scars."

That made her smile. "I love you," she corrected.

"I love you, too." He dropped his head and shook it. "I almost lost you yesterday."

"You saved me yesterday," she disagreed. "Thank you, Brody, for rescuing me."

"I was almost too late."

"Almost only counts in horseshoes and hand grenades," she teased.

"Don't remind me." He combed his fingers through his already disheveled hair and stared at her. "I got lost again. They took Autumn, and I fell into a nightmare.

Dawn was screaming for me to get Autumn back, but I didn't hear her until it was too late."

His head fell forward and rested on the bed beside her. She buried her fingers in his hair.

"Brody, it's not your fault."

"I called the psychiatrist last night. We had a long talk. He thinks now that this is settled, I'll be better able to cope without all this stress in my life. We'll have regular appointments three days a week until I can cope better.

"When you screamed for help and I saw you lying there . . ."

"I yelled for you because I was afraid you'd kill that guy, and they'd take you away from me."

"I lost it when I saw him with that knife, trying to kill you."

"What happened with the police and Dylan?"

"Roxy's boyfriend has been charged with aggravated assault, a felony. He'll go to jail. As for the kidnapping, it's a gray area the prosecutor is trying to sort out. Roxy is the biological mother. We don't have any papers specifying any kind of custody arrangements. Owen is working a deal. He'll try to get Roxy to sign the papers relinquishing her rights to have all charges dropped against her and the boyfriend for taking Autumn. Technically, Autumn was living with me, her father, so Roxy didn't really have a right to take her without my permission or knowledge. At least, that's the case Owen is building.

"We have something else on our side. Don't go ballistic."

"What?" she asked, concerned.

"They charged Roxy with child abuse. She hit Dawn."

"What?" Rain exploded and tried to sit up. Brody held her down. "Is she okay?"

"She's fine. Roxy slapped her, left a bruise on her face. She also shoved her pretty hard and made her fall and scrape up her knees."

"Oh God, Brody. Bring her in here."

"In a minute. They're both fine. Owen and Pop have stayed with them every minute."

The door opened and Owen walked in smiling, wearing a suit, and carrying his briefcase.

"Hi, beautiful. How are you feeling?"

"Great if you tell me Roxy is behind bars."

"She's being released as we speak. Sorry."

"Explain," Brody demanded.

The smile on his face spoke volumes. Things had finally gone their way.

"She signed the papers. Autumn is yours. She also agreed to sell the bar to you, Brody. I've agreed to settle her debts, pay for the liquor license renewal, and give her a cash settlement on your behalf."

"How much?" Rain asked.

"After the payments for the bar, she'll get one hundred thousand. It's what Brody agreed to pay her if she signed the papers and left town for good. Just to get the point across, I've taken out a restraining order. She's not to go within one hundred yards of any of you, including Dawn.

"She'll be gone tomorrow. Robert, the boyfriend, will remain behind bars. He's got an arrest warrant in Nevada for possession with intent to sell. He'll be prosecuted and serve time for both charges as well as the new charges for assaulting you."

"So, it's over," Rain said, unable to believe they'd finally gotten Roxy out of their lives.

"Not quite." Owen opened his briefcase and pulled out a folder. "You need to sign these. I'll file them with the courts at the same time I file the papers Roxy signed."

"What are these?" Rain asked.

"The adoption papers. It'll take a few months to finalize, but once it goes through, Autumn will be your daughter legally." Owen handed her a pen to sign the papers marked by little red arrow tabs.

Rain locked eyes with Brody, her broken hand poised over the papers, ready to sign. He brushed his fingers over her hair and leaned down and kissed her forehead.

"She's your daughter, honey. Sign the papers."

Rain reached up and touched her fingertips to his chest over his heart. The cast prevented her from laying her palm flat. "She's our daughter."

Rain signed the papers. Finished. Over. Finally, they could be a family.

"You know, my daughters have a different last name than me."

She hoped Brody would take the hint and hurry up about asking her to marry him. Impatient to be his wife, she pushed. "Do you have a wedding license application in there, too, Owen?" she asked with a hopeful lilt to her voice.

"I didn't ask you yet," Brody teased. "But I will." Her eyes danced as he grinned at her. Yes, he would ask, and when he did he'd get it absolutely, perfectly right.

Can't get enough of Jennifer Ryan's
heart-stoppingly sexy heroes?

Keep reading for a sneak peek at the newest
book in her bestselling
Montana Men series,

HER RENEGADE RANCHER

Coming October 2016

Her Renegade Rancher

Colt walked into the diner, spotted the only woman to take up residence in his head, and headed for a booth across the room, trying to ignore the tightness in his chest. He should have driven into Bozeman, found some yuppie bar, picked up an underpaid, overworked office girl who wanted to ride a cowboy and have some fun—he was always up for fun. But not tonight. Not most nights these days, because Luna stayed on his mind more than he liked to admit—to himself, never out loud—but she sure as hell wasn't getting into his heart despite the way it leaped every time he saw or thought about her. She wasn't for him. No way. She belonged to his buddy. At least she used to until that night at the bar when everything shifted and changed and became so confusing he was still trying to figure it out.

"Leave it alone," he warned himself under his breath. Easier said than done, especially now that his brother

Rory was marrying Luna's best friend. Sadie kept at Colt, wanting to know what happened between him and the dark-haired beauty with the porcelain face and red lips he could still taste from that one searing kiss. Like now. The damn woman branded him with that kiss.

He glanced over his shoulder as he continued on through the tables to the booth and caught her watching him from behind the counter. Those ice blue eyes with two brown specks in the right and three in the left darted away. The hint of embarrassment and shame in them matched his own feelings about what happened, but the flash of anger he always saw there tore him up. They'd been friends once. He'd ruined that and felt damn sorry about it, too.

"Hey you," Sadie called, walking out of the kitchen.

He ditched the booth idea and headed straight for her, taking a seat at the counter. Luna moved away to deliver her tray of drinks to a family at a nearby table.

"Hey, Mama, how's my niece or nephew doing?"

Sadie smiled and placed her hand over her slightly swollen pregnant belly. "Great." Her hand slid to her hip and she narrowed her eyes on him. The diamond ring his brother put on her finger last week winked in the light. "Did Rory send you after me? I can get home on my own, for God's sake."

He smiled at his soon-to-be sister. Yes, Rory tended to lean to the overprotective side of the line, but he had reason to where Sadie was concerned. At least before that trouble with her brother got settled. Now her brother spent his days locked up behind bars, and Sadie spent her time worry free and her nights in Rory's bed. Lucky bastard.

"I'm sure Rory's pacing the house waiting to get his hands on you, but he didn't send me to fetch you."

The starch went right out of her. "Okay then." She leaned over, planted her elbows on the counter, propped her chin in one hand, and stared right at him, a soft smile on her lips. "How are you, handsome?"

She wasn't flirting. Not really. His brother's girl had become like a sister, filling their family with a feminine warmth that had long been lacking in a household of men. After her father died, he shared his sorrow over his own parents' deaths—he'd been barely old enough to understand they weren't coming home ever again—and they'd bonded.

"It's been one hell of a day. Thought I'd stop in here for something to eat, since you're working late and it's Ford's night to cook." Colt scrunched his face into a sour expression, mocking Ford's mediocre cooking skills.

"That's the only reason you're here?"

He planted his elbow on the counter and matched her gesture of putting his chin in his palm and staring right back at her. "Well, I have been trying to come up with a way to steal you away from Rory."

She put her hand on his cheek and gave him a soft smack. "Never going to happen, cowboy."

He gave her a mocking frown. "That's what I thought you'd say. Way to crush a guy's heart."

"You might stop guarding that heart like it's going to be crushed by pain and loss again . . ." A reference to losing his parents he didn't want to be reminded about. ". . . And consider making up with my maid of honor over there."

Colt sat back in his chair and tamped down the urge to look at Luna again. Urge, hell, it was a compulsion to stare at her pretty face, close the distance between them, both figuratively and literally, and kiss her again. Just one more time. One more moment when everything in his life felt so damn right—before it all went to hell again.

See, he had good reason to guard his heart. The one time the thing pulsed to life over a woman, he screwed it all up. One kiss messed everything up.

"Leave it alone, sis."

"Seems to me you and her have done that for a long time. Apologize."

"It's beyond a simple 'I'm sorry.'"

"You sure about that? Because from where I'm standing, you sneak a look at her. She sneaks a look at you. Both of you act like you've got something to say, but neither of you says anything."

"After what I did, there's nothing to say that can make things right. Sometimes, sis, you can't go back."

"Did you cheat on her?"

Colt shook his head, the thought so distasteful it made him purse his lips. "No. It's not like that."

"Did you purposefully hurt her? Call her a name? Insult her? Run over her puppy?"

He shook his head, smiling despite the seriousness of the conversation. "No. Nothing like that."

"Are you sorry?"

He let out a soft sigh that did nothing to untangle the ever-present knot in his gut. "More than I can say."

Sadie slapped her hands on the counter. "Then I don't know why you can't go over there and tell her so."

"It's not that simple. She was my friend's girl, and I crossed a line."

"Colt, honey, she's not a possession. He didn't own her."

He let his head fall forward and stared at the seam in the countertop. "Well, she sure as hell wasn't mine. I tried to help her out, but I messed it up instead."

"Let me ask you something. Did she cross this line with you, or did you pull her over it?"

Colt sat back and stared up at the ceiling. "What difference does it make?"

"If you both participated, maybe she's sorry and you're sorry and this can be worked out, or at least put to rest, if you just talk to each other."

He gave her a look, putting all his resignation in his face. "Sis . . ."

"Colt, I love you like a brother, so I'm going to treat you like one. You're being an ass. She's going to be helping me plan the wedding. She'll be at the house all the time. Are you going to keep walking away every time she shows up?"

"It's worked so far."

Sadie planted her hands on her hips. "Really? This is working for you? Pretending she doesn't exist and what happened between you didn't happen? Seems to me all it does is make you both miserable."

"She does the same exact thing," he shot back.

Sadie stood and planted her fists on her hips again. "Oh, grow up. You know what you need to do to make this right. Suck it up and get it done. I won't have you two glaring at each other in my wedding photos."

"I'd never do that."

"No. You'd stand next to your brother looking miserable because of the woman standing next to me."

He took a chance, hoping Luna gave Sadie some information, one glimmer of hope that he could make things right. "Has she said anything to you at all about me?"

"Only that she doesn't want to talk about it. The thing is, Colt, she doesn't seem angry."

He perked up at that bit of news. "No?"

"No. More embarrassed maybe. Like she doesn't want to admit what she did, even though I'm her best friend and would never judge her. Maybe it's because I know you now, and I'm marrying your brother."

"She didn't do anything. It was me."

"You take the blame. She takes the blame. Seems to me whatever happened, it was the two of you who did it together."

He didn't know what to say about that. When he thought back to that night, standing in the parking lot, one of her hands on his shoulder, the other touching the aching bruise blooming on his jaw that her ex, his best friend, gave him, he didn't know who moved first. Him? Her?

"Here's what I've learned from dealing with my brother. If you don't take responsibility for the choices you make, things only get worse. Own up to your part. Apologize for what *you* did. Maybe that's all that's needed to at least thaw the cold shoulder you both have for each other."

One tough chick, Sadie didn't back down.

"I see why Rory fell so hard for you."

"He sat across the diner, staring at me for the better part of two years, wishing he'd talked to me. Maybe if he had, we'd have found our way to each other a lot sooner. I'm not saying it's the same between you and Luna, but if you've carried this with you all this time and it's still this raw, maybe you need to settle it before it festers into something so much more than it ever was to begin with."

She had a point.

"I'm afraid it already has. She can't even look at me without me seeing it all in her eyes."

"Maybe because when she looks at you she sees it in your eyes as well. Exactly the way I do right now." Sadie reached out and laid her hand over Colt's. "Don't wait the way Rory did."

"I'm not looking for a wife and a family."

"Maybe not right now, but ask yourself, if you feel this bad about things now, how will you feel if you never make it right and spend the rest of your life wondering what if she was the one?"

"It's not like that," he lied, remembering exactly how he felt when he kissed her. The connection he'd found with her in that moment tugged at him even now to close the gaping distance between him and the woman across the room.

A woman who couldn't stand the sight of him.

"You may not want to admit it, but I see the one thing you try to hide every time you look at her. Something I held onto myself for a long time."

Afraid to ask, but needing to know what she saw but he couldn't figure out, he spoke up. "What's that?"

"Hope."

Next month, don't miss these exciting new love stories only from Avon Books

Hell Breaks Loose by Sophie Jordan

Tired of taking orders, First Daughter Grace Reeves escapes her security detail for a rare moment of peace. Except her worst nightmare comes to life when a gang of criminals abducts her. Her only choice is to place her trust in Reid Allister, an escaped convict whose piercing gaze awakens something deep inside her. Escaping Devil's Rock was tough, but Reid knows resisting this woman could be the end of him.

Why Do Dukes Fall in Love? by Megan Frampton

Michael, the Duke of Hadlow, has the liberty of enjoying an indiscretion . . . or several. So when it comes time for him to take a proper bride, he hires Edwina as a secretary—only to fall passionately in love with her. Edwina had begged him to marry someone appropriate—someone aristocratic . . . someone high-born. But the only thing more persuasive than a duke intent on seduction is one who has fallen irrevocably in love.

His Scandalous Kiss by Sophie Barnes

Richard Heartly has exiled himself from society since the war, plotting his revenge for a terrible betrayal. A masked ball at Thorncliff Manor is intended to be a brief diversion. Instead, he encounters a fascinating young woman as entranced by the music as he is. He can't reveal his identity to Lady Mary. But her siren song keeps drawing him back, and their clandestine meetings could be hazardous to his plan—and to her virtue . . .

REL 0716